Marked by Stone

Deborah Holness

This book is dedicated to:

You!
Thank you for choosing this book to read. I hope you enjoy it.

Steph & Gerry for their unwavering support.
Angie-For coming on the trips that sparked my inspiration, (and for being the first to decode the mystery, even if you still maybe a little unsure.)

CONTENT ADVISORY: This book is intended for mature audiences.

The vocabulary, grammar and spelling of Marked by Stone is written in British English.

Contents

Prologue

Maeve

"That guy gives me the heebie-jeebies." My best friend Tina shudders, as she entwines her arm with mine and hurriedly pulls me toward her aging blue Jeep in the parking lot. It's a miracle the vehicle is still running. Every few weeks, the engine coughs and splutters before the car limps to a halt. Fortunately, Tina's extremely talented brother always comes to the rescue, resuscitating the old girl and giving us a brief reprieve. I couldn't be more grateful for Liam ensuring our means of escape is still running right at this moment, for when I glance back over my shoulder, I see Vince Castillo leaning against his state-of-the-art motorcycle, the one everyone wonders how he can afford. His hair is slicked back with enough product to make it look dull and greasy, and his beady eyes follow my every move as I quickly stash my weekend bag in the back seat of my ride before climbing in the front beside Tina.

"Me to. C'mon let's get out of here."

Tina doesn't need to be told twice. I've barely fastened my seatbelt before she slams her foot on the accelerator and peels out of the lot. As we speed past, my eyes connect briefly with Vince, either he has gas or he attempts a smile, either way, his face contortion doesn't fall far short of being serial killer creepy. Vince is a couple of years above Tina and me at Uni, but rumour has it he's had to resit more than one year of studies, making him older than he should be, which has become a source of intrigue among our friends since he doesn't seem to struggle with any of his coursework. I don't know what his future plans are, but I'll always be eternally grateful that he isn't in any of my classes.

Tina and I don't always head home on weekends; there's much more fun to be had on campus than in the sleepy Vermont town where we come from. But it's Tina's mom's birthday, and she's having a small get-together. Since Tina and I have been inseparable ever since we became friends in kindergarten, I'm going with her, expected to be there as part of the Collins' extended family. Besides that, it's the perfect opportunity to drop by and check in on my brother. Jimmy has been struggling ever since his two best friends were accepted into the highly selective navy SEAL training program without him.

It had been a dream of the three of them for as long as I could remember—ever since they returned home from the movies one night after seeing an action flick they were convinced had changed their lives. Everyone's parents thought it was merely a fad the boys would grow out of, but the excitement and enthusiasm to enlist was something that never went away. They were all supposed to leave town together, but Jimmy's application got declined on medical grounds. He didn't take the news well. Josh, Kurt and Jimmy had been as thick as thieves since before I was born, our moms all lived within close proximity of each other and used to meet regularly, leaving the boys to play together while they put the world to rights over lunch and a bottle of merlot.

I'd crushed hard on Kurt when I was younger. At seventeen, his long lean body paired with the striking green eyes that peeked from the silky mop of dark hair flopping sexily over his chiselled face was too much for my thirteen-year-old hormones to handle. He was the quiet and thoughtful type, nearly always dressed in black, which made him seem dark, dangerous and even more appealing by default. Tina thought I was crazy; she favoured pretty boys with exuberant personalities. Jimmy teased me mercilessly, as older brothers do, while Kurt pretty much ignored me when I constantly trailed after him like a little love lorn puppy. I even stole a photo from my brother's stash, one of the three boys standing together on a camping trip. It was taken on one of the rare occasions Kurt smiled. I drew a heart around his face and stared at the picture every night, imagining I was the one with the camera and that he was grinning back at me. I was never worried about Jimmy or the other guys spotting it, pinned to the wall above my bed, there were too many soft toys and feminine products littering my room for any of them to dare enter, all my girlie stuff seemed to repel testosterone the same way garlic could ward off a vampire.

Josh was the one in the trio that took pity on me, and tolerated me being around. He always offered a kind word or hug when he could see I was hurting, and he acted like my protector, chastising both Jimmy and Kurt when it was warranted. As the largest of the three, the other two listened when he spoke. Josh stood a good head and shoulders above the other two. While they were lean, he had a broad athletic physique that made him stand out in a crowd. Friend or foe, not many people dared to upset him.

Shortly after my sixteenth birthday, Josh and Kurt left town to follow their dreams, and while Jimmy supported them, he was devastated not to be going too. I never got to the bottom of why Jimmy wasn't deemed fit enough to undertake the rigorous training required to join the elite team of highly versatile special ops soldiers. He would never say. I do know that after Kurt and Josh left, Jimmy changed. It's like he didn't know where he fit in the world anymore. Instead of channelling all the energy from his angst into carving out a new career, he gave up. He went out most nights, eventually falling in with the wrong crowd and sometimes staying away for days at a time. He had our parents worried sick; they knew how disappointed and lost he felt. They tried to help, but he kept pushing them away to the point where they finally gave up any hope of his change in behaviour being nothing more than a passing phase. They put up with his surly and sullen behaviour until, in fear and desperation, they issued him an ultimatum. They demanded he either clean up his act or get out. With no money and no place to go, much to everyone's relief, Jimmy decided to stay and try to turn things around. He was still distant and I missed my big brother, not realising how close we actually were until our bond started to unravel.

Tina's dad gave him a job alongside her brother at their family's garage. Jimmy appeared to knuckle down and stopped giving our parents so much cause for concern. Even though most people felt like he had turned a corner and his life was finally headed in the right direction, I knew better. Two and a half years on, the only thing that had changed was that he had become better at covering his tracks.

"So, what's the plan?" Tina glances across at me, "Straight to mine and you'll shower and change there or do you want me to drop you home first?"

"Home, I think. My folks will be pissed if I don't stop by and say hi before the party, and I want to check in on Jim."

"Party?" Tina sniggers, "You've met my parents, right? Two glasses of wine and my mom will think she's Adele and start belting out ballads on the karaoke, while dad tries to recapture his youth by trying not to throw his hip out by breakdancing on the living room floor. Liam's already arranged his escape."

"How?" I giggle.

"He's told them he has to pick his girlfriend up from work at half eight to bring her over. He reckons they're be in full flow by then so won't notice when he doesn't come back. If they do, he's just going to tell them the car broke down or something. I reckon we do the same thing, circulate for an hour, hand out a few drinks to move things along, then you feign a headache and being your very caring best friend, I have to drive you home."

"It wouldn't be right if you didn't," I smirk. "Then you'd have to hang with me until you were sure I was feeling better. I doubt I'll recover quickly; it might take me at least until the party's over."

"Exactly!" With one hand on the steering wheel, Tina offers me her other fist and I bump it.

Plan in place, Tina and I chat amiably the rest of the way. It takes us about forty-five minutes before Tina drops me at the curb outside my childhood home.

"Mom? Dad? Jimmy?" I yell, as I crash through the front door, dumping my bag in the hall.

"In here," Mom calls back, I can tell from the wonderous smells assaulting my senses, 'here' in this case, means the kitchen. It's not unusual to find my mom cooking up a storm when anyone we know is throwing a party. I find her lifting two apple pies out of the oven and replacing the void with a baking tray of cookies.

"Hi mom," I kiss her cheek, and as soon as her hands are free, she sweeps me up in a hug.

"You've lost weight again, haven't you?"

She tells me that every time I see her, convinced that I'm not eating properly since I moved out and she can't feed me a plate crammed full of carbs followed by a healthy helping of fruit steeped in sugar every evening. This time though I have to admit it's true. I have managed to shed a few pounds and I'm finally happy with how I look. I'll never be tall enough to be a model, coming in at a modest five foot four and a half inches, or attractive enough, with what I'd call non-descript mid-brown hair and meh, brown eyes. But thanks to the part-time job as a dog walker I'd picked up, together with the free use of the University swimming pool, I'd finally managed to start shedding some of the puppy fat that had been clinging on from my younger years. Despite my wobbly bits, Tina was constantly telling me I was beautiful and she was envious of my curves, but I wouldn't expect anything less from my bestie. In the past, while I appreciated her comments, I rarely believed them. Recently though, I had been garnering enough attention from the opposite sex to convince me she might actually be right and I might not be the ugly duckling I always thought myself to be. Her constant support and my newfound confidence were starting to make a difference. Not that I'd actually been on any dates—I always claimed I was too busy, though the truth was, I just hadn't found anyone who stirred something in me the way my mean and moody brother's best friend once had. I suppose I was a romantic at heart, craving magic and moonbeams with a healthy dose of fireworks thrown in for good measure—someone who could awaken something in me profound enough to make me believe in a future together. But most of the boys I met seemed more focused on fun, using their Uni years as a playground for fleeting liaisons, trial runs for relationships that might really matter someday.

"A little maybe, and before you ask, yes, I am eating properly. It's all the walking I've been doing, plus Tina and I go swimming a few times a week." I have to look her in the eyes as I'm talking or else I know she won't believe me. She cups my face in her hands and looks me over critically.

"I'll make you up a food basket to take back with you."

"Thanks mom." There's no point arguing so I swiftly change the subject. "Where's Dad and Jimmy?"

"Your dad is just dropping some extra chairs off at the Collins' for later, he'll be back soon." She sighs, "Jimmy is out with one of his *friends.* He said he wouldn't be home tonight and that he'd try and swing by tomorrow to see you."

"Oh, okay." I try to hide my disappointment but my mom's apologetic gaze lets me know I'm not doing a very good job. "I'm going to head upstairs and take a shower, call me when Dad gets back or the cookies come out of the oven."

"You got it." Mum calls, as I disappear before she can see the errant tear that rolls down my cheek.

∞∞∞

By nine thirty, after realising Liam was right about nobody noticing his sudden absence, Tina and I are itching to put our own escape plans in action. I feign a headache brought on by the eighties anthems blaring from a stereo system with more lights and buttons than airplanes cockpit. It's an antiquated piece of machinery that stands dominating the far corner of the living room, taking up much more room than was necessary since the invention of the iPod—Both Tina and Liam have tried to convince their parents of the benefits of upgrading, but the concept of streaming music from an invisible digital cloud was something that they weren't ready to embrace. With speakers at least half my height almost causing the walls of the house to vibrate my bad head is not a hard sell. After being told the youth of today has no stamina, Tina makes a dramatic show of helping me outside and into her car before we take off, pulling to the side just around the corner, as soon as we are out of sight, to let our barely contained laughter erupt safely.

"Well, that went better than expected," I giggle, wiping the tears from my eyes after I finally manage to compose myself.

Tina looks at me and we both burst out laughing again. "Pizza party?" She finally manages to wheeze. I nod and she whips out her phone, ordering our favourites before heading back to mine. We've just parked up when her mobile starts to chime and she glances at the screen. "It's Liam." She answers and listens intently for a few seconds. "Alright, I'm on my way," she sighs, before hanging up. "Liam's broken down, he needs me to grab some tools from home and drop them off to him."

"That's Karma, for lying to his mom on her birthday," I chuckle.

"You'd better hope not, or you'll be getting a migraine later," Tina replies. "You coming?"

"I can't, for one, you're supposed to be dropping me home because I'm not feeling well, what if someone spots us? And two, I need to be here to take delivery of the pizza." I get out of the car and lean back in the open door, "I'll wait here, put the food in the oven to keep it warm. I'll leave my key under the mat so you can just let yourself in when you get back."

Tina tips her head in acknowledgement, "Hopefully I shouldn't be too long."

I nod and slam the car door, watching as she does a three-point turn before disappearing back the way we came. The pizza arrives shortly after, and when it's stashed in the kitchen awaiting her return, I'm heading upstairs to my room when the front door crashes open and Jimmy comes staggering in with his arm wrapped around the shoulders of a tall, greasy looking fellow for support.

"Maeve!" He yells, relinquishing the hold he has on his buddy, before tripping over the rug in the hall as he stumbles towards me and pulls me in for a hug.

"Jimmy? Are you Okay?" I feel my nose wrinkle involuntarily as he gets close enough for me to take in his scent. He wreaks of alcohol and bad decisions.

"I'm fine," he slurs, turning to his friend. "Tony, this is my goody two shoes sister, Maeve."

Harsh.

I'd dressed modestly for the party in a navy fit and flare dress with a high neck, and respectable hemline. It still doesn't feel like enough coverage when Tony starts to leer at me, making my flesh crawl. He seems familiar even though I'm pretty certain this is the first time we've met.

"I can take it from here." I tell Tony resolutely, hoping he'll leave.

"Don't be rude Maeve," Jimmy says as he sways in front of me. "Tony, Vince and I are going to hang here for a bit. Have a smoke and a few beers." He presses his index finger to his lips in an exaggerated 'Shhh' gesture.

"Vince?" I echo with a frown, seconds before all my worst nightmares are realised.

"Tony's brother." Jimmy presents the front door with an arm flourish just as Vince Castillo steps over the threshold. If my skin was crawling before, its positively squirming now.

"Maeve," Vince sneers lecherously causing me to take a step back, "I was hoping you'd be home."

"W... why?" I try to sound strong as I look past him through the front door, hoping Tina will sudden reappear. As if he is sensing I'm looking to bolt, Vince closes the door trapping me inside. I look at Jimmy hoping he can sense my discomfort, his eyes are glazed and his pupils dilated, I'm suddenly acutely aware that alcohol isn't the only vice he has been indulging in. It's clear that whatever is about to happen, I'm on my own, and every one of my heightened senses is screaming at me to get clear because I'm in imminent danger.

"After we've had the chance to relax…" Vince pulls a pre rolled joint from his pocket, lighting it, before taking a deep draw and passing it over to his brother who does the same, "… I thought you and I could get to know each other a little better." He grabs his junk and adjusts himself through his trousers.

Fuck! With nowhere else to go, I turn and bolt up the stairs.

"Eagerly heading to the bedroom I see, make yourself comfortable," Vince calls after me as I retreat hastily, "We'll come and find you when we're ready."

We?

Panic floods my body as I charge into my bedroom and slam the door, with no lock I scan the room for something to push against it. The only item large enough to act as any sort of barricade to help prevent anyone from entering uninvited, is the dressing table standing against the adjacent wall. As music starts blaring downstairs, it takes all my strength to push and shove it into position. Once it's there, I move my bed against it for additional support before I scan the room for my phone. I don't want to call the cops and get Jimmy in trouble, but if I need to, I will. I figure I'll call Tina first to let her know what's happening so she doesn't suddenly turn up alone, and perhaps ask at the same time if she can bring Liam to help extricate me. Unfortunately, it's then I realise my cell is still on the counter in the kitchen, where I left it when the pizza arrived. I find myself with only two options, stay put and hope for the best, or make a run for it. With the bedroom door blocked and no desire to try and sneak past the open-plan living room to the main exit, where I would surely be spotted by either one of the Castillo brothers, my only other means of escape is the window. I dash over and look out, even though I know what I'm going to see. A two-story drop onto an unforgiving concrete patio—assuming I can even slide the largest window open to climb out. Ever since it was repainted last spring, it's been stiff and unyielding.

I settle back onto my bed, curling myself into a ball, and hugging my knees to my chest in an effort to stop myself trembling. I grip the only weapon I can find—a tiny pair of scissors from the manicure set Tina gave me for Christmas last year—while I pray for a miracle and hope that if I stay quiet enough, Vince and Tony will get high enough to forget that I'm even here.

A little over an hour later, Tina still hasn't returned. The stress of the situation coupled with the loud music is starting to make my brain feel heavy and sluggish. I start to wonder if karma is actually about to deliver the migraine I feigned earlier. The air feels thick, like it's being drained of oxygen, making each breath strangely unsatisfying. My limbs are weighted, my thoughts hazy, but I brush it off as fear that it may not be much longer before Vince and his brother come calling. I know I should stay alert, but the battle to keep my eyelids from drooping is one I'm slowly losing. Despite my best efforts, I finally lose the fight and drift off into a peaceful slumber.

I'm not sure what happens next, until I'm roused into semi consciousness by the wailing of sirens and raised voices screaming over each other all around me. I'm no longer on my soft mattress, I'm lying prostrate on a hard cool surface, something is tickling the exposed flesh of my arms and legs, it feels like... grass? As I use every ounce of effort in me to flick my eyes open to check, I find myself staring up and into the intense green eyes of an all too familiar face.

"Kurt?" I try to speak, but my throat is scratchy and dry. What comes out is little more than a gravelly-voiced whisper. My heart stutters, but I'm too disoriented to figure out why. I know it feels like Kurt is kneeling on my chest, which feels heavy and sore, making it difficult to breathe. But I also know that can't be the case since he appears to be behind me, gently holding my head in his hands. His handsome profile is softly illuminated by the strobing lights of the ambulance behind him.

"She's coming to." Kurt barks, before a mask is suddenly thrust over my face and nose. As much as I want to stay awake and find out what's going on, I can't fight it when my eyes crash shut again.

"Let's get them both to the hospital, stat," an unfamiliar voice yells determinedly, breaking through my subconscious.

"Is she going to be alright?" I hear Tina sob a few feet away, "Can I go with her?"

I feel myself being jostled onto a gurney, before someone covers my limp hand with their own strong one, squeezing gently. I know it's not Tina; whoever it is completely encapsulates everything from my fingers to my wrist. My fog-addled brain determines it to be an EMT until a large thumb glides a little too affectionately across the back of my hand a couple of times.

"You're going to be okay, sunshine." A husky, yet comforting male voice whispers, his lips are so close to my ear that I feel his warm breath drift over my skin.

"We need to go." Another voice barks, and suddenly the warmth surrounding my hand disappears. "Where the hell is he going? He needs to get checked out at the hospital." Are the last words I hear before I slip back into the darkness once more.

Chapter 1

Maeve

"**D**on't look at me like that," I chastise Mr Whiskers as I lift him up ready to pop him back into his carrier. "If you hadn't embarked on that whirlwind romance with Mrs Johnson's Siamese… and Mr Perkin's Prize Persian, you might have been allowed to keep your nuts. As it is we are going to have eight to twelve new kittens to rehome soon."

Mr Whiskers mews pitifully as I make him as comfortable as I can before taking him through to waiting room of my clinic. As soon as she sees me, a little girl, about five years old, stops cuddling the Alaskan Malamute lounging on his back enjoying the attention, and comes running over.

"Mr Whiskers, are you Okay?" She asks, wringing her little hands with worry.

I place the carrier on the ground and kneel down in front of the little girl. "Lucy, Mr Whiskers is going to be fine. He is feeling a little sore, so he needs to take it easy until he gets back on his feet. Can you make sure he does that?"

Lucy nods her head enthusiastically, "Can I hug

him?"

I smile, "I think he deserves lots of hugs, but you need to be extra gentle with him for a little while."

"Kay."

I stand, and while Lucy peers in the carrier to coo at her cat, I show her dad over to the reception desk for my assistant, Aiden, to take payment and go through Mr Whiskers aftercare. They are the last customers of the day and once they have left, Aiden and I can shut up shop and head home. I hear a chime and look up to see Tina come barrelling through the main door, dragging a small suitcase on wheels behind her.

"What's this big news then?" She booms.

"Well, hello to you too," I chuckle, scooping her up in my arms for a hug. "How was your journey?"

"Fine. What's the news?" She asks again impatiently. As I draw back and the light catches the diamond in the new ring on the fourth finger of my left hand, she gasps and her hand flies over her mouth. "Tell me you didn't?"

I waggle my hand in front of her face grinning, "I did."

"You can't!" She blusters. Not quite the reaction I was aiming for. I knew she wasn't going to be ecstatic about it, but surely she could feign some semblance of happiness for me. It was a requirement that had to be stipulated in the BFF handbook somewhere.

"Why?" I put my hands on my hips and try to remain calm.

"Because he's an accountant," she blurts out, not even attempting to hide the horrified look on her face.

"So? It's a solid, respectable job."

"Because... because... he keeps his socks on during sex," she shouts incredulously. To my shocked dismay, she isn't finished, "and someday you want kids, how is that even going to be possible when you don't do it enough to conceive."

"Once is all it takes," I shoot back without considering how dire that makes my situation seem.

"You got it right there," Lucy's dad murmurs under his breath.

I hear Aiden snort as he carries on regardless, handing back our customers credit card and trying to pretend he can't hear my friend and her unusually high-pitched voice.

"Jeez, Tina, lets take this somewhere a bit more private, shall we?" I take off my white lab coat and grab my purse from behind reception. "Aiden, are you okay to lock up?"

"Sure boss," Aiden smirks and I glare at him until he resumes talking through Mr Whiskers needs with our client.

"Tiny." I snap my fingers, and the Malamute jumps to attention. Far from tiny, he's on the larger side of the breed, but he wasn't always that way. He got his name after being brought in by a stranger who found him abandoned as a puppy, left in a box by the side of the road the Christmas before last. Back then he was little more than a small, underdeveloped ball of fluff. Aiden joked he was like Tiny Tim from the classic Dickens novel and the name stuck, as did the dog. After spending countless days and nights nursing him back to health, the bond between us was too strong for me to consider rehoming him.

It's summer in Vermont and the temperature is a warm 26 degrees Celsius outside, I don't bother with a jacket, I just storm outside with both Tiny and a sheepish looking Tina hot on my heels.

"Seriously, slow down will you?" Tina puffs behind me, her suitcase bouncing over the grooves in the sidewalk, as she struggles to keep pace in her designer heels.

"No, I'm pissed at you," I snap. The trainers I'm wearing allow me to easily increase my speed further. I can't remember the last time I wore heels. I don't like to draw attention to myself; thankfully, that coincides with the ability to dress for comfort. I'm on my feet for most of the day, and my job as the local vet leaves me almost permanently covered in pet hair, as well as some of the animals' more unpleasant excretions.

"Maeve, please?" Tina wheezes behind me.

"Not until you apologise."

"Apologise? For what?"

"For not being happy for me." I tell her haughtily.

"How can I?" She shouts after having evidently stopped walking.

I turn with my hand on my hips and watch as she flaps her arms in exasperation. "You're my best friend. You are supposed to support me no matter what," I yell.

"Even when I know you are about to make the biggest mistake of your life," she yells back. "What sort of friend would I be if I just kept my mouth shut and went along it without at least trying to discuss it with you first?"

"Discuss it? Is that what you were doing when you announced some of the finer details of my sex life in front of the whole town?"

"Please, what sex life? You don't do it enough to make it newsworthy, and it wasn't the whole town, it was Aiden and two random customers, one of whom probably doesn't even know what sex is."

"Marriage isn't all about sex," I scream. "It's about a healthy respect for one another, loyalty, stability, security."

Tina abandons her suitcase and comes to stand in front of me. "Honey, I get it, you're scared. Derek is a safe option. When the right woman comes along, she'll appreciate his obsessively compulsive, anally retentive, nature. She'll see his flaws as quirks, they'll get married and fall into a routine where every day, week, month and year is mind numbingly monotonous. The biggest decision she'll ever have to make is whether to have toast or cereal for breakfast. For the right girl that'll be heaven. It's just that girl won't ever be you."

"Why? Why can't it be me?" I ask tearfully.

"Because ever since the night you almost died in that fire you've been afraid of your own shadow.

You've become so risk adverse; you're missing out on everything life has to offer. One day you are going to wake up and realise you've been settling for far too long. What's going to happen then? When you wake up and see this isn't the life you wanted for yourself, that you want more? What's going to happen when Derek has the epiphany that no matter how hard he tries he'll never be able to give you what you need? If you get hitched to him, it's not just your life you'll be ruining, it'll be his too. Who wants to be trapped in a marriage with someone who isn't happy? It'll slowly destroy you both.

Everyone has been quietly watching from the wings for years, waiting for you to wake up and start living again. Your parents didn't help at the beginning. Even though they never expected Jimmy to come home that night, and no one could have predicted he and his dumb ass mates would have been so careless with their booze and smokes. They blamed themselves for being out having a good time when the fire started. After Jimmy skedaddled, they couldn't stand the thought of losing you too, so they overcompensated, smothering you with love and never letting you out of their sight. I couldn't get you out of the house for months. Granted I should have realised what was going on sooner, but it took me a few weeks to summon up the courage to face you. I thought you'd blame me for being gone so long when I went to help Liam.

When you finally went back to Uni to finish your degree, I thought you'd turned a corner, but you weren't interested in anything other than studying or animals. You were like a robot. I couldn't even get you to come swimming with me anymore. Even now I can't get you to put on a bathing suit. Why the fuck is that? You can swim like a dolphin and have an amazing body. I don't get it. When you qualified as a vet and got all those exciting job offers, you gravitated back here, the one place we both swore we would never settle. If you wanted to open your own practice, fine. But why here? We always talked about taking a year out and travelling the world. Now, I can't even get you to leave town to visit me in New York for the weekend. You bought that little log cabin out by the lake and live like a hermit most of the time, how you even managed to meet Derek, let alone start dating him remains a mystery to me. When you told me you'd started dating I was so happy. I thought you'd finally met someone who would bring you back out of your shell. Then I met him."

"Don't start in on Derek," I mumble.

"This isn't about Derek, not really," she sighs. "Answer me this," Tina thrusts an old photograph into my hand. It's a copy of the one that used to be pinned above my bed at home. Jimmy, Kurt and Josh on their camping trip. This one hasn't got a heart scrawled around Kurt's face. I flip it over and read the words scrawled on the back. *Don't ever forget me x.* "Do you have even a fraction of the feelings for Derek that you used to have for this guy here?" She turns the picture back over and jabs her finger at

Kurt's face.

Someone had left the photo by my bedside while I was asleep in the hospital the morning after the accident. I liked to think it was Kurt, who had heroically rescued me from the burning building, even though the thought came with the mortification of knowing he must have seen that I had the very same photo pinned to my wall when he saved me. But deep down, I knew it was probably Jimmy. He disappeared the night of the fire and my parents refused to look for him. Even though they were quietly relieved he had managed to get out of the situation unharmed, they were so angry and ashamed they finally gave up on trying to help him. I tried to find him for a short while, but some of his old haunts looked too menacing for me to frequent. I asked around, but either no-one had seen or heard from him, or if they had, they certainly weren't at liberty to share that info with me. I never saw Kurt again either; I almost thought I'd dreamt him being there. Tina confirmed he had been, allaying my fears that I was imagining things, by explaining that he and Josh had been home on leave for the weekend but had returned to duty before I was well enough to be discharged and find him to offer my thanks. I thought the picture had been lost.

"Where did you get this?" I tactfully ignore her question.

Tina shrugs, "The first time I came to visit you, when you were staying in that rental while your place got fixed up, I saw it lying on the floor beside the bed and I took it."

"Why?"

"When we started Uni and other guys started paying you some attention, you seemed to get Kurt out of your system. I guess I didn't want you to put this picture back up and for you to start idolising him again. But now I'm tempted to track him down and ask him to swing by, just to remind you how he used to make you spark. You used to light up like a Christmas tree every time you were around him, I'm sorry but Derek has never made you do that. He'll never be able to give you what you need. You need someone who fans that flame within you, someone who encourages you to chase your dreams, who challenges you and pushes you outside of your comfort zone."

"You're wrong!" I snap.

"Am I?" She asks gently. "Then prove it, take a couple of weeks off and come back to New York with me tomorrow night. Just step off this treadmill you're on for a while and see what else is out there. Give yourself some time to think things through. If you still decide you want to marry Derek after that, I'll give you my full support."

"No! I don't have to prove anything to you. Maybe it's not me that's the problem, maybe it's you and your inability to admit I've changed. I can't just jet off and leave my practice for two weeks, my diary's jam packed. Plus, Tiny would hate it there. I love Derek and I'm going to marry him, with or without your blessing. I asked you here because I thought you'd be happy for me and I wanted to ask you to be my maid of honour. You're my closest friend and I want to do this with you by my side, but only if you can accept my decision."

"I'm sorry Maeve. I can't."

We stare at each other in silence. I don't think there has ever been a time we were together and at a loss for words.

Tiny whimpers, pawing at my leg, eager to get home for his tea. "Well then," I say sadly, "I'm sorry you've had a wasted trip." I turn on my heel and walk away, swiping the tears from my cheeks with one hand, still clutching the old photograph she gave me in the other.

Tiny and I always walk to and from work as it's a good forty-five-minute trek without any detours, so it gives Tiny the exercise he needs to let off some steam. My cabin was bought more for the location rather than its style. It's built close to the edge of a large pond teaming with wildlife, on a small plot surrounded by trees and with one track leading off to the main road. My parents used to think the place was too isolated and worried about me living here alone. That changed when Tiny came to live with me. The property isn't huge but it's large enough for the two of us, it's a single storey abode with the front entrance opening into a large open plan kitchen / living space that has two rooms leading off, a small bathroom and mid-size bedroom. The pièce de résistance, however, is the deep porch that wraps itself around the entire perimeter and has a swing hanging out front, overlooking the pond. Tiny and I have spent many an evening relaxing outside, reading or watching the sun as it dips below the horizon behind the water. There's a fire pit out front that I've always been too afraid to light, and my most recent addition, a hot tub, a treat to myself for my thirtieth birthday last year.

It takes us longer than usual to get home, I amble along with Tiny at my heel and my mind still reeling from my conversation with Tina. As we reach our final approach and I can see my cabin through the trees, Tiny sudden dashes in front of me, stopping dead and almost causing me to crash into him. His hackles rise and he lets out a deep guttural growl, curling his lip back over his teeth. It's the first time I've ever seen him react this way, he is normally so placid and calm. I glance around, nervously scanning the area for a rogue bear or moose that may have strayed into the area. I rummage in my bag for my bear spray, the one my mom insisted I carry, and the one I told her I'd never need. The black bears here are skittish and normally stay hidden deep in the forest, away from the populated areas, even so, it wouldn't be impossible for one to have wandered here. I make a mental note to thank her; I can put up with the 'I told you so's' if it saves me from a mauling. When I don't see anything, I crouch beside my dog and put my hand on his back, only to find he is trembling.

"What's up boy?" I whisper, his eyes are trained ahead of him and I follow his line of sight to the cabin. It's then I see the figure walk across the window inside and panic fills my body. Although the shadow certainly appears large enough to be a grizzly, it's definitely a human form I watch stride past. My pulse starts escalating further, I promised myself that I'd never let anyone corner me like Vince did the night of the fire. That was part of the reason I stopped socialising, meeting new people was terrifying, you never knew who you could trust or what situations you could unexpectedly find yourself in. I suppose it's why I fell for Derek; Tina was right, he was safe. I was the one that actually asked him out, not the other way round. There is a café on the street just opposite my clinic. I watched him pick up his coffee on his way to work every morning, eat lunch there every Wednesday, and treat himself to dinner every Friday without fail. I never got any surprises, that's what drew me to him. He was open and honest from the moment I struck up a conversation with him—I knew everything from how much he earned each month to the name of every pet he'd ever owned. Some people might call him boring, but I called him reliable. He was attractive in a geeky sort of way, and in the bedroom, he was certainly enthusiastic. So enthusiastic I could be seduced at eight and still be sat at the table eating dinner at five past. It wasn't his fault there was no spark; it was mine. Every time anyone got near me, I'd be haunted by Vince and what could have happened if events hadn't unfolded the way they did thirteen years ago. At the time, everyone had been so preoccupied by the fire and how it started, no one had ever asked about the events preceding it, and I hadn't told anyone. I didn't like to relive those moments unnecessarily.

Besides, there was nothing of value in the cabin, nothing that couldn't be replaced, and whoever was inside didn't know I was here. There was only one choice to be made, turn around, head back to the main road and call the police. Let them deal with it.

I stand and start to slowly back away. "Tiny," I whisper. "Come." For the first time in his life, he ignores me. "Tiny," I call a little louder and more forcibly. Nothing. I reach for his collar to give him some gentle encouragement, just as the door to the cabin opens and someone huge steps outside. I pause to look and see if I recognise the silhouette, but I can't see his face clearly; not only is he angled away from me, he is wearing a cap. I can see he is dressed all in black. Combat trousers and boots, topped off with a Tee barely containing the biceps larger than my thighs. The man is definitely stacked, too bad he didn't choose good over evil.

Before I can react further, Tiny suddenly takes off like a rocket, snarling ferociously. The intruder looks up startled and must see my dog charging at him with his teeth bared. He reaches inside his jacket and I only have to see a flash of metal glint in the sun before my fear evaporates and I take off after Tiny. Do what you like to my home, but try to mess with my dog, and it's game on. What is it they say? The bigger they are; the harder they fall, and I'm about to take you down sucker! Obviously Tiny is a lot faster than me, even as I charge through the brush hurdling obstacles like an Olympic champion, he is way ahead of me. So, I do the only thing I can and hope for the best. I scream aggressively at the top of my lungs, hoping the distraction will be enough for Tiny to take down our foe before he gets stabbed or shot.

The adrenaline surging through my body makes my heart pound hard in anticipation of the showdown that's about to take place. My lungs are burning, working overtime as I attempt to outrun the speed of light, trying to catch up with my dog before he gets injured. With all available blood and oxygen being used to power my body, my brain has obviously been starved as I bellow the first words that spring to mind.

"IF YOU HURT MY DOG, I'LL DROWN YOU NAKED IN MY HOT TUB AND FEED YOU TO MY PIG SO THEY NEVER FIND A BODY!"

Let's just analyse this for a second.

1. The man is about two foot taller than me and approximately twice my weight. I don't own a winch. How the hell am I going to get him near the hot tub, let alone drown him in it?

2. Why does he need to be naked? Not that

I'd ever drown Derek, but if I did, I wouldn't want to undress him first. Interesting!

3. I don't own a Pig. I could probably find one to borrow, but explaining the reason I needed it wouldn't be easy.

I'm sure it's the sudden noise rather than the sentiment that buys us the critical few seconds we need. Tiny leaps and the unexpected force of his body colliding against the stranger sends them both tumbling back through the open door of the cabin. When I arrive on the scene there's a hell of a lot of cursing, growling and snarling going on as my malamute wrestles with the intruder on the floor. The man has his arm raised to protect his face and Tiny has clamped down on it.

"TINY. RELEASE. HEEL." This time I speak without hesitation or any hint of nervousness. The authority in my tone makes Tiny obey instantly. As soon as he releases the stranger's arm and is clear, I automatically use the bear spray I'm clutching to subdue our intruder further. He yells in pain as his eyes immediately start to burn.

"Maeve?" He wheezes as the chemicals he's inhaling cause him to start coughing.

I freeze, not understanding how he could know my name. For the first time I take a good look at the sandy haired goliath rolling around on the floor. He looks familiar, he's aged just like I have, it's not... it can't be... "Josh?" I ask tentatively, "Josh Stone?"

"Yeah," he rasps, as he sits up and tries to catch his breath, while rubbing his eyes, which are now inflamed and swollen.

"Fuck! Stop rubbing your eyes." I command. Panicking I've just blinded the guy who used to look out for me when I was younger, I rush over to the sink and fill a large bowl with water before running back. "Open them I need to bathe them."

Josh forces his eyes open and the minute he does all sense goes out the window again as I throw the entire bowl of water in his face. Unfortunately, his mouth is open as he fights to catch his breath from the effects of the spray, and he ends up swallowing a good deal almost choking.

"Jesus, you really are trying to drown me!" He blusters, gagging and spluttering at my feet. "I knew I should have sent Kurt."

"Josh, I'm so sorry," I place my hand at the top of his left shoulder in an effort to placate him, and when he winces, I presume he is repulsed by my touch and it pisses me off. I suddenly decide I haven't actually done anything wrong. "Wait, no I'm not. You showed up here unannounced and broke into *my* house. You were going to hurt my dog; I was defending him." To make my point I take my hand off of his shoulder to use my finger to jab him hard in the chest. Not only do I nearly break my finger as it collides with an unforgiving wall of muscle, I also notice my hand is now covered in blood. "Shit! Josh, you're bleeding."

He gives a response muffled by the hacking and wheezing still underway.

"I need to get this T-shirt off." He doesn't fight me

as I try to pull it over his head, but he doesn't help me either. He is still too busy fighting the effects of my assault and subsequent restorative remedy. I have no option other than to grab the nearest pair of scissors and cut it off him. It's difficult to ignore the ripped torso I'm presented with. He couldn't be further from what I'm used to if he tried. I'd heard of a six pack but his was more like an eight. His hip bones channelled down into his trousers, perfectly framing the treasure trail leading from his belly button to somewhere my wayward mind had no business straying. The butterflies, which I hadn't realised had taken up residence in my stomach, suddenly perform a funny little dance of delight as I take in his physical appearance. If the guy is carrying any fat, I sure as hell can't see it—just a vast expanse of taut skin over toned, humongous muscles. What I can see though, in addition to the bite mark on his forearm inflicted by Tiny, is an open wound on his pec, just beneath a relatively new scar on his shoulder. It looks like it had been packed with gauze and covered with a dressing, but the recent rumble has evidently dislodged both, and now he is bleeding again. "What happened here?"

"Your dog bit me," Josh gripes as I inspect his open wound to see what I can do to repair the damage.

"He was just protecting me," I sigh. "You used to do the same when we were younger."

"I wish I hadn't bothered now," he mutters. Now the effects of the bear spray are under control, I'd definitely say the guy was pissed.

I ignore his attitude and clarify, "I meant the injury to your chest."

"I was pushed through a glass door."

"You were pushed, or you weren't concentrating so you fell?" I joke. Clearly unimpressed by my dog's recent body-slamming him through my door, Josh isn't ready to see the funny side.

"And the shoulder?" I let my fingertips ghost over the angry red dimple in his skin.

"I got shot," he growls.

"I can understand why," I acknowledge dryly, not daring to meet his eye. "Break into that person's house too, did you?"

"No!" He snaps instinctively, before changing his mind, "Well yes, but there were extenuating circumstances."

"Were there *extenuating circumstances* that caused you to break into my place?" When he doesn't answer, I stand and offer him my hand. It's more of a peace offering, there's no way I'm going to be able to heave his huge ass up off the floor. "C'mon, I need to get you cleaned up and I sure as hell aren't going to be able to carry you to the bathroom. You've..." As my eyes involuntarily rake over his half naked body, my mouth goes inexplicably dry and for some unknown reason I struggle to find the vocabulary I need. "...expanded over the years."

"Expanded?"

"Um... yeah, you know," I wave my extended hand around gesturing to his size.

He cocks his head to one side and frowns not

seeming to understand.

"You're... um... bigger than I remember."

He's glaring at me but the corners of his mouth quirk in amusement. The action is so fleeting, I almost think I imagine it. He pushes himself to his feet without taking my hand.

"Maybe you've..." He mocks me by waving his hand at me the same way I did him, "...shrunk, making me seem larger."

I withdraw my olive branch with a huff.

"Which one?" He barks, as he looks across at the two closed doors off to one side.

"Left." I match his tone and then stand mesmerized as he walks away from me. The man really is a work of art, and I'm not just talking about the ink etched into his skin, the sleeve of intricate designs that decorate the highly defined muscles of his left arm. The hard plains of his back are softened by the graceful curves and contours of a rather delectable ass, which fills out his pants in the best possible way.

"Are you coming, or are you just going to keep standing there, gawking at my butt?" He doesn't turn around, so I know the arrogant jerk's just speculating.

"I'm sooo not," I reply dramatically, overtly offended.

"You know I can see you in that mirror, right?"

He points to the wall, and I follow his finger to see the one I'd forgotten was there. Our eyes connect via our reflections, and he smirks, as my cheeks flame.

Busted!

Chapter 2

Josh

Well. Well. Well. Little Maeve Mercer is all grown up! I think! It's hard to tell with what she is wearing. When she comes charging at me with her nostrils flaring, eyes blazing and teeth bared, screeching something about wanting to get me naked in her hot tub even though she thinks I'm a pig, she's like some sex-starved wild woman hurtling through the woods with me as the target she has set in her sights. What the oversized sweatshirt she is wearing doesn't hide of her body; the loose-fitting sweats do. I almost didn't recognise her. It wasn't until I registered the pretty, heart-shaped face—the one I had become so familiar with as a child—that I was sure it was her. I always remembered her as having a gorgeous main of caramel coloured hair, she's not bald, but whatever she has going on up top, is struggling to free itself from the harsh bun that she has pulled so tight it almost looks like she is trying to give herself a face lift. I'm sure if she updated her wardrobe a bit, she wouldn't be prone to taking such desperate measures to get a man.

I've got to say I'm more than a little stunned at the words she yells at me, they cause me to pause and take stock, forgetting every bit of training I've ever had over the last fifteen years. She never used to see me that way. For as long as I can remember she has always had a thing for Kurt, my best friend and now right-hand man in my new business. When we were younger, she was constantly following him around, mooning at him. Not only was she off limits, being the kid sister of one of our best friends, unfortunately for her, she was never Kurt's type. Back in the day, he had a temporary crush on the sister of another friend, she also happened to be Maeve's bestie, that wasn't awkward at all! Since Tina wouldn't give him the time of day, he swiftly decided quantity over quality was the way to go. He went on to favour any woman with a slim, tight body, short memory and loose morals, but that's not my jam. I'm a large guy, always have been. When I hit my growth spurt aged twelve, my parents didn't think I would stop. I finally peaked at just under six foot five and that's without boots. I've always been stocky; when I started training to be a SEAL, fat turned to muscles that just kept expanding. If I take a woman to my bed, I like to know I'm not about to suffocate her or snap her like a twig. Tall or short isn't an issue for me, but she has to have a little padding. I like spare ribs on my plate, not between my sheets, and my dick will only show his appreciation when a woman has a few curves in all the right places. Unfortunately, there's been a few too many times I've been in a one-on-one situation with a woman insecure about the way she looks. I've got more battle scars on my body than any man of my age should, no partner ever seems to mind them, in fact quite the opposite, so why should I care if the person I choose to be with is harbouring the odd stretch mark or bit of cellulite under their clothes.

Maeve startles me so much when she yells, the phone I had just retrieved from my jacket pocket goes flying out of my hand, and when I look up, I see something looking like a wolf emerging from the trees just ahead of her. When it jumps, launching itself at me, my defences are down. The impact of approximately forty-five kilogrammes hitting me at full force, square in my chest, sends me careering back through the open door of Maeve's cabin. As I stumble backwards, I go down, barely managing to keep the beast's canines, dripping with saliva, from tearing into my face. I've just recovered my bearings enough to try and wrestle the dog off me, when the animal's owner arrives on the scene.

Granted, I know I probably shouldn't have broken in, but under the circumstances, I thought it was warranted. This isn't purely a social call; I needed to know she wasn't being held hostage inside, or worse, taken off somewhere against her will. Before Kurt dropped me off and we split up to cover more ground, we had swung by the practice where she was supposed to be working. We found the premises shut with no indication of Maeve's whereabouts. If I had been thinking rationally, I would have waited a little longer before starting to lose my cool. The events of the last few weeks and the healing hole in my shoulder made that impossible. In a whole different story, my neighbour's woman had been in a spot of bother, and I'd stepped in to help, taking a bullet for my trouble. With that incident still fresh in my mind and thoughts of Maeve potentially being in trouble, the protective instincts I once harboured for her surged back to the surface, making my patience evaporate faster than a snowman in a sauna.

Once I'd done a quick recce to put my mind at ease, I was planning to leave and relock the door I'd picked to get in—she was never supposed to know I'd been snooping inside. Trust her to arrive before I could finish what I'd started. While I was in the midst of being savaged, she came running through the door, making me think I was about to be saved. Instead, she throws a pan of liquid in my face. I've got to say, for a fully qualified vet with her own practice, her bedside manner leaves a lot to be desired. Before today, I've been shot, stabbed, burnt, and incurred several broken bones. It's not even the first time I've been maced, bitten, or someone has tried to drown me—such is my life. However, it is the first time I've nearly been taken out by someone half my size and a fraction of my weight, trying to waterboard me with less than a litre of water. I have to give her kudos for originality.

Attempted murder aside, I have to say I like what she's done with her place. It's not the sort of home I imagined her living in at all. For one, it's a simple wooden structure. You would have thought someone who almost died in a house fire years ago would have avoided it like the plague. It tells me she has retained her strength of character since it happened. I knew she would, she always shone way too brightly for a near-death experience to hold her back. Secondly, despite its plainness, her home exudes a charm and resilience that mirrors her own spirit. Lots of soft furnishings and creature comforts make her place a far cry from my apartment back in L.A., which is stacked with boxes I only open if I need something inside. The only two pieces of furniture I possess are the bed and the couch. It would still only be a bed if the couch hadn't been unexpectedly gifted to me by the friend and neighbour I previously mentioned. The one who also has an adorable five-year-old daughter that has me wrapped around her little finger. And I have to say, it's not just me—nearly my entire crew is smitten with her. I only say 'nearly' because she hasn't met them all yet.

My best buddy Kurt and I are in the process of setting up Stone's Personal Security Services. I say 'we', but it's mostly me. I offered Kurt a partnership, but he declined. He doesn't want the hassle that comes with business ownership, and is happy to stand by my side while I take the lead. He isn't interested in paperwork and the social politics it takes to build and maintain a solid reputation. I'm definitely the more easygoing one of the pair of us, not that anyone who didn't know me well would ever call me laid back. Kurt and I have both seen our fair share of action over the years we were serving. After almost fifteen years as a SEAL, we both felt it was time to try something new before our luck ran out. Even though we recognise we can't keep punishing our bodies the way we used to, neither of us is ready to get out of the game completely. We both thrive on challenge and adventure. I'm not sure Kurt will ever want to settle down, but I'm hoping to one day, and when that day comes, I want to have a career that I can fit around my new life, as opposed to having a family that has to survive weeks or sometimes months without me. If I'm lucky enough to have kids someday, I don't want to be an absent father who ends up being relegated to the sidelines watching while they get to call another guy "Dad." But all that is in the distant future. I've got to divorce my first wife before any of that can happen, and I've got to marry her before I can get the divorce.

Neither Kurt or I had heard from Jimmy Mercer since he took off the night his family home caught fire. It was a wise move on his part considering I was looking to tear him limb from limb at the time. So, when Jimmy called to say he was in trouble and needed our help, Kurt and I were curious enough to hear him out. The only details he would give us were that he thought his sister was in trouble and we needed to keep her safe. He wanted us to relocate her and change her name, but he didn't want her to have to go into hiding to do that. Oh no, he came up with the bright idea that one of us had to marry her—temporarily, of course—just until he could sort out the mess he was in. He seemed convinced she would be happy to move to L.A., adopt one of our names, and that if they managed to track her down, the people after him just knowing she was hitched to one of us would be enough for them to leave her alone.

Jimmy refused to give us any more details about what trouble he was in, but he was so panicked on the phone that we agreed in principle, provided he met us face-to-face to give us more information. He reluctantly accepted our terms, but when Kurt and I showed up at the appointed place and time, Jimmy never showed, so we rushed straight here to check on Maeve.

Although we hadn't seen either Maeve or Jimmy in years, we still kept in touch with family back home. The rumour mill was convinced Maeve and Jimmy hadn't seen each other or spoken in years, so I guess deep down, Kurt and I agreed to the plan since we thought she would already be happily married, letting us both off the hook. Imagine our surprise when I got my team to do some digging and they discovered she was still single and living a modest life as a vet back in our hometown. Kurt and I did rock, paper, scissors to determine who would drop the bomb and take the long walk down the aisle. I lost.

During my battle with Tiny, pain flared as I felt the wound on my chest—previously packed and professionally dressed—burst open. So it's no surprise when Maeve points out that I'm bleeding and directs me to her bathroom to clean me up. I was a bit afraid she was keeping good on her promise to throw me naked into her hot tub when she whipped out those scissors and started to cut me out of my clothes. But she did appear to be showing remarkable restraint until I caught her checking out my rear. At first, I thought I must have landed in something when I fell, and brushed the back of my pants with my hand to check if there was anything stuck to them. Then I realised it wasn't curiosity or concern I was seeing in her eyes; it was something resembling lust. The woman really needed to get laid; it didn't seem that any man would be safe until she did. Since she hails from this town that we both grew up in, I'm pretty sure her options are limited. However, she must meet new people when she goes out of town on holiday or for socialising. Surely, she has a little black book—or, judging by her home décor, a pink one covered in hearts and flowers— crammed full of numbers for people she can call for a bit of relief.

I stomp into the closet she calls a bathroom and perch on the closed lid of the toilet, waiting for her to join me. When I do, I catch sight of myself in the mirror by my side, sitting up a little straighter and taking a deep breath, which helps showcase my pecs and abs. I'm pleased my sleeve of tattoos hide most of my battle scars, which are scattered across both my lower and upper arms. Not that I *want* her to check me out again, I just figure a nice deep breath will confirm she hasn't done any irreputable damage to my lungs with her water torture. It's not like I've thought about her at all since I left Vermont to join the navy, I was convinced someone would have snapped her up years ago.

I hold the pose for as long as I can and wait… and wait… and wait. When I feel my face starting to turn blue and she still hasn't joined me, I exhale heavily and shout impatiently, "Are you coming? I could be bleeding to death in here!"

"Chill your jets. I'm just checking on my dog, he's had a bit of a shock," she shouts back.

What the everlasting fuck! "Yeah, you do that, he might need a hand picking my flesh from his teeth." I yell back incensed, expecting her to come running.

She doesn't. "Great call," is the response I get, followed by, "I wouldn't want him to get an infection. Stop being a big baby and just wait your turn, I'll be there in a few minutes."

"People don't usually keep me waiting!" I yell a bit too tersely, I don't mean to come across as arrogant, after all I'm only stating a fact.

"Wow, it sounds like you're quite the celebrity! I must have missed the memo – can I get your autograph, let me just find a pen."

"If I die in here, you'll never be able to move me to get me out. I'll be stinking up the joint for months."

"Don't worry, if it comes to it, I'll dissolve your body in acid and when you've liquified I'll use the shower to flush you down the drain."

For fuck's sake. When did the sweet-natured, compliant little girl from fifteen years ago turn into a sex-starved assassin with no dress sense and clear serial killer tendencies? After another couple more minutes of just hanging around, I start rifling through the tiny cabinet in search of anything I can use to patch myself up. Unless I can work miracles with the variety of lotions, potions and make up products inside, I'm shit out of luck. There is a strip of painkillers, I pop a couple from the blister pack and swallow them whole, tossing the packet back in the cupboard before using my hand as a cup to wash them down with some water from the sink. I find a solitary tampon. One! I'm no expert, but surely she should have more than one. Regardless, I think I might be able to use it to plug the hole the top of my chest somehow. With nothing else available, I figure I'll have to make it work. Before I start, my bladder decides it needs a break, I hold my makeshift bandage between my teeth to free up my hands, it's in a sealed pack so there's no risk of contamination. No sooner have I dropped my pants to point the python at the porcelain than the door flies open and Maeve appears.

It's a good job I've got nothing to be shy about.

"Oooh, s...sorry," she stutters, dropping the medical supplies she's carrying. They clatter to the floor, rolling in all directions. She recovers quickly from her surprise, looking me in the eye and frowning, "You could have asked for me to hang fire for a few minutes. Why have you got one of my tampons in your mouth? Where exactly were you going to put that?"

I spit the offending item out of my mouth and it ricochets off the wall. "And risk waiting another half hour for you to reappear?" I finish what I'm doing and zip up. When I turn, Maeve's rooted to the spot staring at my waist line with crazy looking eyes and a somewhat dazed expression on her face. "Are you okay?" I growl.

"Hmm?" The sound of my voice drags her back from whatever jolly her brain had dragged her off on. Her eyes snap back to my face and her cheeks bloom a fetching shade of pink.

"Can we move this along a bit, I'm starving," I slam the toilet lid closed and sit back down on it. "What's the time?" It was a rhetorical question, but I guess she doesn't notice when I check my wristwatch to see it's nearing seven and realise I haven't eaten since breakfast.

"I'm not sure I'll just go check the cock... clock." Maeve corrects herself before dashing off.

"Are you coming back?" I yell. When I don't get an answer and she doesn't reappear, I retrieve the medical supplies she left behind on the floor, and use them to patch myself up the best I can.

Twenty minutes later I wander back into the main living area to find it empty. A cursory glance through one of the windows lets me know she is standing by the edge of the pond, her dog by her side, staring wistfully over the water. My stomach rumbles and I head to the kitchen area to raid the fridge. There's not much of a choice, a bowl crammed full of animal food and a couple of steaks. I find a couple of potatoes and grab the steaks. It's a lovely evening and the fire pit outside has a grill on top. The sun is just starting to set, and there's nothing better than the flavour of a perfectly grilled steak cooked beneath the stars. Maeve is so lost in thought she doesn't even notice me when I head outside and start preparing the fire. I've just struck my lighter and am about to ignite the kindling when my phone starts chiming from the bushes where it landed earlier. The sudden sound makes both Maeve and I turn in its direction. When she sees the flame in my hand and what I'm about to do, she comes flying at me for the second time today.

Thankfully, this time she's ahead of her dog who doesn't seem to perceive me as a threat since Maeve appears to have accepted me, and I'm also prepared enough for her attack to catch her when she launches herself at me.

"NOOO!" She screams. Batting my lighter out of my hand. Thankfully it extinguishes itself before hitting the dry brush on the ground.

"Shit, what's wrong?" I smell the air for gasoline or any other flammables I may have missed.

She starts batting me with her hands. "Did you forget I nearly perished in a fire?"

"Says the woman who just flicked a naked flame out of my hand onto natures finest tinder." I absorb her blows like the ocean does a raindrop.

She sighs and drops her head, "What are you

doing here Josh?"

"Trying to cook you dinner."

"Not here, here," she gestures to the fire pit. Before splaying her arms wide to indicate she means the overall vicinity. "Here!"

"We'll get to that later; it's been a long day. I'm tired, hungry and my arm and shoulder are hurting like you wouldn't believe. The painkillers I found in your bathroom don't seem to be working. So, here's what we are going to do, I'm going to check my cell to see who that was trying to call me, make us some dinner, then we are going to get some rest. We can talk about my reasons for being here tomorrow." I know she is about to fight me when her lips purse and her brows furrow. I get my defence ready in my head, but when she speaks, she throws me for a loop.

"What painkillers did you take?"

"What?"

"The painkillers, what were they?"

"The one's in the bathroom cabinet." She dashes off, and I'm too relieved to be able to avoid the difficult conversation I was dreading to question it. I grab my phone and check the call log. As I suspected it was Kurt. I dial the number, and he answers immediately as if expecting my call.

"You find her?"

"Yeah, she arrived not long after you dropped me off," I grin, "Want me to say hi?"

Kurt snorts in amusement. "I'll tell her myself when I swing by to pick you up tomorrow."

"What do you mean? Have you found Jimmy? Is

this all just some kind of hoax?"

"No. It's the other thing. If everything's copasetic, and there's no threat here right now, we need to get back to L.A. and finish taking care of things there. We can't keep Darius on ice indefinitely, questions are bound to get asked, and you were adamant you wanted to be the guy to take him in."

Darius Voss was the man stalking and threatening my latest client, and also the idiot who made the mistake of glassing me. Despite terrorising his ex-girlfriend for weeks and frightening the life out of her, the police couldn't do anything since he always found a way to effectively cover his tracks. In desperation, she hired me to keep her safe. Kurt and I planned a sting operation to gather enough evidence to put him away. We meticulously mapped out every detail, from bugging his apartment to tracking his movements, ensuring we left no stone unturned. We were only supposed to be gathering enough intel to get him arrested. But after he made the mistake of trying to assault her in broad daylight, with me stepping in to protect her and earning the laceration on my chest in the process, I decided I wanted to take a more proactive approach in his rehabilitation by having some personal one-on-one time with him before handing him over to the cops. The call from Jimmy came in and bought him some time. Which is probably just as well, for if I hadn't suddenly been called away and given some time to cool off, there might not have been a body left to hand over. The man in question is currently being detained and watched by a couple of my crew at my behest until I return.

Knowing that the anticipation of what's in store for him when I get back is torturing Darius far more than anything else I could do right now pleases me no end. But, deep down, I know Kurt is right—this situation needs to be wrapped up quickly, if only to free up the men I have watching him.

Even though I should be at the helm overseeing my new business since it is still in its fledgling stage, and I have more jobs rolling in than I can comfortably handle with the resources I currently have at my disposal, there's no way I'm about to leave Maeve unless I know she is one hundred percent safe. She's an old friend, and I've done more for people I've known less.

Kurt reads more into the situation as he fills in my silence. "You've still got a soft spot for her, haven't you?"

"What?"

"Don't give me that. We all saw the way you were with her when we were kids, then the night of the fire…"

"I don't know what you're talking about," I bark, cutting him off. "It's you she always fawned over, but that's beside the point. Until we find Jimmy and figure out what's going on with him, Maeve isn't to be left on her own. If anything happens to her, you'd never forgive yourself either, and don't you dare try to deny it. Get a couple of the lads down here to keep an eye on her while with deal with the situation in L.A."

"Ace and Blake do? They can sit on their ass for hours watching paint dry. This job should be perfect for them."

"Yeah. If I'm leaving, I'm not going to mention anything to Maeve about our conversation with Jimmy just yet, I don't want to worry her if there really is nothing for her to worry about. She seems…"

"Josh?" Kurt prompts when I don't finish.

"I don't know, one minute she's like, really nervous and skittish, the next she is ripping me a new one."

Kurt laughs heartily, something he doesn't do often. "Finally found someone not afraid of your sorry ass, eh? This I can't wait to see. What's her boyfriend like? I bet he took one look at you and wished he'd chosen someone else to be with."

"What's that supposed to mean?"

"Well, if I was with the girl you had a thing for, and then you turned up on my doorstep throwing your weight around, I'm not sure I'd be too happy."

"I do not have a thing for Maeve, and it's a moot point because she's living alone. At least, I think she is, I haven't asked."

"Want me to get Axel to check?"

"Not necessary. Boyfriend or not, I'm just here to make sure she isn't in any danger. If he doesn't get back in touch, it's Jimmy we need to find, keep Axel on that and whatever else happens, don't let him get distracted."

"Gotcha."

"And when the guys get here tomorrow…"

"You don't want Maeve to see them or to know she is under surveillance," Kurt finishes for me. That's one of the best things about working with someone you've known for years—the fact that you can pre-empt each other's moves without hardly ever having to explain yourself.

"Where are you staying tonight?" I ask.

"Unless you want me to take the night shift…"

"I got it." I don't mean to snap but I can't help myself, Kurt chuckles.

"Since you don't want me there," I frown at his strange choice of phrasing—I don't need him would have been more accurate. Nevertheless, I don't say anything as he continues. "Liam said I could crash at his, so I've got it covered. We might go out to grab a few beers later if you want to join us."

"Hoping to see Tina are we?" I ask mischievously. He can dish it, but let's see if he can take it?

"She moved to New York."

Damn. "What about Maeve?"

"Bring her with, it'll be good to see her."

"Maybe." *As in, not a chance.* "Text me the details and I'll see what she says, she looks kinda tired so I doubt she'll want to go out tonight."

"Put her on, I'll say hi and check." I can tell by his tone the fucker is smirking.

I bristle but try to remain stoic, "I can't, she's

busy."

"Sure she is," Kurt chuckles again. "I'll see you tomorrow. Have a nice evening." Are the last four overexaggerated words I hear before he hangs up, just as Maeve comes crashing back through the cabin doors, waving the strip of painkillers from her bathroom cupboard at me.

"Please tell me you didn't take two of these?" She demands forcefully.

"Why? What's the problem?" Irritated by her tone, I cross my arms and stare her down.

"Well let's just say you won't be getting pregnant anytime soon," she sighs.

Fuck! I feel myself starting to sweat, and try not to let my panic show as I stare at the serious expression on her face. Instinctively, my immediate reaction is to want to put my fingers down my throat in the hope the drug hasn't been absorbed into my system and I can throw it up. Then I realise that she's a doctor, okay an animal doctor, but surely she is going to know if I'm about to get any adverse reactions or long-term side effects from my mistake. I try to act unfazed as I ask ever so nonchantly, "Ah... so... um... do you think I might get sick?"

"I wouldn't think so? You only get morning sickness when you are actually pregnant."

Wise ass! I cross my arms and try to look threatening, since it works with most people when they try to evade answering my questions. But Maeve just looks like she is about to burst out laughing when I growl, "You know what I mean."

She ponders for a few seconds, "Well, you probably won't have to shave for a few days, you can say goodbye to your nuts, and your boobs probably won't get as big as these..." She pulls the loose sweater she is wearing tight to her frame for a few seconds, accentuating the rather shapely figure of the body hidden underneath. It's a move that shocks me more than it should. From what I can tell, there's definitely more than a handful beneath her chosen attire, a thought that pleases me as I definitely do not have small hands. My wandering mind helps to temporarily distract me from my current predicament as I try not to stare. "...but you should be able to grow a decent pair. Are you okay? You've gone a bit pale."

It's not normal for my legs to give up on me, but as I stagger over to grab Maeve by the shoulders and shake her lightly, they do a great job of resembling cooked noodles. As I come crashing back down to earth, panic sets in and my words come tumbling out in a rush. "What do I do? Is there a cure? Can you give me something? Should I try and throw them up?"

"Jeez," Maeve pushes me away. "I'm just shitting with you, I doubt you've taken enough hormone to throw your body out of balance with just a couple of pills, especially considering the size of you. I can pretty much guarantee there's going to be no long-term effects. I'd lay off them going forward though," she laughs.

"Not funny." I bark, as I push past her to stalk

haughtily back into the cabin.

"Actually, it kinda is," she sniggers, as she follows me inside.

I glare at her and it just makes her giggle more. I grab the steak and potatoes from the top of the kitchen counter where I left them, and make to leave.

"Where do you think you are going with those?" Maeve blocks my path with her hands on her hips.

"Outside to the grill." I try to skirt round her but she blocks me again.

"You can't," she tells me crossly.

I put down the plate of meat and vegetables I'm carrying so I can give her my full attention. "Look Maeve," I start sympathetically, "I know what happened to you when you were younger was bound to leave its mark, but the grill is perfectly safe. I can see it hasn't been used in a while..."

"Try ever!"

"Okay, ever. But it's far enough away from your home or any trees, and there's little to no wind, which makes it even safer. I'm also just about to clear the last of the leaves and dry grass from the perimeter. As long as you treat it with the respect it deserves, in a safe and controlled environment, fire doesn't have to be feared."

"I know that. I just panicked earlier. You've saved me too many times in the past to want to hurt me now. I trust you, you idiot," she sighs. "It's just that..."

"What?" I prompt gently. Puffing out my chest

slightly, proud that she sees me as someone that she can rely on.

"Those steaks are for Tiny," she says way too seriously to be joking.

"You've got to be fucking kidding me?" I snap.

"Language," she barks back.

On autopilot, I immediately reach into my back pocket and hand her seventy dollars.

"What's this for?" She asks, perplexed.

The five-year-old that has me wrapped around her little finger. Well, every time I swear in front of her, curtesy of her aunt's training, she fines me. Ten dollars for her college fund, thirty for her siblings and another thirty for her three cousins. Even though the price has more than doubled since we met, it's plain to see I'm having trouble breaking the habit.

"Nothing." I try to take the money back, but Maeve whips it out of reach. "Na ah, since you were kind enough to give it to me, I'm keeping it as punitive damages for the emotional distress you caused my dog earlier. He might need therapy."

"I'd rather you use it to buy yourself some new clothes." I retort, if she's intent on taking me down, I'm not going without a fight.

"What's wrong with my clothes?" She looks down at herself.

"They don't exactly fit, do they? I could probably squeeze into that sweater." I say, as I cross my arms and eye her smugly.

"Maybe now, but not when your boobs start to

kick in." She comes back, not missing a beat.

I'm ashamed to say, I believe her enough to glance down my own body to see if I am having any adverse effects from her medication. Reassured everything appears as it should, I get back to our dinner options. Gesturing to the two juicy sirloins abandoned on the side, I enquire, "if these are for the mutt, what are we having?"

"Since you turned up unannounced, you'll have to share what I'm having."

"Which is?"

"Salad."

"Those leaves in the fridge?" I cry incredulously. "You've got to be kidding me?"

"I'm trying to lose weight," she snaps.

"Not anymore." I scoop the food up in one hand and when Maeve tries to block my path once more, I use my free arm to pick her up and move her out of my way. She gasps in surprise as I swing her to one side before putting her back down and striding past. She seems to take a few seconds to recover from the shock before she starts chasing after me. It's not a bad thing, since her girly parts being smushed against me incites a reaction I'd rather she not be aware of.

"Wait!" She calls. I don't stop, it's better if she stays focused on the back of me. "Seriously," she calls again, more urgently this time. "If we eat those, what am I going to give Tiny?"

"The leaves," I tell her adamantly. "He had his daily dose of protein when he ripped the pound of flesh from my arm."

"For a someone who thinks they're tough, you sure do complain a lot. He barely broke the skin." She tells me unsympathetically.

I ignore her as I let the door slam closed behind me. There's no way the hound from hell is getting his claws into these steaks. He just turned vegan! Period!

By the time Maeve joins me, the steaks are nearly done. The moon hangs high, casting the only light aside from the glowing embers of the fire, and the shards of light that spill from the cabin windows behind us. She doesn't insist on a chair or complain about sitting on the floor; instead, she throws an old blanket on the ground to protect her clothes and settles beside me. She's armed with cutlery, a plate, two drinks and three bowls: one full of buttered crusty bread, one full of leaves, and one is full of nibbles. I take the plate when she offers it and nod at the bowl of greens. "I hope that's not for me." I swipe a few of the nibbles and pop them into my mouth. They're not bad, even if they're quite hard—kind of like small, crunchy croutons.

"Don't worry, this is mine. You boys can have the steaks. I'm sure Tiny won't mind sharing his biscuit as well, since you seem to be enjoying it so much."

I immediately spit what I'm chewing out into the fire. Maeve hands me an open bottle of beer and I take a deep draw before pointing the neck of the bottle at the salad bowl. "You can't live on that," I say turning up my nose.

"I can't let my dog starve either," she replies.

"Your dog eats better than you do."

"Not really. At least not all the time. I just haven't been shopping for a while and I was supposed to be eating out tonight."

"With who?" I ask abruptly. I don't mean to sound harsh and if Maeve notices the edge to my tone, she pretends not to.

"Tina."

"Tina's in town? Kurt said she'd moved to New York."

"When did you speak to Kurt?" Maeve perks up instantly. Damn, why did I have to mention his name.

"Earlier."

"Is he in town too?"

"Uh huh!" I take one of the steaks off the grill and Maeve starts cutting it up to mix with Tiny's biscuit. When she is done, she slides it across to him and he wolfs it down. While she is busy, I remove the potatoes that have been baking in the embers of the fire, and the other steak from the grill. I cut everything in half, place one of the potatoes and half the steak with the salad on a plate, before handing the perfectly presented dish to Maeve as soon as she is finished. I throw the rest of the steak and potato into the empty bowl her salad was in and start eating while Maeve just stares at me. I point my fork at her food, "It tastes better while it's hot."

She gives me a weird look and cuts her piece of meat in half again, throwing a piece into my bowl.

"You look like you need the calories more than I do."

I don't argue, just tip my chin in gratitude. "Did me showing up ruin your plans?" I ask after a beat.

"No. Tina and I... we had an argument."

She doesn't expand and I wait as long as I can before my curiosity gets the better of me. "What about?"

"My choice of prospective husband."

I swallow heavily, and a piece of food gets caught in my throat. I cough until a swig of my drink helps clear the blockage. "You're getting married?" I exclaim.

Maeve holds up her left hand, pointing to the ring I hadn't noticed with the index finger of her right hand. "What did you think this was?"

I raise an eyebrow. "It's a bit small to make out in this light, but if I had to guess I'd say the free gift from a cereal box."

Maeve lets out a laugh. "Well, at least I didn't have to dig through the cornflakes to get it." She gives me a playful nudge. "What about you? Anyone special in your life?"

"No, not right now. I never thought it was fair while I was serving—I was away for long periods, doing things where my safety was never guaranteed. Since getting out, I've been busy trying to figure out what's next. Right now, I'm in the process of setting up my own business."

"That's great, what will you be doing?"

Fuck! "Um... advising people on security, installing systems, that sort of thing." I don't want her to know my real reasons for being here just yet, so give her the vaguest of answers before swiftly changing the subject. "What about you? Why doesn't Tina like your man?"

She sighs heavily. "Can I just say she just doesn't think we are a good match and leave it at that."

"Sure. What's his name?" I ask casually.

"Seriously?" She raises her eyebrows at me.

"What?" I feign confusion.

"I'm not giving you his name so you can check him out. I may have needed you to look out for me when I was younger, but that was a long time ago." She's waving her arms around angrily as she berates me. "In case you haven't noticed, I'm all grown up now, and I'm quite capable of taking care of myself."

I give her the stink eye. I can agree on the first part; the last however, I'm not so sure.

Chapter 3

Maeve

J oshua Stone is a big scary guy in *every* way. When I accidentally stumbled in on him taking a leak, I felt like one of those cartoon characters you see when alarm sirens sound and they leap in the air with their eyes bulging on the end of stalks. It was hard not to stare, especially when he was so unfazed about having his mammoth weapon of destruction out with me standing there. Derek by comparison has a system, since we've been dating a while, he no longer feels the need to lock the door when he takes care of business, he simply announces he is going to make himself more comfortable, a metaphorical lock to prevent me from storming in on him. Apparently, his equipment looks different in the bathroom to what it does in the bedroom. Not that I often get to see it there either. The shorts come off under the cover of darkness—aka the sheets, and he must be the only man alive that doesn't like a woman to go down on him.

As formidable as Josh must look to everyone else, I remain the exception. It's hard for me to be frightened of a guy who, at seventeen, jumped into the lake near where we lived to rescue a drowning puppy. The same guy who always used to help my mom carry her shopping and, even though he always denied it, left a beautifully wrapped gift under my Christmas tree every year 'from Santa'. He used to tell me it must have been Kurt because he knew how much I wished it to be true back then. But I eventually figured it out after waiting up one night, hiding in the hall closet in an effort to catch my mysterious benefactor.

I'm not sure why he's suddenly turned up on my doorstep after all this time, but it's like he's never been away. I feel so comfortable around him, so safe. I can speak my mind knowing that if I upset him, he might get angry and roar, but he'll never hurt me. I don't have to hold back, I can just be myself, and sparring with Josh gives me the sudden epiphany that it's someone I haven't been for a very long time. I get this deep warm glow in the pit of my stomach when I'm with him, together with this unequivocal need to push his buttons. I want to be the one to challenge the man that I bet everyone else is too afraid to confront. Is that what Tina was trying to tell me I am missing in my life, a partner whose limits I can test, and who tests mine in return? As I stand staring out over the pond in front of my cabin mulling over the conversation with my friend from earlier, I'm aware of Josh bustling around behind me. It seems I'm not the only one who feels comfortable, as from the moment he stepped over my threshold he has made himself completely at home.

When the sound of a phone ringing breaks into my thoughts, I turn and see him about to light the firepit. All my past fears rush to the surface, and a tsunami of panic washes over me. What if the fire gets out of control? What if the wind catches a spark and my cabin goes up in flames? What if the fire isn't extinguished properly and later, while I'm sleeping, it surrounds me, trapping me inside? I know I'm being irrational, but that's the thing about fear— it can consume you if you let it. Suddenly, I can't breathe. If it had been anyone other than Josh there with me, I probably would have gone into a complete nuclear meltdown, ripping the firepit from the ground, and condemning it to a state of permanent purgatory with the person daring to attempt to light it.

Thankfully, when I recover enough to register Josh through my panicked haze, the wave of emotion immediately subsides. I know that whatever happens, he will protect me. His presence gives me the courage to sit beside him in front of a naked flame and enjoy the impromptu feast he cooks up. He even splits his steak with me, whereas many men, even half his size, would have kept the whole one and divided the other between me and my dog.

Despite the shaky start, it's one of the best evenings I've had in a long time. I'm loath for it to end, but I have an early start tomorrow and if I want to get through all my appointments and still have time to get home, shower, and change before meeting Derek for dinner, I need to get some sleep. I fake a yawn and dramatically stretch my arms, hoping Josh will take the hint and leave so I can head off to bed.

He doesn't.

I definitely catch his attention, as he glances up but not far enough for his eyes to actually reach my face. In fact, they hover appreciatively at my chest for a few long seconds before quickly returning to the fire. I would have said the girls had definitely caught his attention when my sweatshirt pulled tight, as I extended my arms while pretending to be tired. For someone that is so afraid of fire, I'm suddenly tempted to play with it.

"Oh shoot," I chirp, as I 'accidently' spill the last of my drink down the front of myself. I quickly whip my jumper off and I'm left in a figure-hugging vest top displaying more than a hint of cleavage. I'm satisfactorily rewarded when Josh's eyes bug so far out, I half expect them to fall out of his head and roll across the floor. I pretend not to notice as I go up on my knees and nonchalantly lean towards him slightly, giving him an even better view. "Where are you staying tonight?" I purr, careful to make the words come out as strategically ambivalent. *I'm* not even sure if I'm either requesting information, or offering a sultry invitation to stay.

Josh's eyes flit quickly to my face before dropping back to my chest. It's clear he's a breast man. Information I store in case I need it at a later date. I wait for him to answer, but he doesn't. He's simply frozen, beer bottle mid air as if he were about to take a drink before his equilibrium was shattered, leaving him in a comical pause.

"Josh?" I call.

Nothing.

"Josh?" I try a little more sternly.

Still nothing. I think I may have just short-circuited the poor guy's brain. In an effort to break the spell I wriggle off the blanket I'm sitting on and wrap it around myself. With a sigh, I reach out and gently lower his arm, hoping to snap him out of his trance. "Hey, earth to Josh!" I say, waving a hand in front of his face. Finally, he blinks and shakes his head, coming back to reality.

"Sorry? What did you say?" A hoarse, husky voice addresses me. He clears his throat, and takes a few large gulps of beer. I guess he really needed that drink.

"Look it's getting late, and I need to go to bed, I'm afraid it's time for you to leave."

"No." That one gruff word incites my wrath like you wouldn't believe. Normally, I'd be the first to offer a friend my bed when they need a place to stay, but his arrogant presumption that he is welcome before the offer is extended riles me. Even if I don't really want him to leave, I'm not going to let him think I am the gentle, mild-mannered pushover most people know me to be.

"Go home!" I bark, putting my hands on my hips. Unfortunately, the movement causes the blanket I'd wrapped round myself to fall to the floor. I instantly lose Josh's attention again.

"Heaven's sake!" I yell, "They're breasts, most women have them." I grab mine from each side, squeezing them together and jiggling them in his face to emphasize what I'm talking about. Not that it's necessary, his eyes are glued to the items I'm presenting. Suddenly there's a deep growl from somewhere in the vicinity. It catches me off guard and I look across at Tiny to see what's bothering him, only to find him sleeping peacefully. When I look back at Josh and see the wild, almost feral expression on his face, I realise the sound must have come from him. My vision blurs as I can't help but notice the way his pants are straining. Remembering the size of what he is packing, my mouth goes dry and all bravado goes out the window. I don't wait for any kind of answer as I leap to my feet. "Stay or go," I shout over my shoulder as I rush off, "but if you stay, you're sleeping outside!"

My usual nighttime routine is completed far faster than normal. I have an uncharacteristically surprising surge of energy coursing through my body. My skin feels hot, causing my face to flush, and parts of my body that have lain dormant for far too long are springing to life. I can't help but peep out of the window every few minutes to see if Josh is still outside, or if he has finally given up waiting for me to tell him he can stay and has left. Every time I look, he is still there, sat by the dying fire and staring out across the pond, deep in thought. Twice I almost go to the door to invite him in before reluctantly climbing into bed. Sleep evades me as I think of him outside and uncomfortable. At three in the morning my conscience finally makes the decision to let him take the couch. I shuffle out of bed, but when I peer out the window he has finally gone. An unknown feeling floods through my body, something akin to disappointment at the thought of him no longer being there, and the realisation that I probably won't see him again anytime soon. Forlorn but relieved that I can finally get some rest, I settle back down, drifting into a fitful sleep until my alarm sounds at six.

It's strange to wake without Tiny by my side. He didn't come with me when I stormed off last night, and didn't scratch or howl at the door like he usually does when he is outside wanting to come in. It was a warm night so I presume he curled up in his bed on the porch under the swing, like he sometimes does when we sit outside together. I'm not worried he may have wandered off; he never goes far from wherever I happen to be.

I get myself ready for work, quickly showering and pulling on a clean pair of Jeans, white T-shirt and large, peach hoodie. I throw some bread into the toaster before pulling my trainers on and fixing my hair while it's cooking. I yawn, tired from my lack of sleep, and decide to make myself an extra strong coffee in my travel mug, hoping it, along with the fresh air on the walk to work, will be enough to keep me awake for the rest of the day. When my breakfast is ready, I sling my bag over my shoulder, grab my drink and hold my toast between my teeth while I grab Tiny's lead and fumble in my bag for my keys. I throw open the door and step outside, almost falling over the gigantic body lying prostrate on my porch right in front of me. Josh is fast asleep with both hands behind his head and the blanket I discarded the night before draped over himself. Tiny is snuggled into his side with his head on Josh's chest. He raises his head and whimpers softly when he sees me.

"Traitor," I whisper to my dog, smiling but confused to find Josh camped out on my doorstep. Tiny thumps his tail against the floor apologetically as I step over the resting form. "C'mon, I'll grab you some breakfast on the way."

I creep off with Tiny hot on my heels.

"I'm pleased to say I can give Noodle a clean bill of health," I tell Clark as he peers over the top of my examination table. Clark beams up at me with a toothy grin, showcasing the prominent gaps where the seven-year-old recently lost one of his top middle and one of his bottom left baby teeth. "You are doing a fantastic job of taking care of him."

"Thank you, Dr. Mercer." Clark's mother grabs a plastic box from the floor as I lift the three-foot royal python from my table, draping him across my shoulder. Leanne places the box in the spot Noodle vacates, then straightens out the pillowcase inside to make a comfy resting place, ready to transport the reptile back home.

I'm just about to hand the snake over when a loud roar comes from the waiting room outside. "WHERE THE HELL IS SHE?"

"Excuse me one moment," I say gracefully, excusing myself from the room.

I stomp into the full waiting room to see a furious Josh leaning menacingly over the reception desk, gripping the lapels of Aiden's shirt in his right hand, nearly suspending poor Aiden mid-air. As I survey the room, I notice children clutching their pets or parents in fear, while the adults shrink back in their chairs. I'm not sure if it's Josh they're afraid of, or Noodle, who stretches, flicking his tongue in and out as he gathers tiny particles from the air, his way of checking out what's going on around him.

"Josh," I hiss through gritted teeth, "Put him down, what's wrong with you?"

"I woke up this morning and you'd gone." Josh visibly relaxes when he sees me, but the ripple of gasps that follows his words have the opposite effect on me. Everyone in this town knows me, and that I've recently gotten engaged to Derek. Suddenly, everyone over the age of twelve is leaning forward in their seats fixated on the entertainment unravelling in front of them, as if they're about to watch the most thrilling episode of a juicy soap opera.

"And?" I flap my arms in exasperation being

careful not to dislodge noodle.

The front door chimes and Tina comes strolling in, "Maeve, we need to talk. I don't want to leave on bad terms... Eww what the heck is round your neck?" She glances to her right and does a double take as she spots and recognises the man mountain whose size dominates the room. "Josh? Holy Hell, you've... developed."

"Developed?" Josh smirks as the door chimes again and when I look across to see whose joining us, so does the rest of the room.

Another giant invades the already shrinking space. He is slightly shorter than Josh, but the same large muscles cover his slimmer frame. When his eyes connect with mine, the intensity of their green gaze is instantly recognizable.

"K... Kurt?" I stammer.

"Whose Kurt?" Someone whispers from the peanut gallery behind me.

"I'm more interested in the one at the counter, what did she say his name was?"

"Josh, I think."

"Do you mind?" I snap at the eavesdroppers, who start opening books and rifling through bags clearly pretending to be busy and uninterested.

Kurt tips his chin at me before looking me over from my head to my toes, his keen scrutiny taking in every detail, making me blush. "Maeve?" He drawls, "You look great."

"No, she doesn't." Josh barks from across the room, prompting Kurt to offer up a rare smile.

"Yes she does!" Tina rounds on Josh with her hands on her hips.

"Nice python," Kurt strolls over and gently lifts the snake from my shoulders, letting Noodle rest along his right forearm while he hugs me with his left arm.

"I thought you were going to wait in the car?" Josh snaps at Kurt.

"And miss the opportunity of seeing my little Maeve here?" Kurt crushes me to his side in an overexaggerated cuddle, almost squeezing all the air from my lungs in the process.

"She's engaged!" It's Tina's turn to snap at Kurt who seems totally unfazed at all the animosity being aimed in his direction.

"But not married, she has options," Kurt retorts before kissing me on my temple and nudging me with his hip, "right babe?"

Babe?

Josh growls, and I round on Tina, pushing myself out of Kurts grip. He wanders off cooing at the python like it's his favourite child. "What's with the change of heart? You were begging me not to marry Derek yesterday?" Another collective gasp from the room causes me to take a stand, I stride over and prise Noodle out of Kurt's embrace, handing him off to Aiden, "Can you take Noodle back to through to Leanne. There's only the consultation fee due then they are free to leave."

"Sure boss." Aiden, obviously upset at missing the show, reluctantly agrees.

"You, you, and you," I point to Tina, Josh and Kurt in turn. "Outside now!"

I storm outside with my posse, Tiny at my heels as usual. It's hard not to feel the eyes of our audience following us, first through the door and then through the clinic window.

When we are as alone as it gets, I'm about to speak when Josh beats me to it. "So, you stayed at Liam's last night?" He crosses his arms and smirks at Kurt. "Have a good time?"

Kurt shrugs, and holds Josh's stare. It's like they are having some kind of telepathic exchange. I frown as I try to work out what I'm missing, then try to take charge again.

"Why are you here?" I ask Josh. Crossing my arms and mirroring his pose.

He and Kurt share another look, and I shove him as hard as I can in the chest in an effort to draw his attention back to me. His taut muscles don't flinch and I bounce back with Kurt catching me before I can land on my ass.

"I came to say goodbye. Kurt and I are leaving town for a while." Josh glares at Kurt whose arms drop away from my sides.

"What's new?" I look between the two men. "You never bothered to say ta-ta the last couple of times you left, at least not to me. I haven't seen or heard from either of you in years. Why the sudden need to keep me apprised of your plans?"

Both men flinch slightly. When they originally left, I guessed they slipped away so as not to upset

Jimmy further. After the fire, I was still in hospital recovering when they took off, but it wouldn't have hurt either of them to swing by.

"I thought you might be worried if I suddenly took off and wasn't home when you got back," Josh says, looking a little hurt at the thought I wouldn't be.

"What do you mean, 'if you weren't home when I got back'? I'm not sure how it can have escaped your notice that we don't live together. Never have. Even last night, you slept out on the porch. Christ, you could have left me a note or texted me."

Kurt sniggers, "She made you sleep outside on the porch?"

"I don't have your number," Josh mutters, trying to ignore Kurt's mocking grin.

"Give me your phone," I say, demanding Josh hand it over. Its not a brand I'm familiar with, but with a bit of patience from all concerned, I manage to save my details in his contacts. "There! Now you can leave with a clear conscience. Just remember I have a fiancé, so if you send me a dick pic, I'm blocking you!"

"Screen wouldn't be big enough," Josh mumbles.

Tina snorts with laughter. If I hadn't seen enough to know he wasn't bragging, I might have too. Since she now has my attention, I move on to her, "Tina, I love you. Always have, always will. You are my best friend and that will never change. We had a fight, it's not the first and it certainly won't be the last. While I appreciate you stopping by, I have a waiting room full of patients and I really can't do this now."

"Dinner? Tonight? I can catch a flight tomorrow?" She asks hopefully.

"I can't," I tell her apologetically, "You know Friday night is date night. Derek has booked a table at the Serenity Springs Tavern for a change, it's been so long since we've actually been out together, I don't want to cancel."

"Date night?" Josh barks.

"I'm done with you." I snap, dismissing him and turning back to Tina. "How about breakfast tomorrow before you leave? I only have a few vaccinations booked in first thing. Aiden is more than capable in handling them; he's been asking for more responsibility now he's fully qualified."

"I guess I could hang for one more night." Tina side eyes Kurt as she responds to me, drawing my attention to him.

"Kurt," I smile at the man who used to haunt my dreams when I was young. There's no denying he looks good—ruggedly handsome, with his black clothes still giving him a dark and mysterious edge. The black ink spiralling up from his wrists before disappearing under the sleeves of his tee is new, as are the bulging muscles, but both suit him. The artwork isn't as intricate as the designs Josh has etched into his skin, but it's just as attractive. When Kurt smiles back, although I'm happy to see him, I realise how much I've changed over the years and how he doesn't hold my heart hostage like he used to. That is until our eyes connect, and I'm reminded of the night he plucked me from a burning building. Then my heart stutters, my soul weeps in gratitude, and I feel guilty for not wanting to enslave myself to him for life. "It's been really great to see you, and if you're ever back in town I'd love to get together and catch up. I know I owe you at least one dinner."

Kurt opens his mouth to speak but is interrupted by Josh saying tersely, "We'd better get going."

"You and me both," I reply, as I catch sight of the window and the open-mouthed stares from my next set of customers waiting expectantly for my return. "Tina, I'll message you," I call over my shoulder as I head back inside, eager to press on with my appointments, but disappointed that my days were heading back to the routine monotony I was experiencing before the three people I'm walking away from all came crashing back into my life for a few hours.

Chapter 4

Josh

Tina disappears soon after Maeve, and I follow Kurt across the street to where our SUV is parked.

"Are the guys in place?" I ask when we are alone.

"Yeah, Ace is on point. Blake's gone to scope out Maeve's cabin, then he's going to get some shut eye since he'll be taking over from Ace tonight. Maeve's dog is the biggest concern, her place is so isolated it'll be easy for him to pick up Blake's scent if he gets too close. We're trying to find a way around that at the moment."

I survey my surroundings, searching for the best vantage points to scope out where Maeve works. The quiet street, lack of towering buildings, and occasional flow of people provide limited hiding spots. Ace needs to be close enough to step in if he is needed, far enough away to be discreet and not get made. Kurt leans against the SUV with his legs crossed at the ankles. He knows I'm trying to find Ace and he takes it as a personal challenge since he was the one who trained him. "I don't see him." I have to finally admit.

"That's the idea, isn't it?" Kurt smirks.

"He's not that good." I narrow my eyes and take another cursory glance around. When I still can't find him, I whip out my mobile and dial Ace's number. There can't be any mistakes in our line of work, and especially not on this job. I listen for the sound of a cell ringing nearby—a classic rookie mistake—but there's nothing but the usual ambient noises even though he answers after the first ring.

"Boss?"

"Where are you? You're supposed where I am, watching Maeve." I bark.

"I am."

"I don't see you."

"That's the point, isn't it?" I glare at Kurt. It seems Ace picked up far more from Kurt than just his tactical training—he could've done without his dry wit.

I raise my arm in the air with my middle finger extended, flipping off anyone who may, or may not be watching. Kurt snorts in amusement, and even though he can't hear our conversation, I know he can guess what's being said. "How many fingers am I holding up?"

"One," Ace answers, "How many am I?"

Smartass!

"Enough to count how many mistakes you can make before you get fired," I growl as I hang up.

"Where is he?" I ask a chuckling Kurt.

"Look up." Kurt jerks his head towards the roof of the café we are stood nearby. To the untrained eye nothing looks suspicious, but it doesn't take me long to spot the tiny camera pointed across the street, aimed directly at the building in which Maeve works. "There's five currently in place, two on the front, two out back, and we managed to get one inside before anyone arrived this morning."

"Ace?"

"Blue transit on the corner."

"The decorating van?"

"Yeah, ingenious, eh? I'd love to take the credit but it was all Blake. Who is going to notice a vehicle like that parked outside a building that's being renovated. With painters going in and out all day, everyone is going to presume it belongs to one of them."

I nod, impressed that the guys got themselves set up so quickly.

"That's why you're gonna pay us the big bucks." Kurt slaps me on my shoulder and smiles as he recognises the expression on my face. Then he jerks his head in the direction of the café, "Breakfast before we hit the road?"

"Yeah, I'm famished."

Twenty minutes later we are tucking into two plates loaded with fluffy pancakes stacked high with sizzling sausages, crispy bacon, fried eggs, tomatoes, and a mountain of golden hash browns. I grab my coffee and take a mouthful before pausing to ask, "So?"

Kurt looks up and cocks his head, frowning. "So, what?"

"You stayed at Liam's last night. Tina rocks up here this morning after having had a fight with Maeve…" I pause to take a forkful of food, washing it down with another slurp of coffee before continuing, "…if she didn't stay with Maeve, and she didn't, because I was there all night and would have seen if she stopped by. I'd say it was a pretty safe bet she turned up on her brother's doorstep last night. Which means you must have seen her."

Kurt studies me carefully, and I know that look. He is trying to work out what he can say without me correctly reading between the lines and working out something he doesn't want me to know.

"We may have… bumped into each other." Kurt tries to hide his smile and it's a giveaway.

"Shit!" I drag my hand down my face. "You slept with her?"

"Nope." Kurt leans back in his chair, sporting the self-satisfied smirk of a guy who has just had a pretty wild night with the one woman who would never give him the time of day… until now, apparently. "Definitely wasn't much sleeping going on."

I groan. "Where the fuck was Liam?"

"He got a call to go and pick up his girl. When he didn't come back… Tina and I… let's just say we had to make our own entertainment."

"And was it everything you ever imagined?"

"And then some. It's a shame she lives in New York; I could have definitely gone for a repeat."

"Says the guy who usually thinks asking for a girls

name is akin to a proposal."

"Tina's different."

"Yeah, you already know *her* name!" I snap, and Kurt eyes me warily. "What about Maeve? How do you think she is going to feel when she finds out the guy she has pined over for years, has diddled her best friend?"

"I shouldn't think she'd care since she is engaged to be married. Besides, it's been years; she had a stupid teenage crush, and who can blame her? I was smart, suave, and sexy even back then. But she's bound to be over it by now."

"Like you're over your little crush on Tina, you mean? And I would say you were more mean, moody and moronic, much like you are now." I love Kurt like a brother, but the thought of him hurting Maeve is pissing me off right now, and he can tell.

"I think you can safely say I put my crush to bed," he grins, "a few times. Relax, unless Tina tells her, it's not like Maeve is ever going to find out what happened last night. With her living in New York, I doubt Tina and I will ever see each other again for it to be an issue going forward." Kurt points his knife out the window and across the street. "Besides, judging by the size of that bouquet being delivered across the road right now, if I wasn't already a distant memory for Maeve, I soon will be."

"Bouquet?" My eyes dart in the direction Kurt is pointing, and I'm just in time to see an ornate display of flowers disappearing through the doors of Maeve's clinic. "What makes you think they're for

Maeve?" I can't help myself as I concentrate on the building across the street, hoping to see one of her clients leave carrying the delivery.

"Who else would they be for?" Kurt chuckles. "Aiden?"

"Anyone who knows Maeve well, knows her favourite flowers are carnations. I didn't see any carnations in that bunch, did you?" I ask absentmindedly, as I continue staring intently at the building across from us.

"I don't even know what a carnation is. How the fuck would I know? And when did you get a degree in horticulture?"

I ignore his snide remark as I have more pressing concerns. "I'm not sure he's right for her."

"Who?"

"Derek." I mumble, distracted as another person emerges from the surgery empty-handed apart from their pet.

"Who the fuck is Derek?"

"Maeve's fiancé."

"You've met him?"

"No."

So, you know this because you got a glimpse of part of a bouquet as it disappeared through a door? A display which you believe, but can't be sure, may not have contained any of her favourite flowers, despite the fact that you can't even be sure he was the one who sent it in the first place?

"Mmhmm," I turn back to Kurt, who is grinning again. I swear the man has smiled more in the last twenty-four hours than he has throughout the rest of his thirty-three and a bit years on this earth. If Tina is the source of all this delight, whatever she did to him, if she could bottle it, she'd make a fortune. I pretend not to notice as I make an impromptu announcement, "I think we should stay another night."

He leans back and crosses his arms, regarding me seriously, "What about the situation in L.A.?"

"That shit can wait one more day. We'll leave in the morning. You heard Maeve telling Tina that Derek was taking her to the Serenity Springs tavern tonight. I propose we swing by for dinner, check the dude out."

"You *cannot* be serious?" Kurt asks incredulously.

"Deadly." I tell him gravely.

"Fine," he sighs. "I'm game. Where are we going to stay tonight?"

"Call Liam, see if you can stay there another night, or get a room somewhere and charge it to the business like the others have. Give Blake the evening off, tell him I'll take the night shift later."

"*You'll* take the night shift? You gonna sleep on the porch again?" Kurt sniggers.

I glare at him. "Tiny knows me, we're buddies. Blake needs more time to figure out how to avoid him."

"Tiny?"

"Maeve's malamute."

"The one that bit you?" Kurt's eyebrows shoot up to his hairline, before his expression changes and he smiles mischievously, "What if she wants to bring her guy back?"

"She won't!" I'll make sure of it.

"What are we going to do all day?"

"I've been thinking about that. We need to go shopping."

"No, we don't, trust me. Foxy set us up with all the electronics we need for the surveillance, and the guys bought their own hardware. I very much doubt there's gonna be that much action that we need to upscale operations further."

"Not that kind of shopping. Grocery shopping," I tell him, ignoring the look of horror on his face.

"Grocery shopping?" He repeats slowly in shock, checking to see if he misheard.

"She's got no food in the house," I explain.

"Who?"

"Maeve."

"So? She's going out for dinner tonight. How much can one woman eat?"

"What about tomorrow?"

"She can go to the grocery store herself."

"Why? When we can go for her today?"

"Who the fuck are you? And what have you done with Josh Stone?" Kurt looks at me as though he is about to have me committed, but I don't care, I'm already compiling a shopping list in my head.

Chapter 5

Maeve

I'm writing up my notes from my last patient when a knock on the door interrupts me, and Aiden peeks around the corner.

"You've got a delivery."

"What is it?"

"You'd better come see." Aiden grins before he disappears. Curiosity gets the better of me and I follow him back to reception. It's not hard to miss the huge bouquet sat on top of his desk.

"Are these for me?"

"Well they sure as hell aren't for me," he quips. "No-one ever sends me flowers."

"No one ever sends me flowers either, so what's your point?" I try to appear unfazed, but my stomach is doing tiny somersaults as I try to guess who sent them. Rifling through the vibrant display of pink larkspur, lavender cremones, blue delphinium, purple limonium, and assorted greenery, I search for a card.

"What's your best guess? One of the two mystery men you chased out of here this morning, or the one you've just got engaged to?" Aiden leans against the counter, watching in eager anticipation as I finally find the little white envelope and rip it open to find the answer.

"Neither. They're from Mr. Jenkins. It's a thank-you for fixing Scottie up. Remember, he slipped his lead and got into that minor altercation with a bike when he dashed cross the road without looking."

"And here was me hoping for some juicy gossip." Aiden doesn't even try to hide his disappointment. I do a much better job. As much as I'm grateful, a small part of me was hoping one of Aiden's guesses had been on point.

"Sorry to disappoint," I force a smile. "You'd better keep these out here and behind the counter, some of these flowers can be toxic to animals. Besides they brighten the place up. Remind me to call Mr Jenkins before we leave tonight."

"Will do."

"Oh, and another thing. Can you open up on your own tomorrow and do the first few vaccinations? I want to have breakfast with Tina before she heads back to New York. We'll only be over the road if you need me."

"Are you kidding? I've been waiting for you to loosen the reigns and give me more responsibility. Why don't you take the day?"

"We've back-to-back appointments until lunch. You can't see them all *and* take care of the paperwork that goes with them. I'd be lost without you helping me keep on top of my admin."

"It's one day, and it's not like there's anything too

taxing booked in. I'll be fine. You always manage when I'm on holiday."

"Barely. I coast until you get back."

"Maeve, you know I love working here, and I love working with you…"

"But now you're fully qualified you want to be doing more than pushing paper around all day while schmoozing our patients?"

The apologetic look Aiden gives me tells me I'm right. I don't want to lose him. When Derek and I get married, I'm hoping to scale back my hours—that's why I hired Aiden in the first place. As the only vet in town, I need backup; otherwise, our clients would have to travel miles to get their pets treated whenever I step back, whether just for my honeymoon or later, when Derek and I want to start a family.

Aiden relocated for this opportunity, and he loves it here. Few people would trade the big-city buzz for the quiet predictability of a small town where not much happens. Most trainees find my practice, focused mainly on household pets, boring—but not Aiden. This place suits him perfectly, and I was both lucky and grateful he applied for the job.

If he leaves to pursue his dream of opening his own practice, replacing him would be daunting—almost impossible. I hope he realises how much he means to this community, and to me. But in case he doesn't, I need to show him. I have to stay true to my word, proving I was serious about helping him build his own client base and supporting him as he grows beyond just being my assistant. I need to start making good on my promise before it's too late.

"Aiden, I get it. I really do. How about I take the morning off and leave you to it? Then, after we close tomorrow, we go out for a drink and try to come up with a plan for how we can improve our situation going forward. Maybe we could clear out the stockroom and set it up as a second consulting room. With the extra revenue that would create, we can put out some feelers for a new receptionist. If we can make it work, we could eventually start doing more house calls, or even consider stretching our wings by getting more involved with the Vermont Fish & Wildlife Department. Perhaps we could get a license to become wildlife rehabilitators. I have plenty of land around my cabin to provide a safe environment to treat animals until they are fit enough to be returned to the wild." As I'm saying it, I can hear the enthusiasm in my own voice. I hadn't really thought about expanding before, but Tina was making me question everything about my life. With Aiden by my side suddenly the possibilities for my business seemed endless, and I was excited to see how we could develop it further.

"Really?"

"Really." I can't help but smile at Aidens's excitement when he sweeps me up in a bear hug. "Put me down you idiot and tell me who's next?"

"Mrs Greyson. Her Great Dane needs his anal glands expressing."

"Want to start being more hands on by taking this

one?" I snigger.

"I can't possibly start treating patients until I've finished getting all your paperwork in order." He beams at me mischievously before pretending to look extremely busy.

"Thought you might say that." I reply smiling. I turn to see a huge dog trying to hide behind Tiny in the waiting room. "Mrs Greyson, would you like to bring Dexter through now?"

The rest of the day is long, but pretty uneventful. Aiden and I finally get to lock the doors and head our separate ways at five sharp. As Tiny and I start our walk home my mind is on my impending date with Derek. My face flushes as I remember Josh's response when I flashed him a bit of skin. I start to wonder if by dressing a little less conservatively, I might incite a similar reaction in my fiancé. Maybe it's my fault our sex life is a bit mundane. After all, you can't expect a car to pick up speed unless you floor the accelerator to crank up the revs a bit! Tina's right, I've been playing it far too safe for far too long, living under a shadow that hasn't been around for years. It's time for me to be brave and attempt to be a little bolder. After all, I'm not alone anymore; I have Aiden at work and Derek at home to catch me if I fall.

I'm still mentally sorting through my wardrobe choices when I push open the front door to my cabin and look around. Everything looks the same, but something's different. I can't put my finger on it; I just have this eerie sense that someone has been inside. I look at my dog, who seems completely at ease, and shove the feeling aside. I have a date to get ready for, and I really don't want to be late. I can't explain why, but my recent interactions with Josh and then Kurt, have left me feeling more alive than I've felt in a long while, and if I'm honest, it's making me a little frisky. I'm determined to have a good time tonight.

I go into the bedroom and lay the dress I'm planning to wear out on the bed, ready for when I've showered. I bought it a while back but never had the guts to wear it until now. It's made of a striking red material that hugs the curves of my body. The plunging neckline gives way to a delicate lace trim that accentuates my décolletage, and the skirt falls to my calf with a thigh-high split on the left side. As I run my fingers over the fabric, a wave of anticipation and excitement washes over me. Tonight's date is going to be special. Derek doesn't stand a chance.

I skip round to the bathroom; fling open the door and freeze. Stacked on the floor is the biggest pile of sanitary products I've ever seen in my life. A variety of every size, shape, and design imaginable.

"What the fuck?" I exclaim out loud, starting to panic until common sense prevails. If anyone were here to harm me, I doubt they would come bearing gifts—no matter how unique and bizarre those gifts may be. And Tiny, he wouldn't be so relaxed if there was someone still around. I immediately go back into the living room and scan the area. The furniture is still in place, but the room looks... tidy. Not that my place is ever usually in that much of a mess. Although owning a Malamute does mean I have to put up with a certain amount of shedding. It's a small price to pay for having such a majestic and loyal companion. Even though I groom Tiny regularly, it doesn't stop me from finding a lot of loose fur around the house at times. Not today, though. It definitely looks like the rug has been hoovered and the couch cushions plumped up. The kitchen has been cleaned too—no toast crumbs on the counter or used mug in the sink. What the hell is going on? I'm almost too afraid to open the fridge. Is this going to be like you see in the movies, when after being lulled into a false sense of security, a poor unsuspecting victim is suddenly confronted with a severed limb on a plate and a creepy note that reads 'you're next'? Thankfully, that's not the case here. When I finally find the courage to take a deep breath and yank the door open, I find it fully stocked. The bottom half is filled with beer—the good kind—while the top is stacked with food. I close the fridge and work my way around the cupboards, which are usually bare, only to find they are so full I'm assaulted by a bag of pasta as it falls from a shelf. Even Tiny has been taken care of, there's a new metal bin I hadn't noticed before now. When I remove the lid and peer inside, it's full of different types of dog food. I smile, it has to be Derek. He's done this to surprise me, he knows that I rarely have time to go out of town for a large shop, he must have arranged this. Aside from my parents he is the only other one who knows where I keep my spare key. I grin and rush back into the bathroom, eager to jump in the shower and transform myself from head to toe. I'll scrub away the day's stress, pamper my skin, and style my hair to perfection. Tonight, I'll step out feeling refreshed, radiant, and ready to take on the world. That man is not going to know what's hit him!

Even though it's warm out, when I leave the house at half past seven, I make sure to cover myself in a long black coat. Not only do I want to surprise Derek with an unveiling when I arrive, but I'm also not confident being so brazenly dressed when I'm alone and around strangers. I stumble in my heels as I make my way to my car. The terrain around the cabin isn't made for tottering around in strappy sandals with four-inch stiletto heels, so I try to make the brief journey from the cabin to the small jeep on tiptoes to prevent myself from sinking into the soft ground. To be fair, it's easier than trying to keep my balance in the delicate shoes that I haven't worn since... well, forever!

I also hadn't figured on how difficult it would be to drive in them. I haven't even made it to the main road before I decide to temporarily ditch them in favour of a pair of dirty boots I find languishing behind the back seat. I figure I can change back when

I'm in the restaurant car park. The heels give my legs the illusion of being longer, with a more slender and toned appearance—essential since the split in my dress's skirt will undoubtedly draw any eyes that aren't already focused on my abundant cleavage.

Once I arrive, even though I don't spot Derek's car in the car park, I make my way straight inside. Serenity Springs Tavern is a beautiful old-style inn. Much like my cabin it's set in a clearing surrounded by woodland and overlooking a picturesque pond. It's just on a much larger scale than my plot. Outside, there are tables on a large veranda overlooking the water. During the evenings, candles on the tables and posts adorned with twinkling lights give the area a warm, romantic glow. It's a huge draw for any tourists that happen to be in the area, and has played host to many a proposal. While it's nice to dine al fresco during the day, locals tend to avoid the area by night, preferring the inside which is no less appealing with its large open fire complementing the rustic charm and cozy decoration. It also has the added benefit of allowing you to dine in peace, away from the midges and nocturnal critters that come alive over the water as darkness begins to fall.

The restaurant's busy tonight, lots of people out socialising, and generally having a good time. There are only two empty tables, the one that I'm shown to, obviously reserved for Derek and me, and the one directly adjacent to it. Our table is tucked away in a secluded nook making it significantly more private than most of the others. A solitary tealight flickers in the centre of the burgundy tablecloth with white underlay, setting the perfect scene for a seduction. I decline the offer for my coat to be taken just yet, preferring to wait for Derek's arrival. Our reservation is for eight and I check my watch to see it's five to. Punctuality is essential to him, so I know Derek won't be late. The waiter pours me some water and deposits two menus on the table before excusing himself, leaving me to peruse the options while I wait for my unsuspecting prey to arrive.

"Maeve, darling," Derek's soft voice breaks into my thoughts a few minutes later. "I almost didn't recognise you. Have you washed your hair? It looks… voluminous."

I don't mean to frown but I can't help myself. My hair is quite thick and easily tamed by pulling it into my usual bun when wet. It took ages to dry it before coaxing it into the loose curls that are currently cascading down over my shoulders. His reaction makes me wonder if all the effort was worth it.

"Don't you like it?" I try to keep my voice even as Derek kisses me on the cheek and takes the seat opposite me.

"I can certainly say you look different."

"Different good?" I'm not usually one to fish for compliments but voluminous…seriously?

"It's not really you, is it? And what have you done to your face; you look like you've given yourself two black eyes."

"You don't like my makeup? I thought I'd try out a new look," I mutter. So the whole sultry, smoky-eyed look I was going for with my eyeshadow obviously hasn't hit the mark either. I only wasted an hour of my life trying to look good for you, jerkoff! "It took a while to perfect, but now I've got the hang of it, I'm sure I could create the same look on you in half the time, and without the aid of brushes." I deadpan.

Derek eyes me warily as I pick up my menu and resume studying it.

"I'm glad you weren't waiting long," he ventures tentatively.

"What makes you think I wasn't?" I answer nonchalantly.

"I wasn't late Maeve," he snaps tersely. "And you still have your coat on."

That I do. With one final rabbit to pull out of the hat, I mellow slightly, "I'm sorry, I guess I'm just a little tired. I wanted to make this evening special so I thought I'd dress up a little for you." I take Derek's hand across the table, "Can we start again?"

His face softens and his fingers wrap round mine. "I'm sorry too. It's been a long day, stressful, but I was really looking forward to seeing you tonight." He waggles his eyebrows confirming we're on for sexy time later. The move dislodges his glasses and they slide down his nose. He pushes them back in place and drops my hand, public displays of affection were never really Derek's thing. "I guess you just surprised me. Why don't you make yourself comfortable?" He gestures to my coat, "then we can go ahead and order."

As if by magic, our waiter appears and starts to pour Derek a glass of water. I stand, making sure to hold Derek's eyes as I do, grasping my moment to slowly unbutton my overcoat before letting it slide off my shoulders. I certainly get a reaction, but it's not quite the one I was expecting. Derek's jaw hits the floor just as the distracted waiter loses focus, causing his aim to drift and spill about half a litre of water into Derek's lap. Derek squeals and leaps to his feet, shoving the table forward and, by default, me back into a brick wall. At least I think it's a brick wall, until it sprouts arms and I'm suddenly encapsulated in a piece of material so large it dwarfs me. "Here, put this on. I wouldn't want you to catch a chill," a deep voice growls sternly.

I'd recognise that voice anywhere. I spin round to see a shirtless Josh staring at me with a face like thunder. "What are you doing you crazy person?" I bellow, trying to fight my way free from the shirt he has me wrapped in. "This is a respectable establishment and you look like a... a... topless waiter!"

"He can serve me anytime," a woman at a nearby table gushes, much to the chagrin of the guy she is with. "Is he going to take his shirt off too?" She waves a spoon in Josh's direction and I peer over his shoulder to see a grinning Kurt hovering behind him.

"No!" Josh snaps.

"Pity."

Kurt throws a wink in the woman's direction,

while I offer her a glare that makes her hurriedly stop gawking at Josh's naked torso and return to her half-eaten dessert.

I hear a snort of amusement from Kurt as he tells Josh, "New business idea for you if the current one doesn't pan out."

Josh throws silent daggers in his direction before turning back to face me.

"Put the shirt on Maeve, you look like you left home in your underwear," Josh commands.

"It's a dress! You told me to get some new clothes!" I shout.

"I meant warmer ones!" He yells back.

I plant my hands firmly on my hips, and growl, "I thought you'd left. What are you doing here?"

"Having a meltdown by the looks of it." Kurt chuckles, answering on Josh's behalf.

There's a gentle cough from behind me. "Maeve, do you know these... gentleman?" Derek asks warily.

"Yes, she does," Josh barks in a tone that makes the question seem like an inconvenience. "Dude, you look like you've pissed yourself, go and get yourself cleaned up."

Derek looks down at himself mortified, then runs off calling a hasty, "I'll be right back."

"Strike one!" Josh holds his pointer finger up right in front of my face. I bat it away instinctively.

"What the hell are you talking about?"

"Sir." The maître de interrupts us, or tries to. Josh ignores him, he's too intent on yelling at me.

"What sort of guy runs off leaving his girl alone with two strange men he doesn't know. Anything could happen?"

"Yes! She could murder one of them." I shout back.

"Sir!" The maître de taps Josh on the shoulder prompting him to turn. The look on Josh's face can't be good, because he shrivels back a few paces.

"What?"

"If you don't put your shirt back on, I'm afraid I'm going to have to ask you to leave. You're upsetting the other guests."

"No he's not!" The woman from before pipes up again. Her date chastises her but she looks unrepentant.

I throw the shirt he was trying to smother me in back at him, and watch as he reluctantly shrugs it on. I have to admit, other than him needing an attitude adjustment, he wasn't bothering me either. I cast an apologetic look at the maître de but I'm not sure he sees as his eyes seem to be stuck due south of my neck. I'm not the only one who notices.

"You better not be looking at what I think you're looking at." Josh growls and the poor man scurries away in embarrassment. Who knew a decent set of boobs held so much power, I start to wonder if I could use them to get a discount off my bill.

Kurt pushes past Josh and gives me an appreciative once over before kissing me on my cheek and plonking himself down at the empty table beside us. "Maeve, you look different, kinda hot.

Who knew this…" he waves his hand the length of my body, "…was hiding under all those layers of cotton and polyester."

I smile at Kurt, and Josh's face goes puce. "She does not look hot! She looks like she could use a jumper!"

He exclaims, scanning the room as if searching for a spare one that someone might have left lying around.

"Excuse me sir, you can't sit there." A waiter nervously addresses Kurt who gives him a blank stare. Not a dazed blank stare, a hard faced— 'I bet you are not sure if I'm about to smile, or leap to my feet, rip your head from your shoulders and kick it around the room like a football'—kind of blank stare.

Kudos to the waiter, he stands his ground and only withers slightly, "this table's reserved."

"Then we'll just borrow it until your guests arrive," Josh answers curtly.

The waiter withers a bit more, "but they just have."

"Kurt. Deal with it!" Josh orders, and Kurt smirks at me before ambling off, with the waiter nervously trailing a few feet behind.

"What do you mean, 'deal with it'?" I round on Josh again.

"Kurt and I are joining you for dinner." Without waiting for a response, he grips the empty table and moves it effortlessly across the floor, cojoining it with one Derek and I are at. With the furniture moved and repositioned to his satisfaction, Josh sits in the seat next to mine, gesturing for me to sit down.

"Un-believe-able!" I flop down in my seat and wave at a waiter across the room. Suddenly, I need alcohol. I don't usually drink—I hate how it dulls my senses. I like to stay in control, ready to react if I ever feel I'm in danger. But given my present company, I'm pretty sure that won't be an issue tonight.

Since Derek's staying over, I'll just go home with him and grab my car in the morning. I've got a feeling one drink won't be anywhere near enough to get me through this evening. "Bring me the strongest drink you've got," I tell the waiter as he arrives. Hearing the urgency in my voice, he doesn't question me—or wait to find out what anyone else might want.

Josh and I sit in silence, glowering at each other until I'm presented with a Long Island Iced Tea. I immediately down half of it, savouring the fiery burn as it slides down my throat. Derek returns at roughly the same time, a little taken aback to see how our cosy table for two has expanded into a larger table for four. He doesn't say anything, simply resumes his place at the table across from me, his eyes gravitating to my chest.

Josh frowns, grabs the corner of the tablecloth, and tucks it down the front of my dress. The gesture is so sudden and ridiculous, I barely have time to react as he attempts to cover as much exposed flesh as he can. I'm so shocked at the man's audacity, as well as the unexpected way my body reacts to the brush of his fingers against my skin, I'm momentarily lost for words. His touch emits a bolt of electricity that shoots down my entire body. It makes my toes curl and my nipples snap to attention as they go on red alert. The fuzzy glow of warm anticipation that starts pooling between my thighs, startles me so much I start flapping my hands like the wings of a demented chicken in an effort to stop him poking around in my cleavage. Kurt swaggers back, sitting beside Derek and opposite Josh, a sly grin plastered across his face. His arrival causes Josh to immediately stop fumbling with my dress. As soon as his hands are clear, I exhale heavily before downing the rest of my drink. With a flushed face and wide eyes, I signal for the waiter to bring me another, preferably two, both made with double measures.

"Well isn't this nice?" Kurt states theatrically, grabbing a menu and asking a stunned Derek, "Do you come here often? What can you recommend?"

Chapter 6

Josh

I pride myself on being cool and calm in a crisis. That attitude served me well when I was in the forces, enabling me to work my way up the ranks before I decided to quit and pursue a different direction in life. But whenever I'm around Maeve, all sense goes out the window. Like now. I couldn't just walk up to her and tell her how amazing she looks. I turn into a complete neanderthal, even though I have no right.

I hate the guy sat opposite her. Hate him! I took one look at him and wanted to launch him out the nearest window. It wouldn't be hard to do either. It'd be like picking up a dart the guy's so lightweight. He looks like a nice enough, respectable, with his polished appearance and his impeccable manners. If a waiter had leered like that at a woman I was with while drenching me in water, I would have been sorely tempted to launch him out of the window too. I check out the expensive suit he is wearing and feel noticeably underdressed even though I'd made an effort tonight, ditching the jeans and combats I usually wear, for a new pair of beige chinos and the black shirt Maeve refused to wear. I never usually care what people think of me, everyone is entitled to their own opinion after all, so why is it so important for me to make a good impression here?

She was never supposed to see me. This mission was supposed to be purely recon. And yet, here we are! Kurt and I were planning to sit at the bar and just keep a watchful eye on the proceedings until we were certain Maeve was in safe hands. But when she sauntered in, looking absolutely stunning it was impossible for me to look away. With her stripper heels, the subtle makeup that accentuated her gorgeous features, and the long silky hair styled to perfection, she looked like she stepped right out of a dream. A dream that turned decidedly wet the moment I saw that dress. When she took off her coat and half the restaurant turned to check her out, something inside me snapped. Suddenly, I knew this night was going to be far more complicated than I'd planned because I couldn't just sit there letting everyone gawk at her.

I didn't even give Kurt the chance to talk me out of it, before I was out of my chair and striding across the room with him hot on my heels. And I should have, because the situation is now beyond awkward.

I watch Maeve down the rest of her drink and flag a waiter to ask for another.

I grab his arm as he turns to leave. I've never been one for cocktails; if I drink, it's usually a straight beer, or on the rare occasion I indulge in the hard stuff, I prefer neat liquor, usually a bourbon.

"What's in that?" I gesture to Maeve's empty glass.

"It's a blend of gin, rum, tequila, vodka and triple sec mixed with cola."

"Hold the cola! And double the measures, I'll have two." Maeve jokes beside me.

At least, I hope she's joking. Christ! I drag my hand down my face. How often does she drink like this? Do I need to drag her off to rehab?

"I can drive," Kurt tells me without asking. We're usually perfectly in sync, but this time I'm not sure if he is offering because he thinks I need a drink myself, or because he thinks she needs to go to rehab too and he doesn't want to be the one to wrestle her out to the car. She's a lot feistier than she was in our youth.

I give a subtle shake of my head, and when the waiter returns with Maeve's drinks, I order myself an OJ. As much as I need a drink too right now, Maeve's clearly on some kind of mission and I need to stay sharp because of my irrepressible desire to keep an eye on her.

Kurt leans across the table to whisper, smiling, "You sure? You really look like you could use something to take the edge off, I can get Blake back in play?" I ignore him, and grab the menu Kurt's holding.

"So, what's everyone having?" I ask jovially, in an attempt to break the tension at the table.

"An aneurysm, I think." Maeve quips beside me, rubbing her both her temples.

"Then you shouldn't be drinking," I tell her

sarcastically, while continuing to peruse the food options and not letting my eyes drift in her direction.

"Maeve? Would you care to introduce me to your guests?" The dick sat across from her simpers.

"No!" She answers him firmly, picking up a drink and taking a couple of huge gulps.

The conversation falls flat again, so I attempt to be the bigger person, extending my hand across the table.

"Josh Stone."

The idiot takes it. Big mistake. I could crush his soft, bony hand in a heartbeat. The acute awareness of Maeve watching our every move stops me, instead I do the honourable thing and let the guy keep his fingers intact. As long as they don't wander anywhere near the woman next to me, he should be fine.

"Derek Dawson."

Derek extends a hand to Kurt. I'm shocked as shit when Kurt takes it. He isn't one for banal pleasantries. When he grins and introduces himself, I feel like I've entered some kind of bizarre parallel universe.

I cough, and frown at Kurt when he looks at me. It just makes his smile broader.

"So Derek..." I ask casually, "What do you do?"

I bet he's an accountant. He looks like an accountant. Not that I know what an actual accountant looks like, having never needed one before.

"I'm an accountant. What about yourself?"

I knew it! I fall back in my chair victorious, trying to ignore Kurt, who is still smiling at me moronically.

"I'm in the process of setting up my own business." I reply.

This little nugget of information obviously gives the man a hard-on, because he suddenly gets quite animated, leaping from his chair and patting down the pockets of his suit until he finds a business card to offer me. He doesn't ask for any further details before he starts in with his sales pitch. "In that case, let me offer up my services. Any friend of my fiancée is a friend of mine."

"Thanks."

I accept the card with a false smile and pretend to slip it into my pocket, while really dropping it on the floor and stomping on it with my boot, pretending it's his face. Maeve must see because it's enough for her to finish her second drink and start on her third. She waves her hand in the air and I say a silent prayer, begging for her not to be about to order a fourth.

"Will you be in town long?" Derek rattles on, "I'd love to get together and look over your business module."

"Leaving tomorrow... early, I'm afraid." Maeve sighs as I speak. I'd like to think it's in disappointment, but I suspect it's more like relief.

"Where are you staying? I'm an early bird myself, perhaps I could pop by before you leave?"

"Maeve's." Even though I've buried my head back in the menu I'm holding so I can't actually see them, I feel the two wide eyed looks of disbelief cast in my direction.

"The hell you are," Maeve bites.

"Strike Two!" I wave two fingers in front of her face. She slaps then away.

"What now?" She's swaying in her chair slightly, the alcohol she has consumed on an empty stomach obviously starting to take effect.

"He should be the one telling me that! Not you," I enlighten her.

"Why would I have a problem with Maeve putting up an old friend for the night?" Derek asks me quizzically.

"Dude, if you have to ask, you need stronger glasses," the woman who was attempting to flirt with me earlier, pipes up once more.

Suddenly, Derek jolts in his seat, his eyes go wide in disbelief and horror. I grin until Kurt jerks his head to something that's going on under the table and realise it's not me causing such an extreme reaction. "Maeve," he chokes out, "We're in public, what's got into you? Control yourself."

I glance beneath the table to see Maeve trailing her foot up Derek's leg, it's almost at his junk when I see red and slap it away. I hold her thigh in a vice like grip to avoid a repeat performance. When I glare at her she gives me an over exaggerated pout and murmurs a drunken, "spoilsport!"

"What the hell do you think you are doing?" I

growl, disappointed I'm not the one sitting opposite her.

"Pumping the gas," she replies cryptically while giggling. "You can stay, but just so you know we're having sex later."

"Lucky you," the unknown female butts in again.

Maeve leans over the table so she can see round me to call back, "Not him and me," she points at me then herself, before waving her hand between herself and Derek, "Me and him."

"Like hell!" I growl, before I can stop myself. I'm hoping in a voice so low nobody heard me. Kurt's smug expression tells me he did, and that he's about to make me regret it. There's a flicker of something behind his eyes—amusement, maybe? It's clear he's relishing this moment.

Maeve ignores me as she continues talking to the woman on the next table. "You can have that one," she points her finger in Kurt's direction. "I'm having this one," she swings her finger round to Derek. "And this one," she jabs her finger at me, "Can go play with himself."

"Don't drag me into this," Kurt chuckles, leaning back in his chair with his arms crossed, clearly enjoying the show.

The man sat with the over expressive woman storms off and she hurries after him, but not before she pauses to dash over and hand Kurt a napkin.

"Sorry Kurt," Maeve giggles, as the woman scurries away. "I was trying to get you laid tonight."

"Maeve!" Derek exclaims forcefully, "You're

embarrassing yourself, and by extension me, please show some decorum."

Kurt ignores him and pokes the bear, "It's ok Maeve, you got me her number." He waves the napkin in the air showing her the digits that have been hastily scribbled on it. Maeve claps her hands in glee and Derek doesn't look amused. "Not that I'll be taking her up on her very kind offer."

Derek and I pick up our drinks and take a mouthful just as Maeve pouts and declares in disappointment, "Why, I bet you've got a very nice penis! It should be admired and shared, not kept tucked away."

In shock, Derek starts choking as his water goes down the wrong way, while I spray my mouthful of orange across the table, narrowly missing Kurt. I'd like to say the trauma was over, but Maeve's not quite done as she rests her elbow on the table and tries to balance her head on her hand. It takes her a couple of attempts before she finds her balance, but when she does, she let's rip again. "He's got a biiiiig penis!" She jabs her thumb in my direction.

"Meh, it's pretty average compared to mine," Kurt chuckles.

"How do you know he has a big penis?" Derek blusters.

"I seen it." Maeve chuckles like a naughty schoolgirl.

"Saw. You saw his penis," Derek corrects her, because of course being grammatically correct is imperative no matter the situation.

"Look! Can we all stop talking about penises. Especially mine!" I snap.

"Sure," Maeve sighs, and slurps another mouthful of cocktail. "It's not like you'll have one for much longer after taking those pills this morning."

"What's this?" Kurt leans forward in his chair, resting his forearms on the table, enthralled.

I give Maeve a warning look, but she's too far gone to notice… or care.

"He took my birth control pills this morning," she slurs. "Two of them!" She sits bolt upright so she can hold two fingers up for emphasis, as she does, she inadvertently jerks the tablecloth still tucked down the front of her dress and everything on the table rattles. She sways unsteadily and I catch her before she can send herself or any of the tableware flying. "His penis is going to shrink like his nuts."

Is that why you bought all those feminine products when we went to the store?" Kurt guffaws, his laughter echoing across the room. "Are you expecting shark week?"

For the love of God! I roll my eyes, trying to ignore the heat rising to my cheeks. I suddenly wonder if that's why I've been feeling so unbalanced and out of sorts, is the transformation actually starting to take place. I grab my junk under the table, relieved to find it still there. "Hang in there buddy," I whisper, much to Kurt's amusement. He bursts out laughing again. The fucker! It's a deep, guttural, full-on belly laugh. I've only ever heard him laugh like this twice in our lives, this instance included. His eyes sparkle with unshed tears as he tries to control himself.

Maeve goes to take another drink and I gently prise the glass out of her hand. "I think you've had enough, don't you?"

She points at Kurt. "He saved my life," she tells Derek firmly.

"When?" Derek looks at her dumbfounded.

"When I was younger. He ran into a burning building to save me. I wouldn't be here now if it wasn't for him." She starts to tear up and Kurt steps in.

"Maeve," Kurt starts. "There's something you should know about that night…"

"Not now!" I bark, interrupting him. He casts me the look of withering condemnation, and goes to speak again, but Maeve silences us both.

"I was so scared. So scared… he…he said he was coming to get me," her hand flies over her mouth and she starts visibly shaking.

"Who?" Kurt and I say in unison.

"Vince," Maeve whispers almost inaudibly. "He said he was coming to get me; he and his brother wanted to 'have fun' with me."

Kurt and I are left reeling by this sudden revelation. We share a look, and it's not a good one.

"Is that why your dresser was pushed up against the door?" Kurt asks.

"Mmhmm." Maeve nods dramatically as the tears start to flow. "I was trying to stop them from getting in." She picks up a fork from the table and starts waving it around haphazardly, and I catch her wrist before she hurt's herself or anyone else. "I was going to try and protect myself..." She starts strong but her voice descends into a whisper, "...but there were two."

"We thought you were trying to keep the fire out," I say dazed.

She shakes her head sadly. "I didn't know there was a fire. Not until after."

"I think we'd better get the bill," I tell Kurt, who nods, then raises his arm to summon the waiter.

"But we haven't eaten," Derek whines.

"Strike three!" I mutter under my breath. "Selfish S.O.B."

"It's okay," Maeve suddenly perks up, a smile spreading across her face. "I can make you something when we get back to mine. I forgot to thank you for all the food." She tries to wink at Derek, but it looks more like an over-enthusiastic blink. Oblivious to Kurt's earlier reference to our spree, she continues, "I'll thankyou when we get home, socks or no socks, I'm going to ride you like the steel vengeance at Cedar point."

"I don't know what that is," Derek says, flummoxed.

"Dude, it's a roller coaster. Used to be called something like the Mean Streak, I think. Let's just say it's hard and fast, with plenty of ups and downs," Kurt chuckles. "And what's this about socks, do you have some kid of fetish?"

"No! I do not!" Derek snaps as he blanches, "And Maeve, you know I like to... er... um..."

"Spit it out!" Kurt slaps Derek on the back so hard, it's only the table in front of him that stops him flying out of his seat, "Any fiancé of Maeve's is a friend of ours, if you have a little problem feel free to share. You never know we might be able to help."

"...be on top, you're a little heavy." Derek finishes, more in fear of Kurt than necessity.

"She is not!" I growl, gently pinching Maeves side. I definitely feel a bit of rib before she doubles over giggling. "Is that why you said you were on a diet?"

Maeve nods emphatically, and I've heard enough.

"What food?" Derek asks, confused. He looks around the table but instead of an answer, he gets a question.

"Whose car did you come in?" I ask him. He arrived a few minutes after Maeve, so I presume he dropped her off at the door before parking and following her inside. Knowing Maeve, I doubt very much she would be able to drive in those heels, and if Derek was planning on letting her get back behind the wheel after drinking as much as she has, it's not just Kurt he needs to be afraid of.

"We came separately," Derek tells me smoothly.

"He didn't pick you up?" I ask Maeve incredulously, prising the glass of alcohol out of her hand for the second time.

"No," she shakes her head sadly, "I always drive myself."

"Is that an escape strategy?" I deadpan, before Kurt pre-empts my next question by cupping his huge hand around the back of Dereks skinny neck, pulling his head close so he can whisper, slow and threateningly in his ear.

"How was she planning on getting home?"

"Um... well... I was going to follow her." Kurt squeezes the hand holding Dereks's neck ever so slightly. It's enough to make him expand his response, "B... but considering how much she has had to drink, I'll drive her."

"That's the right answer," Kurt growls, releasing his hold at the same time as I tell Derek, "No need."

I stand, announcing, "I'm taking Maeve home." Maeve also stands, and I lunge, just managing to untuck the tablecloth from her dress before she upends everything on it. Derek follows suit. If he thinks he is coming with us he can think again. I shake my head. "No need for you to follow."

"But..." He starts to protest and I cut him off.

"I've got her." I warn, as I narrow my eyes.

"If he's not coming, I'm not going!" Maeve says defiantly.

I give Kurt a subtle chin tip, and he responds with a knowing smirk. Then, I pivot fast, and before Maeve can so much as take a step back, I haul her over my shoulder in a fireman's lift. Her startled gasp barely registers before she erupts into furious protests, fists pounding against my back like relentless drumbeats. I snatch up her purse, sling it over my free arm, and stride toward the exit, cutting through the murmur of stunned diners. Maeve writhes in my grip, her voice a sharp melody of outrage. I push through the heavy restaurant door, the night air rushing against my skin as I make a beeline for her car, her fury following every determined step.

"Put me down!" She screams. "You'll hurt yourself you fool!"

What the fuck? It's like I have a sparrow perched on my shoulder. Trying to make a point, I spin in the carpark, pretending to search for the source of the voice I had just heard. "Who said that?"

"Oh God!" She hisses behind me. Two hands sink into my butt cheeks as she tries to steady herself. It's disturbingly arousing. "Do that again and I WILL throw up."

I set her down beside her Jeep and rifle through the contents of her bag for the keys. It's full of assorted paraphernalia, and I sigh in frustration until I find an old photo that catches me completely off guard. I remember this photo well and can't believe she has it. I look at Kurt, Jimmy, and me during better times, out camping one summer when life was easygoing and carefree. I flip it over and see the words written in familiar handwriting on the back before shoving it back into the bag and finally finding what I had been searching for. Maeve watches me in silence the whole time, swaying unsteadily until I bundle her into the passenger seat of the car. She makes no attempt to fasten her seatbelt, so I lean in and do it for her, trying to avoid coming nose to nipple with her breasts at the same time. Once she is secure, I walk round to the other side of the vehicle, climb in beside her and drive her home.

Neither of us speak on the journey back to her cabin. Maeve lolls back in her seat with her eyes closed. I glance across at her a couple of times trying to work out if she is mad or simply resting, but it's too hard to tell, so rather than rile her up again, I keep silent.

When we pull up outside her place, she still doesn't stir. So, after determining she was actually asleep and after several unsuccessful attempts at trying to wake her, I end up lifting her out of the vehicle and carrying inside like a bride. Tiny looks up, but remains comfortably reclined on the couch with his legs in the air, utterly unbothered by our arrival. Since the couch is already taken, I take Maeve straight through to the bedroom, kicking the door open so we can pass through. I put her on the bed and relieve her of her shoes, debating whether I should leave her fully clothed or remove her dress as well before I carefully get her settled under the covers. In the end I decide the dress has to go. It looks expensive, not only will it probably benefit from being hung neatly in the wardrobe, it looks too binding to be conducive to a good night's rest. It has a zip running down the left side, I undo it, and try not to peek too much as I strip her down to her skimpy underwear before throwing her comforter over her, and tucking her in tight so she doesn't inadvertently topple out of bed in the middle of the night.

Once I have Maeve settled, I raid the cupboards I

made a grumbling Kurt help me stock earlier, and cook myself the dinner I'd skipped at the restaurant. After eating and clearing up, I look around. I don't fancy another night out on the porch or on the floor, and Tiny doesn't look like he's going to relinquish the sofa any time soon. I wander back into the bedroom and place a large glass of water on Maeve's bedside table, ready for when she wakes. She looks so peaceful, and I stand there studying her for a few minutes before making an executive decision. With one option already taken and another not being favourable, I'm left with this final choice. I undress and lay beside her on the bed, making sure to stay above the covers. The sound of her soft breathing is almost hypnotic, and I soon drift off into the best night's sleep I've had in a very long time.

Chapter 7

Maeve

I wake up remembering why I hardly ever drink. My mouth is so dry it could give the Sahara a run for its money, my head is throbbing, and where I obviously couldn't be bothered to get undressed properly, I'm as uncomfortable as hell. My bra feels so tight it's a miracle I can still breathe. I'm not sure how long I've been asleep, but I don't think it can be long since it's dark outside; it's easy to tell by the soft shards of moonlight filtering through the partially closed curtains at the window. I have this hazy memory of Josh manhandling me out of the restaurant and into my car, but everything after that is decidedly fuzzy. When I try to sit up, it's a struggle since my covers are pinning me down. I realise it's that, not my underwear, which is creating the pressure on my chest. Then, it dawns on me that this pressure is also being applied to my bladder, creating the unequivocal need to pee. Once I've pushed myself upright, I notice the tall glass of water beside the bed and take a long, grateful drink before gently fighting my way out of bed so as not to wake the sleeping body beside me. I creep back from the bathroom pulling off the rest of my clothes, grabbing a t-shirt on route and throwing it on. I then squint through the darkness, expecting to see either Tiny or Derek on the bed I vacated.

There's no denying the huge sleeping form lying on top of the covers in just his boxers, with one hand behind his head, belongs to neither my boyfriend nor my dog. The moonlight seems to bounce off the hard planes of his body, accentuating the ridges that define the solid muscles making up much of his bulk. The skin of his torso has been marred by the odd battle scar, but it just enhances the raw and primal masculinity he so effortlessly exudes. Each mark must have a story behind it, and I can't help but wonder what horrors he has had to face in the years between us meeting again. It makes me want to hold him, be there for him, like I wish someone had been there for me the morning I woke afraid and alone in the hospital following the night of the fire. I get the sudden urge to repay him with some of the unconditional love and support he provided me when we were younger, even if it's only for a short while.

"Josh?" I whisper into the darkness. He doesn't stir. Concerned he might get cold; I grab a spare blanket from the bottom of the wardrobe and gently cover him. Then, before I can stop myself, I climb under too, resting my head in the handy nook of his shoulder, wrapping my arm around his waist, and hooking my leg over his, giving him the kind of affectionate cuddle I know he would never ask for but undoubtedly deserves. Warm and snug, I drift back off into what feels like the safest and most contented night's sleep of my life.

When I wake for the second time, I'm alone and cocooned back in an abundance of bedding. I'm just starting to think the night had been little more than a dream evoked by my overindulgence in cocktails the evening before, when I notice my glass beside the bed has been refilled. Leaning in front of it is the photo from my bag, the one Tina had given me and I'd tucked away during the walk home after our fight. I pick it up and turn it over in my hand to read the inscription on the other side. For the first time, I imagine the words had been written by Josh, rather than Jimmy or even Kurt. The feelings invoked make me smile before I push them aside, reminding myself this is Josh! He's never shown any interest in me romantically. Sure, he used to look out for me when I was a kid, but that was to be expected as one of your older brother's best friends, wasn't it? Just as it was Jimmy's right as my brother to tease me and Kurt's right as the object of my teenage affection to avoid me rather than be seen as leading me on. Whatever the case, those days were long gone. I needed to remember that!

"Josh?" I call as I fight my way free from the bedding constraining me. I don't get a response, so I get up and saunter through to the main living area. I'm greeted by Tiny and an array of objects set out in a row on the kitchen counter. After making a fuss of my dog, I walk over to find another tall glass of water with a sticky note attached reading 'Drink me!' Beside it is a box of painkillers with the words, 'Eat me!' "Bossy much?" I snigger.

Moving along, there is a piece of paper folded in half with the words, 'Read me!' scribbled on top. Finally, there's another drinking glass, full of fresh wildflowers I can only assume were plucked from the front of the cabin. I smile until I open the note and it makes me frown.

It's simple and to the point:

> *Don't marry Derek,*
> *You deserve better.*
> *J x*
> *PS I've fed your dog.*

I wasn't exactly expecting hearts and roses but what does this mean? Is he coming back later? The thought excites me more than it should considering I'm still currently engaged to another man. I check the clock to find it's already half past eight. I never usually sleep later than seven, usually because Tiny is up and demanding his breakfast before I get ready for work. I guess having already been fed he decided to let me sleep in. Remembering I'm supposed to be meeting Tina for breakfast at nine. I hurriedly ping her a text to say I'm running late and jump in the shower.

Tiny and I have to forsake our normal morning walk in favour of the jeep to meet Tina by half past nine. I promise to take him for a longer walk after seeing Tina and park outside my clinic, taking Tiny inside so he can wait for me there. He isn't allowed inside the café, and the inclement morning weather has made it too damp for us to be comfortable sitting outside.

"Well, look what the cat dragged in." Tina calls, as I push open the door to the café to see her sat at a table with a coffee in her hand waiting for me.

"Do I really look that bad?" I mumble embarrassed.

"You have the face of a woman that was stood on the edge of a cliff for some time, before finally toppling over it." She smirks from behind her mug.

"What the hell is that supposed to mean?"

She shrugs, "I hear you decided to let your hair down a little last night."

There's not much you can keep secret in a small town, even so, the jungle drums must have been working overtime for Tina to have heard about my eventful evening already. "How did you find out?"

"Kurt showed up at Liam's last night, asking if he could crash there." She pauses. "He told us quite the tale, said that Josh acquired a touch of the white knight syndrome when you turned up at Serenity looking like a goddess and offering yourself like a sacrificial lamb to the dark lord Derek. He said Josh threw you over his shoulder so he could carry you off to his castle and have his wicked way with you. Is it true?"

"No, it's not true." I laugh, "Well not all of it."

"Which bit? Please tell me you got a happy ending." Tina waggles her eyebrows salaciously.

"No," I sigh. "Derek went home alone last night."

"I didn't mean with Derek."

"Tina!" I wave my engagement ring under her nose. "I'm engaged."

"You shouldn't be. At least not to the guy you are."

"Let's not go there again, I don't want us parting on bad terms."

"So, what happened? When you got home... no wait. Let's order first."

"I'm not sure I can eat anything," I admit, my stomach feels empty but it's definitely still feeling the aftereffects of yesterday's night out.

"Rubbish. The best remedy for a hangover is a big, greasy breakfast from your favourite diner. Trust me." Tina orders for us both and then continues with her interrogation. "So, spill. What happened when you left the restaurant?"

"I'm sorry to disappoint you but nothing. I have the vague recollection of being driven home, and I woke up in bed this morning with Josh nowhere to be seen." I didn't feel the need to tell her about the near naked cuddling in between. After all, even I couldn't be sure it hadn't all been more than just a dream. "Josh left a glass of water on the side with some painkillers and this note." I hand Tina the piece of paper. "What do you think it means?"

"That I was right and you shouldn't be marrying Derek."

"Not that." I snatch the paper out of her hand. "Is he coming back?"

"Do you want him to come back?" She asks slowly and deliberately.

I don't know how to answer, so I deflect. "He saw that photo you gave me yesterday."

"Please tell me you didn't have it pinned above your bed." Tina looks so deadly serious I giggle.

"Of course not. It was in my bag and he found it when he was searching for the key to my Jeep."

"So you're worried he probably thinks you've been holding on to it and carrying it around with you all these years?"

Shit! What if she's right and he thinks I still have a thing for Kurt. Is that why he doesn't want me to marry Derek?

"Do you think he thinks I still have a thing for Kurt?" I ask Tina.

"Do you?" She asks, earnestly.

"No, don't be daft. I wouldn't be marrying another man if I did"

"Good." Tina shifts in her seat uncomfortably and I know there's something she's not telling me."

"What is it?"

"Kurt and me, we sort of hooked up the other night... and to be completely honest... last night as well." She flinches in anticipation of my reaction.

"What the hell T?" I bluster.

"Please don't hate me," she whispers. "It just... sort of happened."

"Five little words that probably result in at least half of the divorces in this country," I tell her, amazed. "The first time something, 'just sort of happens,' the second is more of a conscious choice. I don't get it. You always hated him when we were kids."

"No, I didn't. I always liked him, but I could never say because you were so invested. It was easier to pretend I didn't like him so he would stay away from me, rather than risk falling out with you. Then the other day, after our fight, I went to stay at my brother's, not realising he had already arranged to put Kurt up for the night, I swear. Liam got a call and disappeared, leaving us alone. Kurt and I started reminiscing over old times, there was a smidge of alcohol involved, one thing led to another, and…

I hold my hand up, "I don't need to know any more."

"Are you mad?" Tina looks at me, crestfallen.

I pretend to think seriously for a few seconds before smiling, "Depends, did all this bonding result in a 'happy ending' for you?" I joke.

Tina's shoulders sag in relief, "It did. More than once."

"Then I'm not mad." I tell her nonchalantly, and she grins, just as our food arrives and we both start to tuck in. After a few bites I ask casually, "Will you see Kurt again? Did he mention what he and Josh were up to today?"

"I doubt it, I'm heading back to New York and Kurt said he and Josh had to get back to L.A. as they had some unfinished business to take care of."

"What sort of unfinished business?" I try to hide my disappointment at not being able to see Josh again later. Then, I realise I gave him my number, and while he never gave me his, I'll have it as soon as he calls.

"He didn't say. Although there was one thing strange that happened last night." Tina stops eating while she recalls the previous nights events. "He kept asking me all these random questions about Vince. You know? Vince Castillo, that creepy guy from Uni."

I freeze; the mere mention of his name chills the blood in my veins. "What sort of questions?"

Tina shrugs as if it's no big deal, "Did I know what he was doing at your place the night of the fire? Did I know what happened to him after Uni? Where was he living now?" That sort of thing.

My stomach drops as I try to remember everything I said while I was under the influence. "What did you tell him?"

"Nothing. How could I? I haven't seen or heard of Vince for years. The night of the fire, by the time I'd rescued Liam and made it back to your place, Kurt and Josh had already saved the day. I was so concerned about you I didn't pay very much attention to anything else that was going on. Apparently, Kurt and Josh were only back in town for a few hours and they called round to check in on Jimmy. It's a good job that they did. The fire was just starting to take hold. At the time, all I knew was that they kicked down the door to get inside and drag Jimmy and his two friends out. I didn't know which friends. They were all semi-conscious, but Jimmy came round and started screaming that you were still inside. Kurt was on the phone to the fire brigade when Josh literally ran back inside the burning building to try and find you. When he got to your room, you'd barricaded yourself inside to stop the fire from getting in. He must have been high on adrenaline because he busted through the door like the Hulk and carried you to safety. By the time I arrived on the scene, you were outside on the lawn being taken care of by Kurt. Jimmy and whoever he had been with had taken off. I was too worried about you to care about that or who he had been with."

"Josh? It was Josh that got me out?"

"Yeah."

"Why didn't you ever say anything? Instead of letting me believe it had been Kurt all these years?"

"I didn't know myself until Kurt let it slip it the other night. He was the one leaning over you, barking at the EMT's and trying to tell them how to do their job. I just naturally assumed he had been the one to go back in and get you."

"But I don't understand why didn't Kurt say anything either up until now?"

"Josh made him promise not to."

"Why?"

Tina shrugs again. "Whoever really understands the inner workings of the male mind? Kurt said the EMTs wanted to take Josh to the hospital to get him checked out, but once you were in the ambulance, he stormed off after Jimmy. Kurt said he never found him, but they both went to the hospital the following morning before they left town. They were both treated for smoke inhalation, and Josh for some pretty serious burns he sustained to his left arm. Josh was certain he saw Jimmy leaving the ER as they arrived, but by the time he'd made it close enough to be sure, Jimmy had vanished. I don't know if he ever found him or what happened after that."

I frown, "I never noticed any burns on Josh's arm."

"Kurt said that's why he started getting inked. Once the scars had healed enough so he could, he covered them to help them disappear completely."

I drop back in my chair, my mind reeling. All this time I believed Kurt to be my hero, and he was to a certain extent, but it was Josh who had gone above and beyond that night. Tina reaches across the table and touches my arm softly, "Maeve, are you OK?"

"Yes," I whisper, already planning the conversation in my head that I'll have with Josh when he calls.

"You know, Liam's single again." Tina looks at me hopefully.

"How many times do I have to tell you, I'm engaged!" I wave my ring finger in the air again. "Besides, I couldn't date Liam, since Jimmy took off, he's been more like my brother too. What happened to his latest conquest... Emma wasn't it?"

Tina nods, and finishes her mouthful of food before grinding out, "Let's just say, Liam didn't much like the attention she started paying Kurt after he arrived last night."

"Neither did you by the sound of it," I chuckle.

"Look, I know you don't want to hear it, so it's the

last time I'll mention it..."

I sigh, thinking I know where this is going.

"Josh, Kurt and Liam have known you just as long as I have. None of us think Derek is the right guy for you."

"Kurt and Liam too?" That little revelation surprises me. "I know Kurt only met the guy yesterday, but Liam has known him ever since we started dating. Why hasn't he said anything?"

"You know Liam—live and let live. He thought we should all just mind our own business until you asked us not to. He said it was your life, and you should be left to live it any way you choose. Although, I think he secretly never thought things would get this far. Maeve, you know I love you and the last thing I want to do is upset you, but if we can all see it... Look at this way, like Kurt said, you're not married yet, you have options. All we ask is that you consider them."

"Options? What options? It's not like I have loads of eligible bachelors beating down the door to get to me."

"Why would you, when it's not like you've been out and about to let any of them know you're available?"

"I'm so confused, I wish the Universe would give me some kind of sign," I sigh.

"It did. It threw Josh at you, and when you didn't take advantage of him like you were supposed to, it made him leave you this note." She widens her eyes and waves the piece of paper he left me in my face.

I giggle, grabbing the paper out of her hand and stowing it in my pocket. "I need another one, something a bit more…"

Tina cocks her head waiting,

"Independent."

"Independent? What's that supposed to mean?"

"Something totally unrelated to anyone I already know, or who already knows me."

"You're crazy, you know that?" Tina gazes at me affectionately.

"I know."

We finish eating and I walk Tina outside to her hire car. She gives me a hug then grabs my hand, raising it in the air. Splaying her arms wide and throwing her head back she shouts at the top of lungs, "Universe, please send my kooky friend a clear sign to stop her making the biggest mistake of her life by marrying the wrong guy."

"Shut up you idiot!" I burst out laughing as Tina, unfettered, goes on.

"If you could deliver it straight to her door because she's going through this phase at the moment and doesn't get out much, all her friends would all be eternally grateful."

"Tina!" I try to prise my hand out of her grip as much to my dismay she's still not done and she's starting to draw attention from passers-by.

"I'm sorry she ignored you when you sent her Josh, but she knows him you see, and their history blinded her as to what could be. So, if you could give it one more shot, and if you could send her an…"

she pauses and side-eyes me, "*independent* sign this time so she doesn't ignore it, we'd all appreciate it. She needs someone adventurous to show her all the things she is missing out on in life. Someone who's patient and kind but fierce enough to protect her when she needs him to. He needs to have a good brain so he can challenge her, be unwaveringly faithful, have a banging body and be great in the sack. Speaking of which, while you're at it, I'd be grateful if you could also remember her best friend who truly only has her best interests at heart, because after she had the best sex of her life the other night, she thinks she might be doomed as far as all other men are concerned and she might need you to prove her wrong. The end!"

"The end!" I laugh.

"Well, how else is the universe supposed to know when you've finished?"

"Valid point."

"I thought so. Let me know as soon as your 'sign' arrives."

"I will, I promise! I have you on speed dial."

"You'd better," Tina snorts.

"Best sex of your life, eh?" I giggle.

Tina doesn't say anything; she just smiles enigmatically as she climbs into her car and drives away, blowing me a kiss as she leaves.

After I've waved Tina off, I pick up Tiny and take him for the walk I'd promised him. I keep looking at my mobile, waiting for a call or message from Josh, but there's none forthcoming.

At one o'clock, I head back to the vets to help Aiden like I said I would. Then, we go out for our drink and I immerse myself in the future plans for my business, if only to take my mind off of the one person who keeps invading my thoughts.

It's gone nine by the time I get home, and Josh still hasn't called. Annoyed, I take the photo he left by my bedside and shove it back in my bag to stop myself from constantly picking it up to stare at his face. It doesn't occur to me that Derek hasn't checked in on me either, until I make myself a snack —courtesy of my fully stocked larder—and settle on the sofa to catch up on some TV before bed. I haven't even been there half an hour when Tiny starts acting squirrely. It's not enough to make me nervous until he suddenly charges toward the front door, barking and growling.

From the way Tiny's reacting, I know it can't be Josh or anyone we know—he wouldn't be this protective if it were someone familiar. I go over to the door and grab Tiny's collar, making sure I have my mobile in my hand in case I need to call for reinforcements.

I'm just about to fling the door open when a loud knock on the other side startles me.

"Hello?" I call tentatively.

"Is that Maeve Mercer? The Vet?" An unknown male voice calls from the other side.

"Yes, you are?"

"You don't know me. I'm just passing through. I found this animal by the side of the road and called the out-of-hours number I found on the internet. Your colleague, Aiden, offered to come out, but when I told him where I was, he said it would be quicker to bring the animal here to get checked out. He said he was going to message you."

My mobile chimes, and I look in my hand to see it's a message from Aiden confirming the stranger's story. We divert any out-of-hours calls to a mobile we share. The phone rarely rings, so there's no fixed pattern as to who has it; it's usually whoever remembers to grab it as they walk out the door. Today, it was Aiden. Appeased and worried about the animal concerned, I unlock and open the door. "Ok one second," I call before my tongue falls from my mouth rendering me mute. Stood in front of me, bathed in moonlight is a tall, disgustingly handsome man, wearing a white t-shirt, blue jeans and a mischievous grin. He is broad-shouldered and athletically built, with a muscular physique that exudes strength and power. Cradled in his strong arms is a tiny grey and white kitten, softening his otherwise imposing presence and making him seem more approachable. As a straight, female vet in her sexual prime, it's a swoonworthy combination. "H... hey," I eventually manage to stutter. When the kitten mews drawing my attention to the small creature, I take him immediately and start checking him for injuries. "Come in..." I look at the stranger realising he hasn't given me his name.

"Blake. I would but I'm a little afraid of your dog. I wouldn't want him to wrestle me to the ground and try to rip my arm off."

I chuckle remembering how Tiny took our last visitor down. "Tiny, it's Ok, stand down." I tell my dog before addressing Blake, "Just let him sniff you and make friendly towards me, then he won't harm you now that you've been formally introduced."

"How friendly?" Blake quirks a brow and smiles at me cheekily.

I feel myself blush from my head to my toes, "You know what I mean." I chastise him playfully, before turning my attention back to the kitten which looks in exceedingly good health.

"Where did you say you found him?" I frown; he has been too well cared for to be a stray.

"By the side of the road not far from here."

"He looks in good shape. I pretty much know all the cats around here and none of them fit his age or description." I sit on the sofa with the kitten on my lap while I continue examining him for any sign of injury. "I'd say he was about eight to twelve weeks. It's a good job you found him, I doubt he would have survived long out here on his own."

"Oh, I'm sure if he hadn't found you first, your dog would have sniffed him out eventually."

"Maybe." I grin at Blake before a terrible thought strikes me. I carefully place the kitten on the floor and it proceeds to start gambolling around Tiny, wanting to play. "You need to show me where you found him, there could be others."

"There isn't." Blake speaks with such certainty; it makes me curious.

"How do you know?" I ask, suspiciously.

"Trust me. That was the first thing I knew you'd say, so I made sure there was only the one."

He doesn't seem the type of man to leave any stone unturned, so I believe him. "Oh, right. If you're sure?"

"Positive."

"Okay then. In that case, would you like a cup of coffee?"

"I thought you'd never ask." Blake smiles and it's infectious.

I trot off to the kitchen and Blake follows me, almost tripping over the kitten playing with the laces of his boots. "So," I sigh, despondently. "I suppose the next thing you are going to ask is if I can rehome him?" With two new litters due soon thanks to Mr Whiskers spreading the love, I'm not sure if I'll be able to find homes for them all as it is.

"Actually, I was thinking, if no-one claims him, I'd quite like to keep him."

"You were?" I ask surprised, before continuing after a pause, "For your... wife, or daughter maybe?" Not that I was fishing.

"Nope. I'm single, no kids. I thought the little guy could keep me company."

"Really?" I slide a cup of coffee across the counter and Blake takes it gratefully.

"Thanks. What's the process? I mean, I don't just want to just run off with him if he already has a home."

"If you leave him with me tonight, I can take him

135

into work with me tomorrow and see if he has a chip. Failing that, I can ask around see if anyone knows where he may have come from. My best bet, is that someone was passing through town like you, they stopped for some reason and he escaped when they weren't looking. If that's the case, unless they come back here looking for him, we might never find out where he came from. Where are you headed? If you leave me your contact details, I can get in touch." I don't mean to leave such a large gap before adding, "if no-one claims him."

Blake smirks, "I don't really want to leave him." Is this guy for real? "Eight to twelve weeks can be a critical age for a kitten to bond with his daddy..."

Jeez, the way he says 'daddy' makes my ovaries sit to attention and my knees almost give way. Presumably hinting I'm supposed to slide to the floor and let him impregnate me.

"... I'm on vacation and was heading up state looking for a good place to camp. If you don't mind the intrusion, I could set up on your land for a few days while we get this straightened out. Maybe down by the pond. That way I could keep out of your way but still be close enough to check in on the little guy."

"No Blake, I really don't think I'd mind that at all," I whisper huskily. We both smile at each other across the top of the drinks we are holding.

Blake drains his cup and walks over to the door, stopping to pet the kitten on route. "I'd better go and get set up then. Thanks for the coffee."

"You're welcome. Isn't it a bit dark to start setting up a tent now?" I purr. Yes, I actually purr like a contented cat, before giving myself a mental face palm. What exactly was I planning to do? Offer to take him in too. I've only known the man five minutes. He doesn't seem like it, but he could still be some kind of deranged axe-murderer.

"It's no problem, I'm used to it." Thankfully, he lets me off the hook before I have to find a way to backtrack.

"Um... Blake." I call, as he opens the door to leave. He turns expectantly, "I'm not great fan of campfires. If you need some extra blankets..."

"I'll be fine," he smiles, almost sympathetically. "Is it ok if I use your firepit to cook myself something to eat while I'm here?"

"Sure." He turns to leave until I say something that stops him and even surprises myself. "Or, you could join me for dinner tomorrow."

"Consider it a date," he tells me, scooping up the kitten that's trying to follow him outside and passing it over to me.

"What are you going to call him?" I ask as our eyes connect.

"Josh." He answers without hesitation and shocks me into nearly dropping the ball of fluff nestled in my arms.

"S...Sorry?" I stutter.

"A friend of mine knew a guy who was too afraid to make his move on this beautiful, intelligent woman he's liked for years. He was called out for being a pussy and his name was Joshua, ergo," he strokes the kitten, "Josh!"

"Oh right." I respond, more than a little stunned.

"Just so you know, I'm not like that. I see something I like and I go for it. No regrets." Blake winks at me and leaves before my brain can formulate any kind of response.

I watch him saunter over to his SUV, trying not to gawp at his flexing muscles as he bends and stretches while unpacking his kit and laying it out on the ground for inspection. When he starts to carry it down towards the pond and is safely out of earshot, I look up to the sky and murmur, "Holy crap you work fast," before finding my mobile and hitting the only number I have on speed dial.

Chapter 8

Josh

In my line of work being late can mean the difference between life and death, that's why I'm always either early or on time. Except this morning, when I keep Kurt waiting outside a full twenty minutes before emerging stealthily from Maeve's cabin.

I can't remember the last time I've ever felt so relaxed. Waking with Maeve's soft curves molded against my body was a surreal experience. I'm not a cuddler, never have been. I'm more of a—we had a good time, now if you don't mind, I need my space so I can get some rest—type of guy. Unlike Kurt, I do at least spring for dinner and ask a woman's name before making a physical connection. Even so, it's easier to leave if you haven't got someone clinging to you like a vine. If I go before my companion wakes, I can avoid the awkwardness that comes the morning after a single tryst.

Today was different. I could have happily stayed in bed, relishing the feel of the warm, curvaceous body melded against me. I wouldn't even have minded if Maeve woke as I was getting ready to leave. In fact, a part of me was hoping she would, so I could say my goodbyes in person rather than having to text once I got back to L.A. I knew there wouldn't be the expectations or demands that often came in the aftermath of a sexual encounter—ones which I usually went to great lengths to avoid—but there was a small part of me that was disappointed. Why? I have absolutely no idea. For this was Maeve. The girl who always used to look past me to pine after my best friend, no matter how many times I would defend her or try to make her laugh and smile.

Saying goodbye wasn't the only conversation I wanted to have; there were other things I needed to discuss. The words, 'He said he was coming to get me; he and his brother wanted to "have fun" with me,' keep playing over and over in my mind. The fear and anxiety in Maeve's voice when she said them made it clear what sort of fun Vince Castillo and his brother had in mind. Lucky for them, they had just been propelled to the top of the most wanted on my hit list.

I knew who she meant as soon as Maeve said his name. I was there the night of the fire, helping Kurt pull him, his brother, and Jimmy from the flames. Now I was going to make Vince regret me ever being there that night. I wanted to have 'fun' with him, the sort of activity that would either make him respect women going forward or guarantee he would stay away from them completely.

"Sleep Well?" Kurt chuckles, the second I climb in the SUV beside him.

"Did you?" I know he stayed at Liam's again last night. I also know Tina stayed there too. If he doesn't feel like discussing what went on between them last night, he can keep his sarcastic comments to himself.

"Touché," Kurt grins. "Although I'll just say one thing."

I give a non-committal grunt, even though I really want to hear what he has to say.

"We've faced some pretty bleak situations over the years, but I've never once seen you lose your cool when it wasn't warranted—until last night in that restaurant."

"Your point?" I look at Kurt to see if he is being serious or toying with me. He glances in my direction without a hint of playfulness.

"You like her... as in you'd like to be more than just good friends."

"No I don't!" I exclaim defensively. "She's a pain in the ass."

"If you say so," Kurt smiles this time. "If it comes to it, maybe I should be the one to marry her then."

The man was talking crazy if he thought I was ever going to let that happen.

"What? You've run out of women on the west coast and now you want to start working your way down the east?" I snap. "No way! Maeve deserves better than someone that's going to be out fucking around behind her back. We both know she's not your type."

"When we were younger, sure. But let's just say

she's… matured nicely. She could be good for me," he says thoughtfully. When I glance at him, I start to believe he's actually considering it, and I start to feel a little nauseous.

"Maeve's off limits. You had your chance when we were kids," I bark.

"So did you," he counters, causing my blood pressure to spike. Then he gives me a knowing smirk. "Don't get your panties in a twist. You're right, but even though I might not be interested in her that way, trust me, she's hot, so there will be plenty of others who are."

"What are you saying?" I growl.

"You snooze, you lose, my friend!" Kurt chuckles, as he side eyes me.

"Can we change the subject now?" It's more of an order than a request. "There's something else we need to discuss."

"Like how we need to find Vincent and Antony Castillo so we can have a little chat about what happened that night? I called Axel to check in this morning—mostly to kill time while you kept me waiting. At first, I was concerned when you were late. That is, until I spotted you skulking around, attempting the feat of invisibility. For a moment, I thought something was wrong—until I realised you were 'casually' plucking flowers from the ground. A scientific endeavour, I assume… or perhaps just another chapter in your newfound passion for horticulture. Definitely not an undercover floral offering to a certain someone you're absolutely, unequivocally not romantically interested in. Nope. No suspicions here." I see Kurt smirk out the corner of my eye but I ignore him. He continues, more serious now. "Anyhow, I wanted to be sure he didn't have any leads on Jimmy before we skipped town. He didn't, but I asked him to dig up some intel on where we might find the Castillo brothers. Told him if he needed a hand to pull Drew in to help."

Kurt glances over again. This time, I meet his gaze.

We might not be on the same page as each other as far as Maeve is concerned, but when it comes to the Castillo boys, we are perfectly in sync.

Kurt and I pull onto the lot of the largest warehouse of a small industrial estate in North Hollywood, late afternoon. From the outside, the building looks plain and unobtrusive. Since this is a relatively new acquisition, we are still waiting for the signage I ordered to arrive and be installed. Golden shards of light cast shadows across the large electric doors at the front of the building. These doors, when opened, lead to a vast storage area, currently unused. It's behind the wall at the back of this space where most of the magic happens. There are doors to both the left and right sides of the property. The door to the right is sealed since it's not in use, so Kurt and I head in through the door on the left. Inside, there is a small waiting area, with a locked interview room to one side and a counter running the length of the space in front of us. There's a button on the counter and a sign reading 'ring for service'—a completely redundant formality, really. We're aware of any visitors long before they step foot inside; the setup is more about putting prospective customers at ease. Sure enough, Kurt and I are greeted by Drew, one of our crew, who was obviously alerted to our presence in advance. The surveillance equipment surrounding the building had already done its job, feeding live updates to the bank of monitors in the back.

"Boss." Drew flips up the hinged lid of the counter, allowing Kurt and me to pass through to the locked door marked "No Unauthorised Access" behind him. There's a digital code that needs to be punched into a panel by the door before it will open. Kurt does the honours and we step into the heart of operations.

Inside is another huge open space. One corner is dedicated to a small kitchen, in front of which are four large couches set around a circular table, perfect for relaxation or informal team meetings. There's a door that leads to a restroom, before the wall is filled with an array of security monitors and TV screens. An elongated desk stretches in front of them, where our electronics expert, Steve Fox, known as 'Foxy', is tapping away at a keyboard. Drew leaves Kurt and me to resume his seat beside him. At the far end of the room, there is a raised platform, above which a desk sits outside two glass offices.

The woman at the desk looks up and beams at us as we enter. Mackenzie Jones, an ex-model and the wife of my A-list actor neighbour, Jared, started off just answering a few calls when I was getting set up. She helped me find this space, seeing the potential that I almost missed, and she soon became an integral member of the team that organizes all of our lives far more than she needs to. I honestly don't know how she manages it on top of wrangling four kids under the age of six, a scary dog named after yours truly, and a husband that she adores. Granted, I got her set up so she could work from home most of the time, but still.

Of the glass offices, one is far larger than the other. Kurt and I share the larger one, while the smaller office is used by whoever we leave overseeing things in our absence. The rest of the space is dedicated to pairs of desks that sit back-to-back, utilized by the team when they aren't out in the field. There's plenty of room for more desks to be added as the team expands. Kurt and I never expected the business to take off the way it has; it was only supposed to be something to keep us occupied after we left the special forces, and with our background, security seemed the obvious choice. We were startled at both the number of people out there who genuinely needed our help, as well as the number of ex-colleagues that wanted to come on board with our venture. Like-minded men who understood that, to get results, they sometimes needed to use their skills in a more unorthodox manner than what the police could offer.

It's not the buzz of activity from the team that brings a smile to my face, but the fact that three of the largest and meanest-looking men in the industry are beavering away while cradling and going completely cuckoo over three babies barely two months old. That can only mean one thing: my queen is also in the building. Kurt and I trot up the stairs to greet Mackenzie, who rises and kisses us both on the cheek.

"Mac, not that I'm not happy to see you, but what are you doing here?" I growl, pretending to be cross.

"Jared had to come to town for a meeting, so I thought I'd swing by to remind everyone what I look like. Besides, your men might be highly skilled in their work, but I believe it's important for them to step out of their comfort zones and learn some nurturing life skills for when they start families of their own." She tips her head towards the men holding her children. "Jared's picking me up shortly. I was hoping you'd get back before we have to leave."

"Where's my queen?" I ask.

"In her office, please note that she insisted on wearing all black to look the part and made me provide her with tuna sandwiches for lunch, since she watched a documentary on seals and presumed you eat a lot of fish just like the animal variety." Mackenzie nods toward my office as Kurt and I chuckle. There is only one other person allowed to share our room, and that person is sitting at a small replica of our large desks. She is dressed in a black

T-shirt with a large pink sparkly heart on the front, combat trousers, and has her hair pulled back into a ponytail. She is bent over her table, concentrating so hard on the picture she is drawing that she is oblivious to our presence. "Do you both want to come over for dinner later?"

"We can't tonight, we have plans." Kurt answers for the pair of us.

"How long are you in town?" I chip in. I came back to deal with Darius, and now I'm here, I want to get it sorted above all else.

"Until Sunday, then we have to get back to the bay as Tia has school."

Jared and Mac spend most of their time in Morro Bay, but they keep an apartment in Hollywood for their city visits. Conveniently—or inconveniently, depending on the day—that apartment sits directly across from mine. With only the two of us occupying the entire floor, it's an unpredictable balance of privacy and good-natured interference since we've become friends.

"If I'm still in town, I'll stop by over the weekend," I promise.

"Great," Mac smiles and shares a look with Kurt before knocking the air from my lungs with her next words. "Bring your bride; I'd love to meet her. It's about time you found a nice woman. I worry about you guys; you need some estrogen in your lives to help balance out all the testosterone flying around you all day."

"I shouldn't worry about that," Kurt grins, jerking

his thumb in my direction, "from what I've heard this one's been taking supplements."

Mackenzie looks at me quizzically but I'm saved from answering as a tiny human starts squealing excitedly when she spots me through the window. In her hurry to get out from under her desk, the nameplate balanced on top reading CEO, goes flying. The only five-year-old in California with at least twenty hard-core ex-service men at her disposal launches herself at me.

"King Josh! I've missed you!" Tia screams as I swing her up into my arms. She plants a smacker on my cheek and I'm a goner. "I've been making sure everyone has been working really hard."

"Yes, you have." Mackenzie smiles at her dotingly, probably wearing an expression not too dissimilar from my own. "You're a right bossy boots. They can't wait for me to take you home."

"Nonsense," I grin at Mackenzie, "It's good to know I have such dedicated advocate protecting my interests when I'm not around."

"Um… Mac," a voice calls from beside the stage on which we are stood, just as a foul stench assaults our senses. "I think Lexi needs her diaper changed."

"I think you might be right." Mac sniffs the air and waves her hand around trying to disperse the smell. "You know the rules."

"Mac… have a heart," Nico pleads.

"Tia," Mac prompts.

"He who holds the baby when he or she poops, changes the baby and learns an important life lesson in the process." The little girl in my arms parrots. Kurt walks into the office behind us to hide his laughter.

"Sorry Nic," I snigger. "The CEO has spoken."

"S'alright," Tia wiggles to be put down, "Mr Nico, I'll show you the ropes, then you can show me what you've learned."

Mac and I both roll our lips to prevent our own laughter escaping as we watch a very distraught Nico being led away by the little girl about to give her very first staff appraisal.

"Anything I should know?" I ask as soon as tiny ears are out of range.

""Nope," Mac smiles, "it's all under control. A couple of calls came in while you were out, but Axel farmed the jobs out to Ethan and Marco. He has the finer details, but from what I understand, they'll be out for about a week. Based on the specs you left me, I've shortlisted about five women for you to interview for a position here. When you're ready to set up a meeting, let me know and I'll invite them in."

"You're the best." I kiss her on the cheek.

"And don't you forget it."

"Mac!" Drew shouts from across the room. "The lucky bastard that married you is just pulling onto the estate; he should be here in two."

"Mr. Drew, you said a bad word!" Tia shouts at him from where she is stood beside Nico. Having inadvertently ripped off the tabs designed to hold Lexi's nappy in place, Nico is improvising with something akin to parcel tape.

Drew must whisper another expletive because, after a pause—during which Tia frowns in concentration, tapping her fingers like a miniature accountant—she yells, "I heard that one too! That's one hundred and forty bucks or three diaper changes!"

"I'd give her the cash," a green and clearly traumatised Nico offers his opinion.

"Two diaper changes." Drew tries negotiating but everyone in the room knows where this is heading. I've seen hostage negotiators crumble under less pressure.

"Four!" Tia puts her hands on her hips, staring him down as she warns. "It'll only go up."

"Fine," Drew sighs, four diaper changes.

"It'll go on your record," she tells him firmly.

I laugh and turn to her mom, saying, "I really should put her on the payroll."

After Mac is helped outside with the children and I've had the chance to greet her husband, I wander back to join Kurt, who is conversing with Axel in our office.

"Did you tell her I was getting married?" I moan to Kurt, ignoring the way Axel's jaw starts swinging in the breeze.

"Nah, wasn't me. Although when she caught me off guard by asking me over the phone the other day if it was true, I couldn't lie. Did you tell Jared?"

I drag my hand down my face and sigh. "Yeah, we met up for a beer before you and I headed back to

Vermont. It may have cropped up in conversation."

Axel gets up and heads to the door. I presume he is going to get a drink until he stops on the platform outside and whistles loudly to garner everyone's attention. Before I can stop him, he shouts incredulously across the room, "Hey guys. The boss is getting hitched."

It's like time stops as everyone freezes. I hear a few muttered expletives and a snigger from Kurt.

I stomp over to Axel and flap my arms in exasperation before making my own announcement, "Is it so unbelievable?"

"Was it Mac?" Drew shouts.

"Was what Mac?" I shout back.

"Did she set you up with... whoever it is?" Nico chips in.

"No, of course it wasn't Mac." I grunt, trying not to sound offended. "I'm more than capable of finding a woman on my own."

"Debateable." Kurt coughs out the word behind me.

"Then congratulations!" Foxy shouts. Everyone relaxes, springing to life and offering me their well wishes. I know I should set the record straight about it being a ruse, but with the prospect of my getting married seeming so implausible, I'm loathe to confirm their suspicions.

"Why would they think Mac set me up?" I ask Axel as we go back into the office to join Kurt.

"Because she told us she is determined to find us all that special someone," Axel groans. "For a moment, we thought she was making good on that promise by starting with you. Have a word with her, will you? Or find something else to keep her occupied."

"I wouldn't worry too much. Mac's good, but she's not a miracle worker. I can't imagine she'd find even one woman willing to date any of you, let alone one for each of you," I quip, rolling my eyes before getting back to business. "So, have you found Jimmy?"

Axel shakes his head solemnly. "No, there's been nothing. The trail got so cold Foxy had to 'accidentally' log into his bank account to see if there had been any recent activity. There's been nothing in or out since the day he called you. I traced the cell number he called from, but it was disconnected the same day. The guy either doesn't want to be found or…"

The room falls silent as we consider Axel's implications. My mind immediately drifts to Maeve. Even though she hasn't seen Jimmy for years, I know in her mind he'll be off living the life of riley somewhere, the prospect of having to break the news that isn't the case fills me with dread.

"What about the Castillo brothers?"

"Oh, they were significantly easier to find. Are the cases connected?"

"Why do you ask?"

"No reason. Except the fact Vince Castillo was serving time in federal prison but was released a couple of weeks before your friend Jimmy disappeared."

"Seems a bit too coincidental, don't you think?" Kurt mutters. "They did know each other."

I have to agree.

"What was he in for?" I ask.

"This time?" Axel widens his eyes—a sign I know isn't good. "Assault with a deadly weapon. It wasn't his first rodeo though. He's already done time for similar offenses, as well as several drug-related charges. His brother Anthony's no angel, but he seems to have inherited the smarts in the family. No one can ever get anything to stick as far as he is concerned."

"Do you know where they are now?"

"Anthony picked Vince up and took him back to his place in Maine. I have the address on my desk."

"That's only about six hours away," Kurt tells me gravely. He immediately pulls out his mobile. I don't need to ask to know who he is calling. Maine is approximately a five-to-six-hour drive away from Vermont, or more specifically, from Maeve. If Vince is after Jimmy, causing him to go to ground, the threat against Maeve could be valid if Vince thinks he can use her to flush Jimmy out. Kurt is calling Ace to alert him.

"We need to get back there," I tell Kurt the minute he is off the phone.

"I'll get us on a flight tonight," Kurt grunts, as he strides purposefully from the room.

"Anything I can do?" Axel asks, concerned.

"Get me everything you've got on Vincent and

Anthony Castillo," I growl. "Then I'd appreciate it if you can keep everything ticking over here until I get back. This one's personal."

Axel gives a dark chuckle, "You say that every time."

"What can I say? There's a helluva lot of people with questionable morals out there determined to piss me off. Although this case *is* different... there's a girl that Kurt and I grew up with who deserves better than getting dragged into whatever shitstorm her brother's involved in."

Axel gives me a chin tip as I continue, "I'll be keeping Ace and Blake in play for now. One of us will be in touch if we need anything."

Axel nods in understanding. "What about Darius?"

"I'll sort that before we leave," I tell him grimly as Kurt re-enters the room interrupting our conversation.

"Flights are booked," he tells me ominously. "We're leaving for Maine in three hours."

"Maine?" I know Kurt wouldn't have diverted us from Vermont unless he had good reason. I wait to hear what it is.

"A body has just washed up on the shore about a mile from where the Castillo brothers are staying."

The bottom falls out of my stomach as I ask, "Jimmy?"

"Too early to tell," Kurt replies. "But it makes more sense for us to stop there and check it out on our way to Vermont, rather than risk sending Ace or Blake, knowing there could be no one watching Maeve if we do."

Lucky for Darius, three hours doesn't give me much time. With Ace and Blake already out of the business and with Kurt and me set to join them, Axel needs all hands on deck while we are gone. "Call the boys watching Darius and warn them!" I tell Axel.

"Let them know you need a few more days?" Axel clarifies.

Kurt smiles, understanding my moves in a way Axel hasn't quite mastered yet.

"No," I growl threateningly, "Tell them—I'm on my way!"

One way or another, the men watching Darius will be back in action tomorrow to help Axel hold down the fort while I'm gone.

Chapter 9

Maeve

A week ago, I was perfectly happy with my life. Now, I feel like I'm walking around in a permanent state of repressed rage. This is why I'm now at work on a Sunday—the one day of the week I don't open the surgery. Usually, Aiden and I just remain on call for emergencies. Not that we ever get any. Blake's call the other night was the first time we had been needed after hours since an incident four years ago... when a moose wandered into the road, a car took a bend too fast, and the two met in spectacularly unfortunate fashion.

In our meeting about the future of the business the other night, Aiden and I decided to dot the i's and cross the t's anyway. Now that he was fully qualified, we decided we would each cover alternate weekends. The theory being, at least one of us could make plans to leave town if we wanted, without worrying about someone needing urgent assistance if we did. Not that I ever left town, and not that I ever minded until Tina opened her big mouth and made me start to question everything about my life and how I was choosing to live it.

Aiden, excited at being given more responsibility, wanted to take the first shift, meaning I wasn't needed today. I had plans to spend my free time sitting on the porch swing, reading. But with Blake swanning around by the pond shirtless and me spending most of the time gawping at him, I decided I needed to find a more productive way to relax.

In an effort to diffuse some of the tension being generated by watching a sexy, half naked man bending and flexing a few feet away, I decided Tiny needed to blow off some steam by being taken on an extra-long morning walk. It culminated in me swinging by the clinic to start clearing out the stockroom I planned to turn into a consulting room for Aiden. The stop proved worthwhile, as emptying, then beating the crap out of a few empty boxes, served as cathartic relief for some of the frustration pent up inside me.

I'm not sure what was getting me so wound up. Ogling Blake wasn't enough of a reason on its own to get me so riled. In the end, I decide there isn't just one reason but rather a combination of factors. First and foremost, I'm pissed at Josh because, despite giving him my number so he could keep in touch, he hadn't used it. I'm dying to ask him about the night of the fire and why he never admitted he was the one who carried me to safety. But since he never gave me his number, I can't get hold of him unless he reaches out first, and he hasn't. No calls or texts to let me know he is okay. No 'I've landed safely' or 'Things are hectic right now, I'll call you soon.' Not even a

'It was good seeing you again, I'll stop by in another thirteen years!' Nothing! Asshole!

On top of that, there's Derek. I haven't heard from him either. The man I'm supposed to be marrying—the one who virtually let me get abducted from the restaurant where we were supposed to be having a romantic dinner for two—hasn't even bothered to check on me to make sure I'm still alive.

Finally, I'm angry at myself. Not only is it profoundly wrong that I'm more annoyed at Josh than the man I'm supposed to be betrothing myself to, but it's also troubling that I'm looking forward to having dinner with Blake tonight far more than an engaged woman should be!

Okay, so there may have been a smidgeon of truth in the words Tina had spoken that day—maybe I did need a bit more excitement in my life. But that didn't mean I couldn't find it with Derek. Maybe I could have the best of both worlds: keep the solid and reliable life I craved, which Derek could provide, and at the same time, find a way to inject the thrill and passion that was missing from our relationship in a relatively calm and controlled manner. I just needed to find a way to set a new equilibrium. Pumped up on adrenaline and driven by a newfound determination, I decide to take the bull by the horns and start by doing something different today. After all, Derek had effectively made the first move by booking us a table at Serenity. Takeaways and cosy nights in were more his style. Perhaps he was feeling the need to spice things up too, and this was his way of gently taking the initiative to see how I would react.

Derek and I never usually see each other on Sundays. I wouldn't mind spending my one free day a week with my fiancé, but he always insists it's a day we should dedicate to pursuing our own individual hobbies and goals. However, after missing his weekly sleepover, I assume he's bound to be feeling antsy and in need of a bit of loving. Surprising him by swooping in and using my feminine wiles to seduce him feels like the perfect thing to do. Not only would it provide us both with the relief we need, it would challenge the mundane Friday night ritual that I hadn't found satisfying for quite some time. I could theatrically sweep everything from the top of the desk in his home office and insist he lay me down and take me there. I know it's technically still daytime, and Derek usually reserves the kind of activity I have in mind for what he considers to be a more respectable hour, but as a guy, surely he should be excited to receive the offer of sex from the woman he recently proposed to. After all, he would be hidden away indoors out of the public eye, he could still be on top with no fear of suffocation, and he would only have to drop his trousers rather than remove them, so his socks would be in good company. It'd also make a welcome change for me to be staring at something other than the cobweb dangling from the beam above my bed— the one I keep forgetting until Derek's getting busy and I have five minutes to contemplate how I can reach high enough to remove it. Hopefully, a bit of mid-afternoon passion would successfully dull my own raging hormones enough to make me less inclined to jump Blake's bones after dinner later. More importantly, it would also take my mind off wondering where Josh was, and what, or who, he had been doing that made him too busy to pick up the damn phone and call. Gah!

After beating one final box into submission and cleaning myself up in the small shower room at the back of the building, Tiny and I set off on the short walk to Derek's place—the house we plan to share once we've wed. It's a beautiful place, one of the largest in town and tastefully decorated inside and out. The garden is huge, and while it isn't the woods Tiny is used to exploring, it's large enough for him to be entertained when we aren't out on one of our daily rambles.

I knew Derek owned his own business when we met, and being one of the few competent accountants in town gave him the cream of the crop as far as his clients were concerned. But I never anticipated how much he was actually worth. He explained it away as being due to the inherent wealth generated from his father's own lucrative business, commissioning and importing souvenirs from overseas that were then distributed to various tourist destinations in this and several neighbouring states.

I didn't account for him not being home when I arrived. After using my key to let myself in, and taking a quick tour to make sure he was definitely not home, it suddenly occurred to me that I didn't actually know what hobbies Derek liked to engage in, or if he was due back any time soon. I figured I had a couple of hours until I had to make my way back to prepare the dinner I'd promised Blake, so after rifling through some of the clothes I had stashed in Derek's wardrobe, I donned some sexy undies that left little to the imagination, and lay in wait like a tiger ready to ambush its next meal.

When I hear Derek's car pull up outside, I hurriedly hide Tiny in the kitchen before making my way to the office, leaving the door slightly ajar before pulling off my clothes to reveal the lingerie underneath, and draping myself seductively across one of the chairs there. I hear the front door open, then close, and am just about to call out seductively when the sound of multiple voices makes me pause.

"So, when are you going to tell her?" The female voice is high-pitched, whiny, and distinctly familiar. It sounds just like Felicia, Derek's stick-thin assistant with razor-sharp cheekbones—the one who always made me feel like an inconvenience every time I visited him at work. The way she looked down her nose at me from over the top of her tortoiseshell glasses was both distinctly unwelcoming and scathing.

"I don't think it's fair to tell her over breakfast or lunch, she'll be devastated. It'll have to wait until we get together next Friday night. I'll book another table at Serenity and hopefully this time we won't get interrupted." Derek's voice filters through to me and I frown, getting up and creeping over to the partially open door so I can hear more clearly.

"Really Derek! She'll just have to get over it!" Felicia grumbles. "I don't want to wait another week! I can't believe you asked her to marry you in the first place. Can't you break with tradition just this once and meet up one evening before then? This is kind of important. If you've changed your mind about us, I have other options you know, I'm done sneaking around while waiting for you to grow a pair!"

Us? The grim realisation about why Derek had unexpectedly arranged to take me out for a meal hits home like a sledgehammer. I know I should be steaming. I know I should go charging from the room and bitch slap the hussy for trying to steal my man. But I don't. My body does flood with emotion, but it takes me a few seconds before I recognise it. It feels a lot like... Relief!

"Baby, of course, I haven't changed my mind," Derek snivels, making me seethe. He always called me by my name, refusing to adopt any terms of endearment that he felt would 'infantilise' our relationship. "If you want to come upstairs with me now, I'll prove it to you."

I hear a gross slurping sound followed by a girlie giggle before two pairs of feet go racing up the stairs. I stand there, stunned, until my brain catches up with the reality of what's about to take place in the room above me. While I may not be upset about the fact that Derek is about to call off our engagement, I am distinctly miffed over the fact that he feels it's okay to cheat on me before he does. After covering my provocative alter ego with my more casual and unappealing daytime attire, I decide it's an excellent time to return the ring I'm wearing.

There's no time to waste if I want to catch them in the act—this I know from personal experience. So, I immediately creep up the stairs, giving them just enough time to get their show on the road. When I peer through the crack in the door, they are already at it full swing. I'm confronted by the pale, almost translucent skin of Derek's ass, bobbing like a half-charged jackhammer atop the warm caramel hue of the body underneath. If I'm totally honest, I'm not entirely sure what *is* actually happening. Felicia's arms and legs seem to be flailing haphazardly as her rigid body bounces on the undulating mattress below her. Derek's familiar grunts come as no surprise to me, but the shrill, cackling squeals coming from Felicia make me question everything I thought I ever knew about sex while almost making me double over with laughter. Part of me wishes Tina were here to witness this moment with me, the pair of us could dine off these images for months. True to form, it's not long before Derek's awkward, jerky trusts gain momentum and I recognise the signs he is about to reach his peak. Seconds before Derek can finish what he started, I fling the bedroom door open and casually stroll into the room, removing my engagement ring and calmly placing it on the bedside table inches away from the pair of their heads. The reaction I get is everything I hoped for.

I'm like a fox strolling into a hen house, watching bedlam erupt all around me.

Felicia spots me first. The wide-eyed look of shock and disbelief is a prelude to her shouting a barrage of expletives and unceremoniously pushing Derek off of her so she can scramble to cover her naked body with the first thing that comes to hand. She grabs a decorative pillow so small; she has to curl into herself like a hedgehog in order to barely cover the essentials. As poor Derek is almost at the pinnacle of operations, this sudden interruption brings with it an obvious wave of discomfort. As he is thrown off balance, he rolls to the floor, landing hard and clutching his crown jewels, prompting him to scream some vibrantly colourful and embarrassingly explicit phrases of his own.

"M... Maeve?" He finally stutters as he forces himself upright, wincing at the excruciating pain he must be experiencing as well as the amount of effort required to complete such a simple task. "What are you doing here?"

"Returning the ring," I tell him bluntly, before attempting to save face with an unpremeditated lie which rolls off my tongue as easily as waves upon a shore. "Josh, one of the men who gate crashed our meal at restaurant the other night, he was insistent I call off the engagement today."

"Why?" Derek's brows furrow in confusion. I

have to admit, I'm caught a little off guard by his questioning. Letting my mouth lead before giving my brain the chance to catch up meant I hadn't had the opportunity to consider any possible ramifications or immediate responses.

Panicking that I'm about to be caught in my deception, I spout the first thing that comes to mind, "He wants to marry me. I know you'll be devastated, but well... I guess you'll just have to get over it." Delighting in the way Derek's face blanches, I breeze from the room leaving both him and Felicia suitably dumbstruck at my audacity.

I grab Tiny and take off. I don't cry on the walk back to my cabin; I'm not even sad. I'm excited for the dinner I'm about to prepare and for the knowledge that the two people thrust together at the whim of the universe are now both single, opening the evening up to all sorts of delightful possibilities. The air feels charged with potential, as though the universe itself is holding its breath, waiting to see what will happen next. It's the kind of night where anything could happen, and I'm ready to embrace it all. "I hope you're ready Blake," I murmur to myself, "Because here I come!"

When I get back to my cabin, Blake is no-where to be seen. I'm not sure if he is ensconced in his tent or if he has taken himself off somewhere. I don't care.

His absence gives me the opportunity to prepare our dinner, the ambiance, and myself before his arrival at six, the time we agreed earlier.

The food fairy had helpfully left a couple of juicy tomahawk steaks languishing in my fridge, and judging by the muscle mass Blake was constantly exhibiting, it looked like he could use the protein. The fact that Derek must have spent a fortune on the meat I was now about to cook for another man to enjoy was just an added bonus. After putting together a bowl of salad and boiling some potatoes to sauté once my guest arrived, I set two plates, ready for dinner, at the kitchen island in the absence of a table. I place two stools at a ninety-degree angle to each other along two edges, making it easy for Blake and me to converse and get close should the mood allow. I use the flowers Josh left me and a candle I find under the sink as subtle decoration before changing out of my sweats and into a short summer dress I hope my date will like. I'm just touching up my makeup when at precisely six o'clock there's a knock at my door.

My stomach does a funny little flip as Blake's eyes skate appreciatively down the length of my body, then when his eyes meet mine, I recognise the conspiratorial twinkle that accompanies his mischievous smile. Even though he is dressed casually in blue jeans and a navy T-shirt, the man oozes charm and sex appeal.

"C'mon in," I breathe, as his cologne assaults my senses, giving me a pleasing head rush.

"Don't mind if I do," he replies, leaning in to ghost his lips across my cheek in a welcoming kiss. "Where's my little man? How's he doing?"

"He's around somewhere," I giggle. "Just be careful if you sit on the couch, he likes to hide underneath the cushions and I nearly squished him earlier."

As if he heard us, Blake's kitten mews and climbs up onto the sofas arm. Blake catches him before his inquisitive nature almost sends him toppling over the edge. As he holds him close, tickling him under the chin and cooing endearments, I'm sure it the closest thing to vet porn that can be achieved without the presence of a naked body. I'm startled by the sudden rush of oxytocin that floods my body.

"I hope you're hungry," I scuttle off to the kitchen before I make any unscripted changes to the menu. Blake looks just as tempting, if not more so, than the steaks set out ready for the grill.

Blake greets Tiny before wandering over still cradling the kitten, "Anything I can do to help?"

"No, it's all under control. Help yourself to a beer and make yourself comfortable. Is steak, okay? I mean, you're not a vegetarian or anything?" I ask, suddenly horrified that I made an assumption base on appearances.

As if he senses where my head is at, Blake smirks and tickles my ribs as he brushes past me on his way to the fridge. "Steaks fine. What are you drinking?"

"I'll have a beer too," I giggle shamelessly.

As I start searing the steaks and toss the potatoes

in a pan to finish cooking, Blake pops the cap from a couple of bottles before handing me one.

"Glasses are in the cupboard over there," I say automatically. Derek always thought it uncouth when he saw people drinking without decanting the liquid first.

Blake grins, "Let's live life on the edge tonight, shall we? Save on the washing up, it'll give us more time to get to know each other later."

It's a loaded statement that makes me respond with one of my own as I glance back over my shoulder to ask him seductively, "How do you like it?" The atmosphere sizzles even more than the tomahawks as I add coyly, "Your steak I mean."

"Surprise me," Blake smirks and takes a draw from his bottle, placing the kitten he's holding on the floor and coming to stand beside me before whispering in my ear, "I'm sure I'll love whatever you're planning to serve up."

Suddenly, it's not just the heat from the stove that's making me feel so hot and bothered. Sensing my reaction to his close proximity, Blake withdraws and goes to sit at the island. I finish cooking the steak and potatoes, plate them, and place one dish in front of Blake before sitting beside him with the other. Blake fumbles in his pocket for a lighter and uses it to ignite the candle in front of us. Tiny lies at our feet, letting out a contented sigh as the kitten clambers all over him.

Blake makes no attempt to start eating, instead he holds my eyes as he leans towards me. I jolt slightly when I feel his hand on my knee and as his fingers gently roam an inch up the exposed skin of my thigh. "Look's delicious," he drawls sexily.

I feel my cheeks flood with heat and the tell-tale prickle of goosebumps as they scatter across my skin. I don't realise I've unconsciously run my tongue over my lower lip until Blake's eyes dart down to momentarily focus on my mouth. In an instant, the atmosphere is electrified and my heart starts to pound in anticipation of what's about to come. Infinitely slowly, some kind of invisible force starts drawing us together, and when I feel Blake's warm breath on my face, I know it's about to be game on!

"How can I thank you for dinner," he murmurs, when his lips are barely a millimetre from my own.

I can think of a few ways—the words are on the tip of my tongue, but they just won't come out. There's no doubt I'm attracted to Blake; he has made me feel more alive in the last few minutes than Derek did in all the years we were together. Even so, something feels off. I can't quite put my finger on it. It's not that I feel uncomfortable or unsafe; it's more like we are two pieces of the same jigsaw, pushed together only to find we are slightly out of alignment. I don't know how else to explain it. As good as he looks and as nice as he is… we just don't fully match up.

The problem is, now I've had that epiphany, I don't know what to do next and my mind goes into overdrive, completely overthinking the situation. Do I let him kiss me and see if it's just nerves holding me back? What if it's not, and he wants more than I'm prepared to give? What if I pull back and he turns nasty like Vince? Fear floods my body, and Tiny, sensing my sudden discomfort, instinctively sits up to rest his head on my knee in reassurance. As he does, he nudges the hand already there nearer to the apex of my thighs. I feel like it's a sign and relax instantly. Tina's words come back to haunt me: *You've become so risk-averse; you're missing out on everything life has to offer*. In that second, my mind is made up. I'll never know anything for sure unless I'm prepared to put myself out there, try new things, and see what happens.

I'm just about to seize my moment when an indestructible force causes the cabin door to fly open. It's like the open void acts as a vacuum, sucking all the air from the room. Blake and I spring apart with a gasp to see a furious Josh standing in the doorway, his hands are clenched into fists at his sides, the anger rolling off of him is palpable. He strides towards Blake who stands to meet him head-on, and I watch as they stare each other down like two championship boxers before a fight.

Kurt strolls in casually behind Josh. Ignoring the tension in the room, he sniffs the air, takes Blake's seat at the island, and declares, "Looks like we arrived in the nick of time," before picking up a knife and fork and proceeding to tuck into Blake's dinner.

"W... what are you doing here?" I stutter, as my hand flies to my tummy in an effort to soothe the swirling mass of butterflies that have suddenly decided to take up residence there.

No one answers me. Blake extends a hand to Josh, who takes it slowly but doesn't shake it. He merely holds it firmly, narrowing his eyes as Blake offers up his name.

"And what do you do, Blake that we've never met before, and who we shouldn't be meeting here particularly under these circumstances?" Kurt asks with a playful grin plastered across his face, attempting to make conversation as he forks a piece of meat into his mouth, chewing it carefully.

I throw him an incredulous look for his bizarrely exaggerated greeting.

"I... er... I work for a firm based in L.A.?" Blake offers cagily.

"Do you?" Josh challenges wryly, "You kinda look unemployed to me."

Kurt snorts in amusement, and I get the feeling I'm missing something as a bead of sweat trickles down Blake's temple. I watch as his hand starts to turn white under the force of Josh's grasp and feel the need to intervene somehow.

I pick up the kitten gambolling at my feet in an effort to diffuse the situation. "Josh, meet Josh," I giggle, waving the furry bundle in front of his human namesake.

"What?" Josh frowns, temporarily distracted, "You named your cat after me?"

"No, it's not my cat, but it's a funny story..." I say, trying to sound upbeat rather than borderline hysterical.

"Maeve," Blake whispers firmly, I get the sense he is trying to stop me, but since my diversion appears to be working and Josh's attention is focused on me, I continue.

"It's Blake's, he named his cat after a guy he knew called Josh, he said he was a bit of a pussy for not admitting his feelings to the woman he loved."

Josh's eyes go wide, and Blake's face goes paler than a ghost as Kurt's laughter causes him to inhale a piece of food and start choking. I don't know which way to turn; Josh looks like he is about to murder Blake for some reason. But if I throw myself between them and don't get Kurt the water he desperately needs, he could keel over too. I can only save one of them. I decide Kurt is the safer option, getting caught in the crossfire of the two alphas looking ready to start kicking seven bells out of each other could result in my own demise. I dash to the sink and fill a glass, handing it to Kurt who takes it gratefully, downing the entire drink.

"What are you doing here?" Josh whispers threateningly. He still has Blake's hand in a vice like grip, and I can see the muscles in his forearm straining as he ratchets up the pressure. Over my shock at Josh and Kurt's sudden appearance, and out of concern for my guest's well-being, my patience suddenly wears thin.

"I invited him!" I yell. "I didn't, however, invite you to come storming into my home to start interrogating my guest. For heaven's sake, Josh, let him go."

Startled by my outburst, Josh lets Blake go but crosses his arms defensively. Blake rubs his hand and talks to me without taking his eyes off Josh for a second. "Maeve, since you have company, I'll be heading out..."

"You don't have to," I interrupt, annoyed at my unexpected visitors and making it glaringly obvious by throwing them both a look that could curdle cream.

"It's fine," Blake answers slowly, like he feels he needs to justify his reasons for being here, which is ridiculous. "You've been so kind in letting me stay to keep an eye on the kitten I found wandering outside. Your dog is so perceptive it was lovely to be introduced so I could stop by without him worrying you or taking me down any time I happened to be nearby."

"What?" I look at him, baffled by his response. Between his and Kurt's elongated responses and Josh's overbearing behaviour, I'm starting to think all the testosterone in the room has fried their brains. He doesn't notice my reaction because he is still eyeing Josh warily.

Josh grunts but doesn't look all that impressed either. Neither of us have the chance to comment, since a chaste knock on the still open door of the cabin draws everyone's attention that way.

"Derek!" Kurt chuckles, striding over and pulling him inside to join us. The colour drains from Derek's face as he spots Kurt, who wraps his arm around Derek's shoulders, giving him an unwelcome, robust squeeze. "What are you doing here, buddy?" He eyes the garbage bag Derek is holding with interest.

"Returning Maeve's things," Derek snaps, dumping the bag on the floor so it spills open. Some of my more discerning underwear topples out into plain view. Blake's kitten jumps in the mix and embarrassed, I scramble to untangle him and stuff my lingerie back into the sack, out of sight.

"Who the hell is this?" Blake rounds on Derek, his hands firmly on his hips.

"Another one of Meave's men," Kurt offers with a wink to me.

"Really?" I growl incredulously, giving him a death stare back.

"Fine," he chuckles. "This is Derek, her fiancé."

"Ex-fiancé," I correct him, waving my ringless finger in the air.

"I thought you would have known that since she announced she is going to marry him instead," Derek barks at Kurt, pointing to Josh at the same time. I suddenly feel a little faint, wondering if I can climb into the sack I'm still holding, and hide until everyone leaves.

"You two," Blake waves his finger between Josh and I, "are getting married?" He frowns in confusion and horror.

I push myself up, wringing my hands anxiously as I stand, frantically trying to come up with a way I can get myself out of the hole I'd dug myself. "I can explain…"

"This should be good," Kurt is beaming brighter

than the sun as he takes a seat on the couch, leaning forward with his forearms resting atop his legs ready to enjoy the show. "This is better than an episode of the Kardashians."

Shocked by his admission everyone turns to look in his direction. He shrugs as if it's no big deal, "It's my guilty pleasure, what can I say?"

Blake looks at me waiting for a response, I look at Josh apologetically, Derek is still looking at Kurt as if he has just grown two heads, and Kurt is surveying the room waiting to see which of us is going to break first.

"We are." Josh suddenly addresses Blake while watching for my reaction. "So I suggest you get the hell out of here and make sure Maeve and I never catch you in our sights again unless you're invited."

Blake doesn't need to be told twice, immediately walking over to give me a hesitant peck on the cheek, "Let me know when I can come back and collect my cat," he murmurs, side-eyeing Josh on his way out.

"You know, in light of the circumstances I thought you were making it all up," Derek sneers. "I actually came round to see if we could work things out."

"Work things out," I scream. "After I caught you plonking your secretary in our bed?"

"My bed." Derek yells.

Kurt claps his hands in glee, "Now we're cooking," he sings excitedly from the sofa. "Who started cheating first."

"Well, it wasn't me!" I shout.

"How do I know that?" Derek screams back. "Flick and I have only been seeing each other a few months, you could have been seeing this... this... brainless, muscled moron in secret for years."

"Who are you calling a brainless moron?" Josh snaps, stepping forward and looking as though he is about to use some of those muscles Derek was talking about to hammer him into the ground. As Derek shrinks back, I jump between them. This is definitely my fight, and I want to be the one who ends it.

"MONTHS!" I scream, incandescent with rage, "You've been cheating on me for months?"

Derek looks so smug and unrepentant, I fly at him with my right hand curled into a fist, punching him hard, right between his eyes. He staggers back stunned.

"Dang!" Kurt cheers, "Nice form."

"SHUT UP!" I turn on him and he draws his mouth closed with an invisible zip, locking it before throwing away the key. Once he is silenced, I turn my wrath back on Derek. "For your information this man..." I shove Josh in the chest without looking at him, "...is nether brainless, nor a moron. He is sweet and kind, intelligent, adventurous, brave, but above all else, he's LOYAL. We've known each other years but only reconnected a couple of days ago."

"You forgot handsome," Josh leans forward to whisper in my ear, clearly amused by my rant. Kurt scoffs and I ignore them both.

"So, if your meeting up again was so sudden, when did you decide to marry him?" Derek yells.

"When I saw the size of his penis and it made me realise how you'd been short changing me all these years!" The words come tumbling out before I can stop them.

"Again, with my penis!" I hear Josh sigh behind me. He must cast a look in Kurt's direction, as Kurt reinforces the fact his grinning mouth is zipped closed, before widening his eyes and raising his arms in resignation.

"I don't believe you. You're lying," Derek gloats, he knows he's caught me out and is just waiting for me to admit it.

"She is not," Josh steps in to defend me like he always has in the past.

"Prove it. When's the wedding?" Derek challenges with a smug, victorious look on his face. "I suppose you're about to tell me you haven't thought that far ahead, or it's none of my business."

"Next week." Josh counters without missing a beat.

Derek looks Josh over in disdain before crossing his arms and huffing, "Nope, still not buying it!"

"Then come along and watch for yourself," Josh says casually, miraculously with no hint of the contempt I can feel dripping from his pores.

I smile. There's no way Derek will agree, Josh has him backed into a corner, so he can't do anything other than concede.

"Alright, I will! Send me the time and place of

these supposed nuptials, and I'll be there to watch the show. Maeve has my number."

Before I get the chance to argue, Derek turns on his heel and marches out of the door. I'm left standing with my jaw hanging open and my anxiety levels rising astronomically by the second.

Kurt rises from his seat, walking over and clapping both Josh and me on the shoulder at the same time. "If I'm allowed to speak now," he chuckles, "May I be the first to congratulate the happy couple."

I stare at him dumbstruck as spots start dancing in front of my eyes. He turns to an equally shell-shocked Josh, telling him jokingly, "You're one lucky son of a bitch, you know that?"

Josh tips his chin silently in response before his eyes lock onto mine. From his expression, I know his thoughts are mirroring my own—*What the hell just happened?*

Chapter 10

Josh

Maeve looks like she is about to puke.

If you had told me twenty minutes ago that this wedding was actually in the works, I would have looked like I was going to puke too. Marriage was something for my future—my very long and distant future. But Maeve? She was all set to take the plunge with dismal Derek. I have my flaws, but I'm definitely a better catch than that idiot. Would it be so bad marrying me? She was singing my praises a few minutes ago, making my chest swell with pride at the thought of her recognising some of my more redeeming qualities, rather than seeing me as one of her older brother's best friends who upped sticks and deserted him when he probably needed him the most.

Walking in to catch Blake about to kiss her made my blood pressure spike to a dangerously high level. I liked to think it was because he had defied a direct command to stay out of Maeve's way, but deep down, I knew there was more to it. The green-eyed monster had inexplicably reared its ugly head. I was still annoyed that she had used the flowers I'd left her to stage a romantic dinner with another guy when that sleazeball, Derek, showed up —insulting me and claiming Maeve had told him we were getting hitched. I'd picked those flowers with my own hands, doing my best to avoid Kurt's gaze —and the certain ridicule that would've followed if he saw me. Which, of course, he did. Jealousy made it feel almost natural to go along with her lie in front of both Derek and Blake—especially since she'd chosen me, not Kurt, as her fall guy. Although to be fair, my acting skills are considerably better than Kurt's, so it wasn't all that surprising to have been the one picked to be presented as her faux groom. And really, what better way to wipe that smug smile off Derek's face while also ensuring Blake kept his distance?

Kurt's right, I am one lucky son of a bitch, but not for the reasons Maeve thinks right now. Kurt and I had spent the better part of the last six-hour drive from Maine trying to come up with a way to convince Maeve to give up her life for a few weeks and come back to L.A. with us—just until we got to the bottom of whatever mess Jimmy had gotten himself into. The best we could come up with was slipping her one too many drinks until she was as inebriated as she was at the restaurant the other night, waiting until she fell asleep before throwing her in the back of the car, and then, when she woke up in a different state, trying to persuade her she'd insisted we take her on an impromptu road trip.

Neither of us had taken the marriage idea

seriously when Jimmy originally suggested it, not really. When an unknown number flashed on my personal cell, I planned to ignore it. I still don't know what made me answer. Probably the fact it was my personal phone and not the one I reserved for business—very few people had that number, so I was curious to see who was calling. When the agitated person on the other end announced themselves as Jimmy, the guy I had intended to beat the crap out of thirteen years ago and who had been hiding from me ever since, I thought I was being punked. I immediately put the call on loudspeaker, believing Kurt had set me up. I wanted him to know his little charade wasn't going to work. The look of shock that flashed across his face told me the caller was genuine—more than that, it was clear he had just recognised a voice he hadn't heard in a long time. One that dredged up memories, both good and bad, stirring something deep within him.

Kurt and I have been around enough people in dire situations to know the difference between real desperation and feigned distress. Even though we hadn't parted on the best of terms and hadn't heard from Jimmy for over ten years, the fear in his voice was enough for us to give him the benefit of the doubt. When he started rambling about one of us having to marry his sister, we would have said anything to keep him talking long enough to find out what was really going on. If we decided to get involved in whatever shady deal Jimmy had messed up, we needed all the facts before we could come up with an alternative plan that made more sense. Jimmy's call got cut short when his frantic whispers let on that he had to make a quick escape or he was about to be discovered. Who he was hiding from, where, and why remained a mystery. We asked him to meet us at one of the old haunts we used to frequent when we were kids before he suddenly disconnected, leaving Kurt and I confused and more than a little concerned.

Even though we were worried, it had always been in our nature to try and playfully push each other's buttons on a regular basis. Knowing how hooked Maeve had been on Kurt when we were younger, I kept goading him into being the one to take the plunge Jimmy had suggested. I could see marriage and kids in my future one day, but Kurt couldn't see either in his, so I knew I would successfully rile him up. Eventually, he called my bluff and challenged me to the duel I lost. That was supposed to be the end of the madness. We both knew there was no way we could rock up unannounced after a thirteen-year absence and get Maeve's agreement to marry either of us. And why would we need to? We're in security, for Christ's sake. If we had to get her out of town for her own protection, we'd either have to tell her the truth and hope she'd see sense, or find another way to convince her it was a good idea. We had more than one trick up our sleeves, and even though we were struggling to find one that would work with Maeve, the answer would present itself eventually. Either way, we were hoping it would be a moot point. Unfortunately, our trip to Maine persuaded us otherwise, and, much to Kurt's glee, Maeve herself inadvertently provided the solution to the problem that had Kurt and me stumped. It was an ironic twist of fate that had led us back to the same plan Jimmy had laid out at the beginning.

"I… I'd better go check on Blake," Maeve's dazed voice breaks into my thoughts.

"No," I grab her wrist as she turns to leave.

"I'll go, let you two start planning your upcoming nuptials," Kurt chuckles.

I throw him silent daggers, and Maeve incorrectly assumes I'm glaring at her.

"I… I can explain," she stutters nervously.

"I got the gist, so I'd rather you sit and eat your dinner, you've not touched it and I didn't spend a fortune on those steaks for them to go to waste," I say, before muttering, "or for you to feed them to a random stranger!"

"Wait," Maeve frowns, "*You* left me all that food?"

"Your cupboards were empty, and you were eating leaves. From the look of them they'd probably been plucked from outside your door! I was just replacing what I ate the other night and leaving you some supplies to tide you over until you had the chance to get to the store."

"That was… thoughtful," she looks genuinely surprised. "Why did you leave all that stuff in the bathroom?"

"You only had one tampon."

"So?"

"He thought he'd better stock up before he got his first period and needed to borrow some," Kurt chips in helpfully.

"Why are you still here and not out kicking Blake's ass?" I bark.

Kurt grins and disappears out the door.

"Why would he need to kick Blake's ass?" Maeve rounds on me with her hands on her hips.

"Figure of speech, you know, since you always wanted to be his girlfriend I thought you might like to see him warn off the competition," I tell her, thinking on my feet.

"For heaven's sake Josh, that was years ago," Maeve flaps her arms in exasperation, having seemingly believed me.

"Eat your dinner," I say again.

"I'm not hungry."

"Maeve you need to eat," I tell her a bit more forcibly.

"Bossy much?" She widens her eyes at me defiantly.

"When we're married, you'll do as I say." I quip.

Maeve's eyes turn into saucers that almost eclipse her entire face.

"Too soon?" I chuckle, heading to the fridge to grab myself a beer.

"What are we going to do?" Maeve whispers, her anger suddenly deflating.

"Go through with it," I say simply, adding a one-shoulder shrug for good measure. "Invite the prick along to watch, then you can come and stay at my place for a couple of weeks after. You can say we are going on honeymoon. While we're in L.A. we'll get the marriage annulled, then you can come home and tell everyone whatever you like. I'm away working, or we had a fight and went our separate ways. I don't care; it's not like it's real."

As I pop the cap off the bottle I'm holding and take a deep draw, Maeve immediately starts searching the room for something.

"What are you looking for?" I ask, curious.

"My emergency medical bag. I can't cure crazy but I'm pretty sure I have something in there that I can use to sedate it," she tells me seriously, and I can't help but huff out a laugh.

"Well, what do *you* want to do?"

"I don't know," she sighs. "Fess up?"

"Sure, we can do that?" Time to employ a bit of reverse psychology. "We'll do it together, call in on Derek at work tomorrow so we can kill two birds with one stone. If he's not busy banging his secretary, we can let her know at the same time."

When her face falls, I know I have her. When a lone tear rolls down her cheek, I know she has me.

"What?" I have her in my arms in an instant, holding her tight and stroking the back of her hair like I used to when we were kids and she was upset. It feels so familiar, I'm immediately transported back to my youth. "Maeve, what is it?"

"I just thought…" she snivels into my shirt.

"You thought what, baby?" Something about those four little words set her off again, and I shake her gently. "Maeve, talk to me. What did you think?"

"Nothing. You'll think I'm being silly."

"When have I ever thought that?" All those times she used confide in me about her feelings for Kurt when we were younger, I never judged. I always took her seriously and gave her the support she needed. I guess she must remember that too, since she looks up at me with her sparkling eyes before confessing her fears.

"I just always thought that when I got married, it would be for life, you know? That I'd find someone I loved, who loved me back, and we would have a big fabulous wedding then ride off into the sunset to build a wonderful life together."

"You can still have that."

"It won't be the same. After a quickie wedding and a fake honeymoon, I'll be a divorcee."

"Not if we get an annulment. It'll be like it never happened."

"To us maybe, not to anyone else who happens to be there," she says sadly. "If Derek wants to watch, I'll have to invite my parents because he'll expect them to be there, then they will insist on telling our friends."

"So, we'll elope."

"We can't. If Derek doesn't witness it, he'll never believe we went through with it. It would be just as mortifying as if I confessed to fabricating the entire thing right now."

"Okay, so let's go the other way."

"What do you mean?"

"Let's have the big, fabulous wedding. Make it look as legit as possible by giving everyone a day to remember. Blow anything you and Derek were going to do out of the water."

"You're kidding, right?" Maeve looks at me as though I've completely lost my marbles. Maybe I have.

"Nope. Here, I'll give you my card..." I forage around in the back pocket of my jeans until I find it, then press it into her hand, "...and you can arrange the wedding of your dreams. On the proviso that you agree to come back to L.A. with me for a few weeks afterward to keep it looking credible. When it all ends, I'll take the blame. Your friends and family will never believe you were at fault and everyone will have some beautiful memories to look back on."

Maeve takes a deep breath, her eyes searching mine. After a long pause, she finally nods. "Alright. Let's do this."

"That's my girl!" I give her a squeeze. "I'm popping outside to get Kurt up to speed. Meanwhile, you can call your folks to give them the good news."

I grab two more beers and stroll outside, finding Kurt assisting Blake with the final touches on packing up his camp by the pond.

"Change of plan," I announce, causing both men to stop and look in my direction. Blake eyes me warily. I hand him a beer as a peace offering and he takes it gratefully. I give another to Kurt and gesture for them both to take a seat. We drink in silence for a few minutes while I try to organise my thoughts, but just as I'm about to speak, Kurt pre-empts me.

"You're actually going through with it aren't you?" He smiles.

"Yep." Is the best I can up with as I take another swig from my bottle.

"So, apart from the fact you've gone insane, what's changed?" Kurt quirks an eyebrow at me inquisitively.

"Everything," I sigh.

"Everything?" Kurt echoes.

"I'm going to stay here with Maeve as planned. Since we told Derek the wedding was next week, she is going to need my help in getting everything arranged in time. Getting the licence, finding someone to perform the ceremony etc. etc." I wave my bottle in the air as I speak, helping to emphasize the last few words. "I know we were going to send Ace to Maine with Blake, but I need it to be you."

"Okay, care to elaborate? Why me?"

"A quick trip to city hall has been taken off the table, and since Maeve still has her practice to contend with, I've a feeling she is going to have me running about doing errands for the next few days. That means I can't be with her keeping her safe twenty-four seven. She knows you," I tip my bottle at Kurt, "She also knows you now," I tip my bottle at Blake and narrow my eyes as I speak. "But she still doesn't know Ace is in play and he is all set up to watch her throughout the day. So she doesn't get suspicious, I propose Ace stays here with me and you two head to Maine. It makes more sense anyway."

I tip my bottle back towards Kurt, "You know both Jimmy and the Castillo boys, so you might recognize anyone coming or going from Anthony's place. That could save Axel a lot of time in identifying them before he can run any checks. I want you running point there for now. Plus, if Jimmy does show up, he'll trust you."

"You think he's still alive?" Blake voices the thoughts Kurt and I are too afraid too. "Kurt said the body that washed up was an acquaintance of your friend's. If they were together when he was killed..." He doesn't have to finish.

Kurt and I were relieved when the body was identified as a stranger. But our relief turned to sorrow when we learned he was barely twenty— far too young to meet such a brutal end. Billy Jenkins, as he was identified, had been badly beaten before being killed by a single gunshot to the head. His body was then tossed into the water, presumably hoping the local marine life would erase the evidence. Axel made some checks and we weren't happy when we discovered that five years ago, Billy had been in regular contact with the same number Jimmy had called me from just before he disappeared. Then, nothing—radio silence for years. Until suddenly, just days before Billy's body was discovered by a dog-walker on the beach, he made several calls to Jimmy's mobile. One of them lasted nearly an hour. I'd have given anything to know what was said.

I look at Kurt. "Jimmy's a scrapper. When he isn't

high, his mind is sharp—like a steel trap. If he didn't think he was going to make it, he wouldn't have called. Neither of us have heard from him in over a decade, which means he got us involved for a reason. He knows that once we start looking for him, we won't stop until he's found. Whoever is after him has to be pretty ruthless—they know exactly what they're doing. The fact that Jimmy believes they'd use his estranged sister as leverage says everything about how far he thinks they're willing to go. I have a feeling this is a dangerous game, one he doesn't want his sister caught up in. And now we're walking straight into it, whether we like it or not. Jimmy wouldn't have reached out after all this time unless he was desperate, which means we could already be in deeper than we realise. He'll be banking on us to bring everything we've got to the table—so we can outmanoeuvre whoever's pulling the strings and beat them at their own game."

Kurt gives me a chin tip.

"We still don't have definitive proof that Vince or Tony are actually the ones after him." I take a slug from my beer. "We need to know for sure. I want them watched around the clock. Get Foxy to send you some toys to help with surveillance. If either of them so much as scratch their ass we need to know about it."

Both men raise their bottles in confirmation, and we sit in silence for a few seconds while I search for a way to lighten the sombre mood that's descended.

Eventually, I say thoughtfully, "Axel will be

pleased."

"How so?" Kurt asks.

"Well, Mac's on a mission to get everyone at the firm partnered up, so he asked me to find an alternative way of keeping her occupied. I'm going to hook her up with Maeve and get her to help with the wedding prep."

Kurt widens his eyes. "How big is this event going to be?"

I shrug. "I'm not sure, I gave her free reign as long as she agreed to come back to L.A for a few weeks after."

"Tell me you didn't give her your credit card," Kurt laughs.

I shrug again absentmindedly.

"You are so whipped," he murmurs, as the three of us take a drink from our bottles.

"Josh," Maeve calls from the door of the cabin, "Which do you prefer: swans or peacocks?"

I immediately spray the contents of my mouth out in shock. Maeve must see my reaction, as she follows through with, "Gotcha!" before laughing and going back inside.

"You are in so much trouble," Kurt laughs.

"So are you," I counter.

"How do you figure?"

"I need a best man."

"If he's the best you can find, you really are in trouble," Blake chuckles.

"No way," Kurt blusters. "I'm allergic to weddings. Ask Jared."

"Mac won't like that," I say, ready to play my ace.

"Why?"

"They're married, and isn't it customary for the best man to hook up with the maid of honour?" I smirk, waiting for him to figure out who is going to be Maeve's obvious choice.

It's a beautiful moment when the penny drops, and I watch as Kurt's internal struggle plays out across his face.

"I don't mind helping you out now that the bride's off the market," Blake grins.

"Not necessary," Kurt snaps in a tone that would make lesser men crumble. "Send me the details, and I'll make sure I'm there."

"Don't worry." I clap Blake on the shoulder and joke, "The bride will be back on the market in a few weeks."

"Sure she will," Kurt mutters with a knowing smile that I find unsettling.

Chapter 11

Maeve

"Am I crazy?"

"No. Crazy would have been marrying that other fool."

"Tina. You're not helping." I sigh down the phone.

"Have you got a maid of honour yet?"

"I wasn't going to have one."

"Why?"

"There is only one woman I'd want for the job and since when I asked her the last time she declined, I thought I'd leave it."

"Aww. Ask her again."

"No, she already turned me down once."

"Because you were marrying the wrong guy."

"Wait! So let me get this straight. You flat out refused to stand by my side at my real wedding, but you're willing to take time off work and fly out here to support me at my fake one?"

"Derek wasn't the love of your life."

"Neither is Josh."

"How do you know?"

"What?"

"How do you know he isn't the love of your life and the person you are supposed to be with?"

I giggle, "Because it's Josh! You know we've never had that kind of relationship—he's never shown any interest in being more than friends."

"Hasn't he? Or were you too blind to see it because you were always so hung up on Kurt."

I think for a second. "Nope, definitely never liked me that way."

"Really?"

"Really."

"Okay, if you say so." I can here the disbelief in her tone and it makes me curious.

"Tina, spit it out, what's on your mind?"

"I was just wondering who that other guy was then."

"What guy?"

"The one who threatened to beat up nearly everyone on the school football team when your boobs came in and they finally started noticing you. Or the one who offered to take you to every school dance when you couldn't get a date because of it. The one who was basically on speed dial whenever you had a problem you couldn't solve yourself, and who would drop everything in a heartbeat to be there for you. Or the one who sent you an anonymous Valentine's card every year to soften the blow of never getting one from Kurt. Boo, I think it's pretty clear he liked you, even if you didn't see it at the time."

"He was the one who sent me all those cards?"

"Who did you think it was?"

"You! When no-one else showed any interest in me, I thought you were just being kind."

"You would have recognised my handwriting."

"I always thought you got Liam to write them for you, and how do you know he threatened the football team?"

"Liam told me he overheard Tommy Malone joking at the garage one day about how you had a nice rack and how he was planning to convince you to let him take you out so he could pop your cherry in the back of his car. He told Jimmy, who got pretty pissed and was planning to warn Tommy to behave himself if you agreed to go on a date with him. Jimmy must have been with Josh at the time, because Josh found out and went postal. He told Jimmy there wouldn't be a date, so there was nothing to worry about. Then he stormed down to the diner where Tommy and his mates used to hang out and made sure Tommy—and anyone else thinking along similar lines—stayed far away from you."

"I always thought I couldn't get a date because no one liked me."

"Maeve, everyone liked you. I kept telling you that."

"But you're my best friend; you had to say those things. Plus, I wasn't shown any evidence to the contrary."

"Duh. Once Josh laid down the law and the rumour mill took over, no one was brave enough to approach you. Are you mad I didn't say anything? I promised Liam I wouldn't, and it didn't seem like a big deal at the time. Especially since I was pretty mad at Tommy too."

"How is it that I'm just finding all this stuff out now? It's a lot to take in, and if I'm honest, I'm not sure how I feel about it. Maybe if another guy had paid me some attention back in high school, I might not have stayed hung up on Kurt for as long as I did."

"Another guy did, but you were just oblivious."

"Josh was Jimmy's best friend. Jimmy told me he was off limits."

"So was Kurt. But despite your little crush I bet Jimmy never warned you off him."

I have to admit, she had me there. "No, he didn't."

"Ever wonder why?" Tina's voice carries a hint of amusement, the kind that makes it clear she already knows the answer.

"Tell me."

"Because Jimmy knew he didn't feel the same way, he was never a threat. Josh, however, despite denying liking you, was a different story. Jimmy knew that with a little encouragement, Josh's attitude would change. He didn't want you falling for someone who was pursuing a career that demanded long months away and daily risks to his life. Things are different now. Jimmy's not in the picture, and you're not crushing on Kurt anymore. We are all older, wiser, and better equipped emotionally to face the challenges life throws our way. The timing wasn't right for you and Josh back then. Your lives were heading in different directions, and both of you were so determined and focused on your careers that you didn't have time for each other."

She giggles and I tilt my head expectantly waiting to hear what she finds so funny. Finally, she lets me in on the joke. "If you need another sign, just look at how it all panned out, I mean, who better to be paired with a SEAL than a vet?"

I giggle too, "You and your blinking signs! Although I have to agree that's a good one."

Tina continues, turning serious again, "You both needed time to grow, and let's face it, the man has grown in all the best ways. He was always a hottie, but now..." Tina lets out a long exaggerated breathe, like she is fanning herself with her hand at the other end on the phone, "...phew, when I saw him the other day he was smoking. He could be just what you need to bring you back out of your shell a bit. Hell, he's only been back in your life for a couple of days, and he's already convinced you to leave the state for a few weeks. Weeks! I've been trying for years to get you to visit me in New York—just for a long weekend—and I couldn't even get you to leave town. I think the Universe is being pretty clear, I asked for it to send you a better man and it did."

"It sent me Blake."

"No. It sent you Josh first and you ignored all the signs. So, I asked for it to try again and it sent you Blake, who just so happened to have a kitten named JOSH. What are the odds? When you were still

197

being too dense to pick up on that little nugget, it sent the man himself back to propose before you got in too deep with the wrong guy again."

"He didn't propose. He just backed me in a lie I told Derek to save face.

"Whatever!"

"I take it back. I don't think I'm crazy. I think you are."

"Did he really give you his credit card?"

"Yeah, but I don't get it. I'm the one who got him into this mess. I thought he would just show up on the day, considering I'm planning to arrange and pay for everything. And that's exactly what I'm going to do, by the way—it's not fair to expect him to."

"What about your parents? Won't they want to help?"

"They wanted to, but I told them Josh had already offered to cover everything. I feel like enough of a fraud without taking their money. Funnily enough, I called them before calling you to give them the news, but they didn't seem as shocked as I expected about the sudden change of groom and my desire to rush down the aisle. He wouldn't come right out and say it, but I'm pretty sure my dad thinks Josh knocked me up," I sigh. "Regardless, I'll cover everything."

"Can you afford to? I have some savings set aside if you need some."

"Now you are offering to help pay for my fake wedding?" I ask bemused.

"Think of it as a bribe."

"Oh, I see where this is heading," I chuckle. I know what she is waiting for so I give it to her, "Tina, I'd be delighted if you would agree to be my maid of honour for my fake wedding?"

"Hell yeah! I'll book some time off tomorrow and fly back to help with the preparations. Meanwhile, is there any reason why we can't have a little fun?"

"What do you mean?"

"Have you told Josh you intend on footing the bill?"

"Not yet. I was a little stunned, still trying to process everything, when he handed me his card and then disappeared outside to talk to Kurt."

"Kurt's there?"

"Ah, now I see why you're so eager to come back."

"Very funny. Are they together now?"

I walk over to the window and peer outside. "Yeah, the pair of them are sat outside having a beer with Blake."

"So, you have Josh's credit card and he thinks he is paying for everything..." Her voice trials off and it takes my brain a few seconds to catch up.

"What are you saying?"

"I dare you to ask him if he wants Swans or Peacocks at the wedding."

"Swans or Peacocks?" I burst out laughing as the penny drops, "Oh Tina I couldn't. Could I?"

"Do it. I double dare you."

Without any further encouragement, I open the front door and shout, "Josh, which do you prefer: swans or peacocks?" I'm too far away to see anything other than his body going rigid before he almost chokes on the mouthful of beer he has just taken. I can't contain my giggles as I yell, "Gotcha!" before closing the door again.

"What happened?" Tina screeches in my ear, and I tell her before the pair of us descend into laughter again.

"Let me know the date as soon as you have it and I'll see what time off I can get. This is going to be a riot!"

We say our goodbyes, and I flop down on the couch, my mind reeling with all the new information I've gathered over the last few days. I think of the Valentine's cards Tina mentioned—the ones I know are in the keepsake box tucked away on a shelf in my bedroom closet. Now that I know who really sent them, they've taken on a whole new meaning, one I'm eager to explore.

After pouring myself a large glass of wine, I head to the bedroom and pull out the box. Settling onto the bed, I lift the lid and rummage through until I find what I'm looking for. There are four cards. I'd received one every year from the age of fourteen until I left home at eighteen to go to university. I study the envelopes first. There's nothing remarkable about them—no postmark, which is partly why I'd always assumed they were from Tina. They are all just plain envelopes, each with a single word scrawled on the front in a handwriting I know I've seen before but just can't place where: Maeve.

The first two cards depict humorous cartoons

and the message inside is sweet but succinct. *To someone who makes the world a little brighter just by being in it,* and, *to someone whose beauty and radiance shine brighter than the sun.* Both are signed *Happy Valentine's Day from your secret admirer (Not Kurt!).* I smile as I remember how excited I'd been to receive them before I'm suddenly transported back to the night of the fire and the words whispered in my ear as I lay on the gurney, moments before being taken to the hospital, 'You're going to be okay, sunshine.' Sunshine? Josh never had a nickname for me when we were younger, but the words seem oddly familiar now. My heart races as I start to piece together the connection, the tender nickname aligning with the sentiments in those cards. Was Tina right? Could Josh really have liked me more than he let on? The thought both surprises and warms me, painting the memories in a new light as questions swirl in my mind. Why hadn't I realised it sooner? And, more importantly, what if anything, will it mean for us now?

I pop them back in the box and pick up the next one. It's more romantic than fun—a couple sharing a candlelit dinner for two. The words inside make more sense now that I believe them to be from Josh, who would have already left town to join the navy.

Roses are red, Violets are blue, Every moment apart I'm missing you. The days feel longer, The nights colder too, But my heart stays warm, Just thinking of you. From your secret admirer. (Not Kurt).

Reading the words and wondering now if they

were heartfelt instead of simply a playful gesture aimed to soothe my aching heart, I feel a new weight to them. The longing in the poem suddenly feels deeply personal, reflective of a young Josh grappling with distance and emotions he perhaps didn't yet know how to fully express. My heart tugs at the thought of him penning those lines, his feelings hidden behind the anonymity of a card, and I can't help but wonder how different things might have been if I had known the truth back then. It also makes me wonder who his co-conspirator was. For the card to have been hand-delivered, he must have left it with an ally in town who ensured I received it on time.

> *Roses are red, Violets are blue, You've stolen my heart— Now what do I do? Love your secret admirer. (Not Kurt!).*

In the final card the word 'love' suddenly screams out at me, a substitution for the word 'from' as used in the others. I study the front, it's the slushiest of the four, all hearts and roses.

"Maeve?" Josh's voice sails through to me from the living room. I hurriedly stow the cards back in the box, hiding it under the bed just before he appears in the doorway. I'm not ready to admit to him I know the truth, not yet. It was all such a long time ago and so much has happened since. I need some time to organise my thoughts and wrap my head around it all. Josh leans against the doorway, his easy smile tugging at my heart, and for a moment, I wonder if he already knows what I've discovered. "Whatcha doing?" he asks, oblivious to the storm of memories and emotions swirling inside me.

"Um, wondering how I can reach that cobweb hanging from the ceiling." I grapple for the first excuse that comes to mind, forcing a smile, and resolving to ask him for the truth—but only when I'm ready.

"Here, I can help." Josh strides over, and as I climb off the bed, I'm barely upright before two strong hands grip my hips, hoisting me into the air as if I weigh nothing. I gasp. Before my conversation with Tina, his touch wouldn't have affected me like it is now. I probably would've just laughed, brushed away the web, and moved on as if nothing had happened. But now—now my body is reacting in all sorts of unfamiliar ways, and I'm not sure what to do for the best. The heat from his hands seeps through the thin fabric of my dress, igniting my skin and sending flames licking throughout my body. My heart starts racing erratically and in an effort to calm it down, my breathing adjusts becoming deeper and faster. My boobs feel as if they've suddenly gained an extra ten pounds and don't even get me started on what's going on at the top of my thighs. I suddenly start to feel light headed. "Can you reach now?" Josh's voice breaks through my haze of arousal.

I open my mouth to speak, but my brain is too overwhelmed to find the right words. With everything else it's struggling to process right now, no sound comes out.

"Maeve?" Josh shakes me gently, and every sensation I'm feeling intensifies to the extreme. I need him to put me down and more importantly let me go, but I know how stubborn he can be. The quickest way to get what I want is to finish the task he's so determined to help with. Swiping my hand across the ceiling, I finally clear the cobweb—the room's only source of entertainment for far too long. Once my feet are firmly back on the ground, I excuse myself, scurrying to the bathroom under the pretence of washing my hands.

I close the bathroom door and my fraying nerves manifest in the overwhelming urge to pee. I drop my panties and sit on the throne just as the door flies open and Josh strides in.

"Are you okay?"

He is totally unaffected by the sight in front of him. I however, am not used to having a spectator and momentarily freeze before going into complete meltdown.

"What the fuck Josh?" I yell, scrambling to grab a towel off the rack nearby and using it like a blanket to shield myself from the waist down. Not that I really needed to worry as my dress was already providing sufficient coverage. I grab a box of tampons from the floor and launch them like a missile at Josh, who swats them away with his hand. I thought he would leave, but he doesn't. He doesn't even look embarrassed, he looks amused.

"What's the problem? I've seen a woman take a leak before."

"When?" I snap, a tidal wave of jealousy catching me off guard as it washes over me.

He just chuckles without answering, so I try to shrug it off before he starts to question my erratic behaviour.

"That may be, but you've never seen me..." I bob my head, unable to even finish the sentence. Derek's bathroom etiquette used to be so regimented, all to ensure we never crossed paths—I'm surprised he never went as far as to create a schedule.

"You caught me with my pants down, this makes us even." He smirks and my stomach does a backflip. "Besides we're getting married, it's important to show that we're comfortable with each other on an intimate level—otherwise, people might start asking questions."

"And that includes watching me pee?" I raise my eyebrows at him.

He folds his huge arms across his chest, a mischievous smile playing on his lips. "It includes everything, babe." My stomach flips again at the unexpected term of endearment, only to drop as I scramble to decipher what he means by 'everything'.

"What did you want?" I ask, squeezing my thighs together in the hope my pelvic floor muscles are strong enough to stop the dam breaking before my audience departs.

"I just wanted to make sure you were alright, you were acting a bit... strange, in there a minute ago." He jerks his head back in the direction of the bedroom.

"What do you mean by strange?" *Please don't say horny, please don't say horny!*

"A bit... distracted."

"I'm fine. I've just got a lot on my mind right now."

"Like what?"

"Can we talk about this in a minute after I've finished here?"

"Sure."

I wait for him to leave. Yet again, he doesn't. He leans against the door frame, smirking. If I could stand, I'd probably march right up to him and slap him, either that, or climb him like a tree and kiss him senseless, jury's still out.

"Are you going?" I ask finally.

"Nope. Are you?" He flat out grins this time. He knows I'm restraining myself, the thought of him hearing a less than delicate tinkle is mortifying.

We stare at each other for a few more seconds. "I can't 'go' with you standing there watching me."

"Nature will have to take its course eventually, and I've got nowhere to be, I can wait," his eyes crinkle with mirth and I feel my lip curling into a snarl.

I try to pee quietly before cleaning myself and getting redressed beneath the towel—like a prude getting changed on a busy beach. Then I wash my hands and try to stalk past him. He hasn't moved the entire time, and his huge frame blocks the doorway, making it impossible to pass. His presence makes the small room feel claustrophobic. Until I can make sense of these new feelings I'm experiencing towards him, I daren't get too close. I take solace in the fact that he and Kurt will be leaving soon. When he's out of my proximity, I'll take the time to sit and consider our situation and my emotions in greater detail.

"Shall we go and sit down," I try to shoo him out of the doorway without touching him. He knows as well as I do, I would normally just shove him out of the way so I can barge past.

"Maeve, what's wrong?"

"Please Josh, can you let me by," I'm hoping he doesn't pick up on the strain in my voice.

He frowns before pushing himself from the door jamb and meandering back into the living room. I follow, and just when he is about to plop himself on the couch I scream at him.

"STOP!"

He freezes mid-air while I rescue the kitten peeking out from behind one of the cushions.

"He has a new name, you know," Josh says as he settles at one end of the couch.

"Oh yeah? What would that be?" I ask, clutching the small bundle of fur to my chest, its warmth grounding me like a safety blanket. I sit on the opposite end of the sofa, angling myself to be as far away from Josh as I can get. It isn't very far though, considering it's a small couch and Josh is a very large man. Our knees are almost touching, and I can feel the heat from his body radiating onto mine.

"Derek," Josh says, his lip quirking as he utters the

name.

"Derek?" I giggle.

"Blake said after meeting both me and that other dweeb, Derek seemed a more fitting title."

I chuckle, relaxing slightly. "Where are Blake and Kurt?"

"Blake left—his boss sent him on an urgent job, and he had to leave immediately. He asked me to tell you to call him when you're ready to let him have Derek back, and he'll make arrangements to collect him. Kurt has gone to see a friend." It's not a lie, both Blake and Kurt have gone to see Ace and fill him in on what's going on before they both leave town.

"Oh right, where are you staying tonight?" I ask absentmindedly, as I try to unhook the kitten's claws from my top.

"I would have thought that was obvious." Josh answers just as casually. "I'll be staying here."

I freeze, my heart pounding as I look at him. "I'm not sure that's such a good idea right now."

"Why?" His eyes lock onto mine, and the hairs on the back of my neck stand on end. The blood surges through my veins in anticipation of being stuck in such close quarters with him for a newly extended period of time. "We stayed together the other night and it makes sense. We need to start arranging the wedding and if we want to make it look believable, we need to act like we're in love."

"I'm not sure that's a good idea either." A fake wedding to a platonic friend is one thing. A fake wedding to a friend I'm suddenly attracted to is something else entirely.

"The wedding?"

"Um… yeah." Some fleeting emotion flashes across Josh's face. It's gone so quickly I almost believe I imagined it.

He sighs, "It's Kurt, isn't it? You wish you were marrying him."

I burst out laughing. "Are you being serious right now? Tina would kill me."

"You know about Kurt and Tina," Josh looks at me gobsmacked.

"Of course I know. We tell each other everything."

"Not everything," Josh murmurs almost inaudibly.

"Why? What else don't I know?" I seize the opening, hoping he might come clean and confirm some of the new information I've recently uncovered.

"Nothing." He changes tack effortlessly. "What's changed within the last hour? Not so long ago you were asking me if I wanted swans or peacocks at the wedding."

Not wanting to admit the real reason, I deflect—just like he did—joking, "My dad thinks you knocked me up."

"Could be arranged." He deadpans the words, and for a moment, I look at him like a deer caught in headlights. I know he's joking, but the response hits me like a freight train. My body betrays me, flooding with arousal as my mind is suddenly filled with vivid thoughts of us together. I'm overwhelmed.

I need space to think. In my tiny cabin, there are barely any places to hide. Other than the bathroom, there's only one other room to escape to without leaving entirely.

I cough, trying to cut through the sudden tension suffocating the air between us. Then I stand and announce, "I think that's enough talking for tonight. Let's just go to bed."

Josh's jaw drops slightly, and I realise with a jolt that he thinks I'm implying I'm taking him up on his offer. Time slows as the startling realisation hits me: maybe I am.

Chapter 12

Josh

H *oly Shit!* Is Maeve saying what I think she's saying, or is my brain hearing what it wants to hear since it became starved of oxygen when all the blood in my veins hurtled south?

By the time I've recovered enough to ask, she's gone. Hidden behind the closed door of the bedroom while I remain seated outside wondering what the hell to do.

She's joking. She has to be. In all the years I've known her, through all the things I've done to make her feel happy and safe, she's never shown any interest in being anything more than friends. I accepted my fate a long time ago.

Kurt and I used to laugh about her teenage crush on him—until she grew older. Then, it didn't seem so funny anymore. As she blossomed and other guys started to take notice, I hated it.

I remember dragging little Tommy Malone out of the diner on Maple Street. His scrawny legs were kicking, and his mouth was running faster than his brain ever could. When I'd found out what he wanted to do with her in the back of his car, I went nuts. It helped that his friends were watching when I finally caught up with him. Once I warned him to stay away, word spread like wildfire: she was off-limits unless whoever had the guts to ask her out was prepared to face me.

Even when I left town to train as a SEAL, my memories of her kept me going. The training was brutal—physically and mentally—but at least I wasn't alone. My best friend was by my side, and we pushed each other through every gruelling trial. Still, it was Maeve I saw in my mind. I used to picture her waiting to welcome me home, and every time I felt like giving up, her face would appear in my thoughts, driving me to push just that little bit harder.

Kurt and I weren't supposed to be in town the night of the fire—it was pure chance that we were. We had received orders to deploy the next day for a mission: infiltrating a remote island compound controlled by a dangerous arms dealer smuggling experimental weapons. The mission promised to be intense, and it was our first major test of skill. The compound was heavily guarded, surrounded by dense jungle, and fortified with state-of-the-art surveillance systems, making a high-stakes firefight almost inevitable.

Before deployment, we were given a couple of days leave to spend with loved ones. After Kurt and I checked in with our parents, I asked him to make one last detour—I told him I wanted to catch up with Jimmy.

It wasn't Jimmy I truly needed to see. Fearing it might be the last time I ever saw her, I had to see Maeve one final time. Neither of us expected to arrive and find their house engulfed in flames. It took all of Kurt's and my strength to break through the front door and drag Jimmy and the others to safety.

When I learned Maeve was still inside, no force —man or beast—could have stopped me from going back for her. The smoke was so thick it was nearly impossible to see or breathe, but I fought my way through. When I reached her room, the door wouldn't budge. It took every ounce of strength I had to force it open, where I found her unconscious on the bed.

As I scooped her into my arms, my eyes caught one last thing—the picture above her bed, with a love heart drawn around Kurt's face.

I carried her outside, flames searing my skin and the acrid smell of burning flesh invading my senses. I shielded her as best I could, forcing my way through the inferno until we were clear. Once outside, I laid her gently on the grass and stayed by her side while Kurt checked her vitals. We waited anxiously until the EMTs arrived a few minutes later.

I stepped away for just a moment to wave down the approaching ambulance. In that second, Kurt shouted, "She's coming to!" Relief flooded through me, indescribable and overwhelming, but by the time I returned to her side, she had slipped back into unconsciousness.

I couldn't go with her to the hospital. Something told me Jimmy was responsible for putting Maeve in danger, and one way or another, I needed answers. Unsurprisingly, he and the others had bolted before the police arrived. I spent the rest of the night trying to track him down. He should be grateful I never found him that night.

Kurt and I had to leave the following day, but not before he dragged me to the hospital to have my wounds professionally treated. While Kurt was busy charming one of the nurses into giving him an impromptu 'physical', I slipped away. Maeve was alone, sleeping peacefully, when I said my goodbyes.

Walking away from her that day, I knew I had to let her go. She needed time to heal—from Kurt, from everything that had happened—and I needed time to heal from her. As much as it hurt, I knew leaving for good was the right thing to do.

I never contacted her after that. I'd hear snippets about her through Liam, but I avoided the topic, burying myself in work and fleeting distractions until I convinced myself I could be satisfied with the friendship she was willing to offer.

But now... just when I thought I'd made peace with it all, one throwaway comment—probably meaningless—has completely unravelled me. It's left me questioning everything I thought I'd come to terms with, and I don't know if I can keep pretending I'm okay with where we are.

I walk over to the bedroom door, my hand

hovering hesitantly above the handle. I can hear Maeve shuffling around inside and my thoughts wander to forbidden places as I imagine her undressing before slipping into bed. I'd like to do nothing more than join her, wrap her up in the warmth that's flooding my body. As I begin to open myself to the thrilling possibilities of what's to come, my heart starts to beat double time. My dick is throbbing relentlessly, urging me on to my most important mission to date—a moment so pivotal it could define the future between Maeve and me for years to come.

I'm poised, mere milliseconds from opening the door, when I'm stopped by the sound of an incoming text on my mobile. More specifically, the unmistakable tone reserved for urgent messages from my crew—signalling that I'm needed or there's a critical update I must know about. I pull my phone from my back pocket and glance at the screen. The message is from Axel. I open it to read:

"I've got a few details I need to clarify on my sister's surprise party. Can we touch base when you're alone and preferably outside? Walls have ears."

To the untrained eye, the message appears innocuous. But since Axel doesn't have a sister, I know he's trying to warn me of something far more serious. The fact that he wants me alone means Maeve, and any other civilians that might be around, must be out of earshot. And the last comment—it unsettles me the most. Axel knows where I am and he fears that Maeve's cabin might be bugged.

My training kicks in, and I'm immediately on high alert. I turn off the lights and methodically check each window for any signs of movement outside. Everything looks calm and still. Tiny is sleeping peacefully, which reassures me that whatever 'surprise' Axel is warning me about pertains to information, not an immediate threat.

Slipping outside, I move as far from the cabin as I can while staying in the shadows. I settle where I can keep the entire perimeter of the structure within my sightline as I dial Axel's number.

"Boss." Axel answers on the first ring. "Is Kurt with you?"

"He's on his way to Maine with Blake." Axel doesn't waste time asking questions about the sudden change in plans.

"Driving?"

"Yep."

"Let me just patch them in."

I wait while Axel conferences Kurt and Blake in to the call and ensures they're able to talk freely.

"Have you found Jimmy?" Kurt asks immediately he knows the line is secure.

"Not yet, but I've found out some information that doesn't make much sense to me and I'm hoping you guys might be able to help me shed some light on what's going on. Do either of you know a man called Derek Dawson?"

"We do," I growl. "We met him recently, on a meal out with Maeve."

"Jimmy's sister? The girl you grew up with? Is she

involved with him do you know?" Axel asks warily.

"She was going to marry him. She came to her senses and now she's not!" I say bluntly.

"Can I ask why?" Axel probes further.

"Because she's marrying me now." I growl.

There's a stunned silence before Axel asks in genuine surprise, "That's who your marrying? I thought you were just there keeping an eye on her."

"He is," Kurt chuckles, "a close one!"

I hear as Blake snorts in amusement.

"Axel," I bark, "Can we get to the point? Why all the questions about Derek? He is a small-town accountant with little to no nads."

"He may not have much in the way of balls, but he has an extremely large bank balance for a 'small town accountant' as you put it."

"Go on."

"When you asked me to find out all I could on the Castillo boys, I started delving into their past starting with the reason for Vince's most recent incarceration. It's not so much what he was in for as much as the fact he only had two visitors all the time he was inside."

"One was obviously Tony," Kurt chips in.

"Not even close." Axel says.

"I'd go with Billy Jenkins and Derek Dawson," I surmise, based off the information we have so far.

"Close, but no cigar. Billy Jenkins and Douglas Dawson, Derek Dawson's father."

"Billy's definitely the connection between Vince and Jimmy," Kurt growls. I'd like to agree but I need something more concrete, Axel gives it to me.

"Here's what I know so far. About a month before Vince was sent down five years ago, phone records show he got in touch with your pal Jimmy. Prior to that, I couldn't find any connection between the two men, and I went back at least ten years. Then, out of the blue, there were about half a dozen calls between them over a span of two weeks, after which all communication stopped again."

"You didn't look back far enough," Kurt says, "Jimmy knew Vince of old, although it sounds like they went their separate ways for a while. What else did you find?"

"Not long after Vince and Jimmy stopped talking —this most recent time," he clarifies, "Vince started reaching out to Billy Jenkins. They spoke every day, often multiple times, until Vince was arrested in an alley outside a club, caught trying to cave someone's head in with a baseball bat. Vince was locked up, and about a week later, Billy visited him with Douglas. Not long after, Douglas returned alone. That was the only visitation Vince got—until Douglas showed up again, just a week before Tony picked Vince up following his release.

Here's the kicker. Jimmy only moved to Maine about six months before Vince hooked up with him. Jimmy got a job working at a local boatyard, fixing up fishing vessels and charter boats. He kept his nose clean and in his spare time, he even became a mentor for at-risk teens, giving talks and organizing activities to help steer kids away from the kind of trouble he saw growing up."

"Let me guess, Billy Jenkins was one of the teens Jimmy was working with!" I growl.

"Got it in one. I don't want to be the one to say it, but Jimmy had access to enough boats to have been the one to dispose of Billy's body."

"No," I snap. "He wouldn't do that."

Wouldn't he?" Kurt bites back. "I'd like to think not, but we haven't seen him in a long time. People change. He was already starting to change when we left him behind in Vermont and decided to sign up without him."

"No!" I say again, more forcefully. "It doesn't make sense. Jimmy was holding down a blue-collar job and trying to help rehabilitate troubled youths. If he was up to no good, the last thing he'd do is draw attention to himself by inviting you and me to the party. No matter how dire the situation looks, his actions don't align with someone who has something to hide."

"Unless he has been holding a grudge all these years and is out for revenge. He could be trying to set us up, wanting to make us pay for abandoning him.

"Axel, what did his financials show?" My gut is telling me Kurt's wrong, but I can't ignore the possibility.

"Nothing out of the norm," Axel says. "He lived moderately and hardly ever went out. He spent most of his time working, picking up whatever overtime he could get. It looks like he was saving for something big—every spare penny he earned was being transferred into a savings account in his sole name. He'd managed to accrue about six thousand dollars. The same can't be said for Tony Castillo. Did you stop by his place when you were in Maine?"

"No, why?"

"Because when I checked his address, I was surprised to find that, for someone who has never done a hard day's work in his life, he's living in a ten-million-dollar home. It was bought with a series of rather hefty cash deposits, which are being made regularly to a shell corporation registered offshore—and in Vince's name."

"Where's the money coming from?"

"I'm still trying to trace that back to its roots."

"Where does Derek fit into all this?" Kurt asks the question already on my lips.

"I'm not sure, other than the fact Derek is both Anthony Castillo's accountant and Douglas's son. Anthony is paying Derek well over the odds for his services and guess where the money is coming from?"

"The offshore account in Vince's name." Kurt beats me to it.

"Right again," Axel confirms. "Derek is skimming a percentage from every transaction and funnelling the rest into a joint account he holds with his father. With everything we've uncovered, I can't ignore the possibility that his meeting Maeve wasn't just a coincidence. Tony Castillo has a reputation for being shrewd—dangerously so. If Derek is on his payroll, there's a real chance he orchestrated their encounter for a reason we haven't yet uncovered."

There's silence as we all mull over the information.

"I think you should get Maeve out of there for a while, just until we figure out exactly what's going on," Kurt says, voicing my own thoughts.

"I agree, although it's not going to be easy without letting her know what's going on in detail. She's got her business to consider, and I'm pretty sure she's going to want us to get married here so she can make sure Derek attends."

"Derek is going to your wedding?" Axel asks incredulously.

"Long story," I sigh.

"I'm pretty sure I can help with the first part; the second, you're on your own," Axel says.

"I'm all ears," I reply. "Ace followed your girl on Saturday. She went for a drink with the guy she works with."

Your girl? The words make me smile until the second part of what I'm told registers. "Aiden?" The name comes out sharp with jealousy, earning snickers from at least two of the three men listening in.

"Relax," Axel says, clearly amused. "From what I understand, it was all business talk. Aiden's eager to get more involved now that he's a fully qualified vet. I'm sure he'd be delighted to be left to his own devices for a few weeks. The only roadblock I can foresee is that Maeve is going to be advertising for a new admin assistant, and I doubt she'll want to leave until she's filled the position. If we could help with that, I think she'd be more open to leaving town. You could arrange the wedding remotely, fly back to tie the knot, and then take off again for the honeymoon."

"Who have we got free at the moment?" I ask, even though I suspect the answer already.

"No-one. We're rammed; I'm having to turn jobs away."

I drag my hand down my face as I think. "Listen, Mac has a list of new applicants wanting a job at the firm. They've already been shortlisted due to the list of specs I gave her. I want you to interview them with her."

"Why with Mac?" Axel asks curiously. I've only ever asked him to interview potential hires on his own before.

"They're all women and you're both be looking for different traits." I say cautiously.

"Are you implying I'll only be hiring based on physically appearance?"

"Not at all," I admit. "I'm implying that you'll be so wrapped up in their technical abilities that you may not recognise some of the softer skills that may be of value to us."

"What sort of skills?" Axel asks.

"People skills," I say tactfully.

"I'm a people person." Axel flares aggressively, clearly offended.

"Sounds like it," Kurt sniggers.

"Let's put it this way..." I pause, choosing my

words carefully. "You've never been that great at reading certain people—namely women."

Axel bristles at the implication. "I'm not that bad."

"Dude, the last time you had a date, Obama was in office." Kurt cuts to the chase. "It's no wonder Mac thinks you need help with your love life."

"Fine." Axel barks. "But if Mac starts nitpicking about nonsense, I'm calling you."

Deal," I say with a slight smile. "I'll call her in the morning to smooth the way—make sure Jared's at home to help with the kids. I'll get her to arrange the interviews at a location that suits her. If it's out of town, anyone unwilling to travel can be cut right away. We'll recruit the best two on a probationary basis. I'll come up with a backstory convincing enough for Maeve to hire one of them for the position she's advertising. That way, we'll have someone on the inside to keep an eye on things while we're gone. The other can team up with Ace, handling round-the-clock surveillance of the area and keeping tabs on Derek, ensuring there are no surprises by the time we return. Ace will act as their handler, providing on-the-job training. Tell them both it's a foot in the door—an opportunity to prove themselves, and if they don't fuck it up, they'll each be guaranteed a formal job offer at the end of the term."

"Isn't that a bit risky? Letting them loose before they've had any official training?" Axel, always the voice of reason, raises his concerns.

"I think the bigger risk will be leaving Ace in sole

charge of two females," Blake chuckles.

"He doesn't chase everything with a pulse," I retort, "unlike some." A subtle dig at the compromising situation I recently walked in on between Blake and Maeve.

"I wouldn't be so sure about that," Blake says amicably, more amused than worried at my attempt to reinforce my displeasure at the situation I found him in.

"Kurt, can you call Ace and fill him in on what's happening?" I ask.

"Sure."

"I can call him if it's easier?" Axel offers.

"I think it's better if Kurt does it," I say, and Kurt chuckles.

"Any particular reason?" Axel, still smarting from the reminder of his less-than-stellar track record with women, is obviously still feeling the sting.

"Because I have even less people skills than you," Kurt deadpans, his voice suddenly low and dangerous. "And while Josh might trust Ace to play by the rules when he takes the newbies under his wing, he knows I'm here to provide a little extra... persuasion. Just to ensure he stays on track."

Axel and Blake fall silent. They both know Kurt isn't a man to cross, and I'd wager they're silently relieved it's Ace in the hot seat, not them right now.

"So," I say jovially, trying to lighten the mood a little. "Let's recap. Kurt will call Ace and fill him in on what's going on..."

"When you speak to him, let him know not to

panic if any of the cameras get triggered at Maeve's surgery tonight. Foxy is on his way," Axel interrupts. "Sorry, I forgot to mention it earlier. He hopped on a plane a couple of hours ago. Considering everything, I thought you'd appreciate him doing a sweep of both Maeve's surgery and her cabin to confirm they're clean. Once that's done, he's heading to Maine to help set up surveillance. When we realised the property was much more impressive than we were expecting, he wanted to see firsthand what we're dealing with. I think it's safe to assume Tony has some kind of security in place. At this stage, we don't know just how extensive it's going to be."

"Great," I confirm. "Axel, call him when he lands and tell him I'll meet him at the cabin after I've dropped Maeve at work in the morning."

"Are you sure you trust me to?"

"Ha! Ha!" I roll my eyes. "Kurt will phone Ace. Axel, you'll call Foxy. I'll call Mac, fill her in on what we discussed, and get her to call you, Axel, to make the necessary arrangements. Like I said, we need to move fast on this. Kurt and Blake, you'll start active recon on the Castillo brothers. I want daily updates unless it's something significant—then I want to know immediately. No one is to make a move without my say so. If anyone hits any kind of trouble, the code word's 'porpoise.'" Spotting one off the coast of Maine is rare but not impossible, making it an easy yet subtle word to slip into a conversation.

"I'll be moving Maeve out of the area tomorrow —how and when is yet to be determined. I'll let you know more when I know myself, she can be as stubborn as a mule these days so I'm not sure how I'm going to be able to persuade her on such short notice. Everyone clear?"

Axel and Blake agree immediately. As much as they fear Kurt, they know there's one man who commands even greater respect—and fear. Kurt doesn't respond; he doesn't need to. His loyalty to me is as unwavering as his watchful eye, ensuring no one ever questions who's truly in charge, even if I see him and me as equals. He knows I watch his back as closely as he watches mine—and that I wouldn't hesitate to lay my life on the line for him or any other member of my crew, if it ever came to that.

We end the call and I immediately ping a text to my friend and neighbour in L.A., Jared.

U up? I need a favour.

A few seconds later my cell starts to ring and I answer smiling.

"Dude, I have triplets under six months old; I sleep less than you do. This favour—is it a 'can I borrow fifty bucks' kind of favour, or a 'remember I took a bullet for you once' kind of favour?"

"The latter," I chuckle.

"I was afraid of that," Jared sighs. "What do you need? Although if it's a part in my latest blockbuster, please remember I wasn't lying when I said you had a face for radio."

"Worried I might upstage you, pretty boy?" I banter back before getting to the crux of the matter. "I do need to borrow something, but it's not money."

"What do you need?"

"Your wife. I want to ask her if she'd help me out by interviewing some candidates with Axel for a job at my firm. I also need to know if she'd be up for helping with a bit of wedding planning."

"Why are you asking me?"

"You know what Mac's like—she'd say yes even if she was taking on too much. Then you'd get pissed and be chasing me down to either rip me a new one or get the CEO to fire me from my own company for stealing away her mom. I thought I'd bypass that stage by checking with you first to make sure you'd be around to help with the kids for a few days. I need a pretty quick turnaround on both requests so I'd kinda need her from tomorrow if she agrees."

"Go for it. I'm just reviewing scripts at the moment, so I won't be away filming for the foreseeable future. Plus, my sister and brother-in-law can help out if I need them to. It'll do Mac good to get involved. She only went into the office the other day because she was worried you might think she can't handle the responsibility now that she's had the triplets. When you first mentioned you were hiring, she started worrying you were planning to replace her. Then, when she saw the specs you outlined, she panicked, thinking you felt she wasn't up to the job. Since she was only supposed to be helping you out while you got the business up and running, I swear she thinks you're looking to let her go."

"The CEO would never allow it."

Jared barks out a laugh. "You know, she made me help her put up a chart on the wall in her bedroom. She's replicated the good behaviour chart we have in the kitchen, but hers has the names of all your employees on it. Someone called Nico didn't get a smiley face yesterday. When I asked why, she wouldn't say—just told me you made her sign an NDA. When I asked if she knew what that meant, she said, 'No Daddies Allowed', and told me to stop asking questions because Kurt said she mustn't spill company secrets."

I can't contain my laughter as I shake my head and huff out, "I love that kid!"

"Do you want to speak to Mac now?"

"Only if she's free."

"The girls are all down, but Ben's fussing, and she is trying to settle him. I'll go take over and leave you to it."

"Thanks man. I'll make sure to let Mac know how much she's appreciated."

"Does this mean we're even. You know over the whole shooting thing?" I know he's only joking; that incident was put to bed a long time ago. It's part of the story of how we met and forged what I consider a lifelong connection. I like to remind him about it every chance I get—just like he loves to tease me about how I'm utterly at the mercy of his five-year-old's demands. The banter is just part of our camaraderie. His family has become as important to me as my own.

"Not even close!" I deadpan, as he passes the

phone to his wife so I can tell her what I need.

Fifteen minutes later I creep back into the cabin. I walk straight over to the bedroom and stop just before I open the door. I need to be on my A-game right now. As much as I want to go inside, I can't be distracted by Maeve and what might happen between us until the issue surrounding Jimmy is resolved. I rest my forehead on the closed door as I remember the night she spent curled up beside me, her soft curves and the way her warmth seemed to melt into mine, as if she was meant to be there. The faint scent of her hair still lingers in my memory, a reminder of how her presence made everything else fade away. My fingers twitch at the thought of reaching for her, of feeling her close again, but I force myself to focus. This isn't the time. I look back to see Tiny has already commandeered the couch and sigh. The floor isn't the only thing that's hard, and I already know it's going to be an impossibly long night.

Chapter 13

Maeve

I really thought he'd come. Shortly after I'd left him speechless, I caught something in his eyes —a fleeting look I almost missed. His pupils dilated, and he swallowed hard. In that split second, he looked so consumed by lust, I thought he was about to eat me alive. The intensity of the moment made my core pulse with need. A feeling so potent it caught me off guard, stealing my breath and sending me scurrying into the bedroom—out of his orbit— just so I could regain my composure.

Once there, I stood listening behind the door, my heart pounding in my chest until I heard him rise and start toward me. The sound of his movement jolted me into action—I tore off my dress and positioned myself on the bed in nothing but my sexiest underwear, determined to leave no doubt as to what I wanted, in case words failed me when he appeared.

I waited, steeling myself for his arrival—knowing our future hinged on what happened next, hoping I wasn't about to make a monumental mistake. But as the minutes ticked by—ten good ones, to be exact—

the door stayed shut. No movement. No arrival.

Finally, I go in search of my man—only to discover he's gone. Just like that. Gone!

I don't know where he has disappeared to, or if he'll be back. All I know is that I feel stupid, embarrassed, and like I'm spiralling out of control. He may have liked me years ago, but that doesn't mean he feels the same now. After all, I was borderline obsessed with Kurt once, and now his good looks and dark demeanour only stir the warm affection reserved for a good friend with a shared history. It's probably the same for Josh—any feelings he may have had for me are long gone. Rather than hurt me, he does something so typically Josh: he walks away, giving me a chance to hold on to my dignity. I know he'll wait until I'm asleep, and tomorrow he'll act as though nothing happened. He'll do nothing to acknowledge that moment when his eyes bored so deeply into mine, I could have sworn they caught a glimpse of my soul. It must have been little more than a look of affection that I mistook for desire, my judgment clouded by my own longing.

The problem is, I don't want to be in the friend-zone anymore. I want a chance to see what could happen between us—I deserve that, especially after just finding out the truth about what happened all those years ago.

I come to the conclusion that there are two ways I can handle this predicament. I could be blunt, lay my feelings on the line, and pray Josh doesn't run for the hills before I've had the chance to come clean to my parents and Derek about our marriage being a sham. Or, I could explore these new feelings by seducing him slowly, reeling him in to the point of no return by stepping out of my comfort zone and seamlessly integrating myself into his life—even if it does mean traveling back to California to learn about his new business and the man he is today after the wedding. I know I've already tentatively agreed to leave with him for a few weeks on our pretend honeymoon. But until now, I was secretly hoping I could convince him to stay within the comfort of my familiar world.

For me, the thought of leaving my hometown to explore unknown pastures has always felt like stepping out of the sun and into a storm without an umbrella. Since the night of the fire, I've clung to my safe routines, avoiding even the smallest ventures. Not even my best friend could coax me into visiting her for a short break—stories of New York's crime rates only fuelled my fears.

But this is different. When Josh came crashing back into my life, he brought an effortless ease and warmth I hadn't felt in a long time. The thought of traveling with—or for—Josh exhilarates me; when he's by my side, the shadows of fear lift, and I can finally breathe deeply. He's always been my anchor, my safe haven.

The idea of stepping out into the world with him feels less like a risk and more like a promise of something greater waiting on the horizon. And now, with my feelings for him escalating exponentially, it's my chance to show him how much he means to me. In the process, I can hopefully rediscover parts of myself I thought I'd lost. So, it's a no-brainer, I quickly decide on the second option. For him, I'm determined to take the leap.

Josh can be stubborn and pig-headed at times, and I've learned the best way to handle him is to let him think he's making all the moves. I'm still fairly inexperienced with men in general, so I still need to figure out how to pull that off effectively. As I drift off to sleep, my mind races through all the things I need to accomplish before the wedding, because once we leave town, I want to shift my focus entirely to him—or more accurately, my goal in becoming an 'us.'

The next morning, I wake up alone, disappointment settling in as I realise Josh never returned last night. I guess the first phase of Operation Irresistible is finding my target—but not before my morning coffee. Stretching, I stumble out of bed, still in the underwear I fell asleep in, and fling open the bedroom door. The next thing I know, I'm nearly face-planting as I trip over a body sprawled on the floor just outside.

"Whoa!" Josh catches me before I hit the ground, manoeuvring me so I land on his fully clothed body with a thud. I know he thinks he's doing me a favour, but honestly, I think the hardwood floor might have been a gentler option than the rock-hard muscles I've just collided with.

"What are you doing out here?" I wheeze as I try

to catch my breath.

"I didn't want to wake you."

"That excuse didn't stop you sneaking into my bed the other night, what's changed?" I regret the words instantly when Josh's face clouds over and I feel him flinch beneath me. I know this isn't going to be the way to get what I want so change tack, "Never mind, I think I may have punctured a lung."

Josh snorts in amusement, then starts tickling my ribs until my squirming and giggles assure him that's not the case. "I think you'll live," he says.

He opens his mouth to speak again but suddenly seems at a loss for words when he registers what little I'm wearing, and more specifically the cleavage that is now tucked just under his chin. I see my chance and seize it, putting my hands on his biceps and pushing myself up to give him a better view. I'm rewarded by a sharp intake of breath which I pretend not to notice as I feign innocence at my behaviour. I fake a shiver, letting my breasts shimmy in front of Josh's face.

"It's chillier than I thought out here," I lie.

"Feel's pretty hot to me," he murmurs.

Bingo! The girl's have definitely caught his attention. I push myself up so I'm straddling him as he lies on the floor. Pretending to be positioning myself ready to stand, I slide my body down his until my core is perfectly aligned with his groin. I'm taken aback by how noticeable his hardness is already, but figure he may have had a certain degree of morning wood to get him started. Feigning an attempt to gain the momentum required to push myself upright, I gently rock back and forth a few times. Josh tries to mask a groan which escapes on a whisper as his eye lids momentarily flutter closed. The feeling of having complete control over such a large and commanding presence empowers me, and I raise myself slightly before 'accidently' slipping to rub against him a little harder. The feeling is so good it's like a drug. I've been so caught up in watching Josh's reaction, I didn't realise how hooked I'd become myself. Like an obsessive on the verge of addiction, I'm caught between taking my next fix and walking away before I'm unable to control my urges.

"You're playing with fire princess," Josh growls, his voice scratchy.

"Then save me," I whisper, surprised at my husky tone. I'm desperate to add, "just like you did all those years ago," but something holds me back. Instead, abandoning all plans for a slow seduction, I tease, "Maybe I don't want to be your princess. Maybe I want to be your queen," just to see his reaction.

"Sorry princess, that titles already been claimed."

What? My core temperature plummets, ice flooding my veins at what he's implying. I always assumed he was single—he never mentioned being involved with anyone. He was the one who suggested taking me back to L.A., the one who picked up the reins of my lie, agreeing to take us over the finish line by marrying me. The thought that I may have lost him before he was ever truly mine crushes me. I feel sick to my stomach as I ask apprehensively, "Does she… does she know about the wedding?" If she does, she's a fool. If he were mine, he'd be marrying another woman over my dead body, no matter who she was or the reasons why.

"Not yet. I'm not sure how I'm going to tell her if I'm honest," the ass smirks, while still fixated on my boobs. "I think she's hoping it will be her sometime in the future."

"Who is she?" I snap, my voice sharp and abrasive. I don't mean to slap him—it's an automatic, impulsive reaction, driven by the urgency to grab his full attention.

"What the fuck was that for?" Josh sits up and at the same time grabs my butt cheeks, dragging me forward so I'm smushed against him, our faces millimetres apart. I can feel his breath on my face and his heart pounding against my skin. His fingers are digging into the soft flesh of my behind, the sweet sting reigniting the flames within me. I want to kiss him, mark him as mine, he is so close it would be easy to do. I lick my lower lip in anticipation and see Josh's eyes follow the movement of my tongue. The atmosphere between us hangs thick with desire, making me feel as though I'm about to combust. I'm wondering if he feels the same, but before I can react further, I'm haunted by the memory of walking in on Derek and Felica. I know I can't be that woman —the one that sleeps with another girl's man behind her back.

"I can't marry you," I say abruptly, trying to

unsuccessfully pull myself out of Josh's firm grip.

"Why?" Josh looks at me like he is genuinely baffled.

"You already have a queen," I say sadly. "I get that you were only doing it to help me out but it wouldn't be right. Not if she didn't know."

"She'll get over it. It's not like there was ever that kind of future for us." His lack of compassion riles me, but before I can challenge his response, his face changes. It's like I'm watching him have a major revelation—though I can't quite tell what it is. His confusion suddenly morphs into something akin to... mischievous ease? He redeems himself slightly when he adds, "It's not a conversation I feel I can have over the phone. I want to look her in the face when I explain things to her."

"Then you need to go and do that before we take this charade any further." I tell him seriously. Jealousy making me bristle and try unsuccessfully to wriggle out of his hold once more.

"I will, if you come with me," Josh grins. "I want her to meet you. She'll always be a part of my future so I think it's best you guys at least try to get along."

I frown, unable to believe what I'm hearing. Is he trying to suggest some kind of ménage à trois? I feel like I'm being played, like he's sensing my discomfort and taking a little too much pleasure in it. I'm pretty sure he's just teasing, testing my limits, pushing to see if he can make me confess I'd indulge in whatever warped male fantasy his sly expression suggests is bouncing around in his brain.

He definitely thinks he has the upper hand, that I won't pick up the gauntlet he's thrown down. He seems a little too confident I'll fold and withdraw myself from the situation, accepting it for what it is and letting him off the hook for never mentioning he was already in a relationship. The ball's in my court. Do I give him what he wants and admit defeat, or do I start fighting for what I think should be mine before he has the chance to tell 'his queen' there's a new piece on the board—one ready to claim checkmate if given half the chance? Neither. I raise an eyebrow and play Josh at his own game, calling his bluff. "Alright," I tell him. "Let's go."

"You're joking, right?" He looks at me astounded. "I never thought you'd go for it."

"Well, I did," I tell him resolutely, expecting him to immediately try to talk me out of it.

"Great," he slaps my ass. "As much as I'm enjoying the lap dance, now's not the time or place. Get off me and go get ready for work. I'll drop you off then sort us out some flights for later today."

"W...what?" I stammer, completely overlooking the comment about the lap dance, which clearly wasn't as subtle as I'd hoped. Josh stands, pulling me up with him. "I can't leave town today," I blurt out, panic starting to set in.

"Well, we told Derek we were getting married next week, that doesn't give us a huge window of opportunity. We'll leave this evening." He says it like my skipping town is already a done deal.

"I can't." I repeat in a daze.

"Why?"

"My business. I need to ask Aiden if he can cover for me for a start. Then I need to finish setting up his consulting room. I only started clearing a space on Sunday. That needs to be finished, then I need to buy an examination table, scales, a second set of tools. He has his own stethoscope, otoscope and ophthalmoscope but not much else. Then I'm going to be advertising for a new receptionist. It's not fair to take off and leave him in the lurch. For every patient we see, records need updating, supplies need checking, and stock needs reordering. Plus, there's the wedding itself, we need to go and get the licence, book a venue, and make sure any guests receive an invite."

"Don't forget the swans." Josh tells me seriously.

"Exactly!" I heave a silent sigh of relief.

"If I could get all that organised by the end of today, you'll come?" Again, it feels more like a challenge than a request, but I know pulling everything together in such a short space of time will be an impossible task. Aiden and I won't have time to finish clearing out the stock room since we have a full diary, some of the equipment I want to order is specialised so not available for immediate delivery, and Josh can't magic up an employee for a job that hasn't even been posted yet.

"Sure," I tell him, masking my relief with a nonchalant shrug.

"I'm going to grab a shower, write down what you need." Josh tells me unfazed, or at least pretending

239

to be.

"Okay," I tell him, as I try not to laugh at his naivety.

Ten minutes later I try not to drool as he emerges from the bathroom wrapped in possibly the smallest towel I own. I feel my pulse quicken as heat floods my body at the sight of all the toned muscle on display. It's frustrating how I can no longer seem to control the way my body reacts when I'm around him. Josh stops in his tracks when he sees me. It's not surprising when I feel like I must be glowing red enough to be a warning light on the dashboard of his life. "You're staring?"

I try to avert my gaze but I'm captivated. "Uh huh." Is the best my scrambled brain can come up with. He strolls over arrogantly, stopping as close as he can be without touching me. I can feel the heat radiating off the ripped plains of his abs which are glistening, still slightly damp from his shower. The floral scent of the soap I use, mixed with the raw masculinity oozing from his pores makes for a heady aroma.

Like what you see princess?" Josh leans in to whisper the words in my ear. His breath travels down my neck like a warm caress, making me shiver before leaving goosebumps in its wake. My nipples stand to full attention as my mouth goes dry, leaving me unable to answer his next question. "Have you made your list?"

I know it will be dangerous to hang around longer than necessary, so I thrust the paper I've written my demands on into his hand, before dashing past him into the bathroom and closing the door. When I've caught my breath, I take a cool shower, and when I exit the bathroom myself, Josh is no-where to be seen. Since Tiny has also disappeared, I assume he has taken my dog out to do his thing. Derek mews pitifully at the door evidently distraught at being separated from his new best friend, so I scoop him up and take him through to the bedroom with me while I finish getting ready for work.

I've just made myself some toast and am taking a bite, when Josh comes barrelling back in the room, stealing my breakfast from my hand and grinning like a cheshire cat.

"You ready?" He asks, with a smug smirk. "We've a busy day ahead."

"Yeah, yeah." I roll my eyes, stealing back my toast before heading out the door. "I've got to get going, I'm running late."

"There's plenty of time, I said I'll take you."

"It's fine. I usually walk so Tiny gets his exercise. That way he'll settle while I'm working."

"After I've taken you to work, I'm going for a run. I'll take him with me."

"You are?" I ask surprised. I was pretty sure he would be killing himself trying to work through my list. Then I realise he must know it's unachievable and be feigning confidence until he has to admit defeat at the end of the day. I could be the bigger person and let him off the hook but I find myself prodding the bear instead. "Where's your running gear then?"

"In my go bag, back of the car."

"What's a go bag?" I've never heard a holdall or suitcase called that before.

Josh freezes, like he knows he's said something wrong. "I meant my travel bag."

He doesn't look embarrassed but he definitely looks like he's hiding something, and there's only one thing I assume it could be. I wait as long as I can before envy gets the better of me, and the words come tumbling out, "Did your queen pack it for you?"

"What?" Josh looks like I've just handed him a winning lottery ticket. "No," he beams, "I packed it myself."

"Well, if you're sure?" I say distractedly, trying to work out why my unease is causing him so much joy.

"Yes, I'm sure I packed it myself." It almost feels like he's gloating, but of course he would be, wouldn't he? Knowing he has a queen back home, and even if he thinks the idea of him and me being together is ridiculous, he must find my attention flattering, feeding his ego in a way that only a man with two women lusting over him could appreciate.

"I meant about taking Tiny for a run," I try to sound upbeat but don't think I do a very good job.

"Of course, we need to spend some quality time together. We need to bond if we are going to be around each other a bit more. If he tackles me every time he sees me, people will start to get suspicious."

"Once." I hold my index finger up in the air as I

manage to crack a smile. "And he hadn't gotten to know you then."

Josh walks over and slings an arm across my shoulders, leading me towards his car. "C'mon princess, let's get you to work. I said I'd catch up with a friend this morning and I'll take Tiny for a run after. Then I've a few calls to make, text me when you know what time you'll be taking lunch and I'll come and pick you up so we can go and get our wedding licence."

"What's the rush?"

"We're leaving town tonight remember."

"Oh yeah," I say, humouring him. "I forgot."

"You don't think I can do it, do you?" Josh side-eyes me, his tone daring.

"Do what?" I ask, feigning innocence.

"Complete your list."

"Not a chance." I reply, dipping my chin to try and hide my smile.

"Love you."

"I love you too Randy." I chuckle at the African grey parrot stood on my examination table.

"I'm sorry," Mrs Jacobs apologises on behalf of her pet. "I don't know where he picks it all up from."

"I'd say Mr Jacobs," I say with a smile. Mr. and Mrs. Jacobs were high school sweethearts who have been married for fifty years and are more in love now than ever before. It's what I'd always hoped for myself. Still, I think with a sigh, maybe next time around. "What seems to be the problem?"

"Show the nice lady your foot Randy," Mrs Jacob's addresses her parrot who immediately tucks one foot under his body, hiding it from view.

"Ouch." Randy hops about on the table dramatically.

"Randy," Mrs Jacobs, tells him calmly but sternly, "Show Maeve your foot."

Randy puts his leg down and stretches it out in front of him so I can see the small abrasion atop his front toes.

"How did this happen little guy?"

"Ouch." Randy squawks solemnly.

"He was watching a horror movie with his dad the other night. I think he was just dozing off when there was a loud bang that startled him, he bashed his foot in his panic."

"Horror movies, eh?" I say in amusement to Randy, who bobs his head up and down in agreement. I take a pencil out of my pocket and offer it to Randy who easily grips it with his injured foot. "His movement doesn't appear to be restricted and the wound looks superficial. I'll just give it a good clean then apply some ointment to help it heal and prevent any infection. Keep an eye on it, and if it looks like it's getting any worse bring him back in for another look. Though, I'm sure he'll be fine."

"Thank you. What do you say Randy?"

I grab a swab and go to clean the injury. "No!"

Randy starts skittering back, away from me. I chuckle and reach forward, but before I even make contact, Randy mimics a blood curdling scream. Its so loud I jump in surprise, Mrs Jacob's however doesn't react until the door to the consulting room flies open and a lion in human form bursts in, visibly alarmed and poised for action.

"What the fuck is going in in here?" Josh roars.

I jump for a second time, Randy loses control of his bowels and poor Mrs Jacobs, fearing she is about to be attacked, crumples to the floor.

"Josh! What the hell?" I catch my breath before rushing to Mrs Jacob's aid. "Get me some water, hurry."

Josh assesses the situation quickly and, after determining there is no threat, rushes to fill a glass with water from the sink in the far corner of the room. As Mrs. Jacobs starts to stir, I keep my gaze on her while reaching behind me for her drink. Unfortunately, I'm a second too late, as Josh misinterprets my intent and showers her with the cool liquid.

"Fuck!" I gasp, shooting Josh daggers before turning my attention back to the older lady—now fully awake, albeit drenched. "I'm so sorry."

"What?" Josh asks in amazement. "That's what you did to me."

"You're not a seventy-year-old woman on the verge of having a heart attack!" I bark back.

"That's alright dear," A contrite Josh helps Mrs Jacobs stand on two very wobbly legs, and she brushes herself down as she tries to regain her composure. "And just for the record, I'm sixty-nine."

"My favourite number," Josh gives the woman an award-winning smile and I can tell by the way she grins back he is already forgiven. I roll my eyes wondering if he has that effect on all women.

"What are you doing here?" I growl at Josh. "I texted to say I'd be taking lunch at one o'clock, it's not even twelve."

"Change of plan," Josh tells me decisively.

"What do you mean change of plan?" I put my hands on my hips and glare at him.

"You're in trouble, you're in trouble!" Randy parrots humorously, like a naughty schoolchild on a playground.

"That maybe, but at least I didn't just shit myself!" Josh retorts, only for Randy to squawk indignantly.

"Josh! I'm with a patient," I snap, bundling him out of the room. "Wait outside and I'll see to you in a minute."

Randy blows a raspberry as I close the door in Josh's displeased face.

Ten minutes later, I reopen the door to find Josh still leaning against the wall outside, muscular arms folded across his chest. He doesn't look amused but I don't stop to acknowledge him as I walk Mrs. Jacobs out to Aiden, confirming there will be no fee for Randy's treatment. Aiden sniggers, making it clear he knows the reason why without needing to ask.

"Who's next?" I ask.

"Um," Aiden shuffles back and forth

uncomfortably. "Your man asked if I could see the next few clients while he whisked you away for a couple of hours."

I feel my eyes widen. "He did, did he? What about your lunch?"

"He's arranged for it to be delivered—today and every day for the next couple of months, actually. I'll eat between appointments and take a break when you get back. It's not like we haven't done that before to help each other out. Besides, if I'm going to be holding the fort after today, as well as teaching the new girl the ropes when she arrives tomorrow, it's only to be expected while you're away for the next few weeks."

I feel my mouth opening and closing like a goldfish, too stunned to reply, as Josh appears beside me just as Aiden hands me my bag across the counter. "Ready?" Josh asks, slinging his arm around my shoulders and steering me out the door with an air of nonchalance.

I don't say a word as I'm ushered outside and into Josh's car.

"Where's Tiny?" I suddenly ask concerned.

"Back seat," Josh chuckles.

I look behind me to see my dog sprawled out almost unconscious.

"What did you do to him?" I ask in horror.

"Took him for a run like I said," Josh looks at me grinning. "Thought he'd have more stamina if I'm honest."

"If you've broken my dog, the weddings off!" I

grumble. "Where are we going anyway?"

"Get our licence. I told you this earlier. You really will have to learn to listen when I speak if you are going to pledge to love, honour and *obey* me correctly." I snort, unamused, as Josh continues a little too jovially.   "We have to go now since I have to get back to finish clearing out Aiden's consulting room before his new equipment arrives later."

I stare at Josh, dumbfounded, but he simply puts the car into gear and drives off without giving me a second glance. He's bluffing. He has to be!

Chapter 14

Josh

Maeve thinks I didn't clock the look on her face. It was all I could do to stop myself from bursting out laughing.

After dropping her back at work, I returned to her cabin to meet Foxy. He quickly checked her small space to ensure it wasn't bugged. Before he left to meet up with Kurt, we set up a discreet camera disguised as a clock in her living area. The feed is designed to trigger a response back to base if anyone enters while Maeve and I are out of town—it's purely a precautionary measure.

Then, I made a few calls. Before she started working for me, Mac was a highly renowned model. She's now married to an A-list actor, the sister of another, and friends with the one who happens to be her husband's biggest competition at the box office. Over the years, the four of us have built enough influential connections between us to make almost anything possible. And when our friends can't help, it's almost a foregone conclusion that they will know someone who can. Which is how I've managed to arrange for every piece of equipment Maeve requested on her list to be sourced and delivered in record time. I've also bribed the decorators working on the house across the street from the surgery to pop in and give the old stock room a fresh lick of paint before they leave at the end of the day. Axel and Mac have confirmed that after some heated debates, they've already whittled our job applicants down to five, and I have their assurance that the best two will be on a plane heading in Ace's direction before the day is out. That just leaves the wedding. Once we get to L.A. and they've been introduced, Mac is going to help Maeve arrange everything from there, freeing up my time to help Kurt in any way I can.

She doesn't know it yet but Maeve won't be heading home again for a while. Once we have our licence and I drop her back at work, I'll head back to the cabin to make sure it's secure and pack a bag for her. Then it's back to the vets to finish getting it set up for Aiden before we head straight to the airport to catch our nine o'clock flight.

I like Aiden. He's loyal to Maeve, and while I hit some resistance when I first outlined my plans, after convincing him of how much it would mean to her—and assuring him my intentions were honourable, even if I couldn't reveal all the reasons —he eventually came around. Now, with everything falling into place, it's only a matter of time before Maeve realises that our leaving today is a done deal. That's the second time I've had a problem she's unwittingly resolved. Kurt's words come back to haunt me: I am one lucky S.O.B—and as it turns out, in more ways than one.

I know I should stop being such a jerk towards her. I've been around enough women to recognise when they're flirting, and this morning, Maeve was definitely trying to get my attention. Normally, she would've screamed and run off, mortified, if I'd caught her in a similar state of undress, but she brazenly pushed her chest in my face like an offering too good to refuse. Then when she asked why I hadn't joined her the night before, her disappointment was unmistakable. I could barely contain the surge of elation when she started to grind against me, leaving no doubt—she was mine for the taking. It was all I could do not to blow in my shorts, every fantasy I'd clung to for years was unfolding right in front of me. And yet, I couldn't help but crave a little payback—for all those times in the past I'd tried to make it clear how much I liked her, only to have her never once feel the same way I wished she would. When I'd joked about the queen, and she misunderstood, thinking I already had a lover, her jealousy became the trigger I needed to convince her to leave town, making it easier for me to protect her. Once the mystery of Jimmy's disappearance is resolved, and I can finally let my guard down, I'll admit the truth—that I like her too. She deserves my full attention because I don't want anything short-term, not with Maeve. Now she is back in my life I want her to stay. It'll be good for her to see my place in California and explore my life there, so she can understand how much I've grown—from the boy she once knew to the man I've become. If she still likes what she sees, I'm all in. Until then, I'll have to ignore the way she glances at me when she thinks I'm not looking, the subtle ways she tries to touch me, and the unspoken desire that lingers between us. For now, I'll keep my distance, focus on keeping her safe, basking in the knowledge that when the time is right, I'll finally get the chance to show her just how much she means to me.

"Penny for them," Maeve strokes my thigh to get my attention and I resist the urge to grab her hand—to hold it there, to keep her close.

"I was just thinking how much I have left to do once I drop you back to work," I glance across at her smiling.

"That you have," she chuckles. "I wouldn't think any less of you if you wanted to admit defeat now." There's unmistakable hesitancy in her voice, and it makes me think she might actually be starting to worry I'll be able to meet the challenge she set.

"Never!" I reply staunchly. After a pause I glance over again, adding, "You only agreed to come away with me because you thought I'd fail to complete all the tasks you gave me, didn't you?"

"No!" She exclaims in a tone that really means 'yes', and this time I actually have to bite the inside of my cheek to stop myself from laughing out loud.

Two hours later, license in hand, I drop Maeve back at work before heading to her cabin. There's still plenty to organize, starting with packing her a bag.

I search everywhere, but come up empty handed. It's like she never goes away. Even when Derek returned her stuff it was all in garbage bags. What does she use when she goes on holiday? Or when she goes to visit Tina in New York?

The last place I check is under the bed. There's nothing there except for a box. Intrigued, I pull it out and flip the lid—only to fall back onto my haunches, stunned by what's staring back at me. The valentine's cards I sent her all those years ago. The one's I thought would've ended up in the trash the minute she realised they weren't from Kurt. I can't believe she kept them all this time. As I read the words I once wrote, memories flood back—of the love I felt for her then and the hope I poured into every pen stroke, the yearning I felt for her to see me differently. And now, after all these years, I wonder what they meant to her, why she kept them, if she ever worked out they had all been sent by me. Closing the box, I slide it back where I found it—valid questions for another time. Right now, without a suitcase, gym bag, or any other practical option in sight, I need to go to the store.

Forty minutes later, I'm back and facing a new dilemma—I've never had to pack for a woman before. My thoughts drift to the essentials I always keep in my go bag—the one that's always packed and ready for me to leave on a mission at a moment's notice, no matter the circumstances. I start with a change of clothes. Los Angeles is significantly warmer than Vermont year-round, with its Mediterranean climate of mild, wet winters and hot, dry summers. Vermont, by contrast, has a humid continental climate, marked by cold, snowy winters and warm, humid summers—Maeve's wardrobe reflects the difference. I don't find much in the way of summer clothes, so I throw whatever I can find into the case and make a mental note to ask Mac to take her shopping and get her properly kitted out once we arrive.

I move on to underwear, disregarding the thermals and anything that looks like something my mom would buy, in favour of anything lighter and more appealing. I always thought women loved shoes, but not Maeve, apparently. Apart from the strappy heels I saw her wearing at the restaurant, I only find a few pairs of boots. The shoes go in the case, but the boots stay—she won't be needing those where we're headed.

Toiletries. I step into the bathroom and scan the shelves. Everyday items like shampoo and shower gel, she won't need—I've already got those covered. It's the lotions and potions that baffle me. I pick up a small tube, squinting at the label. Age-defying lip volumizing serum. What the fuck? Who knew this was a thing? Curious, I pop the cap and smear a little on my lower lip. It starts to tingle almost immediately, and panic sets in—I scrub it off under the tap before tossing the tube in the bin. She doesn't need that; she's perfect just the way she is. In fact, most of the items I find make elaborate claims about transforming this or improving that—each one more absurd than the last. She doesn't need any of it. I grab the makeup bag she often rummages through, along with a box of tampons I spot on the floor as an afterthought. Just as I'm about to zip the case, a soft mew catches my attention. Derek, the stowaway, peers up at me from inside the suitcase. Smiling, I lift him out gently and scoop him into his carrier—he's coming, just not packed in with the clothes.

Once I've finished, I stow the suitcase in the boot of my car and secure Derek's carrier to the back seat. Tiny decided to stay with Maeve when I dropped her off—probably worried I'd take him for another run.

It's four in the afternoon by the time I make it back to Maeve's clinic. Aiden greets me as I step inside. "You wouldn't happen to know anything about the four painters just finishing up out back, would you?" he asks, smiling.

"Not a clue," I deadpan, handing Derek's carrier over the counter. "Can you take care of this little man until we're ready to leave? He's got a long journey ahead, so if you could feed and water him, and maybe wear him out a bit before we go, I'd appreciate it."

"No problem. You're still leaving tonight, then?" Aiden asks, raising an eyebrow. "Only Maeve seems to think she'll still be here tomorrow. I heard her telling Mrs. Johnson she'd pop round to give her pregnant Siamese a once-over."

"Can you take care of it?"

"Sure, but…"

"No buts. Maeve and I are leaving tonight. You have my word there'll be a new receptionist on your doorstep by the time you open in the morning. I'm sorry to add to your workload by having you train her, but I'll make sure you're well compensated. You have my number, so feel free to call if there's any problem, large or small. I'd rather you didn't worry Maeve unless it's absolutely necessary."

"I hear you," Aiden says with a grin. "You really do care about her, don't you?"

"I do," I reply sincerely as a large delivery van pulls up outside.

Aiden clocks the truck and furrows his brows as he scans the computer. "I'm not expecting a delivery."

"Yes, you are," I say, heading out to meet the driver.

By the time everything has been unloaded and is in place, Aiden has become my new best friend as he marvels at his new consulting room. I haven't seen Maeve since I got back—she's been tied up for at least an hour with her last appointment of the day. A young golden retriever with a sprained leg, if Aiden's quick update is anything to go by. I glance toward her closed door, hearing soft voices and the occasional bark, wondering what she'll say when she finally sees what I've accomplished.

"What time are you leaving?" Aiden asks.

"As soon as Maeve's done here," I reply.

"Before she has the chance to talk you out of it, you mean?" He chuckles.

"Something like that," I agree, just as she strides into the reception area, a lively dog with a bandaged leg hobbling cheerfully along behind her.

She doesn't even get the chance to tell Aiden what she needs before his excitement bubbles over. "Maeve, go check out my new consulting room! Thank you so much—I don't know how you managed to organise it so quickly. We were only talking about it the other day!"

"What?" Maeve replies, her expression perplexed.

I stare at the ground, avoiding all eye contact, hoping to go unnoticed as the realisation starts to dawn on her.

"You didn't..." I think she's talking to me, but since I'm still not looking at her, I'm not sure. I only glance up when she suddenly scurries out of the room. I follow her, leaving Aiden to go over her notes and see the last customer out.

I find her in the new room, her hand pressed over her mouth, her eyes wide in shock. "How did you... I mean... Josh, this is all brand-new, high-end gear," she breathes. "I can't afford this—some of it is more advanced than anything I've already got. You'll have to send it back."

Walking up behind her, I wrap my arms around her waist, and she sags back against me. "Call it a wedding present."

"You can't afford all this," she protests gently.

"You said you were in security. That doesn't pay much, does it?"

"It pays more than you'd think," I chuckle, pressing a kiss to her hair. "I offer a bespoke service that people are willing to pay a premium for. And while I was in the service, my expenses were minimal—I've managed to put away a good amount in savings."

"Savings for your future," she murmurs. "Not mine."

Her stomach growls and I whisper into her ear, "If it makes you feel better, I'll let you buy me dinner."

"Josh be serious," she turns in my arms, looking at me, her face full of worry and unresolved questions. There's something in the way she looks at me—a mix of gratitude and resistance, as if she's unsure whether to accept or argue further. I offer her a soft smile, fully expecting her to smile back. But she doesn't.

Instead, her hands reach behind my head, her fingers threading through my hair with a gentle but deliberate touch. Before I can even process what's happening, she catches me off guard, her lips— thankful and unyielding—meeting mine in a kiss so full of feeling it leaves me momentarily stunned. For a moment, the world around us falls away. Her warmth and the way she leans into me speak volumes, answering all the questions I didn't even know I was asking. I pull her closer, deepening the kiss, wanting to hold on to this fleeting, perfect moment for as long as possible. She responds fervently, making me greedier—it's like a dam has burst inside me, and all my repressed emotions are flooding out. I crave her attention, desperately, like a parched earth soaking up every drop of rain. Each whimper, each sound she gives feels like a lifeline, and I can't get enough. She matches my enthusiasm, until the tension becomes unbearable and we start clawing at each other's clothes. She lets out a small moan, and my reaction is visceral as I push her back towards the recently delivered examination table.

"Maeve?" Aiden's voice rings out, breaking the spell we're under. He stands frozen in the doorway, his brows knitting together in a mixture of surprise and amusement. The moment shatters like glass, and we spring apart, our breath shallow, our faces flushed. Dishevelled and shaken, we exchange a glance—equal parts shock and disbelief at the intensity of what just happened.

Maeve coughs in embarrassment, "Um… yes?"

"I just wondered if you were ready to lock up and leave," Aiden smirks. "Or should I just go and let you close up when you're done?"

"No… no, we're coming," Maeve stutters.

"So I see," Aiden chuckles as he walks away, Maeve scurrying behind him, while I struggle to suppress a smile at his cheek.

I follow the others back through to reception where Aiden is bundling Derek back into his carrier.

"What's he doing here?" Maeve asks confused.

"He didn't want to stay home alone," I quip.

Maeve gives me a puzzled look. "C'mon, let's go.

It's been a long day and I'm exhausted—I could do with a nice soak in the bath before dinner." The three of us leave, and while I shake Aiden's hand, thanking him for the task he's about to take on, Maeve, blissfully unaware, bundles Tiny and Derek into the back of my car.

As Maeve climbs into her seat, she lets out a weary sigh and rubs her temples. "Don't let me fall asleep before dinner," she murmurs, her voice heavy with exhaustion.

We pull out onto the road, and before we set off, Maeve calls to Aiden out of her open window, "Bye. See you tomorrow." He opens his mouth to respond, but as he catches the look on my face, he simply raises his hand with a knowing smile.

Maeve slouches back in her seat and closes her eyes, the tension melting from her features. Her tiredness works in my favour; it ensures she doesn't notice when I take an unexpected turn away from her cabin and head toward the airport instead.

When she finally opens her eyes, she sits bolt upright in panic, repeatedly slapping my knee as though I might not have noticed she's suddenly alert and aware of her surroundings. "Josh, where are we going?"

"The airport."

She lets out a funny little squeak. "Why?"

"If I completed everything on your list, you said we could leave tonight. I did. In fact, I went above and beyond to make sure you couldn't weasel your way out of it, so we are."

There's a stunned silence, and I can feel her eyes boring into me. The quiet is unnerving, so I feel the need to elaborate before she combusts.

"I finished clearing out the stockroom, had it repainted, and kitted it out in line with your minimum specifications. I checked with Aiden to make sure he was okay covering for you while you're out of town. I even arranged for his lunch to be delivered every day for the next few weeks, in case he gets a rush on and is too busy to leave the clinic and pick it up himself.

I hired a temporary receptionist to help him, and she'll be ready and waiting outside the clinic for his instructions first thing tomorrow morning. He has my number in case there are any issues. I took you to pick up our wedding license, have my executive assistant on standby to help you arrange the wedding of your dreams when we reach Los Angeles, and called in a few favours so Tiny and Derek can travel with us in the cabin instead of the hold of the plane."

The rest of the journey doesn't go as smoothly as I would have liked. Maeve is constantly on edge, asking all sorts of ridiculous questions in an effort to get me to turn around and take her home. Did I remember to pack her hairdryer? Nope, but I'm sure they sell them where we're headed. Was I certain I locked up before leaving the cabin? Yes. Did I throw out the perishables in the fridge? *Mmhmm. Note to self: get Ace to drop in and take care of it.*

Things don't improve much once we're on the

plane. I recline back in my chair with my eyes closed, trying to relax, while Maeve bounces nervously in the seat beside me. She jabs my arm. "We need to get off. Tiny's shaking."

"He's excited—he's never flown before."

"Derek's crying."

"Give him a cuddle. He'll be fine."

She only relaxes when the seatbelt sign goes off, and I can rearrange us so she's safely tucked under my arm. For a while, she's still, her breathing evening out as the tension drains away. I finally feel her shoulders relax against me, and I let out a breath I didn't realise I was holding.

Just as I think we might make it through the flight peacefully, she stirs again. "Josh," she murmurs, her voice laced with sleep and suspicion, "You're sure we've got everything?"

I can't help but grin. "I've got everything I need right here," I reply, giving her a squeeze and pressing a kiss to her temple.

Twelve hours later, we pull up outside a sprawling five-bedroom property in Morro Bay, a charming coastal city roughly two hundred miles northwest of Hollywood. It's just past six in the morning, and the day already feels warm and promising—so different from where we've come from.

"Why are we here?" Maeve asks as we pile out of the car. "I thought you had an apartment near Hollywood."

"I do," I reply. "But the whole point of this trip was for you to meet my queen."

"She's here?" Maeve asks, panicking. "I can't meet her now."

"Why not?" I ask, amused.

"Josh, I look like a train wreck. I've barely slept, my hair's a mess, and I've been wearing the same clothes since yesterday. I need a bed, a shower, and a meal—not necessarily in that order. And before any of that, the animals need attention."

"You can do all of that here," I say reassuringly.

Maeve rounds on me, hands on her hips. She does look a little travel-worn, but somehow it's endearing.

You don't want to meet the woman you're competing with looking and smelling like something the cat dragged in," she snaps. Derek meows pitifully from his carrier, and Maeve quickly adds, "Sorry, Derek."

"Competing with?" I raise an eyebrow, feigning innocence. "What do you mean?"

Maeve flushes, clearly embarrassed and at a loss for words. Before she can respond, the gates beside us begin to part. The front door of the mansion swings open, and Mac comes charging down the path to greet us. She's wrapped in a pale green silk robe, her nightwear still visible beneath it. Soft curls cascade down her back, flowing like she just stepped out of a salon—despite what must have been a restless night caring for three babies.

"Holy shit!" Maeve exclaims in horror, "She's stunning."

"Ex-model," I confirm as Maeve's brows furrow,

"She looks really familiar."

"She would do," I whisper. "Before she got married, you couldn't flip through a magazine or watch an ad without seeing her face. She was everywhere."

Married?" Maeve repeats, her confusion deepening as Mac throws herself forward, wrapping Maeve in an enthusiastic hug.

"I'm so glad you made it," Mac gushes. "We've all been dying to meet you."

"We?" I query, my stomach sinking. The way Mac says the word makes me feel she is talking about more than just Jared and her kids. I look up towards the house in time to see the front blinds spring closed.

"I'm sorry," Mac says, looking at me apologetically. "Jack called yesterday. When I mentioned you were coming and bringing your bride-to-be, he decided to drive down with Jaime to meet her."

"Just Jack and Jaime?" I growl, scrubbing my hand down my face.

The Jack Mac is referring to is her brother, Jackson Longe—a man who left his acting career at its peak after a personal tragedy. Good looks clearly run deep in that family, and Jackson is no exception. Built a lot like me, he's a formidable presence who doesn't tolerate nonsense. Still, it's not Jackson I'm worried about. His wisecracking best friend and neighbour, Mitchel Dalton, is another story. Mitchel took the spotlight when Jackson stepped away and is now dominating the box office. To the outside world,

Mitchel is rumoured to be the sworn enemy and biggest rival of Jared Jones, Mac's husband. In reality, though, those rumours couldn't be further from the truth. Despite their rocky start, Jared and Mitchel are close friends. I know I should warn Maeve so she is prepared for who she's about to meet. She thinks she's about to walk into a room of strangers, but she's in for quite the shock. What Maeve doesn't yet realise is that she is going to be walking into a glittering circle of Hollywood royalty—and when her world suddenly collides with theirs I'm not sure how she'll react.

I met both Jack and Mitchel through Mac, and while I consider them friends, I know all too well that they're quick-witted troublemakers. Despite their fame, they're as down-to-earth as they come. Jack has a quiet strength and Mitchel a mischievous charm, but neither takes themselves too seriously. Spend five minutes with them, and you'd forget they're household names—they're just two regular guys who love a good laugh and don't let the glitz of Hollywood go to their heads. Jack's here to give me a hard time—and there's no doubt he'll milk the fact that I'm getting married for all it's worth, especially after all the times I swore I'd never fall prey to a woman's charms like he did. I just hope Jackson didn't bring Mitchel along to double the pain —those two together are an unstoppable force when it comes to torment.

"And Harper," Mac confirms. Relief washes over me. Jackson's one-year-old daughter I can handle.

But that sense of calm is short-lived when, after a hesitant pause, Mac adds, "With Mitchel, Jen, and Zach." I groan loudly, but she's still not done. "Plus, Jared's sister Ava is here with Grant and their brood."

"How?" I ask, utterly astonished, glancing at my watch. It's not even seven. Grant and Ava live within walking distance of Jared and Mac's place, but getting their whole crew out of the house before we arrived must have been a Herculean effort. When awake, their identical twin boys, around ten years old, are a whirlwind of mischief, and their daughter Olivia, about the same age as Mac's triplets, is just as spirited. The thought of facing them all this early in the morning has me bracing myself. It's no wonder Maeve looks like she is about to pass out.

"Maybe we should go to a hotel and get cleaned up first," I say backing away from the house.

"And disappoint your queen?" Mac goes for the jugular. "She'll be raging if she doesn't get to see you before she has to leave."

"You coming in or do you have to go back to Vermont and find your balls first?" Mitchel's unmistakable voice comes sailing out the house amongst a chorus of giggles.

"I can't meet all these strangers looking like..." Maeve trails off, gesturing down the length of her body. "This!"

"Nonsense," Mac says with a reassuring smile, wrapping an arm around Maeve's waist and guiding her up the pathway toward the house. "You look lovely."

"But… but I have animals!" Maeve protests weakly, her gaze fixed on the pristine property ahead. "Tiny moults, and Derek—well, he's a kitten. He's playful. I wouldn't want them damaging your house."

"We love animals," Mac replies warmly. "The queen has a dog, and let me tell you, when we first got him, the damage he did…" She pauses dramatically, sucking in a breath. "If this house can survive him, triplets, and a five-year-old on a daily basis, a kitten and a few stray dog hairs will be no trouble at all. Besides, Mr. Josh could use someone to play with."

"Who's Mr. Josh?" Maeve asks, still dazed.

"The queen's dog. She named him after that big lug," Mac says, thumbing back toward me as I trail behind the two women. "He's a Cane Corso. Are you familiar with the breed? Wait… what am I saying? You're a vet, aren't you? Of course you are."

"You know I'm a vet?" Maeve asks, clearly surprised.

"Of course! Josh never shuts up about you," Mac replies with a grin. "He's always telling us how gorgeous you are and how proud he is of you for running your own veterinary practice back in Vermont. Honestly, I think it's so romantic—the way you knew each other in high school, drifted apart, and then reconnected all these years later. You're like a pair of star-crossed lovers, torn apart by fate, only to be thrown back together by destiny."

"Really?" Maeve glances back at me, her eyes wide with wonder. "He thinks I'm gorgeous?"

"Mac," I bark sharply.

"When he told us you were getting married, I wasn't surprised."

"You weren't?" Maeve whispers. "How do you think the queen will take the news? That's why we're here—so I can meet her and we can explain our... situation. Josh didn't want to do it over the phone."

"Your situation?" Mac looks at me puzzled, she says something else I don't hear as the sound is drowned out by the piercing scream coming from the mini tornado hurtling toward me.

"KING JOSH!"

I barely manage to scoop the little girl into my arms before she flings herself at me. She hugs me so tightly it's hard to breathe.

"That's your queen?" Maeve barks, her face darkening like a thundercloud.

"Yes, that's Tia, Jared's and my oldest," Mac replies, laughing at Maeve's sullen expression. "Is something wrong? Wait... he didn't lead you to believe 'his queen' was a romantic entanglement, did he?" Too shrewd for her own good, Mac stops mid-motion, releasing Maeve so she can turn to me with a knowing grin. "Josh Stone..." Her words linger, heavy with amusement. "You've got it worse than I thought."

I frown, not quite grasping her meaning. As Mac guides Maeve toward the house, my phone starts to ring—the familiar ringtone I can never ignore. Fishing it out of my pocket, I glance at the screen and see Kurt's name flashing.

"I'll be right there," I call after Mac and Maeve as they disappear inside. I set Tia down gently. "Honey, can you look after Maeve for me? Introduce her dog to Mr. Josh and make sure they get along. He'll also need something to eat and drink."

Tia nods eagerly, reaching for the cat carrier I set down to be able to search for my phone. "I'll take this, too."

"I can bring it in a moment—it's a bit big for you," I say gently.

"I'm not four!" She retorts indignantly.

It's hard to suppress my smile as I hand over Derek, making sure she has a firm hold while still being able to see where she is going. "Careful now," I tell her.

"I've got him," she whispers, her tone reverent, as though speaking too loudly might break him.

Once she's safely on her way, I turn on my heel and step away from the house. Answering the call, I skip the pleasantries and get straight to the point. "What do I need to know?"

Chapter 15

Maeve

Where the hell has Josh disappeared to? I thought he'd keep me safe, yet here I am, being led by this woman—nice as she seems—into an unfamiliar house full of strangers. And where's Josh? Nowhere to be seen. He seems perfectly fine with it, even though anything could happen. At least Tiny stays loyally by my side, his steady presence a small comfort as I rest my hand on his head, trying to soothe my rapidly fraying nerves.

"We haven't been formally introduced," the woman gripping me speaks, making me jump slightly. "I'm Mackenzie Jones. But my friends call me Mac. I work for Josh."

Hi, I'm Maeve." I let out a nervous giggle as we pause in the large hallway. I extend my hand for shaking. Mac hesitates, then pulls me into a tight hug, muffling my next words: "Are you his executive assistant?

"That's quite a posh moniker for what I actually do, but yes, I help him out by answering calls and handling various administrative tasks."

When Mac releases me, I glance around. Several

doors lead off the hallway, but only one concerns me. I can hear numerous voices behind the door to my left, and the sound makes my anxiety spike. In an effort to delay the inevitable meeting of the clan hiding behind it, I try to strike up a conversation. "If you don't mind me asking, how did you two meet? You seem like much more than just work colleagues."

Mac smiles at me kindly, as if sensing my apprehension. "My husband owns the apartment across from the one Josh bought in Hollywood. Before we married, he lived there full-time. Now he keeps it because it's a handy crash pad for work or whenever any of us visit the city. When Josh moved in, he knocked to introduce himself, and Tia insisted on drawing him a picture to take over. He was so sweet with her. He'll make a great dad one day. He has a lot to learn on the practical side, but we're doing our best to educate him. The first time he changed a diaper..."

"He changes diapers?" I can't hide the surprise in my voice, and Mac picks up on it, smiling.

"He tries," she giggles. "Let's just say he's come on leaps and bounds from his first attempt."

"He has?" I exclaim, still surprised.

"I have triplets, so it's all hands on deck during a poop fest. No one's safe—not even you," she jokes, her words making me feel warm and unexpectedly calm inside. After all, if Josh's stamp of approval is enough for her to trust me with changing one of her newborn's nappies, then by the same token surely I can feel safe in her hands, knowing she won't spring any unwelcome surprises my way. "Anyhow, shortly after Josh moved in, Jared and I ran into a problem that he helped us solve. Things kind of grew from there."

"You have triplets?" I say, stunned again. "But you look fantastic."

"That's so sweet of you to say," Mac looks genuinely touched. "I must admit it's all down to a mix of good genes and your man Josh."

"Josh?"

"You can imagine what having three babies inside your belly does to your body. Not that I minded, I hasten to add. I just wanted to try and get back in shape as quickly as possible after the birth. I asked Josh if he'd be kind enough to put together a training plan for me that I could work around the triplets. I get distracted easily, and when I'm in the gym, Jared usually has to watch the children—unless his sister is visiting—so he can't always be there to keep me on track. Then, during a work call one day, we got chatting, and Josh somehow became my unofficial personal trainer. Before I knew it, he was training with me four times a week. When he's not able to join me in person, we train via video call. He's even recruited Tia as his trainee fitness instructor to help me stick to my routine when he's not around," she laughs. "She has a notebook, and the pair of them are always huddled in a corner giving me very serious looks whenever he visits. I've still got a way to go before I hit my goal, but he's always phoning with words of encouragement to help me stay motivated."

"Wow!"

"Why do you sound so surprised?"

"I don't know. I guess I shouldn't be. He was always kind and thoughtful towards me when we were young, always looking out for me. But with other people, at times he can be a bit…"

"Big and scary?" Mac laughs, and I nod with a smile. "He's definitely a force to be reckoned with if you end up on his bad side, that's for sure."

"I hadn't seen him in so long. I suppose I was just afraid that his job and everything he's been through over the last thirteen years might have hardened him a little too much. But I'm glad to see it hasn't. The old Josh is still there, even if he keeps him tucked away most of the time."

"Would you still have said yes to marrying him if you thought the Josh you once knew had disappeared completely?"

"Our marriage… it's complicated."

"Honey, the way he looks at you and the way you look at him—it doesn't seem all that complicated to me." Mac gives me a knowing smile, as if she can sense the way my heart swells when I think about him. "Josh is strong-willed, fierce, and doesn't suffer fools gladly, but when it comes to Tia… they've forged a bond where there's nothing he wouldn't do for her. Most people do whatever she says—not because she's the scariest five-year-old on the planet, but because when they look over her shoulder, Josh is there daring them to defy her. And the only other woman who has that effect on him is you! I know you're going to say, 'How do you know when we've only just met?' But Josh and I, we've talked —a lot. I think he feels he can open up to me more than he can the guys. And believe me when I say, the man's absolutely gaga for you. He'll never admit it outright, but whether you want it or not, you've got that big, lovable oaf wrapped around your little finger." Mac smiles at what I assume is yet another one of my astonished expressions. "Now, are you ready to meet everyone? The whole gang is so excited to meet the woman who's melted our Mr. Stone."

"I'm not sure," I answer honestly, hoping she's not offended. "I'm not good with large crowds—or people I don't know, for that matter."

Just then, the patter of tiny footsteps draws our attention to Tia as she appears, gingerly carrying Derek's pet carrier—a welcome distraction.

"Here, let me help you," I say, scrambling to take the large box from her tiny hands. She looks up at me shyly.

"I think your kitten would like to get out and play with me," she whispers timidly.

I glance at Mac, who gives a subtle nod with a smile. "I think he would really like that."

"Take him in with the others, but keep an eye on him. Get Uncle Jack to help you," Mac tells her daughter softly.

"I will in a minute. King Josh says I should get

Maeve's dog a drink and something to eat. Who's Maeve?" The little girl looks up at her mom.

I kneel down so I'm at eye level and introduce myself. "Hi, I'm Maeve, and this is my dog. He's had a long journey, so I really should feed him and take him for a run."

"Did he come with you?"

"Yes, we all took a plane together—me, Tiny, Derek, and King Josh."

"Who's Tiny and Derek?"

"Tiny is my dog..."

"But he's huge!" The little girl widens her eyes at me as Tiny, seemingly aware he's been introduced, licks her cheek, causing her to burst out giggling. "I like your dog."

"Thank you," I grin. "Derek is the cat, but he isn't mine—I'm just looking after him for a friend."

Mac snorts in amusement. "That's a funny name for a kitten."

"I think it's a lovely name mommy," Tia looks at her frowning.

"You would. And no, I don't think your dad would like it if we got a cat." Mac pre-empts the question, clearly forming on Tia's newly pouting lips, before apologizing when Derek mewls indignantly from his carrier. "Sorry, Kitty."

Tia looks at me thoughtfully. "If you had a long journey, you must be tired, so I'll help you." She grabs my hand and drags me away from the closed door I had been so afraid of, the one with all the bustling activity behind it.

275

Relieved, I follow willingly with Mac accompanying us. We enter a large, open-plan kitchen and family room with the largest sectional sofa I've ever seen. The room is littered with baby paraphernalia and toys.

Mac groans. "I made everyone shift into the front room so we'd make a good first impression—trust Tia to derail my plans. I'm sorry. We've got six children here under the age of two at the moment. They kind of take over the place."

"King Josh says if people don't like you for who you are, stuff them." Tia doesn't even glance up as she scoops dog food into a large bowl, pushing it under Tiny's nose with practiced ease. She then hands her mom another bowl for water, which Mac dutifully fills before setting it down beside Tiny's food.

I cough out a laugh as I scan the room. Two giant glass sliding doors showcase the huge garden beyond. A large dog, tall and muscular, rushes to the closed doors as soon as he spots us. His sheer size and the intensity in his gaze make him appear fierce, almost intimidating, as he stares through the window with an expressionless face. He doesn't bark, nor does he growl—he simply watches us, his commanding presence impossible to ignore. Yet the steady, wagging rhythm of his tail leaves me reassured that he's friendly and not about to cause any harm.

"That's Mr. Josh," Tia informs me.

"I can see why you named him after your king,"

I chuckle, taking in the dogs large and imposing stature.

"Right?" Mac giggles. "Although, like his namesake, he's a big softy too. Once Tiny's eaten, I'm sure Mr. Josh can keep him entertained while giving him plenty of exercise in the garden. He's still just a youngster, and while Tia does her best, she only has two legs to his four. It'll be good for him to have someone who matches his speed and energy to play with. And it'll give Tia the chance to take care of Derek and give you a break. Does he need feeding too?"

"He's been fed, but he may need to use the bathroom. I know he'd appreciate being let out for a play afterward. I have a tray I can set up for him if you could just show me where would be best."

"I think he would like it in my bedroom," Tia pipes up.

"I don't think he'd like to poop in there," Mac says gently. "If his poop smells anything like Charlotte's, it'll linger, and you'll never sleep tonight. How about we set it up in the utility room for now? If it's okay with Maeve, you can still show him your room later."

Tia nods, and we all trundle off to the largest utility room I've ever seen. In fact, I'm pretty sure this room alone is larger than my entire cabin back home. Once Derek is settled with his tray and water, Tia watches over him while Mac and I head back to the kitchen.

"Wine?" Mac grabs a bottle from a chiller and waves it in my direction.

"Please." She pours me a large glass, and I accept it gratefully, relishing the cool, crisp flavour. "Are you not having one?"

"Well, other than the fact it's a little early for me…" I flush when I realise it's barely seven in the morning, with the time difference and the fact I've been awake almost twenty-four hours it feels much later. "I can't. I'm still breastfeeding on and off. With three, it's hard, but I do my best to give the little ones what I can. You, on the other hand, looked like you needed a drink."

"I did?" I answer, mortified that my nervousness might have come across as rudeness. "I'm sorry, really, it's not you," I garble in panic.

"Hush now." Mac comes to stand beside me. "Did Josh ever mention me, or the fact that I was married to someone else before I met Jared?"

I shake my head.

"Well, I was. I gave him everything, and in return, I was left with nothing. He… well, let's just say he turned out not to be a very nice man. But I'll never regret marrying him, because without him, I never would have met the love of my life and built the amazing life I have now."

I frown. "Why are you telling me all this?"

"Because I see the woman I used to be in you right now. Something happened to you, didn't it? In your past. Something that's been weighing you down, making you anxious in certain situations."

I nod, my movements robotic and unthinking as I swipe away the lone tear trailing down my cheek.

"Does Josh know?"

I shake my head. "Some, not all. I was in a fire years ago. He was there at the end, but not for the events that preceded it."

"I just want you to know you're safe here— probably the safest you'll ever be in your entire life. Do you think Josh would have left you alone if he thought anything might happen to you?"

I shake my head again, too choked up to speak. This woman's perceptiveness is remarkable.

"No. Because we're not strangers to him; we're more like family. And family looks out for, supports, and protects each other unconditionally. Being part of Josh's life means you're automatically part of that family, and I just hope you'll give us all the chance to prove that to you."

There's something so sincere in the way she speaks that I can't help believing her. I smile at her just as three more women burst through the door, one of them waving an empty mug in the air.

"Oops, sorry, we didn't realise you were in here." The one with the mug speaks first, and it's obvious she's tipsy.

"Sure you didn't," Mac mutters under her breath, giggling as she shoots me a sly glance. "Maeve, meet my sister-in-law, Jaime. She's no longer breastfeeding, so last night she decided she needed to make up for lost time by trying to drink enough for the rest of us. The effects haven't quite worn off yet, and we've been plying her with coffee ever since she rolled out of bed this morning."

"Oh, thank goodness," Jaime exclaims, placing a hand over her heart when she spots the wine in my hand. "A kindred spirit—finally, someone who understands my plight! Now, tell me, are you a red, white, or 'whatever's closest' kind of girl?"

"Um… whatever's closest?" I answer with raised eyebrows.

"That's the right answer," she says with enthusiasm, swooping me up into a warm, slightly tipsy hug that catches me off guard but leaves me smiling. "Now, tell us what we're all dying to know — is Josh's dick really as big as his ego?"

"Jaime!" One of the women exclaims, gently nudging her aside before pulling me into another friendly hug. "You'll have to excuse her. She doesn't often drink, but when her husband started vying with mine for the 'World's Greatest Dad' title, she decided to take full advantage." Grinning, she adds, "Honestly, I'd have done the same if Zach would hit the bottle as fast as that one," jerking a thumb in Jaime's direction. "But he's like his dad and definitely a boob guy. I'm Jen, Mitch's wife."

"And I'm Ava, Mac's other sister-in-law—Jared's sister." The last of the three wraps her arms around me, giving me a comforting squeeze. "What a beautiful dog." All three pause to make a fuss of Tiny.

"Nice to meet you all," I say, genuinely meaning it. The women exude nothing but kindness and authenticity, making me feel totally at ease.

"So, back to Josh?" Jaime smiles mischievously,

jerking her eyebrows a couple of times for added effect.

"I'd say it's bigger," I confirm, joining in the playful banter just as Josh appears.

"There you are," he sighs with relief, his gaze shifting to the glass in my hand, then to his watch. He frowns, takes the glass from me, and tips its contents down the sink, much to my horror and everyone else's amusement. Then, with an interested tone, he adds, "What's bigger?"

"Your penis," I reply honestly but sharply, much to the wide-eyed glee of everyone else in the room.

"Fuck's sake!" He drags his hand down his face as all the women burst out laughing before he can make his hasty exit. "I'll be in the other room having a more grown-up conversation—with the kids."

As he disappears, Tia comes running out of the utility room with Derek in her arms. "Mommy, Derek's pooped, so I'm taking him to show Tyler and Jacob now," she announces, darting past. Fixing her gaze on Josh as she chases after him, she calls out, "King Josh, you owe me seventy bucks!"

"Tyler and Jacob? Seventy bucks?" I glance around at my new friends, who are doubled over with laughter again, obviously sharing some kind of inside joke. Their infectious amusement makes me eager to be let in on the fun.

"Tyler and Jacob are my twin boys," Ava explains. "They're ten, identical, and have a knack for pretending to be each other around newcomers. I've written their initials on the backs of their hands with Sharpie so you don't fall victim to their antics this morning." She grins before adding, "And as for the fines—Tia charges anyone who swears. When it started, it was just aimed at me, Grant, and Jared, and it was thirty bucks total—ten for each of the kids. But since then, the family has grown," she gestures around the room, reinforcing what Mac told me earlier, "and so has the price."

"Remind me not to swear," I say, as Mac replaces my lost drink with a coffee and hands one to Jaime as well. I nod in thanks as she offers me some cream.

"Don't worry, we've got you covered," Jaime giggles. "Watch this." She calls Tia, and as she comes running, Jaime points at me and says, "Maeve said a bad word. She didn't mean to, but it just slipped out."

Tia rounds on me, one hand on her hip and the other outstretched, waiting. "That's seventy bucks."

"She forgot her purse—like I do all the time," Jaime adds with a sly glance at me. "King Josh will pay you."

"Okay!" Tia accepts the explanation without question and bolts off, calling Josh's name. I burst out laughing, genuinely feeling at home and part of the gang.

"Are you ready to meet the guys?" Mac asks.

"Of course, she is," Jaime says, entwining her arm with mine and steering me across the room. We all leave en masse and head toward the room I had avoided earlier.

As I step through the doorway, Ava's twins immediately catch my eye, they're busy keeping three youngsters entertained in the corner of the room while Tia excitedly shows them Derek. They look up as I enter, smiling and waving in unison. "Hi, Maeve," they say.

As they return to playing with the babies, my gaze locks onto Josh's. He looks uncomfortable, and the sight instantly puts me on edge. Josh is never anything but in full control of every situation. My eyes shift to the figure standing on his left.

"Holy..." I exclaim loudly, hurriedly correcting myself as Tia stands to attention, her fingers flexing, ready to pounce. "...Moly! You're Jared Jones!"

"I am. Pleased to meet you, Maeve," he says, strolling over and kissing me on the cheek. I instinctively raise my hand to cover the spot, silently vowing never to wash my face again. "This is Grant, Ava's husband," he continues, gesturing toward a man who nods from the couch. He has a baby reclining in his lap and two more in his arms.

"Sorry, I can't get up right now," Grant says with an amicable grin.

"No problem," I whisper, still dazed from meeting my second-favourite actor.

"This is..." I don't let Jared finish as my eyes land on the towering figure walking toward me.

"Jackson Longe," I croak, as he kisses my other cheek. My jaw drops open as I mimic my earlier reaction, raising my free hand to cover the freshly kissed spot.

"What are we doing? Impressions of that kid from Home Alone?" Mitchel Dalton, my favourite actor in the whole world, bounces into the room and taps me on the nose as my jaw drops even further and the room begins to spin.

"Happens every time. You've either got it or you haven't," Mitchel's casual observation is the last thing I hear as my knees buckle. I feel a pair of strong arms wrap around me, catching me, just before everything fades to black.

Chapter 16

Josh

"**W**hat are you jabbering on about?" I snarl at Mitchel, lunging across the room to catch Maeve as she falls. Unfortunately, Mitchel, being closer, beats me to it, sweeping her up into his arms like the hero from one of his action flicks.

"I exude sex appeal. I can't help it. One whiff of my pheromones can make even my harshest critics swoon in my presence," he declares.

"She smelt something, alright," Jackson smirks. "Not sure it was pheromones, though."

Mitchel avoids a fine from Tia by flipping Jackson off behind her back.

"It had nothing to do with you, you idiot," I say, shaking my head and rolling my eyes. "She's tired, that's all. She hasn't slept for nearly twenty-four hours, and someone…" I shoot a pointed look at Mac, "…gave her wine before she's even had breakfast."

"She had one sip," Mac laughs. "Before you got all protective and whipped it out of her hand."

"Tired?" Mitchel teases. "What was she doing on the seven-hour flight here—burpees? Or…" he waggles his eyebrows for effect, "were you two initiating yourselves into the mile-high club after pulling strings with Grant to get that upgrade?"

I glance to make sure Tia is still distracted with the kitten before giving him the middle finger salute. "It's the heat—she's not used to it."

Ava's husband is a pilot, and while I don't usually ask for favours, I knew Maeve wouldn't have been okay with Tiny and Derek being transported in the hold. Besides, since I sprung our departure on her, I wanted her journey to be as pleasant as possible. I shoot Grant a dirty look for letting Mitchel believe there was more to it, but he simply smiles, feigning obliviousness as he focuses on the babies in his care.

"Nor are you, if the look on your face is anything to go by," Jackson sniggers.

"Where shall I put her?" Mitchel asks Mac, jerking his head toward the woman passed out in his arms.

"Guest bedroom, please," Mac replies with a smile.

"I'll take her—you'll drop her," I say, stepping closer to take Maeve from Mitchel. But before I can get near, he turns and marches off.

"Relax, big guy," he chuckles. "I haven't dropped my wife once."

"It's true," Jen laughs, trying to reassure me further.

"You can bring the bags," Mitchel calls behind him.

"Why? We're not staying," I say, perplexed. "We're going to check in somewhere."

"You most certainly are not!" Mac says sternly. "You're staying here with us. For one, we all want to get to know Maeve better, and if the girls and I are going to help her plan your wedding, it makes sense for us all to be together. For another, if you get one of those calls that send you scurrying off to deal with some business emergency, I won't have Maeve left in an unknown place, alone."

"I would never just abandon her," I say, affronted, before growling, "And you don't have the room— not since a gaggle of uninvited guests descended on you." Though I secretly concede, after my recent phone call with Kurt, that if I had to leave in a hurry, I would feel more at ease knowing Maeve was surrounded by our friends. After all, Mitchel is trained in multiple martial arts, and Jackson can be nearly as intimidating as me when it comes to protecting his own.

Mitchel chuckles.

"We've made room," Mac says firmly.

"It's true," Mitchel adds. "She reserved the main guest room for you last night—no one was allowed over the threshold."

Mac pushes the door open, revealing a cheerful, sunny room that rivals the most elaborate hotel suites. The bed is immaculately made, guest towels are neatly laid out, and on the side table sits a handmade card welcoming Maeve. The colourful drawing and childlike handwriting are unmistakably from my queen, but it doesn't stop me from teasing as Mitchel gently lays Maeve on the bed.

"I see you left us a card," I say with a smirk.

Without missing a beat, Mitchel grins, "Well, I figured you'd need something colourful to hold your attention for more than five seconds."

"Seriously, Mac, it's not that I'm ungrateful, but where have you put everyone?"

"Jared, the babies, and I are staying at Ava's. Jackson and Jaime are in our room. You and Maeve are here. Mitchel and Jen are in the second guest room. Harper and Zach are in the triplets' room, and Tia's here because she claimed she wanted to sleep in her own room—but I suspect she really wanted to make sure she was here when you finally arrived."

"Rubbish!" Mitchel scoffs. "That kid adores me. Once I showed up, there was no way she was leaving."

"Forget it. I'm not chasing you and Jared out of your own house." I give Mac an affectionate squeeze to show her I appreciate what she's trying to do.

"You're not," Mac assures me. "We spend half our time over at Ava's anyway. It's really no big deal. When the babies are older and need their own space, it might be different. Although Jared's been thinking about building a guest house at the bottom of the garden to accommodate everyone in the future."

"That was my idea," Mitchel announces proudly.

"Jack's solution was to buy a couple of bigger houses near him and move us all to Santa Monica," Mac giggles. "But we like it here. The kids are settled in school, and they have friends of their own."

"They'd make new ones," Mitchel counters, making Mac smile.

"It's not practical right now. Besides, you can have too much of a good thing. I love visiting you guys down by the beach—it makes it more special somehow."

"If you're sure," I say, drawing Mac's attention back to me.

"I am. Plus, I don't see Tia giving that kitten up without a fight, do you? Thank heavens Maeve told her she was only minding it, or I think Jared would already be shaking his head in defeat, resigned to the fact that we were about to adopt a new member into the family."

I glance toward Maeve, who's still out like a light. "Could you watch her for five minutes while I make a quick call? I won't be long, then I must admit, I could do with getting my head down for a bit."

"Of course," Mac replies. "Make sure you grab something to eat before you come back."

"I could watch her for you," Mitchel says with a mischievous grin.

"Not a chance," I say, cuffing him lightly on the back of his neck and pushing him out of the room ahead of me.

"You do remember I'm married, right?" He sniggers, letting me push him away from my woman.

"Yes, and I'm sure I just heard your wife calling you," I reply smoothly. I know I'm being irrational. There's no way Mitchel would cheat on the wife he so obviously adores. On top of that, I know he despises adulterers. Still, I can't help but feel this primal need to stake my claim by escorting him away from Maeve.

Once I've delivered Mitchel safely back to the others, I ignore all the smirking faces and excuse myself. I escape to the garden finding sanctuary to call Axel. Tiny trails me out, only to be eagerly pounced on by an exuberant Mr. Josh, who clearly wants to play. Satisfied they'll get along, I pull out my phone and dial Axel's number. As usual, the call has barely connected before he answers.

"Boss."

"Everything okay back at base?"

"All under control, but I get the sense that's not why you're calling." Axel chuckles.

"I'm back in Cali, but I'll be staying with Mac in Morro Bay for a few days. Keep liaising with her as normal, and I'll get her to fill me in on anything routine."

"Uh-huh."

"I spoke to Kurt a while ago. He and Blake have hooked up with Foxy, but the job's more complicated than they first thought. Foxy's going to have to stick around in Maine until they sort it out. Tony Castillo's security system is state-of-the-art—even Foxy had trouble hacking it. He managed to access the camera feeds to give us visuals, but we'll need to go in to get audio. Tony's got a couple of armed guards at the gate, and from what we can tell, at least two more patrolling the grounds with an unknown number inside."

"Makes you wonder what he's so desperate to

protect, doesn't it?" Axel growls.

"It does," I agree, my tone solemn.

"Do they need back-up?"

"Not right now. Kurt says they've got it under control. They're monitoring the video locally for now, since you're short-handed, and reporting directly to me. That said, we need more intel—what's being said behind closed doors—so as soon as they get the chance, they'll go in to set it up and look for any evidence Billy or Jimmy were ever there. They've snagged stills of some people coming and going. Foxy's doing background checks on them, but if they need more, they'll send you and Drew the data to dig deeper and work your magic. This has to take priority over everything else for now."

"Got it."

"When Kurt and Foxy go in, Blake will stay on the ground, monitoring the situation from the outside. He's under strict instructions to notify you the moment Kurt and Foxy make their move and to check in with you every ten minutes until the mission's complete."

"No problem. But why me? I thought you wanted to handle it yourself."

"I did. But right now it has to be you. I've got too many distractions around me to monitor the job effectively. Should anything go wrong, you're the one I trust to make the right call when it counts. Just send me a message before they go in and another once the job's done and they're in the clear."

"Understood."

"I should be back in town in a couple of days. I'll see you then."

"Boss."

As I disconnect the call, my stomach growls loudly. I head to the kitchen, which is a hive of activity. Grant, Ava, and Jared buzz around, trying to get the oldest three children ready for school.

"Who's doing the school run today?" Jared asks Grant while stuffing a couple of books into a pink knapsack.

"I want King Josh to take me," Tia exclaims, jumping up and down excitedly as I walk into the fray.

Jared crouches down, tapping his daughter affectionately on the nose. "King Josh had a long journey and is really tired, peanut."

Tia pouts, and I can't stand to see her upset. "How about he picks you up later instead?"

"Can we make waffles?" Tia asks slyly.

"Sure." I'm rewarded with a beaming smile as Ava hands Tia and the twins their lunches before they scurry out to the car.

"I got this," Grant says, swiping the keys before Jared can reach them, following the kids out.

"Here, I made sandwiches for you and Maeve while I was preparing the lunches," Ava says, sliding a plate laden with food toward me. I navigate around the kitchen island and kiss her cheek.

"Thanks," I reply, accepting them gratefully. I pour a couple of coffees and two glasses of orange juice, adding the food and drinks to a tray alongside some fruit. "Where's Derek?" I ask, glancing around, mildly worried Tia might have snuck him into her backpack to show her friends at school.

"Don't fret. She left him in Jackson's care for the day—much to his chagrin and Mitchel's amusement," Jared says with a knowing smile, reading my mind. "Go get your head down for a couple of hours, and tell Maeve not to worry. We'll take care of her animals."

I jerk my head in gratitude before heading out the door with my tray of goodies. When I return to the guest room, Maeve's awake, chatting amiably with Mac. I set the tray down on the dresser and march over to where they're both perched on the edge of the bed. "You're awake?" I state the obvious to Maeve before whipping my gaze to Mac, peppering them both with questions. "Why didn't you call me? What happened? Were you ill? Is she okay?" I try to press my hand against Maeve's forehead to check her temperature, but she bats it away with a frown.

"Will you stop, you lunatic? Of course I'm okay." Her cheeks flush slightly, clearly betraying her embarrassment at being caught off guard by her body's recent betrayal.

"I'll leave you two to it," Mac says, giggling as she excuses herself. "Have something to eat, take a nice hot shower, and grab some rest. We'll see you downstairs when you're ready." She closes the door behind her, leaving us alone.

Maeve spots the bags I left in the corner of the room. "Should we go check in to a hotel?"

"No need." I grab the tray of food, pleased when Maeve starts eating without prompting. "Mac is putting us up here."

"You're joking?" She stops mid-chew, looking at me in horror.

"What's wrong?"

"She's married to Jared Jones, that's what's wrong. And she currently has Jackson Longe and Mitchel Dalton in her sitting room!"

"So?"

"I can't stay here with them."

"Why?"

"They're... they're... and I looked so... then I fainted..." She rambles, catching me off guard as she starts pummelling my chest. "Why didn't you warn me?"

I catch her wrists. "Warn you that they're normal human beings who put their pants on one leg at a time, like the rest of us?"

She growls. Actually growls. It's so cute, I have to roll my lips to keep from laughing. "Eat your sandwich," I say, trying to contain my amusement. "Then we'll grab some shut-eye. You'll feel better after some sleep." She nods reluctantly, and I let go of her wrists.

"Where are you sleeping?" She asks, her brow furrowing.

"In here with you." I grab a sandwich and take a bite.

"I don't think so," she says firmly.

"Have to," I say with a grin. "There's no more

room at the inn. Besides everyone knows we're getting hitched so assumed we'd be fine bunking together."

Maeve nods to the en-suite bathroom, "Are we sharing that too?"

"Yup."

She gulps audibly. "Fine, I'm too tired to argue."

"Argue about what? We were sharing the bathroom back at your place, and we've even slept in the same bed before."

We finish our food, and I strip down to my underwear before sliding beneath the sheets on the bed. I lay back with my chest exposed, one hand behind my head. A sigh escapes me as I close my eyes and sink into the bed's comforting embrace—it feels like heaven. That is, apart from the incessant pacing at the foot of the bed, which disrupts my tranquillity.

"What's wrong? Worried you won't be able to keep your hands off me?" The pacing stops suddenly, prompting me to crack one eye open. Maeve doesn't answer, but her horrified expression makes it clear I've struck a nerve. I try not to smirk as I reach across, flipping back the sheet next to me. "Will you just get in the damn bed!" She hesitates then starts to climb in beside me fully clothed. I push myself up onto one elbow, eyeing her incredulously. "Really? Aren't you going to make yourself a little more comfortable?"

She pauses, sat on the edge of the bed. "I'm shy."

I feel my eyebrows shoot up towards my hairline.

"Shy?" I laugh out loud. "Since when? This morning you were straddling me in your underwear and riding me like a cowgirl at a rodeo."

"That was different," she snaps. I can almost feel the heat radiating from her glowing face.

"How so?" I ask, flopping back onto the bed to resume my earlier position. When she doesn't answer, I fill in the silence for her. "Oh, I see. This morning you wanted to get some and I was the only guy available," I tease.

"Yes," she answers quickly, then follow that with, "No," just as fast. "Just keep your eyes closed."

I hold three fingers up to my temple in acknowledgement. After a few seconds I feel the mattress shift as Maeve stands, there's some shuffling and eventually she slips into the bed beside me. I open one eye to see she has turned her back towards me, I know she is still wearing her bra as the straps are visible on the shoulders peeking above the top of the sheets. I smile and wait until she starts to relax before rolling over and in one swift move, wrapping my arm around her and dragging her flush against my body so we are spooning. She gasps in surprise, tensing for a few seconds before finally relaxing against me.

"Now sleep," I order.

"Yes oh lord and master!" She snaps, her tone a mix of astonishment and indignation.

"I'm glad you're learning your place in this relationship," I tease, nibbling her neck until she giggles and starts writhing against me. "It'll make my life so much easier when we're married." She stills abruptly, sucking in a breath when I cup her one of her breasts and whisper in her ear gruffly, "Later, we practice cuddling without the bra."

A few hours later I wake with Maeve still in my arms. It feels right, and I'm loathe to move. I don't remember falling asleep, or how long after me it took Maeve to succumb to her own exhaustion. I lay there for a few moments, taking in the warmth of her body pressed against mine and the faint smell of her shampoo as it lingers in the air around me. Eventually, I gently extricate myself from her embrace and pull on a pair of sweats, not wanting to shower before I've hit Jared's home gym. It's been a while since Mac and I worked out together, so I figure I'll go and ask her if she wants to join me. I don't bother with a shirt or shoes as I go in search of her. I find her in the garden with the others, clearly enjoying the sunshine as they laugh and joke amicably. A small marquee has been set up to protect the little ones from the sun, their tiny forms lined up inside, all sleeping peacefully for a change.

"Here he comes," Mitchel is the first to spot me. Taking in my near-naked appearance, he quips, "What happened to your shirt, mate? Did it finally give up on trying to cover up all that 'potential'?"

"Don't worry, when you finally find a gym, I'll

sponsor your first session. It'll stop your shirt from trying to hide your excuses," I banter back.

Jackson and Jared scoff good-naturedly as Mitchel, clearly unoffended, continues, "Where's the woman of the hour? Still reeling from my charm?"

"More like recovering from exposure to your aftershave," I shoot back with a grin. "She's still sleeping. The scent was obviously way more potent than any of us realised."

"I'm not wearing any," he fires back. "Told you, it's my pheromones!"

"Or an allergic reaction to delusion," Grant chimes in, and all the men laugh. It's only then I realise the women are all being suspiciously quiet. I glance around, noticing that, aside from Mac—who's used to seeing me like this when we train—the rest are openly gawping.

"Ladies," I schmooze, flashing a grin. Jen coughs awkwardly, and the others glance around, clearly amused at being caught checking out my abs. Jackson and Mitchel shoot their wives furious looks, while Grant winks at his, making Ava blush. Jackson is cradling Derek in his huge arms, the tiny kitten softening his imposing stance.

"You can put him down you know?" I tell him.

"He won't. I've tried," Jaime answers for her husband. "He's too afraid to face Tia's wrath if Derek hides and he can't find him." Her tone makes it clear this fear stems from a near-miss that's already happened.

"I came to see if you wanted to hit the gym with

me?" I ask Mac.

"Sure," she smiles getting up from her chair. "I'll just go change." She glances at Jared, "Will you be okay watching the children?"

"Course, go do your thing."

Mac leans down and gives him a lingering kiss before dashing off.

"You're letting your wife wander off with that... While he is only half dressed?" Mitchel asks Jared incredulously, just as his own wife announces, "I could do with some exercise, I might join you both."

Mitchel's jaw drops, closely followed by Jackson's, when Jaime chimes in, "Me too," and they both bolt before they can be stopped.

"I guess I may as well join them," Ava whispers before slipping away.

"Why aren't you upset?" Mitchel rounds on Grant, who's grinning. "You know they're all only going to ogle him," he says, waving vaguely in my direction, "while he works out."

"If he revs her engine ready for me to reap the reward, I'm all for it," Grant chuckles. "Besides he's already taken, you'd be blind not to see it."

His answer doesn't seem to appease Mitchel—or Jackson, as both men throw silent daggers in my direction.

"You've either got it, or you haven't," I throw Mitchel a wink before turning on my heel and following the giggling women back inside the house.

It's no surprise when Mitchel and Jackson join us

about ten minutes into the session. What begins as a straightforward workout quickly morphs into a playful display of macho bravado, much to the women's amusement. They pretend to exercise but are clearly more entertained by watching me effortlessly outdo Mitchel in both pull-ups and bench presses.

Jackson, however, proves to be a tougher opponent. His relentless determination pushes me to my limits, but I still manage to come out on top, maintaining an air of composure as though the victory required little effort. Jackson takes the loss in stride, his handshake carrying a subtle hint of admiration.

Mitchel, on the other hand, launches into a barrage of excuses, drawing laughter from everyone before his wife drags him off to tend to his supposedly pulled muscles. As they leave, Mitchel throws us a sly wink, making it clear he's successfully duped his wife into some impromptu 'adult time.' I can't help but feel a pang of envy as I watch them go—wishing that Maeve were here to laugh at my excuses, should I ever need to make any, before whisking me away too.

The rest of us wrap up our session and I grab two coffees before heading back to my room to shower and change. When I walk through the door its all I can do to keep myself in check when presented with the heavenly sight I find stood before me.

Chapter 17

Maeve

I'm going to kill him!

When I woke up alone in bed, I thought it wise to hop out and take a shower before my roommate returned. I can't deny I missed him when I woke—how is that even possible? I've survived thirteen years without him, yet now that he's back, even knowing he's somewhere in the house, the distance feels more unbearable than anything I experienced during all those years apart.

My face warms at the memory of him holding me, my body soon following suit, its nerve endings tingling as I recall the last words Josh whispered in my ear before falling asleep with his large frame enveloping mine in a warm, comforting hug. It was as if I were surrounded by my own personal, impenetrable forcefield. I've never felt so safe and coveted in my entire life.

Which is why he can't see me like this. I look like a hot mess— hair sticking out in all directions and the remnants of the single, swipe of mascara I'd applied hours ago somehow smudged across my face. I saw the way other women looked at him when we were traveling here, and if I don't want to lose him to the competition, I need to show him I'm a prize worth winning. I may not be ready for him to see me naked, but I can blow out my hair and dress to impress rather than distress.

And let's not forget the rest of the house. After arriving looking like I'd been dragged through a hedge backward, then fainting in front of half of Hollywood's elite, I need to up my game if I don't want them to think I'm a complete disaster.

That's why I leapt out of bed and into the adjoining shower posthaste. The room was completely dry, and the towels Mac lent us yesterday were still folded neatly on the counter where I'd left them. It makes me wonder where Josh has disappeared to—and why he had to leave in such a hurry if he didn't even have time to shower before he left. Not that I mind having the place to myself for a moment—it's easier to think when there's not a six-foot-five distraction roaming around.

I switch on the shower and scan the toiletries while I'm waiting for the water to heat up, I gather everything I need and wash quickly, wrapping myself in a towel before doing the same with my hair. It's surprising how much a good sleep followed by a warm, soothing shower can revitalise you. I peek around the door to make sure the room is still empty before stepping out in my skimpy towel. Throwing the case Josh packed for me onto the bed, I unzip it and fling the lid back.

What greets me is an impeccably packed mix of

complete impracticality. Growing up in Vermont, where the climate rarely demands anything lighter than a sturdy sweater, and working with unpredictable animals on a daily basis, my wardrobe has always been more about function than fashion. I know that left Josh with slim pickings when he packed this case for our California trip, but really?

Inside, I find an assortment of mismatched, thin, summery items that I assume Josh felt screamed 'warm weather', together with one lone pair of high heels that are about as practical for daily wear as snowshoes. When I look more closely, I see most of the items are either underwear or thin silky nighties. It's clear his main criteria were 'attractive' and 'lightweight', with no thought given to how any of it actually goes together—or how I'd survive a full day in those heels.

I sift through the contents with a mix of amusement and disbelief. I mean, I appreciate the effort, but did he not think I'd need at least one jumper or pair of trousers? And one pair of flats wouldn't have gone a miss? He was clearly so focused on the California weather, or my boobs judging by the number of bras he's included, that he forgot humans still require functional clothes.

I'm going to kill him! I pull out a nightie and try to convince myself it'll pair well with the trusty sneakers I wore here, but being honest, there's no way I can make any of it work. I'll have no choice but to hide in our room until either a miracle turns this mess into a wardrobe, or everyone is so distracted helping me dispose of Josh's body they won't notice I'm dressed like I'm auditioning for the cast of Moulin Rouge.

The door suddenly swings open, catching me off guard. I turn, one of the more revealing bras dangling from my forefinger, and freeze as Josh steps in. My mouth opens, ready to challenge him on the questionable items he packed, but the words die on my lips as I take him in.

He looks like he's been working out—his hair sexily mussed, beads of sweat rolling down his toned torso before disappearing beneath the low-slung waistband of his sweatpants. He's holding two mugs of coffee, but he stops in his tracks when he sees me.

Forgetting all about my own lack of clothes, I assume it's the underwear I'm inadvertently waving in his direction that's thrown him off. Heat rushes to my cheeks as I fumble to hide the bra behind my back and close my mouth before I start resembling a goldfish.

Josh recovers first, stalking forward to kiss me on the cheek while handing me one of the mugs, "Morning gorgeous, I'm just going to jump in the shower then we'll strip," he purrs.

Holy Shit. He's not messing this morning! I look up into his eyes and see the lustful gaze bearing down past my face and onto the swell of my breasts peeking from the top of my tightly wrapped towel. "Strip?" I ask nervously.

"The bed," he answers mischievously, totally

unaware of my undulating emotions. "Be nice to have a fresh set of bedding for when we've both cleaned up, don't you think?"

"Oh right," I answer, hoping to hide the disappointment in my voice. Clearly, my brain needs a cold shower more than he does.

"Just so you know, if *you* wanted to strip for me, I'd be open to it," he whispers. His words are like a warm caress that has me pressing my thighs together, trying to suppress the arousal coursing through my body as he walks away, disappearing into the bathroom and tapping the door closed with his foot.

The sound of the shower starting snaps me back to life and I suddenly remember what I was so desperate to talk to him about. I figure he'll let the water warm as I did before stepping under, so I burst through the door before he has time to undress. "Um Josh…" I start with renewed determination.

"Yeah?"

I'm thrown off kilter again when his voice sails over the sound of the spray and through the lighted frosted glass that does little to obscure the naked form behind it. He has his hands outstretched, resting on the tiled wall in front of him while his head is bent forward to allow the water to cascade over the nape of his neck. I blink, once again forgetting why I barged in here in the first place, my brain seems to have short-circuited. Apparently, coherent thought isn't compatible with this view.

He turns his head slowly in my direction,

"Maeve?"

I'm almost in a trance-like state as my body moves toward the screen door, opening it to reveal the treasure behind. Josh stands tall, turning to face me. My eyes are automatically drawn to the semi he makes no attempt to conceal before snapping up to his face. I roll my bottom lip into my mouth and bite down hard, prompting a muttered expletive from Josh as his eyes bore into me.

"Are you dropping that towel and joining me? If you are, I'll turn up the heat. If you're not, you need to leave, because standing there looking like that is doing nothing to help my cause right now." He jerks his head to his waist and I follow his line of sight to see his appendage is now fully erect. In a reflex action I release my lip, wetting it with my tongue and inciting a groan from Josh. "Babe, you're killing me here."

I reach out, grazing my fingertips beneath the freezing spray. A shiver runs through me as I wonder how Josh can endure such an icy blast. Without saying a word, I lean in and adjust the thermostat, waiting until the water reaches a more bearable temperature. Then, I step into the cubicle and close the door behind me. Josh immediately reaches for my towel but I catch his hand to stop him.

I whisper, embarrassed, "I'm not ready for you to see all of me, I'm..." My voice is so low that I'm unsure if he hears me until he responds abruptly with, 'What?'"

"You're so..." I gesture to his firm, toned physique,

then to my own, which is noticeably softer. "And I'm so…"

Josh frowns, clearly displeased with my answer. "Babe, you're beautiful," he says, reaching for the second towel still wrapped around my head. He pauses and asks, "May I?" The towel has absorbed so much water that it's heavy and uncomfortable, so I nod. Josh frees me from its confines, tossing it aside, and I use both hands to push my hair back from my face. He catches a stray piece of hair, tenderly tucking it behind my ear, "What now?"

I place my hand over the fresh, round scar on his shoulder, tracing its rough edges with my index finger. "You got shot?" I ask, avoiding his gaze. His closeness is both comforting and strangely unnerving.

"Yeah," he says simply.

I slide my hand down letting it rest beside the fresher wound on his chest. I'm pleased to see it appears to be knitting together nicely. "Glassed?"

He grunts an affirmative.

I glide my hand down to his ribs, tracing a thin, elongated scar—much older than the first. "What happened here?"

"Stabbed," he replies quietly.

I turn to his opposite forearm, running my hand along its length from wrist to elbow. The skin, covered in tattoos, feels rough and marred in patches—far more than the work of an artist's needle would ever create. "Here?"

"I got burned," he whispers. He doesn't elaborate

or mention that he was the one who fought the flames that nearly claimed me.

Looking up into his eyes, I feel his hand taking mine. "You missed the most important one," he says, placing my hand over the unblemished skin covering his heart. Confused, I stare at him. "I've been in love with a girl for as long as I can remember," he murmurs, "but she never loved me back."

"Love?" The intensity of the word shocks me, yet fills me with joy at the same time.

"Uh huh," he replies, awkward and uncertain.

For the first time in all the years I've known him, this massive, fierce giant looks... vulnerable.

And suddenly, I see.

Everything sharpens, like the world has been blurry until this very second. I can't explain where this sudden clarity comes from, and I don't care. There's only one thing that matters—being honest with the person standing before me now.

"Josh," I begin, his face radiating optimism and hope. "I don't want to fake-marry you." I watch as his expression clouds over with sadness, and his eyes drop to the floor. Gently, I cup his cheek, tilting his face so his eyes meet mine again. "I want to marry you for real. I'm sorry I never realised it sooner, but it's you. It's always been you." In an instant, his face transforms, and he beams brighter than the sun. Unable to control himself he lunges forward, claiming my mouth is the most heated, passionate kiss I've ever experienced. With his body crushed against me and my libido about to combust, I reach between us desperate to start pleasing my man. I'm surprised when Josh stops me, capturing my hand in his before raising it above my head and pinning it against the tiles behind me.

"Not like this," he growls, his eyes aflame with heat and desire. "I want our first time to be special."

"What did you have in mind?" I pant, my body taking on a life of its own as it writhes against him seeking relief.

"Our wedding night."

"Our wedding night?" I giggle. "Are you worried I won't respect you in the morning? Or were the rumours about you in high school untrue?"

"What rumours?" He pulls back, baffled.

"The ones about you bedding half the girls in your year."

"That was Kurt," he blusters, his cheeks tinging pink.

"No, he bedded the other half," I chuckle.

He doesn't respond. Instead, he leans in, gently biting and sucking the sweet spot above my collarbone. The action drives me wild, and I reach for him again with my free hand.

"I want to wait," he says, capturing my second hand and pinning it with the first, repeating the same move as before. His voice is steady, but his eyes betray something deeper— a storm of excitement, restless desire, alive, just waiting to be unleashed. "I want to be able to take my time with you. No interruptions."

"How will we know if we're compatible?" I ask breathlessly.

"Oh, trust me, we'll be compatible," he says confidently, smirking mischievously.

"What if I don't want to wait?" I whisper, squirming impatiently as I try to free myself.

He kisses up my neck, across my cheek, and to my ear, caressing the shell with his lips before whispering, "You made me wait thirteen years, so now I'm going to make you wait for thirteen days."

"Thirteen days?" I croak.

"Seems to be our lucky number."

"But we told Derek we'd get married next week."

"I don't give a fuck about what we told Derek. That was different. This is about us now—and me giving my wife the wedding she deserves."

My heart swells and I relent, "Okay, you can let me go. We'll wait."

He gives me a cocky grin before transferring my two small hands into one of his much larger ones, still keeping me restrained. I look at him quizzically.

"You've seen the goods, I think it's only fair I get to see what I'm getting in this deal." Before I get the chance to protest, he tugs at the towel covering me and it falls to the ground, exposing my flaws to his scrutiny.

"Fuck! You're gorgeous," he exclaims, my face flaming as his eyes roam my naked body.

I watch as he takes his hardness in his hand, stroking himself, quickly increasing his grip and pace. I'm still incapacitated and can do little more than watch in awe as he jerks off right in front of me. After about a minute, his face scrunches up and his body goes taut before he explodes, shooting his release up my torso and over my breasts, marking more than just my body. As he comes down from his high, he trails his essence over my skin before it can be washed away. Covering every intimate area before finally running his finger across my lips.

"Open," he commands.

I do as I'm bid and he pushes his finger inside. I can taste the saltiness on his skin as I close my mouth around him, sucking him clean as he slowly withdraws.

"You're mine now," he growls. "And no-one else gets to touch what's mine."

"Are you mine?" I ask, needing to be sure.

He lifts my chin, leaning in, making sure he has my full attention, "Every single part of me," he whispers before kissing me again then releasing my hands. "Now let's get cleaned up, we've a wedding to arrange."

After a quick shower brimming with unfulfilled desire, restrained longing, and whispered promises of what's to come, Josh throws on a white T-shirt and black combat trousers before I send him off to find Mac. Wrapped in a dry towel, I wait. It's not long before she comes running, and Josh finds the two of us staring incredulously into the suitcase he packed.

"You did this, didn't you?" She asks, pointing into the suitcase while trying not to laugh.

"What's wrong with it?" He retorts defensively, looking more than a little disgruntled.

Mac flaps her arms in exasperation. "Men! Where are the clothes? What's this poor woman supposed to wear?"

I stifle a giggle at the puzzled look on his face.

He picks up a thong, and I snatch it out of his hand, much to his amusement. "You've got the underwear more than covered," I tell him. "What am I supposed to wear over it?"

He rifles through the suitcase and extracts a wide, black leather item, handing it to me. "How about this skirt?" He starts.

"Um…" Mac interrupts, causing him to pause and frown at her.

"It's a belt," I inform him.

He holds it up, baffled. "For who? A WBA heavyweight champion?" He tosses it aside and dives back into the suitcase. "Fine! How about this dress?"

"Um…" Mac begins, and Josh lets out a strangled expletive.

"What now?" He growls.

"That's a nightie," I enlighten him.

"Honey, why don't you go and find the others?" Mac speaks to him like she would her five-year-old. "Maeve, follow me. Let's go to my room and see what we can find."

I glance at her tall, slim frame. "Don't take this the wrong way, but I'm a little shorter and a tad more… curvaceous than you. I'm really not sure you'll have anything that will fit me," I sigh.

"If I haven't, one of the other girls will. But you'd be surprised," she says kindly. "I stayed out of maternity wear for as long as I could when I was pregnant, so I have a whole closet stashed with all sorts of bits and bobs in varying sizes. We'll have a rummage and see what we can find to tide you over until we can go shopping."

Forty minutes later, I look better than I ever have. Mac blow-dries my hair, styling it into soft curls before applying some natural-looking makeup to my face. We find a beautiful summer dress with spaghetti straps and a loose, flowing skirt that I manage to squeeze into without feeling uncomfortable. The only item missing is a more practical pair of shoes.

"What size are you?" Mac asks, tapping her chin thoughtfully.

"Seven. It's fine—I can wear the trainers I arrived in."

"And ruin the look? I don't think so. You're the same size as Jaime; let's see what she brought with her."

"Won't she mind?" I ask nervously.

"Of course not. We're always borrowing each other's stuff."

I follow Mac reluctantly, and she finds a gorgeous pair of sandals that complete the look. Despite my lingering embarrassment about making a fool of myself when I arrived, I'm feeling pretty good as I step outside to join the others in the perfectly manicured garden.

As soon as Tiny spots me, he comes bounding over to greet me, with his new best friend, Mr. Josh, hot on his heels. I'm so busy fussing over him that I almost miss the way every head turns in my direction—and the appreciative looks from the men as they check me out.

Mitchel immediately stands and meanders over, dramatically pretending to faint at my feet. Laughter erupts around us as he opens one eye and squints up at me.

"Now we're even," he says, throwing me a cheeky wink.

"You better not be looking up her skirt," Josh growls from his seat a few feet away, sparking another round of laughter from the crowd.

I extend a hand to help Mitchel up. "I'm sorry about yesterday…" I start, but he stops me by pressing a finger to my lips.

With exaggerated theatrics, he kisses the back of my hand like an actor in an old-fashioned movie. "It's the pheromones—it couldn't be helped."

"Really? And here was me thinking I was simply overwhelmed by the size of your ego," I say with a smile.

"If you've got it, flaunt it," he quips, throwing his arm around my shoulder and leading me over to the chair he just vacated.

"Nice sandals," Jaime grins. "I've a pair just like them."

"Actually…" I start uncomfortably.

"We had a situation," Mac interrupts smoothly.

"Say no more," Jaime winks at me, pressing a finger to her lips to urge me to stay silent as Jackson looks the other way.

After twenty minutes of reintroductions and general chit-chat, the women migrate to the kitchen. It's my chance to ask Jaime about all the secrecy over the shoes. Jen is the one who answers.

"Her husband is a nutcase, that's what," Jen giggles. "They were having dinner out one evening when a woman strolled past wearing a pair exactly like them. Jaime excused herself to go to the restroom, and by the time she returned, Jackson had almost gotten himself arrested for trying to take a picture of the woman's foot! He sent the snap to Mitchel's personal assistant, demanding he track down a pair for Jaime. When Dale asked what colour, Jackson told him to get one of each. The next morning, Jaime woke up to a delivery of seven pairs of that sandal. She now has them in black, white, gold, rose gold, silver, blue, and khaki. I mean, who needs seven pairs of the same shoe?"

"Who even has room to store them?" I laugh.

"She does," Ava teases, thumbing in Jaime's direction. "Her closet is the size of this kitchen."

I look at Jaime, bemused.

"It's true," Jaime admits. "And if Jackson heard you'd borrowed them, he'd have a replacement pair ordered and would've paid over the odds to have them delivered tonight—just in case I wanted to wear them later."

"If you need them, just say the word," I say hurriedly.

"I won't," she says kindly. "Keep them as long as you need. Forever, if you like."

I smile gratefully, finally understanding why Josh is so fond of these people and relishing the warm feeling of being accepted into the fold.

"So..." Mac starts, "Let's all grab a drink and start prepping for this wedding, shall we?"

Mac pours two large glasses of wine and three mineral waters before we all settle on the large sectional couch. She sets her glass down and flips open a pad, ready to take notes.

"Have you set a date yet?" She asks.

"Sort of," I reply. "Josh wants to get married thirteen days from today. He says that's our lucky number."

Jaime sucks in a breath. "That doesn't give us a lot of time."

"It's not going to be a large affair..." I begin, but stop when everyone starts exchanging looks. "What?"

"Josh said you wanted swans," Ava tells me, and I burst out laughing.

"That was a joke," I say, and everyone visibly relaxes.

"Joke or not," Mac replies, "He said he wanted you to have your dream wedding, to spare no expense, and to charge everything to his card. So spill, lady—let's start with the dream and go from there."

"I don't feel comfortable maxing out his card. I know he plays it down, but he can't be making that much money just advising on and installing security systems. I have some money set aside, but even so, I want to stick within a reasonable budget." I stop and glance around as the room falls silent. "What now?"

"How much do you know about what Josh does for a living?" Mac asks carefully.

"Not much—just what I've told you. Why?"

"It's not my place to say, but I think you should talk to him before you get married," Mac replies. "Remember I work for him and I think he might be making a lot more money than you give him credit for."

I furrow my brow as Jaime steers the conversation in another direction. "What about the honeymoon? Can you get some time off and leave straight after the wedding? Where would you like to go?"

"I guess I can get the time off. I'll need to check in with Aiden—the vet who's covering for me. I haven't really thought about where I'd like to go, but it has to be somewhere special, considering it will be the first time we… you know."

Four jaws drop so fast in disbelief, I'm surprised the floor tiles don't crack under the pressure.

"You haven't had sex?" Jaime finally splutters.

"He wants to wait until after we're married," I reply coyly.

"Who wants to wait for what until after you're married?" Jackson asks casually, appearing out of nowhere as he strolls past on his way to grab more beers from the fridge. He pops the cap off a bottle and takes a deep draw.

"Josh," Jaime answers with a grin, "He wants to wait until after the wedding before they have sex."

Jackson freezes, lowering his bottle infinitely slowly. "Are you saying... he's a virgin?"

I roll my eyes. "Yes, he's a virgin," I reply, not expecting in a million years to be taken seriously.

Jackson gathers up an armful of beers and heads out of the room, moving like he's in some kind of trance.

"He isn't, not really... is he?" Jen chokes out, wide-eyed. "I mean, what a waste."

"Of course he isn't," I laugh, shaking my head. "You really think Josh would've survived this long without releasing some of that testosterone? Rumour has it he'd deflowered half the girls in our town before I'd even hit puberty."

Everyone rolls about laughing until Mac calls order and we get back to some serious wedding planning. Jaime keeps topping up our wine glasses and the more I drink the looser my lips become. Mac keeps scribbling notes as I start spouting my ideas for what my dream wedding should look like.

It's not long before Josh comes striding in, pinching the bridge of his nose and looking distraught.

"What the hell did you just tell Jackson?" Josh

looks around the room, exasperated. "Seriously, a virgin? Now everyone's trying to give me tips on what to do between the sheets!"

Mac bursts out laughing, almost dropping her notepad, while Jaime raises her glass in mock salute. "Well, at least you're learning from the best."

I stifle a giggle. "Relax, it was a joke! I never expected him to take me seriously." The look Josh gives me makes it clear he doesn't believe a single word. With my best faux angelic smile, I add, "Still, I firmly believe it's in my best interest to make sure your technique gets a thorough review—purely for the sake of perfecting it, of course."

Chapter 18

Josh

I t's five-thirty the following morning, and the house is still quiet except for its youngest residents, their mom, dad, and me. We're gathered on the sectional couch off the kitchen. Jared and I are bottle-feeding the two baby girls, while their brother, already satisfied, is being gently burped over his mom's shoulder.

"I've sent your schedule to your phone," Mac tells me as I coo at Lexi, who's calmly drinking her milk. She is hands-down my favourite of the three —placid, quiet, nothing like her demanding siblings. Cradled in my huge arms, she looks so tiny, like she's made of porcelain. If you'd told me a year ago I'd be here, in this exact moment, I probably would've looked you dead in the eye, laughed maniacally, and staged an intervention—certain you were tripping on something illegal.

"I've got a schedule?" I ask absentmindedly.

"Josh, as much as I appreciate your help this morning, I really need you to focus on what I'm saying right now," Mac says, slipping into her mom tone. Jared chuckles as I lift my head, pulling an exaggerated look of concentration that's guaranteed to earn a raised eyebrow from Mac. "I've tried to keep it light, just in case you get called away on business. Speaking of which, you really need to have a discussion with Maeve about what you actually do. You're aware, aren't you, that she thinks you're nothing more than a glorified security consultant —handing out flyers, giving advice, and maybe installing the occasional alarm system?"

I shrug, deliberately nonchalant. "That is part of my job."

"Is it?" Jared smirks. "When's the last time you went door-to-door handing out leaflets?"

"I will," I counter, "if business ever gets bad enough."

"Sure you will," Jared replies with mock disbelief.

"Don't try to act smart with me, Josh Stone. She deserves to know the truth. Do you have any idea how I felt when she told me how relieved she was that you'd finished your time in the service? That she no longer had to worry every single day whether you'd come home in one piece—or several pieces?

Just talk to her. She adores you, and you'll work it out. You don't want to start your lives together with some silly misunderstanding hanging over you."

"She adores me, huh?" I say, unable to suppress my grin.

"You know she does," Mac replies softly with a smile.

"It's the whole virgin thing," Jared chips in smiling. "Drives her wild thinking you're about to let her pop your cherry."

I glower at him as Mac continues, "Maeve told us yesterday that you wanted to get married thirteen days from that date, so we pencilled it in for Saturday the twenty-second. Since you seem to have an affinity with that number, we figured the ceremony should be booked for thirteen hundred hours."

"Nice touch," I smirk.

"Maeve and I will be working on securing a venue today. I need a guest list from you as soon as possible so I can send out the invitations ASAP. We aren't giving people a lot of notice, so I want to get them out quickly. This weekend is stag and hen. Thursday, you, Maeve, Mitchel, Jen, Jackson, and Jaime will all drive to Hollywood to get things set up. The rest of us will follow on after school ends on Friday."

I groan, cutting off Mac mid-sentence. "Why can't the comedians travel up with you guys on Friday?"

"Because I've seen your place," Mac replies. "Jen's coming to help Maeve furnish and if needed, redecorate the place. One bed, one couch, and a few unopened boxes do not an apartment make. Don't worry—they'll all be staying at their own place across town. Jackson and Mitch have family and friends to catch up with while they're there, leaving the girls free to take Maeve shopping and find her the perfect dress. Once that's sorted, she'll let us know the theme so I can organise your suit and anything else you may need."

"Theme?" I ask, baffled, as Mac continues.

"Tia and I are hosting a pizza party at our place Friday night while you boys head out for your bachelor party."

"Head out where?" I ask, still dazed.

"Who knows," Jared chimes in. "Mitchel volunteered to plan everything."

"Great," I mutter, running my hand through my hair as I already start imagining the worst. "Maybe I should hire my own firm for protection."

The other two exchange amused looks before breaking into knowing smiles.

"You'll all have the day Saturday to recover before taking over the childminding duties at four, so us girls can get ready for Maeve's hen party. I need to know if there's anyone outside our group you think she'd want us to invite."

"Definitely her best friend Tina. She lives and works in New York, but I'm sure she could fly in for the weekend. I'll get her number for you. Actually, we'll call her together as I need a favour. Where are you all planning to go?"

"Josh," Mac sighs, looking exasperated, "we only started piecing the plan together yesterday. Give a girl a chance!"

"Sorry," I chuckle.

"Oh, while I think of it, can you let Axel know your phone will be off from six p.m. Friday until at least ten a.m. Saturday? I'd do it myself, but unless he hears it straight from the horse's mouth, he'll just nod, humour me, and then panic when he can't reach you."

"Will do," I smile. "Since Maeve has such a packed schedule, I'll swing by the office Thursday and tell him in person. Actually, if you don't need me until Friday evening, I could relieve him of duty for a couple of days' R&R. Do you want my guest list now?"

"Sure," Mac juggles her son, balancing him on her lap while jotting down notes in her notebook.

"My queen and her family, along with the rest of the motley crew who've been helping us pull this together at such short notice."

Mac smiles. "I'm glad you said that, considering Maeve already invited us."

"Kurt's my best man, so make sure you send him the final details. He knows he'll need to step away from the job he's on for a couple of days. I'll speak to Axel, and together we'll arrange backup for Blake when that happens. Send a blanket invite to the firm for anyone who can make it without compromising its integrity by abandoning a job they're currently handling. My parents and Kurt's parents—that'll be plenty. If Mitchel is coming, it'll already be enough of a circus without making it even more chaotic."

"Do you know how I can contact Maeve's brother Jimmy?"

Mac's words throw me for a loop as I ask, "Why?"

"Because when she was tipsy last night, she let slip that she'd really like him there. I know you've all had your differences in the past, but I'm so glad Jackson and I reconnected when we did…"

"Mac," I cut her off mid-flow, "the truth is I don't

know where Jimmy is right now. Maybe I should have said something earlier, but this job Kurt's on... let's just say it involves Jimmy. Trust me when I say, we want to find him as much as you do."

"Does Maeve know?"

"No, and I'd like to keep it that way, at least for now. When we find him, I'll tell her—I promise. But for now, I don't want to worry her over nothing."

"Okay," she sighs, her voice carrying a hint of doubt. "I trust you. I just don't want this to blow up in your face if she finds out you've not been totally honest with her. She's the best thing that's ever happened to you."

"Believe me, I know." I exhale heavily. "I'm not trying to screw this up—I'm just trying to protect her the best way I know how."

Over the next few days, I truly begin to understand what it feels like to be part of a couple in love. For once, it's nice not to be on the outside looking in. Maeve integrates herself into the group effortlessly, and it warms my heart to see her so relaxed and at ease around everyone. Her sharp wit and keen mind are more than a match for both Mitchel and Jackson combined, their endless bantering often leaving the rest of us in fits of laughter.

Jaime and Jen even extend an invitation for us

to visit them after our honeymoon. I can't help but wonder what Maeve will think of their palatial beachside properties, nestled side by side in one of Santa Monica's most exclusive neighbourhoods.

Nights are both the sweetest escape and the cruellest torment, leaving me to constantly question my decision to abstain from sex until our wedding night. Since our shower together Maeve has become much more comfortable in her own skin. Watching her lingering looks as she parades around in little to no clothes getting ready for bed pushes my resolve to the extremes. Our goodnight kisses are so passionate they are accompanied by an electric tension that lingers in the air, a pull so potent my daily check-ins with Kurt become my escape—a convenient excuse to step away and make a phone call, giving me the time to cool off so I can maintain my vow of chastity.

Not much is happening in Kurt's world right now. He's simply waiting, biding his time for the perfect moment to strike. Vince and Tony haven't left their place in days. With people coming and going at all hours, it's made it nigh on impossible for him and Foxy to make their move. Their instincts tell them that something big is brewing, yet the lack of inside information makes it impossible to predict the details of what's about to unfold. The faces they see are unfamiliar and seemingly insignificant—mostly hired muscle, the kind brought in to do the dirty work with no questions asked.

On Thursday, Maeve and I head to my apartment

in Hollywood. I'm both eager to show her my place and anxious to hear what she thinks. She laughs at the sparse furnishings but isn't discouraged. Spurred on by Jen's enthusiasm, the two of them throw themselves into transforming my blank canvas into a home we can hopefully share. We still need to figure out where we'll base ourselves after the wedding. With our businesses located on opposite sides of the country, it's a logistical nightmare we know we'll have to tackle eventually. But right now, we're far too wrapped up in each other to care.

With Maeve distracted and in Jen's safe hands, I head into the office. After catching up with the team, I relieve Axel from duty as planned, making sure to familiarize myself with the two potential new hires before catching up with Ace to see how they're faring.

At six p.m. sharp on Friday evening, I switch off my mobile and hand it to Mac for safekeeping before stepping through the door to my apartment—and almost walking right back out, not recognising the place. The once sparse, impersonal space has been completely transformed. Where there had been cold emptiness, there's now warmth and charm, thanks to Maeve and Jen's creative touch. Cozy furnishings, thoughtful accents, and splashes of personality breathe life into every corner, turning it into the sort of retreat I never thought I'd have the pleasure to own.

With Maeve inside waiting for me, I'm reluctant

to leave, but we part ways when Mitchel, Jackson, Jared, and Grant usher me off to meet up with some friends at a rooftop bar in a private club. Scantily clad women serve drinks as we're entertained by a celebrated drag act. Given the nature of my job, it's rare for me to indulge in more than a couple of beers. But tonight, everyone seems to be on a mission, plying me with enough alcohol to lower my guard —so much so that I end up belting out "I'm Every Woman" alongside Fonda Dix, Miss Taken Identity, and Barbie Q as my enthusiastic backing singers.

Just before midnight, we head to the casino in the basement. By then, I'm too far gone to remember how I got home. Waking up shirtless, sprawled on the couch with a pounding head, wrapped in a red feather boa and with wadges of cash stuffed in my pockets, is enough to tell me I had a good night.

"Look at the state of you," Maeve giggles, setting a cup of black coffee on the table beside me.

My eyes drop to the red feather boa, and panic sets in. I don't want her to think I'd been up to no good. I rip it off, tossing it aside, wincing as the sudden movement jars my aching limbs. "It's not what it looks like," I bluster apologetically.

"It's exactly what it looks like," she mocks. "I've seen the video."

I groan, sinking back onto the sofa, dragging my hand down my face while carefully avoiding the eyeballs which feel set to explode. "There's a video?"

"Not just one," she confirms cheerfully, as I mentally calculate how much I'll need to pay Foxy to hack into people's devices and erase all traces of the evidence from last night's shenanigans.

"There's some painkillers in my bag," she says, tossing it onto my chest. I groan at the impact, even though her purse is tiny and practically weightless. Maeve chuckles, "I'll go fetch you a glass of water."

She disappears, and I rummage through her purse until I find the blister pack. Popping two pills, I wash them down with a slug of coffee. I toss the pills onto the table in case I need more later, then close my eyes, praying they kick in quickly so I'm not frozen to the couch all day.

"Not again," Maeve says incredulously as she returns with the water, setting it down by my mug.

I force my bloodshot eyes open to watch her rummaging through her bag. She finds a box and waves it at me. "These, you idiot!" I glance at the discarded pills on the table, then at Maeve, my brain struggling to piece together what she's trying to tell me. It must be an iconic moment when the lightbulb finally goes on, illuminating my face with the horrific realisation that I've just downed two of the wrong medication... again!

"That's right," she says, her voice laced with disbelief. "You've just managed to leave me short on contraception again this month. She sighs witheringly, "Mac, Tia, and I are going to walk the dogs. Ava's staying with Jared, Grant, and the little ones. I'll tell her not to count on you for backup."

I wave a hand lazily in confirmation as she bursts out laughing and disappears through the door and across the hall, with Tiny hot on her heels. Once silence reigns, I lay back down on the couch, drifting into a restful slumber without a care in the world.

I'm not sure if Maeve returns before I wake again in the early afternoon, feeling much more like my old self. I down a pint of water and head to the shower. I've barely had time to dress and make it back to the living room, before there's a knock on the front door. Checking the monitor I installed when I first moved in, I spot Tina outside and glancing around nervously. She's holding a small blue bag, and I can't help but smile, knowing exactly what's inside.

"You got it?" I ask as I open the door.

"Hi, Tina. Welcome to my home, Tina. It's so lovely to see you, Tina," she parrots, handing me the bag.

"Sorry, Tina," I chuckle. "Welcome! It's lovely to see you."

She kisses me on the cheek. "I knew you'd come through. You two were meant for each other."

"Are you sure she'll like it?" I ask nervously.

"Trust me, she'll love it. It's the one she's been dreaming of since she was sixteen years old. All you need to do now is get set up. Oh, and I dropped off my case while you were comatose on the sofa earlier —I'm staying with you, by the way. At the same time, I convinced Maeve to take the outfits we're wearing later next door, pretending Mac could help us with our hair and makeup so I can keep her out of the way until five. Jaime's sending a car to pick us up at six, so you'll have an hour to get through all the gushy stuff. Jared took pity on you and ordered the flowers; they're in the lobby, ready to be brought up whenever you give the word. I'd better head back before she notices I'm gone." She opens the door to leave, then pokes her head back in with a grin. "Five o'clock," she reminds me before disappearing back behind the door and pulling it closed.

I check my watch to see its already nearing four, I don't have much time so immediately set to work.

Maeve steps through the door, calling back over her shoulder, "Where did you say you left it?"

"Living room, I think," Tina's voice carries in from the apartment opposite.

Maeve turns, and her eyes widen in surprise as she surveys the room. The warm glow of countless candles fills the space, their light dancing off the walls. It had taken me ages to light and arrange them in clusters, carefully crafting an atmosphere of romance and intimacy. Among the candles, several bouquets of red roses interwoven with delicate white gypsophila are scattered throughout the room.

One large bouquet—a striking mix of red, white, pink, and orange carnations, with a single cheerful sunflower standing tall in the centre—takes pride of place directly in front of me. I'm topless, with last night's feather boa draped over my shoulders for comedic effect. From Maeve's viewpoint, I appear completely naked, the largest bouquet strategically positioned to create the illusion.

She pauses in the doorway, her brow furrowing in confusion as Derek darts between her legs. The mischievous kitten prances around, momentarily catching her attention, before leaping onto the table and batting at the edge of a candle. With a gasp, she lunges forward, snatching the candle just as it teeters dangerously, threatening to set fire to his tail. Startled, Derek bolts, accidentally stepping on the remote for the sound system as he flees. The subtle romantic ballad, carefully chosen to complement the ambiance, suddenly blasts at an unbearable volume.

Maeve scrambles to save both our hearing, fumbling with the remote until the music is restored to a more acceptable level. The near-disaster makes her laugh nervously, though she's still entirely bewildered by the scene before her.

"What's going on?" She whispers, her voice tinged with curiosity and confusion.

It takes me a moment to answer. Standing there in her high silver heels, wearing a short, cream, figure-hugging dress, subtle makeup, and with her hair pinned up—soft tendrils framing her pretty face—she looks like a goddess. The candlelight bathes her in a warm glow, her beauty stealing the air from my lungs and rendering me temporarily speechless.

All my prior plans to tease and play with her a

little fly out the window as I automatically stroll over to her before dropping down to one knee. Clearing my throat to ensure my voice doesn't betray me, I hold her gaze as I reach into the pocket of my jeans.

"I looked at your hand the other day, and I didn't like what I saw." I start a little hoarsely.

"My hand?" Her brow furrows as she holds her hands in front of herself, studying them for any unappealing marks or blemishes she thinks I might be referring to. "Which one? What's wrong with it?"

I pause dramatically, pulling a small velvet box from my pocket. "The left one. There's no ring."

Maeve's left hand flies to her mouth, covering her lips in shock.

"It suddenly dawned on me that I never proposed—not properly. And a woman as stunning as you is bound to draw attention. I know you've already hinted that you were mine, but it's not enough. I need to know for sure and I want the world to see it. Maeve, will you promise to accept this ring and me along with it, for the rest of your life?"

I open the box, revealing the ring—praying Tina got it right and it's the exact one Maeve has been dreaming of. Her breath hitches, and as her eyes lock onto mine, I see the realisation wash over her. She takes in the candles, the bouquets, the music, and, most of all, the emotion etched onto my face.

For a brief moment, she stares straight into my soul, recognising the depth of my feelings for her. If she didn't before, she knows now, without a shadow of a doubt, how long I've silently loved her. How those Valentine's cards I sent years ago, when she was pining after someone else, were born from love and longing, even though I believed I didn't stand a chance.

I can tell she feels it too—the vulnerability in this moment, the way I'm baring my heart and asking, with everything I have, for hers in return.

Happy tears make her eyes shine, but before she can respond, Derek decides he's had enough of our moment. He leaps onto my arm, claws scrambling to climb higher, knocking the velvet box out of my hand. It lands on the floor with a muffled thud, and I frantically scoop it up, frowning at the interruption while Maeve dissolves into laughter.

I quickly regain my composure, holding the box out once more. "You didn't answer me," I say softly, my normally abrupt tone replaced by a voice filled with love and hope.

"Yes," Maeve whispers, her voice trembling. "A thousand times, yes."

She steps closer, allowing me to slide the ring onto her finger. I stand, pulling her into my arms as Derek circles our feet, clearly unimpressed at not being the centre of attention.

I kiss her tenderly, but as I go to deepen the kiss, she pulls back, her expression suddenly serious. My heart skips a beat as I wonder what's wrong.

"There's one stipulation I must insist upon," she says.

"Name it," I growl, determined never to let her slip

away.

"You have to stop taking my contraception," she teases.

"Deal," I laugh before claiming her mouth once more.

By the time Tina, Mac, and Ava come knocking to whisk Maeve away at six, both of us are looking pretty dishevelled. I'm forced to hide behind the enormous bouquet when they arrive, attempting to shield myself from their amused scrutiny.

Thankfully, my attempts at keeping my unzipped jeans and rock-hard erection out of sight are successful, going blissfully unnoticed amid their excitement over the item glinting from Maeve's hand. The moment they spot the ring, all other distractions vanish, replaced by squeals and heartfelt congratulations. I'm so hyped up the minute they all disappear I take to the shower, relieving the pressure in my balls over my memories of Maeve's naked form and the imagery of how I plan to covet it on our wedding night. I've always prided myself on having a stronger willpower than most, but when my orgasm hits, the feeling is so intense that I wonder if even I have the capacity to last the next seven days without my dick seeking the haven it so desperately craves.

Half an hour later, I meander next door with a box of beers tucked under one arm and Derek under the other.

"King Josh!" My queen yells triumphantly as I walk through the door.

Six babies recline contentedly in their bouncers, watching Mitchel with rapt attention as he sits in front of them, reading from a script like he's auditioning for a panel of the world's harshest critics.

"What's going on in here, then?" I chuckle.

"It's a good way to learn my lines. Plus, they all stop crying when I perform," Mitchel explains, waving his arms about dramatically. Whatever he's trying to emulate is completely lost on me.

"They're in awe," Jared scoffs. "Never seen such bad acting before."

"Or they're constipated," Grant quips.

"Here's hoping," Jackson deadpans.

"I hear ya," Grant agrees, clinking his bottle with Jackson's. "I could do with a night free from toxic waste."

I set the beers and Derek down. He immediately runs over to greet Tiny who has been at Jared's with Maeve for most of the day. "Where are the twins?"

"Bedroom playing video games," Grant replies.

"Or watching porn," Mitchel chuckles. "If you feel the need to join them to take a few notes, no-one here will mind."

I ignore the ripple of laughter that follows, "Anyone ordered food?"

"Chinese and pizza's on its way," Jared answers this time.

"Odd selection," I say, quirking an eyebrow at him.

"Well, we all voted for Chinese…" He's interrupted by his eldest daughter.

"But I wanted pizza."

"Didn't you have pizza last night, little lady?" I laugh, swinging her up into my arms and settling her on my knee as I sit on the couch.

"It's my favourite," she giggles playfully.

"We negotiated," Jared tells me with mock seriousness. "She could have pizza if she agreed to be in bed by seven-thirty without any argument, and promised not to spill all our secrets to her mom when she gets home. Oh, and there's one more thing —you're on bedtime story duty."

"I think I can manage that."

The smile I'm rewarded with is dazzling, her little face lighting up with pure excitement. It's the kind of smile that makes you feel like a superhero, even if all you're doing is reading a children's book.

"Can we make it a long one?" She asks, her voice hopeful and filled with mischief.

I glance over at Jared, who raises an eyebrow as if to say, *Good luck with that.*

"We'll see," I reply, chuckling, ruffling her hair as she snuggles closer. "But only if you promise not to correct me every time I get the voices wrong."

She giggles again, her laughter warm and infectious. "I'll try," she says, though her tone suggests otherwise.

An hour and a half later, I'm barely halfway through my story before Tia falls asleep. I make sure she's tucked in tight, pressing a gentle kiss to her temple before quietly slipping out of the room.

"Did Mac tell you where she left my phone?" I ask

Jared as I rejoin the main group.

"It's in the top drawer of the desk in my office," he replies.

"Do you mind if I grab it? I told Axel I'd switch it back on this morning, and, as you know, that didn't happen."

Jared laughs. "Be my guest."

I wander over to his office and locate my phone. When I switch it on, I expect a few notifications, but instead, I'm bombarded by a cacophony of alerts. I sit at Jared's desk, resting my forearms on the table as I scroll through the notifications.

Multiple missed calls, voicemails and messages, from Kurt, Axel, Blake, and Ace flash across the screen. My chest tightens with concern as I head to my messages, hoping to shed some light on what's been happening while I was out of action. I figure the most urgent communication would come from Kurt, so I open his single voice message first.

My eyes dart to the timestamp: 7 p.m.—roughly an hour after I switched my phone off last night. That would've been 10 p.m. for Kurt, given the three hour time difference. My thumb hovers over the screen for a second, then I press play. As is Kurt's usual style, he doesn't waste time on pleasantries.

His voice is tense, clipped, and straight to the point. *"This could be it. Vince and Anthony had one hell of a blowout. Vince stormed off, and Blake tailed him to the airport. He boarded a flight to Vegas. I pulled Blake back—my gut says Vince is just going to blow off some steam. Tony's had him cooped up since his release;*

I reckon he's getting stir-crazy.

But here's the real deal: Tony's place is a hive of activity right now. Half his crew peeled out shortly after Vince left. Foxy followed them as far as Portland and managed to plant trackers on two of their vehicles when they stopped for a bite. Tony and the rest look like they're gearing up to join them. Soon as they're out, I'm going in. We need ears on the inside. If Foxy doesn't make it back in time, I'm going solo."

I blow out a breath. Kurt going in alone isn't ideal and if I'd known in time I would have stopped him. He is stubborn and pig-headed and wouldn't have listened to anyone but me. I can only hope Foxy made it back in time to join him. I cut to Axel's messages. They start off short and succinct but grow in length and worrying intensity with every word I read.

9:30 p.m. *It's happening. Kurt and Foxy are making their move.*

I blow out another breath, relieved Kurt is not alone.

10:10 p.m. *Devices in place. Transmitters set to pick up audio—getting ready to evac.*

10:17 p.m. *Tony's back unexpectedly—with Derek Dawson and several heavies in tow. Kurt & Foxy still inside.*

10:22 p.m. *Blake checked in late. He's lost all internal comms with the others. External sound and visuals compromised. We're blind. He's gone in for a closer look against orders.*

10.32 p.m. *Radio silence from Blake.*

A wave of unease crashes over me as I process Axel's last message. My focus sharpens when I notice he's created a new group chat. I tap into it, scanning the messages rapidly, searching for answers amidst the chaos.

10:37 p.m. *Nic/Bear: You're on a flight in thirty minutes from LAX—ETA to destination seven hours. Forward final address when you land. Mission to establish location of and if possible extract Kurt, Foxy and Blake from enemy turf. All parties MIA—Unknown If they're alive. Check in the moment you arrive for further instruction.*

10:40 p.m. *Ace: You're closer. Tony's place is your priority. Backup's inbound—DO NOT go in alone. Tell the rookies this is their time to shine in your absence. NO SCREW-UPS any issues to contact me directly.*

11:15 p.m. *No further updates received from Kurt, Foxy, or Blake. Situation's critical. Everyone Move fast.*

11.30 p.m. *Boss—check in when you can.*

I look at my watch, that message was sent nearly twenty-one hours ago. I don't check the messages from Ace or Blake before calling Axel to get an update on the situation. I hit dial and press the phone to my ear, each ring grinding on my nerves. When Axel finally picks up, I'm met with the sound of his heavy breathing. "Boss," he says, his voice sharp with tension.

"What's going on, Axel?" I demand, my throat dry. "It's been nearly a day since your last update, and I haven't checked Ace or Blake's messages yet. Tell me everything."

"Everyone's accounted for," Axel begins, but there's a pause—long enough to twist my gut. "Apart from Kurt."

I suck in a breath, forcing my voice to stay level. If I panic, the team will too—and mistakes will follow. I can't let that happen, not when my best friend's life might be on the line. "What do you mean? Apart from Kurt?"

Axel exhales hard, his voice heavy. "He threw himself into the line of fire. Gave Foxy and Blake the chance to get out unseen."

"And them?" My voice rises despite my effort to stay calm. "Foxy? Blake?"

"Fine," Axel says, a note of relief slipping through. "They made it out clean after Kurt convinced Tony he went in alone looking for your friend Jimmy. They managed to retrieve intel, too. It's bad, Boss, real bad."

"Tell me."

"Vince and Tony," Axel begins, his tone grim. "They've been running a smuggling operation, using Dawson's souvenir imports as a front to bring drugs into the country.

Tony's smart, though. He's the one pulling the strings, but he's made sure nothing can be traced back to him. Dig deep enough, and everything leads straight to Vince—a fact Vince has finally woken up to. And it's starting to grate on him. A lot." Axel pauses briefly before continuing. "It seems Vince tried to go rogue behind his brother's back and got caught. When he ran into Jimmy before he got sent down, Vince saw an opportunity. He tried to coerce Jimmy into helping him set up a new distribution network using the kids Jimmy works with. We think Vince wanted to skim off some of the profits he believed Tony owed him."

I frown as Axel exhales, his voice heavy.

"When Jimmy refused point-blank to get involved, sending Vince on his merry way, Vince didn't back down—he went behind Jimmy's back and recruited Billy Jenkins anyway. When Vince got put away and Billy stopped hearing from him, we think Billy went looking and found his brother instead. Tony stepped in, taking Billy under his wing. Over time, Tony leaned on Billy more and more, rewarding him generously for jobs well done and handing him greater responsibility. Everything ran smoothly—until Vince's release. Jealous and eager to reclaim his place in the hierarchy—the one Billy had settled into—Vince tried to shove him aside. He may have been young but Billy stood up to Vince because he was convinced Tony would back him. He was confident Tony needed him more than he did Vince. But blood is thicker than water, and the fact all the bank accounts are in Vinces's name meant despite their dysfunctional relationship, Tony backed Vince, demoting Billy— a fact Billy didn't take well after five years of loyal service. Angry and bitter, Billy started throwing his weight around, mouthing off to anyone who would listen. We know he called Jimmy just days before his disappearance—maybe to come clean about what he'd been up to, or maybe to pit Jimmy against Vince in hopes of getting his old job back. Whatever the reason, Billy's loose lips pissed Tony off. And in the end, Billy had to be silenced—before someone actually started listening to his rants and brought too much attention Tony's way.

When Billy's body washed up, Jimmy must've figured out who was responsible and why. Knowing he might be the only one able to connect the Castillo brothers to Billy, he must have gone to ground—terrified they'd come after him to tie up loose ends.

Tony's got a shipment coming in within the next few days, and he's jumpy—real jumpy. With Jimmy still out there, he's a liability.

Pulling out all the stops, Tony switched the drop-off point for his latest consignment at the last minute. He must be worried Jimmy knows more than he should about his operation. To throw off anyone watching, he sent a decoy team to Portland docks—hoping that if Jimmy tipped off the authorities, they'd still believe the drugs were coming through there.

Axel takes another breath. "That's the group Foxy tailed to Portland—but it was all a distraction. The real shipment has been redirected to Searsport."

I grip the edge of the desk, my knuckles whitening.

"That's not the best bit though," Axel says darkly. "Vince was supposed to oversee the Portland delivery, knowing full well the drop location had changed.

But Tony—fed up with his brother's constant demands and reckless behaviour—decided it was time to cut him loose. Permanently.

He planted a small percentage of the merchandise, just enough to make it look like a win when the authorities intercepted it. Then, he planned to tip off the DEA himself, cementing his credibility as a law-abiding citizen while seizing the perfect opportunity to get Vince out of the picture—for good."

"He was planning to frame his own brother?" My voice carries the weight of disbelief.

"Sure seems like it," Axel growls. "However, Vince must still have some loyal friends and somehow, he found out what Tony was planning to do and flipped. He threatened to drain the offshore account Tony set up in his name. The two had it out—big time. After just getting out of federal prison, Vince knew getting caught with even a fraction of the merchandise would be his end. Discovering Tony's plan to use him as a scapegoat clearly shook him."

Axel exhales sharply before continuing. "Vince's only leverage is the account Tony's using to launder their profits. Tony put everything in Vince's name, so he could distance himself if things ever went wrong. While Vince was inside, it was never an issue—Tony had full control. But now Vince is out and having to watch his back, he's blocked Tony's access to safeguard himself. Tony's given him an ultimatum—find Jimmy and silence him for good, or transfer the money into a new account Tony can manage so they can go their separate ways."

Axel pauses. "Vince obviously took umbrage at his brother's constant assumption that he gets to call all the shots. He didn't take kindly to being told what to do, so he bolted for Vegas—with a wad of cash in his pocket.

My guess? He needed space to figure out his next move. And while doing that, he thought he might as well enjoy some of the money he felt he was owed.

Tony's furious—and that probably explains why Douglas has suddenly shown up"

"I guess Douglas is worried Vince has stopped his cash flow too." I let out a low whistle. "And Kurt?"

Axel hesitates, the silence stretching unbearably. "Changing the shipment's destination at the last minute wasn't easy—it caused delays.

At first, we thought Tony was heading to Portland to join the rest of his team. But in reality, he was meeting a contact in Searsport to grease the wheels there.

He came back early, bringing Dawson and some of his muscle. They interrupted Kurt and Foxy while they were setting up our gear. Foxy said Kurt created a distraction, giving him just enough time to find a safe place to hide until the coast was clear—so he could escape and summon reinforcements."

Axel exhales sharply, his voice raw with exhaustion and defeat as he continues. "Tony's paranoia made him have his tech team tear the place apart until they found every device we'd installed. That knocked out our comms. Concerned, Blake went in but Foxy managed to intercept him. They were outmanned. Outgunned. They couldn't reach Kurt—they needed time to regroup, to plan their next move." His voice drops lower. "Kurt created the diversion the others needed to get away. He set on Tony, taking down five of his men in the process. Foxy and Blake slipped out just as he was being dragged away. There was nothing they could do. But... Josh, Tony was incensed and threatening all sorts, we don't know if he made it."

The words hit me like a hammer, leaving me cold and numb. My head spins as I try to process the layers of betrayal and danger. Kurt's actions weigh heavily on my mind, but I shove the emotions down. There's no time for that—not now.

"What's the plan?" I manage, my voice steady despite the turmoil.

"We're regrouping," Axel says. "Nic, Bear, and Ace are on the ground, gathering intel from Foxy and Blake about the property's interior layout. But Boss..." He pauses, his voice heavy. "They're rattled. Losing Kurt has shaken them to the core—they need you."

Axel exhales, the tension clear in his voice. "They're divided. Half want to storm the fortress immediately, desperate to search for Kurt while there's still hope he's alive. The others are insisting on taking the time to plan a strategic attack. They need you to lead them, Boss. You're the only one who can unify them and make the call."

There's no time to hesitate. "Get me on the fastest

flight out there—I'll be at LAX within the hour."

I thought you'd say that," Axel replies. "There's a jet on standby, ready for wheels up as soon as you arrive."

Chapter 19

Maeve

I've never felt so happy and relaxed in my entire life. Jaime—or should I say Jackson—booked a private room for us in a restaurant above a club in one of Hollywood's most elite areas. We've indulged in a sumptuous five-course meal, and those who could partake savoured some of the city's finest wine. Lord knows how much it must have cost. Jackson assured me not to worry; he insisted it was an engagement present from him and his wife. He said his goal was for us all to unwind and enjoy ourselves without interruptions. Jaime, however, corrected him with a playful jab, explaining the location had been carefully chosen so Jackson didn't have to fret over other men hitting on her while she was out. Not that he'd ever need to worry. Jaime only had eyes for her husband—it was plain for anyone within a five-mile radius to see.

Mitchel's popularity, coupled with his wife's tall, statuesque beauty, meant she always turned heads. His solution? Employing two burly security guards to trail us at a "discreet" distance—though discreet might be a stretch. They were clearly there for his peace of mind more than anyone else's, a testament to how much he adored his wife.

"He thinks I don't know they're there," Jen giggles as we sit at our table, laughing and joking together. She's clearly referring to the two muscle-bound men loitering on our periphery, failing to blend into their surroundings despite their best efforts.

"Not exactly subtle, are they?" Tina chuckles. "I can't remember the last time I saw two people so clearly out of place. Did he hire them from Josh's firm?"

"No," Jen sighs, smiling. "Atlas is the one posing as the very stern looking sommelier in the black Armani suit, and Jed's outside somewhere, keeping watch. I'm sure Mitchel thought if he hired someone from Josh's firm, Mac would spot them immediately."

"How do you know all this, if it's supposed to be a secret?" Tina laughs.

Jen rolls her eyes, feigning exasperation. "Mitchel must have been so proud of his plan, he forgot I'd already met them both. What can you do? His heart's in the right place."

"I don't think he'd have found people with the skills this job requires working at Josh's firm," I chime in, joining the conversation.

"What do you mean?" Tina asks, her brow furrowed in confusion.

"Well, I imagine all the men working for him are adminy types," I reply with a shrug.

"Adminy types?" She scoffs, raising an eyebrow.

"Does Kurt look like an adminy type to you? What exactly do you think Josh does for a living?"

Mac's gaze starts to drift, her eyes connecting with anyone in the room but me.

"He advises people on security, fits intruder alarms—that sort of thing," I reply, shrugging. "He mentioned he's in the process of starting his own firm, so I figure he does most of the grunt work alongside Kurt. Mac helps out with the phones, payments and scheduling, while a few others handle marketing and stuff."

"Have you ever seen his office?" Tina asks somewhat cagily.

"No, but Mac has. Tell her," I prompt the woman squirming uncomfortably in her chair.

The awkward pause that follows tells me I'm missing some vital information.

"Mac?" I urge her to speak.

She takes a deep breath, then starts slowly before her words spill out in a rush. "What you said... is only a small part of what he does. I mean... he fitted our security systems after finishing another job for Jared and me. Other than that he provides a very bespoke service, using skills from his previous profession to help others solve problems—problems that sometimes need a more unconventional approach. Your man has quite the reputation in certain circles for getting things done when local authorities can't, using their more restricted methods." Her words tumble out faster as she continues. "His services are so sought after that his business, although still in its infancy, is expanding rapidly. He currently employs eighteen highly trained men he used to serve with. Recently, I helped him interview two new recruits—both women—to diversify his team. They're currently on probation."

I fall back in my chair, stunned. Mac hurries to reassure me. "If it's any consolation, the reason he started the business was to create a solid foundation for settling down and having kids in the future. But he also wanted to use his experience to help people while building something stable. His ultimate goal is to run the office, while training up the next generation for the hands-on work. So he ends up in a role where he won't have to travel or risk throwing himself into danger constantly, and he can come home to you every night." She exhales heavily, like a weight has lifted from her shoulders. "It's a conversation he promised he'd have with you. I think he's been so happy lately that he was afraid telling you might spoil that."

"What was the job you originally hired him to do?" I ask a little testily as I struggle to digest all this new information.

"Jared tried to hire him to protect Tia and me," Mac giggles nervously trying to inject some humour into the otherwise tense conversation by adding, "It was before we'd met him and Kurt basically shut Jared down. Then we met as neighbours and Tia won him over."

I don't respond, so she hesitates before

continuing. "My ex-husband turned a little... unhinged. He held Ava and me at gunpoint." Her voice falters as she adds, "That's how Josh got the scar on his shoulder. He took a bullet meant for Jared while rescuing us." My mouth falls open as she goes on. "Unfortunately, my ex got away. The police couldn't track him down, and he ended up kidnapping Jen and one of Ava's twins before Josh and Kurt finally stopped him. They made sure he could never bother any of us again." When I still don't answer, she finishes weakly. "I know it sounds bad, but it's all behind us now, I promise." She lets out a nervous laugh, glancing away like she's waiting for my reaction.

"Babe," Tina nudges me with her elbow. "Remember, this is Josh we're talking about. The Josh who sent you anonymous Valentine's cards every year when we were kids, just to make you smile—even though he knew he wouldn't get anything in return. The Josh who had to bribe Liam to hand deliver them on his behalf, just so he'd be sure you got them on time. The Josh who ran back into a burning building to carry you to safety, only to let you believe for years it was someone else because he thought that's what you wanted to hear." I hear a few startled gasps around the table as she continues, "The guy who called me in New York so I could find the ring you always dreamed of. And let me tell you, he spent more than I earn in a year on it." She leans closer, her voice softening. "There may have been a gap in your relationship where you both changed and grew, but fundamentally, you're still the same people. He still loves you—quirks and all. Your habit of talking to animals like they're people, your questionable taste in music and the way you always hit the Karaoke believing you can sing—none of it fazes him. And I've never seen you happier than you've been since I got here." She exhales, a little laugh escaping. "When he told me to bring the ring to Cali, I nearly fainted. When I found out he actually convinced you to leave Vermont, I knew. I knew he was the one—and that you loved him, too." Tina glances at me, her eyes filled with sincerity. "He's protected you your whole life. So is it really so surprising that he kept certain parts of his work from you to stop you from worrying?"

I guess not," I sigh. "But he has to stop. I'm a big girl now, and I want him to be honest with me."

"Then talk to him," Tina says with a reassuring smile. "Tonight, when you get back."

"I will," I smile, and Mac exhales in visible relief. "But right now, it's my hen party, and I want to dance! Anyone fancy seeing if we can get into that club downstairs?"

"Hell yeah!" A tipsy Jaime raises her glass as Tina claps her hands in excitement. The others need little convincing, and soon we're all trooping downstairs—two thoroughly unamused security guards trailing at a respectable distance, exchanging worried glances behind us.

Twenty minutes later, the club is alive with the pulsating thrum of bass-heavy music. Neon lights casting their kaleidoscopic glow across the packed dance floor. Our little group, however, is having the time of its life in our own glorious bubble of chaos. The half of us still nursing their young sip elegantly on colourful mocktails garnished with elaborate fruit skewers, while the other half are consuming cocktails that come with umbrellas so absurdly large they could double as parasols.

Tina is in the centre, spinning in circles and flailing her arms like a windmill caught in a tornado, while a giggling Jaime attempts to teach her the 'right' way to dance. The so-called 'right way' involves moves that resemble someone trying to dodge imaginary flying objects. It's hard to tell which one looks more ridiculous, but the laughter between them is infectious.

Meanwhile, the security guards—Atlas and Jed— hover near the edge of the dance floor, their stony expressions betrayed only by the faintest hint of bewilderment. Having barely talked their way past the bouncers, they are now halfheartedly swaying back and forth, trying to blend in but looking like oversized trees lost in a forest of clubbers. Every now and then, one steps closer to our group in an attempt to deter admirers, only to stumble awkwardly as Tina's wildly waving limbs come dangerously close to taking them out.

"Is this their idea of camouflage?" I whisper to Mac, who is pretending to choke on her drink to suppress her laughter. One particularly bold admirer, undeterred by the looming security duo, saunters over and attempts to join the group. Jaime, quick as ever, forms an impromptu human shield, pulling Tina and Jen into a synchronized dance routine so erratic it could've doubled as an aerobics class. The poor admirer takes one horrified look at the flailing arms and retreats with a polite nod, leaving us howling with laughter.

"Mission accomplished!" Tina crows, raising her glass in triumph before tripping over her own feet and collapsing into a fit of giggles.

The night's young, the music's loud, and though half the group have had to reluctantly surrender to mocktails—admittedly superior in their decorative flair—we're unstoppable. Even Atlas and Jed eventually give up their stoic facade, resorting to small, embarrassed smiles as we finally admit their cover has been blown before we drag them into the chaos of our dance circle. Their moves are— let's say—unique, but nobody cares. This is a night for dancing, laughter, and building memories with friend's new and old.

By one a.m., the club is still alive with pulsing music and laughter, but the energy among our group has shifted. Exhaustion mingles with the buzz of cocktails, and I'm more than eager to return home to my fiancé. The memory of his perfect proposal lingers vividly in my mind—the way his voice trembled with emotion as he asked me to spend forever with him, the warmth in his eyes reflecting nothing but love. Our heated kisses before I was swept off for this celebration play on repeat, igniting an ache in my chest that only his presence can soothe. It's this thought that makes the noise and chaos around me feel so distant, almost insignificant. Jaime calls for our transport to meet us out front. As everyone gathers their belongings, I feel the familiar pressure of too many drinks and decide to make a quick detour. "I just need to go to the restroom," I announce with exaggerated drama, earning a chorus of giggles from Tina, who's also bouncing on her heels.

"Me too," she says, her voice light and bubbly. "We'll meet you guys outside in a sec."

After an exuberant, heartfelt parting of the ways, Jen and her entourage help an alcohol-fuelled Jaime stumble away toward their car in a flurry of hugs and laughter. Their voices rise above the thrum of the music from the club as they remind my own fuzzy brain about tomorrow's packed schedule. It's the kind of bond that feels unbreakable, forged in the glow of a fabulous night out.

"Don't forget, Maeve! We've got a hundred things to sort tomorrow!" Jaime calls over her shoulder, her organizational skills somehow intact despite the amount of alcohol she has consumed. Her tone is light, yet full of the determination that's become her hallmark over the past few days.

Jen hovers just long enough to wave back at me with a warm smile as she catches Jaime when she stumbles, her promise to help find me the perfect wedding cake lingering in the air as they turn and head toward their waiting car. The camaraderie between us feels effortless, the bonds of friendship solidified by their unwavering support for my fast-approaching nuptials.

Since they're staying at their own place in a different part of town, I watch as they disappear into the night, their goodbyes echoing like a fading melody. Mac and Ava follow them out quietly, fresh-faced and steady despite the late hour, their responsibilities as new mums keeping them in check throughout the evening. They exchange knowing smiles with Jen before offering quick waves in my direction and slipping out the front to wait for us in the car we're sharing. As soon as Tina and I are alone, we make our way to the back of the club, navigating the dimly lit corridor that leads to the restrooms.

The passage stretches ahead, its shadows rippling faintly under the glow of neon lights spilling from the club behind us. The thrum of bass fades with each step, the lively chatter softening to a dull murmur as the cooler air presses against my skin. The quiet feels eerie and a stark contrast to the chaos of moments before. A sudden unease begins to creep along the edges of my thoughts, prickling at the back of my neck, until we push open the restroom door and are once again engulfed in pandemonium.

The air is thick with cloying perfume and the hum of overlapping voices. The mirrors are fogged from the heat of too many bodies crammed into the small space, their movements frenetic as they retouch makeup or wait impatiently. Tina groans audibly, her gaze fixed on the long line snaking toward the stalls.

We wait patiently for our turn, "I'll wait for you outside," I tell her as I hit the front of the queue, my voice raised to compete with the noise.   She nods, already distracted by her phone, and after I've taken care of business, I slip back into the corridor.

The quiet hits me like a wall. The passage is still spookily vacant, the muffled sounds of the club barely audible now. My heels click against the tiled floor, the sound clipped and lonely. I glance back toward the restroom, hoping to see Tina's silhouette appear, but the door remains closed and the space empty.   The same prickling sensation as before creeps along the back of my neck, the unmistakable feeling of being watched. My breath quickens, and I force myself to turn back toward the passage, scanning the shadows for any sign of movement. The silence presses in, heavy and oppressive, amplifying the pounding of my heart.

"Maeve," an unmistakable voice calls from the darkness, low and familiar. My breath catches. The sound slicing through the quiet like a blade, freezing me in place. Slowly, I turn, my pulse roaring in my ears.

Vince Castillo steps forward, his face half-lit by the dim overhead light. His twisted smile drenches me in terror, transporting me back to a place I thought I'd buried—a place where I was a petrified young girl, bracing myself to fend off his advances all those years ago. "You're a hard lady to find," he says, his tone casual, almost amused. But his eyes—those cold, calculating eyes—betray his intent.

Fear roots me to the spot. My mind races, grasping for a means of escape, but my body refuses to move. Vince closes the distance between us in a heartbeat, one hand darting out to cover my mouth and nose with a dampened cloth. As his other arm coils around me, locking me against him, panic detonates in my chest—sharp and suffocating. I twist and thrash, every muscle screaming to be free, but his grip is unrelenting. No matter how hard I fight, I can't break free. Suddenly, a noxious, chemical scent floods my senses, searing through my nose before embedding itself in the back of my throat. It burns and chokes me as I attempt to lash out. My vision blurs, the edges darkening as I continue to struggle. Colours start to swim, bleeding into one another, disorienting me and making me feel nauseous. My limbs grow heavier by the second, becoming sluggish and unresponsive, it's as though I'm sinking slowly underwater with my lungs screaming for air. Tears spill freely, not just from the assault, but from the crushing knowledge that I may never see Josh again. The fear that our future together—the happiness we finally found—could be snatched away at the last moment overwhelms me. The thought of never sharing the night we had waited so long for—the night he promised would be worth the wait, a gift he wanted to make more special by saving our most intimate union for our wedding day—shatters me as I fight to keep the darkness from closing in. Through the haze, I hear Tina's voice, shrill and panicked. "Maeve!" She screams, her footsteps echoing as she rushes toward me. But she's a fraction too late, and Vince knows it. The last thing I see is his arrogant smirk as he pulls me backward out of a fire escape and into a dark and foreboding alley, slamming the door in Tina's distorted face before I finally have no option other than to let myself free fall into oblivion.

My senses stir listlessly, my mind's groggy, my body disoriented. Darkness smothers me, and for a moment, I can't tell if my eyes are open or closed. My wrists and ankles are bound tightly, the restraints digging into my skin as my body contorts in a cramped space. I try to scream, but duct tape across my mouth pulls at my skin, stifling the sound and leaving me snorting in desperation. I struggle to move, but my limbs feel foreign, heavy, and uncooperative. How long have I been out? Minutes? Hours? Days? The thought constricts my chest, but the void offers no answers.

Suddenly, a blinding light cuts through the darkness, forcing me to blink against the glare as my vision fights to adjust. With a jolt, I realise I'm crammed into the trunk of a car, my body pressed against cold, hard metal. My heart pounds violently as Vince's face looms above me, his evil grin sharpened by the blinding floodlights overhead. I squint against the brightness, my surroundings gradually taking shape—a private airstrip, the tarmac gleaming under the artificial light and humming with the low vibration of a jet engine. A shiver wracks my spine, my trembling escalating with each shaky breath I struggle to take.

"Rise and shine," Vince says, his tone dripping with mockery as he grabs my arm. I thrash weakly, my movements clumsy and restricted by the bindings. He hauls me out of the trunk with ease, my feet scraping against the gravel as he steadies me upright. "Don't make this harder than it needs to be," he snaps, his sweaty fingers digging into my arm like a vice. He bends, ruthless in his movements, and doesn't take any prisoners as he rips the tape from my ankles, taking with it the top layer of skin. The pain is instant, blinding, forcing a strangled, muffled sound from my throat. I convulse against the agony, terror twisting in my gut—petrified that if I throw up, the duct tape across my mouth will cause me to choke.

The jet looms ahead, sleek and menacing, its open cabin door spilling harsh light onto the ground below. My chest tightens further as Vince forces me up the steps, my muffled protests swallowed by the night. I try to resist, planting my feet and twisting against his grip, but he overpowers me effortlessly. He shoves me into a seat with such force that my head snaps back, and he wastes no time buckling me in. He lets his hands linger on my shoulders, his fingers gliding up my neck to stroke my cheek with a mock tenderness that makes my stomach churn. I suppress a shiver, my skin crawling at his touch.

"You're not going to cause any trouble, are you?" Vince asks, his tone almost casual as he leans closer, his eyes cold and calculating. I glare at him, my breathing erratic behind the tape. He chuckles low, the sound laced with cruelty. "Didn't think so."

From his pocket, Vince pulls out a syringe, the needle glinting under the cabin's light. "In your profession," he says, a cruel smirk curling his lips, "you'll know exactly what this is." My eyes dart around the cabin, landing on a small discarded bottle. The label catches my attention, and my stomach drops as I recognize the drug—a powerful sedative designed to render even the strongest animals helpless.

Muffled cries escape me as I shake my head frantically, desperation clawing at my chest, but Vince doesn't falter. "This is just to help you relax," he murmurs, his voice dripping with mock concern. I flinch as the sharp scratch of the needle pierces my arm, the cold liquid spreading through my veins like ice. My pulse slows as dizziness sets in, my head lolling as sleepiness takes hold. My eyelids droop despite my resistance, and I barely register Vince tucking a stray lock of hair behind my ear. "Sleep tight, duchess," he whispers, his voice smug and condescending. "You'll need to conserve your strength for later." His lips graze my cheek with a soft kiss, the gesture landing more like a threat just before I lose the fight for consciousness and my eyes crash shut once more.

The next time I wake, I'm lying on a queen-size bed, disoriented and with a relentless pounding in my head. Forcing myself to sit up, I switch on the lamp beside me and instinctively press a hand to my temple. Memories of the night before surge forward. My gaze falls to the deep red rings around my wrists and ankles, tender bruises left in their wake. I run my fingers over the marks—they're sore, yet not painful. Relief washes over me as I notice, aside from my shoes, my clothes are still in place —untouched and intact. The tension in my chest eases, but only slightly, as my mind remains alert to the dangers surrounding me.

The room around me is steeped in shadows, the blind firmly drawn over the window. Without a watch, and with my phone stashed away in my purse, wherever that may be, time feels lost. My eyes sweep across my surroundings. The room is opulent but minimalistic—no clock, no hint of what hour it might be. Apart from the bed, there are matching side tables with lamps, a dressing table with a small stool tucked beneath it, a wardrobe, and a rug. Two doors break the monotony of the walls.

I swing my legs out of bed. The floor is cool beneath my bare feet as I make my way unsteadily to the first door. It opens to a bathroom—large, cold, and devoid of personality. The white tiled walls gleam starkly against the black marble floors. A bath, a shower, a sink, and a toilet sit neatly arranged, but the space is otherwise barren. No toiletries, no personal touches to suggest someone's presence or care. The emptiness sends a chill through me as I pull the door closed.

The second door doesn't open. I shouldn't be surprised—it's locked from the outside. My fingers hover over the old-fashioned keyhole, but the key has been left in the lock on the other side. Frustration overwhelms me. The mechanism feels antiquated, an odd choice for a house with such sleek and modern design.

I cross to the window, heart pounding, and lift the edge of the blind just enough to peek through— desperate for any clue about where Vince has taken me. Sunlight spills across the landscape, though the sky remains dull—clouds hanging heavy, a vast difference to the Californian sunshine that greeted me yesterday.

I scan my surroundings. I'm at least one story high. Escape this way would mean risking a broken limb—or worse. Below is a courtyard, edged by walls that open onto a perfectly manicured garden. Trees line the perimeter and stretch as far as the eye can see. The rhythmic crash of waves hums nearby, if nothing else I know that I'm somewhere near the coast. I scan the horizon for something, any beacon of hope—but there's only an endless expanse of nature.

There's a lone tray on the dressing table. An unappetizing sandwich sits on a paper plate, its corners curling at the edges where it's been left uncovered. No cutlery, nothing I could use as a weapon. I'm not hungry, but even if I were, I wouldn't touch it. I've been drugged twice already—I can't risk the food being tampered with. The bottled water beside it looks untouched, the seal appears intact, but I can't be sure. Dehydration feels like the safer gamble. If desperation strikes, I'll take my chances with the tap water in the bathroom.

I open the wardrobe, hoping to find something useful. Inside, I find only a pair of folded towels and a few cheap, plastic coathangers hanging empty. I shut the door with a hollow thud. Like I'm going to shower or bathe here, in this place where anyone could walk in—or worse, where hidden cameras might be watching my every move.

I sink onto the edge of the mattress, cradling my pounding head in my hands. My fingers rake through my hair, only to snag on something. I untangle myself and stare at the offending object: the breathtaking ring Josh gave me. Tears blur my vision as thoughts of him flood my mind. Tina must have raised the alarm by now. Josh—my beautiful protector—will be going out of his mind with worry, torturing himself for not being there when I needed him most.

The thought of his suffering ignites something deep within me. Fear twists into anger, then hardens into unshakable determination. I don't know how I'll reach him—or how I'll even escape this room—but I know one thing for sure: I have to try. Vince stole thirteen years of my life, forcing me to live in fear of my own shadow. But now that I've had a taste of what I've been missing, I won't let him take another second. One way or another, I'll either find a way to set myself free, or die trying. If Vince wants a fight, this time, he'll get one. I just need to make sure I'm ready.

Chapter 20

Josh

I'm on the final leg of my flight when the satellite phone rings. My pulse quickens; Axel chartered this jet at the last minute, so I know the call must be serious. The aircrafts network's unfamiliar, and he's as aware as I am that transmissions like this can be intercepted. We agreed to radio silence until I was safely on the ground—unless there was an emergency.

I brace myself as I answer with a sharp, "Stone," prepared to decode whatever cryptic message I'm about to receive.

"Josh." Relief floods through me as I recognize Mac's voice. But the slight strain I hear makes me tense. I presume Maeve's back and wondering where I am. I'm guessing Mac's calling to ask me what she should tell her. When I shot out of Jared's apartment earlier after speaking to Axel, I told the guys it was a work emergency—nothing unusual for them, given the nature of my job. Disappearing without explanation is something they've come to expect.

However, Maeve doesn't know the full extent of what I do. I curse myself for keeping her in the dark. If one of the guys let anything slip, she'd likely be furious she got the information second hand. I should've come clean before now—but hindsight is no help when you're flying thousands of feet above the ground.

"How mad is she?" I ask, eager to hear Maeve's voice, even if she's about to rip me a new one. She's the spark that'll ignite the courage I'll need to face whatever horrors lie ahead.

"You need to come back." Mac's trembling voice cuts through the noise of the jet engines—things must be worse than I thought.

"I can't. Not right now. Put her on. Let me speak to her to explain." My jaw tightens, my tone urgent.

"I can't." Her sob cracks across the line like a whip. "I tried to find her. I really did."

The words slam into me like a physical blow. I struggle to focus, gripping both the phone and the armrest of my seat as if the force could anchor me. "What do you mean? She's run off?" I ask, clinging to a shred of hope, though the dread pooling in my gut warns me there's a darker truth.

"She was taken." Mac's voice fractures again, trembling with guilt. "Josh, I'm so sorry. I never should have left her." Her frantic, uneven breaths hitch as she continues, "We were getting ready to come home. Ava and I were waiting in the car while she went to the restroom with Tina. Tina was just in time to see her being dragged out back by someone she thought she recognised—someone called Vince. We alerted security, and they tried to go after her, but she was already gone. They called the police, and Tina gave them a description, but since they haven't got much to go on, they don't seem to be any closer to finding her."

Rage suddenly consumes me, a blistering heat, a white-hot fury clouding my vision. Adrenaline surges, propelling me to my feet. I pace the narrow aisle, the lava in my veins colliding with the altitude, turning my world unsteady. Dizziness slams into me like a freight train. I press a hand to the wall, forcing myself to breathe, grounding myself as I squeeze my eyes shut. When I do I see Maeve's face, frightened and alone. Her words from the restaurant all that time ago come back to haunt me: 'Vince... He said he was coming to get me; he and his brother wanted to 'have fun' with me.' I swallow the bile that rises in the back of my throat. If he touches her. It'll be the last thing he ever does.

"Put Tina on," I growl, trying to keep the fear and anger out of my voice.

"Josh, I'm sorry," Mac sobs again, her voice shaky.

"It's okay. It's not your fault—it's mine." I rub my temples, the weight of guilt settling like lead on my chest. As I say the words, I mean them. I let my guard down. I got so caught up in my feelings that I forgot all about Jimmy's warning and the real reason Maeve and I were together. But there's no time to dwell on that now. I need to act fast. "Please, Mac. Put Tina on the line," I ask, softening my tone.

"Okay," she whispers, her protests weak. "But she's really upset. I've already told you everything she knows."

"Please, Mac. It's important." I wait, impatience gnawing at me as Mac hands the phone over. I take a deep breath, forcing myself to sound calm and in control.

"Vince has her," Tina cries, her voice breaking. Before I can respond, she bombards me with questions. "What does he want? Why was he even there? We haven't seen him in years! I couldn't get to her—I tried, I really did. What does he want?" Her words tumble out in a frantic rush, the same question repeating like a desperate mantra.

I grip the phone so tightly my knuckles turn white. The rage inside me escalates, threatening to spill over, but I can't lose control—not now.

"Tina, it's okay." I soothe as best I can. "I'll find her. But I need your help—and Maeve needs it even more. I need you to calm down and tell me exactly what happened."

There're a few sniffles then Tina repeats verbatim what I had already been told by Mac. Nothing of any value except for the time it all happened: just after one a.m.

"Tina, I really need you to focus. Close your eyes and take a deep breath. Block out everything except the moment you first realised Maeve was in trouble. I want you to describe what you saw in as much detail as possible. Can you do that... for Maeve?"

A whimper escapes, followed by the sound of a deep, shaky breath. "I walked out into the corridor and I heard a scuffle..."

"Good girl," I prompt, "go on."

"I looked to see what was going on and that's when I saw her... Maeve, she looked terrified."

"Describe the scene to me," I encourage her along.

"Vince had one arm clamped around Maeve's waist. He was dragging her backward, toward the fire escape at the rear of the building."

"Was he alone? Did Maeve scream, try to draw attention to what was happening?"

"I didn't see anyone else. She couldn't, Vince had his hand over her mouth and nose. Maeve was clawing at his arm, like she couldn't breathe."

"What was he wearing? Did you hear him say anything?"

"I don't remember. It was dark and he sort of blended into the shadows, so whatever he was wearing must have been dark too, right? He didn't speak, he just sort of gave me a creepy smile. There was a funny smell though."

"What kind of smell?"

"I don't know, it was sweet, but it had a sharp, chemical edge."

"Okay, go on. What happened when he dragged her through the back door? Did any alarms go off?"

"No, no alarms,"

"Could you see anything past the door?"

"It opened onto an ally. There were some large commercial bins. I remember because Maeve tried to kick one as she was being hauled outside."

"Tried to?"

"Her movements were slow and... weak. Like she

was giving up."

"Was the alley narrow or wide."

"Wide."

"How do you know?"

"There was a car parked out back."

"What sort of car?"

"I'm not sure."

"What colour was it?"

"Black."

"Small or large."

"Medium. That's all I saw before Vince slammed the door in my face."

"You're doing great Tina. What happened next?"

"I tried to open the door, but it was stiff and heavy. By the time I'd got it open they'd gone."

"Gone where? Where could they go?"

"I don't know." I looked around but they'd vanished. There was no where for them to hide, I couldn't understand it."

"What about the car Tina, was it still there?"

"No. It was driving away."

"But there was only one person inside."

"How do you know?"

"I could just see the driver."

"As you came out of the club which way did it go?"

"Left, then it turned right onto the main road."

"Did you notice anything else? The licence plate, did it have anything in the windows?"

"Do you think Maeve was in the car?" Tina's voice rises, panic overtaking her words.

"Tell me about the car Tina." I say as calmly as I

can.

A heavy silence lingers before Tina speaks again.

"It was a Toyota Corolla—I recognised the emblem."

"Are you sure?"

"Positive. My family owns a garage, remember?" She adds, a hint of defiance in her voice."

I manage a brief chuckle at her insolent tone, despite the gravity of the situation.

"Anything else? The plates? Any distinguishing marks or stickers?"

"I didn't catch the number, but I'm sure they were Nevada plates, and I can't be sure but I think there was some sort of sticker in one of the rear windows."

"What sort of sticker?"

"I'm not sure. It wasn't a picture—just a set of stripes. Small, and I only saw it for a moment."

"That's great Tina. Is there anything else you remember?"

"No... I don't think so," She sighs despondently. "Did I help?"

"More than you realise, Tina. You've been a huge help. Can you pass the phone back to Mac?"

"Hi," Mac's worried voice comes back on the line. "Jackson and the others want to know if there's anything they can do to help? Josh what are we going to do?"

"There is something you can all do for me," I know they won't all want to be sat around twiddling their thumbs while they're waiting for news, but there is no way I'm putting any of them in Tony or Vince's line of fire.

"Name it," Mac sounds relieved, grateful to be able to help.

"Did Maeve tell you everything you'd need to pull off her dream wedding?"

"I think so," she sounds baffled.

"Then that's what I need you to do. Keep up the illusion that it's business as normal."

"But…"

"No buts. Maeve and I are getting married in six days. I'll find the bride. I need you to handle everything else, set it all up while I'm gone. Can you do that?"

"I guess. Are you sure? I mean…" Her voice trails off but she doesn't need to finish.

"I'll find her Mac. And bring her home. I just want you to be ready for when I do."

"If you're sure," she confirms hesitantly.

"There's one more thing. I promised my queen we could go for ice-cream. Tell her I'm on a secret mission, and Maeve needs her help. Ask her to look after Tiny and Derek until I bring her home."

"Will do," she whispers. "Josh," she calls just as I'm about to hang up,"

"Yeah?"

"Be careful."

As the line disconnects, the dam breaks. The incandescent rage, the frustration, the fear—all surge forward at once. I yell, a guttural release of everything I've been holding back, stomping through the cabin with such ferocity I'm sure the pilot must feel the plane shudder under the force.

I splash water over my face in the restroom before meeting my own gaze in the mirror, resolve tightening in my chest. Kurt. Maeve. My team. They're all counting on me. There's no room for doubt. It's time to focus, to remember my training, and to come up with the plan that can save two of the most important people in my life, even if they are almost three thousand miles apart.

Judging by Foxy and Ace's tense expressions, the anger radiating off me is still palpable as I barely wait for the plane to stop before flinging the door open and jogging down the steps toward them. Foxy leans casually against a car, biting into an apple. He tosses it away the moment he spots me, swiftly opening the front passenger door of a sleek black SUV for me to slide in. He climbs into the backseat without a word. Ace slouches behind the wheel, his attention elsewhere. But the moment I approach, he sits bolt upright, fires up the engine, and prepares to peel out of the lot. Once I'm seated, I message Axel to phone me on a secure line. Buckling my seat belt, I glance at Ace, who greets me with a curt, "Boss," before accelerating away. He looks like he's about to speak again when my phone rings. I silence him with a raised finger and answer the call.

"Boss!" Axel barks, his tone sharp, ready for

instructions.

"Maeve was taken by Vince Castillo last night." My words hang heavy in the air, and I feel the shift in everyone's demeanour—their attention snapping to me as I continue. "She was abducted sometime after 1 a.m. from a club in West Hollywood. I'm sending you the GPS coordinates now." I pause briefly to send the information.

"It's an exclusive venue. Vince was already inside, and when he pulled her out through the fire escape at the rear, the alarms were never triggered. I believe he used a drug to subdue her—chloroform, judging by the description. There was a black Toyota Corolla with Nevada plates waiting out back. It vanished at the same time they did. The car had a black sticker in the rear window, likely a barcode rental companies use to track inventory.

My guess? Vince flew into Vegas to throw off anyone watching him, rented a car, and drove to California with one purpose in mind: to take Maeve. He knew where she was, the exact moment to strike, and he was let into the club carrying whatever drug he used to control her. That means he had help.

The car sped down the alley behind the club before turning east onto the main road. The friends Maeve was with alerted security the moment they realised what happened, and now the police are involved. You need to stay ahead of them."

My voice drops, low and commanding. "I don't care what it takes. Find them—whatever it costs. And send someone to the club. I want to know who helped Vince.

We need to act fast. Tony won't want to draw attention to himself with his next shipment so close. I believe that means Kurt is still alive—likely being held as leverage to keep Jimmy quiet and lure him out of hiding. When Tony finds out Vince has Maeve, Kurt will become expendable. But the tension between the brothers means Tony won't make any rash moves until he's in full control of the situation. I glance at my watch. "It's half five. Too risky for me to move in for Kurt before tonight. I need time to brief the team and prepare. I'll need a bargaining chip to ensure Kurt's safety until then."

Axel's voice crackles on the other end of the line, sharp and inquisitive. "What do you have in mind?"

"Get me Derek Dawson," I growl, my tone dark and ominous. "Whether they're united or divided, the Castillo boys can't move their merchandise without Douglas. Let's send him a message—one large enough for him to keep both men in check. Douglas won't risk sacrificing his own son to call our bluff. But even if he does, Derek's the one disguising the origin of everyone's funds to make them look legit. Without him, this carefully constructed empire will start to crumble."

"How am I supposed to get to Derek? Ace is with you in Maine. If he leaves now, even with little to no traffic, it'll take him nearly four hours to make it back to Vermont," Axel points out, his voice clipped.

"There's a faster option. We already have eyes up there," I reply evenly.

"Boss," Ace interrupts, concern lacing his tone as he takes his eyes off the road briefly to glance at me. He knows exactly where I'm going—as do the others.

Before Axel can voice further objections, I cut him off. "We don't have a choice. We need to use the rookies. I've read their jackets—they're both more than capable."

"What if they're not willing?" Axel grumbles, his irritation clear.

"Talk to them," I instruct firmly. "Make sure they understand the gravity of the situation. If they're uncomfortable, tell them they can walk away, no hard feelings. But the reality is, this is the kind of job we face on a regular basis. If it's not for them, it's better we know now.

Essentially, we only need to create the illusion that we've got Derek and then keep him from contacting the others to set them straight. Andrea has access to the drugs at the clinic, there's bound to be something that can be used to knock him out long enough to stage a few incriminating photos. After that, they just need to keep him out of the way for a few hours. I'll leave it to them to decide how they want to handle the situation, but make sure they know we've got their backs. Call me back within the hour."

After I disconnect, the mood in the car lightens slightly.

"You really think Kurt's still alive?" Foxy whispers from the back seat, his voice tinged with hope. "He took one hell of a beating... for Blake and me."

"I do." My tone is firm, leaving no room for doubt. "Kurt knew exactly what he was doing. He saw you were outnumbered.

Telling Tony he was alone and searching for Jimmy wasn't just part of a ruse to help you and Blake escape—it was strategic. Yes, it ensured you got out so we could get the intel we needed, but it served another purpose too. By admitting Jimmy had been in touch, Kurt gave Tony a reason to keep him alive.

Tony won't rest until he knows exactly what Jimmy told Kurt—about his operation and who else might be in the loop. And if Tony thinks they're still in contact, he knows Jimmy will come looking when Kurt goes silent.

Tony won't kill Kurt. Not yet. He'll use him as bait.

You know how stubborn Kurt can be. He won't break easily—especially knowing you got away. He'll hold out for us to go in and get him."

I fix my gaze on the road ahead. "Even so, I don't want him in there longer than necessary. Tony has a nasty streak. Kurt won't have an easy time in there.

That's why I need the girls to deliver on Derek. If they do, we can use him to take the heat off Kurt and buy ourselves time to prepare.

Once we meet up with the others, I'll go over the plan."

"I hope you're right," Ace murmurs beside me.

"I am," I say resolutely.

"How can you be so sure?" Foxy asks, almost hopeful.

"Because he did exactly what I would have done," I whisper back.

Forty-five minutes later, I get a text from Axel: *The girls are on board. Be in touch when there's more to say.*

An hour after that, I'm holed up in a motel room in Brunswick, having just imparted my plan to extract Kurt to the team. Nico has already left to fill Bear in on what's happening—he's still watching Tony's place for any developments—Foxy and Blake are about to head out to source some specialist supplies, and Ace and I are finishing off the last of a pizza when a series of alerts flash across my cell screen.

Everyone stops, turning as I open Axel's messages. There are four pictures of Derek Dawson. He doesn't look pretty. My eyes widen in shock. I tilt my phone, showing the photos to the men surrounding me. They react just as I did—stunned. I immediately call Axel.

"What the hell did they do to him?" I bark.

"Nothing," Axel chuckles.

"Doesn't look like nothing to me," I growl.

"That's what I said," Axel chuckles again. "And do you know what they said?"

"Go on," I prompt impatiently.

"That's supposed to be the point, isn't it." Axel mimics the tone of an indignant woman.

I feel my lips quirk before I can control them. "Tell me what happened."

"You know how he stops for coffee every morning at the café opposite Maeve's surgery?"

"Yup."

"Well, Andrea happened to bump into him and must have accidentally spilled some of the medication she was carrying into his drink. She had to rush back to work, not realising that after he left the café, Derek took ill. Thankfully, Chloe happened to be passing by and offered to drive him home. She just got him inside and up to the bedroom when he passed out."

"Fancy that," I joke seriously.

"Anyway, while he was having a nap, someone— I'm not sure who, probably his girlfriend..."

"Probably," I agree.

"Hogtied and gagged him before using her previous skills as a makeup artist to create those rather artistic-looking photos. After she'd had her fun, she cleaned him up again, leaving him tied to the bed so when he wakes up, he'll believe he had the best time of his life but just can't remember it. I'm sure when he wakes up in a couple of hours, he'll want to call someone to tell them all about it. But if he does manage to get free, I bet he'll find his landline disconnected and his mobile missing. In his confused state, he must have hidden his cell and any keys lying around in the garbage out back."

"What about the secretary he's actually plonking? Any chance she might pop round?"

"She might. Although, when she left for work this morning, she noticed she must have driven over some nails or something the night before—her car had a puncture in all four tyres. She called and left a message on the work voicemail saying she'd be in late. Needs to wait for the local garage to pop round and fix the problem. Rumour has it, you know the family that owns the garage…"

"I do. Maeve's best friend Tina—her family runs the garage. I'm well acquainted with her brother Liam; he handles most of the breakdowns. Let me guess—you want me to give him a call and persuade him to take his time."

"It'd be appreciated. Chloe will be keeping an eye on Derek's place to run any interference if needed, but Andrea has to be at the clinic to help Aiden and keep him from getting suspicious. We could use another set of eyes."

"Consider it done." I let out a long breath, finally allowing myself a chuckle. "Tell the girls—outstanding work. However this plays out, they've got a guaranteed job at the firm when this is over. If they want it, of course."

"Gotcha."

"Any leads on Maeve?" My heart twists, but I won't let my emotions take control—I won't be any good to her if I lose focus now.

"Not yet. She was bundled onto a private jet, no flight plan filed. I'm pulling out all the stops to figure out where they took her. But there's one thing that's bothering me—where Vince was getting his information. He paid off a bouncer at the club to let him in and switch off the alarms, but that doesn't explain how he knew she would be there that night. The bouncer swears Vince approached him that morning, only a few hours after Jackson Longe had booked the venue."

"Keep on it. Let me know the second you have anything. In the meantime, get the number for Douglas Dawson. Send him the pictures you sent me—with a warning that we have his son and are willing to make a trade. That we'll be in touch. Make sure the number you use is untraceable."

"Who are we trading for—Kurt or Maeve?"

"Leave the message ambiguous. We don't know yet if Tony is aware Vince has Maeve, and Tony captured Kurt after Vince left for Vegas so he may be in the dark about that. With the fractured trust between the brothers, they'll both be playing their cards close to their chests. I'd say Douglas will be hedging his bets, waiting to side with whoever comes out on top. He'll have a foot in both camps, and we'll use that to our advantage. If he doesn't know which brother we're targeting, he'll have no option but to speak to them both—that should keep both Kurt and Maeve safe for now. Let me know when it's done."

I disconnect, and everyone except Ace leaves.

"Seems you did a good job with the new recruits," I tell him when we're alone—credit where credit's due.

"Appreciate it, boss. Just doing my part to uphold Kurt's legacy."

The mood turns sombre as our thoughts shift to his mentor and his current predicament. As my mind cycles through recent events, along with the plan I just laid out to the crew, some of Axel's words begin to weigh heavily on me.

Ace is more like Kurt than either of them would ever admit. In the absence of my best friend, I need the insight of someone just like him. "If my hunch is right, and Vince flew to Vegas for one reason—to hire a car so he could drive down and take Maeve. It means he must have known not just that I took her to California, but exactly when and where she'd be at her most vulnerable. He wasn't guessing. He knew enough to plan ahead. He made sure someone at the club was ready to help him. And why take a flight to a neighbouring state— it's like he knew he was being tailed. What's your gut telling you about that?"

"You won't like it." Ace leans forward, resting his forearms on his knees, pinning me with a hard, disgruntled stare.

I tilt my head in response, urging him to spill whatever's on his mind.

"I'd say it sounds like we have a traitor within our own ranks."

"That's exactly what I was afraid you'd say." I growl. "And if that's the case, then Tony walking in on Kurt and Foxy—that might not have been an accident either."

Ace exhales sharply, his jaw locking, eyes flashing with fury. "What are you saying?" He demands, voice tight with barely contained rage. I meet his gaze, my voice steady. "I've got a feeling we're being played. And if we are, we're about to walk straight into a trap."

Chapter 21

Maeve

There are only two ways out of this room that I can find. The door and the window. I'm not brave, nor am I stupid. Vince may want to harm me but I'm not going to risk greater injury by throwing myself out of a first floor window without the aid of a net. That leaves the door. I initially thought the fact it was an old style lock and key might help me. I've seen the movies where the key is forced out of the lock so it's drops onto a piece of paper that's slid under the door so the captive can set themselves free. That won't work here. For one, despite triple checking the room there is nothing I can slide under the door to catch the key when it falls. For two, the carpet on the other side of the door appears too plush. It fits snugly up against the base of the door preventing anything from sliding beneath it easily. The door appears to be really heavy duty. Solid wood. Josh might be able to force his way through but the reality is I don't stand a chance. I need to get Vince to open the door. That way I can just stroll right through it. I just need to figure out a way to make that happen.

I'm still sitting on the end of the bed, staring at the door, trying to figure out my next move—when the sound of the key turning in the lock makes me snap to attention.

Fear makes me instinctively shuffle further back up the bed as the door swings open and a face I wasn't expecting comes into view. The lecherous look he gives me chills me to the bone.

"You're awake." Tony Castillo leans on the door jamb, letting his eyes rake over my body. I grab the comforter from the bed, pulling it over myself like a shield. He enters the room closing the door behind him before approaching the end of the bed and making a grab for my foot. I try to kick him away, but he's too quick. His strong hands capture both my ankles, dragging me down the bed towards him. "Long time no see, Maeve Mercer," he drawls. "Welcome to my home." I can feel my breaths coming in short sharp bursts as he goes on. "Imagine my surprise when Douglas told me you were getting engaged to his son. I'm not surprised you dumped him. He wasn't man enough for a woman like you." He slides his hands to my thighs, pinning them down, almost painfully, like he knows my legs will lash out at him the first chance they get.

"Y... you know Derek's father?" I stumble over the words.

He grins almost manically. "Let's not waste time talking about him right now. I'm much more interested in hearing how you plan to repay my kind hospitality for putting you up right now."

His words make me balk and he can tell, anger flashes in his eyes as he releases one thigh to be able to grip my jaw. Bearing down on me he spits, "You always did think you were too good for me and my little brother. Well, I'm about to show you you're not." He releases my jaw and starts tearing at his clothes. That's when I finally find my voice and let out a blood-curdling scream. It startles him enough for me to draw my free leg back and kick him hard in the groin. As he stumbles back in pain, I seize my chance, dashing for the door. I pray I can reach it first, locking him inside to buy myself precious time to escape. As I fling the door open, my heart sinks as I run straight into the arms of Vince, obviously alerted by my screams and coming to see what the fuss was all about. I barely have time to register Vince's grip on my arm before he yanks me back inside, throwing me to one side like a used rag. Instinctively, I brace myself for the backlash, expecting him to round on me—but his glare isn't aimed in my direction.

"What the fuck are you doing in here?" Vince growls, his voice low and dangerous. "I told you she was mine."

Tony straightens, unfazed, his lips curling into a slow, taunting grin. "Relax, brother. I was just going to welcome our guest properly." He gestures lazily toward me, as if I'm nothing more than a toy that's fair game.

My stomach twists, but I force myself to remain still, watching. Vince's fists clench, his entire body wound tight like a predator about to pounce.

"You think this is a joke?" Vince steps closer, towering over Tony now, his face dark with rage. "While I was locked up, you were playing king. Having whatever you wanted, living the high life. And now you think you get to have her too, after I risked everything to get her here."

Tony sighs, shaking his head in amusement. "Oh, Vince. You always let your emotions get the best of you. Face it, brother—you'll always be chasing my scraps while I feast at the table. Unlike you, I don't beg for what I want—I just take it."

I catch a subtle shift in Tony's stance—a readiness, a taunt just begging for Vince to lose control. And he does.

Vince's eyes go crazy just before he launches himself at his brother, punching Tony hard enough in the stomach to make him double over in pain. Recovering quickly, Tony slams Vince backward into the doorframe, their scuffle spilling into the hallway. Voices rise, curses fly, the tension morphing into outright hostility.

I act instantly, removing the key from the outside of the door, silently pushing it closed before locking myself inside. If they're so intent on fighting each other, maybe—just maybe—I can turn their rivalry into my salvation somehow. At least this way I've bought myself some time in case the victor decides to return. I press myself against the door, trying to hear what's going on above the sound of my shallow breaths.

The low hum of angry voices outside tells me Vince currently has the upper hand. I'm not surprised—he's leaner and fitter than Tony, who has the softer physique of a man with a hearty appetite and little to no discipline.

"You really think you can waltz in here and take whatever you want?" Vince growls, his fury barely contained. "You've been living the good life while I was rotting away—and it shows. Lounging in luxury has made you weak, brother. I had nothing else to keep me occupied but pushing my body to its limits every day, proving to people like you just how strong I am. I wouldn't recommend underestimating what I'm capable of—or what I'll do to make sure what's mine stays that way. If you think you can have Maeve, think again. For once in your life, you don't get to take what you want—not from me. She's mine, until I decide otherwise, and you'd be wise not to forget that."

Mine?" Tony laughs, the sound dripping with mockery. "You sound pathetic. You were never on my level, brother. While you were locked in a cage, I was building something real—making something of myself. I don't lose, Vince. I take what I want, and nobody—not even you—can stop me."

My stomach twists as the fight escalates—their voices sharp, venomous. A crash echoes through the hall as one of them slams the other against the wall. I hear a grunt of pain, the scuffle of shoes on carpet, and then the sound of a fist slamming into something—or someone.

Suddenly, a phone buzzes, interrupting the foray. "Wait!" Tony demands a pause in the conflict. "It's Douglas."

Silence follows.

"What?" Vince barks, short-tempered and impatient. "Let's finish this."

There's a guttural sigh, weighted with frustration, then another pause—long enough to build unease—before Tony curses under his breath.

Their voices lower, urgent and tense. It's clear something's happened—something that demands their immediate attention. I strain to hear, but the details slip away as their footsteps hurriedly retreat down the hall, their anger suddenly united and redirected.

I wait, holding my breath. One second. Two. They forgot to check the door. They never noticed I locked it from the inside. My heart pounds as the realisation hits—this is it. What might be my only chance to escape.

Slowly, carefully, I ease the door open, checking the coast is clear before slipping into the main body of the house. I relock the door behind me and take the key. If one brother returns, they may assume the other took it in an act of defiance. It doesn't matter what they think. If I can keep them out for as long as possible, it'll buy me precious time. I have no idea what waits for me beyond this point—but one thing is certain.

I'm not staying.

I move cautiously through the dimly lit house,

my steps light, my breaths so shallow I'm barely aware of them. Every creak of the floorboards feels deafening, every shadow a potential threat. My nerves are frayed, my heart's pounding so hard I'm afraid I'll pass out. I cling to walls and peer round corners. The stairs are the hardest to navigate, they're too open, too exposed, making a single wrong move a disaster. I creep down, then at the base, voices drift from a nearby room—low, muttered. I recognise one of them instantly. Vince. The sound sends a chill snaking down my spine.

I freeze as footsteps echo a few feet away, growing in intensity on the wooden floor as they near. My heart's hammering so hard I fear the sound will give me away. I duck behind a large plant pot beside a hefty wooden cabinet, pressing myself deep into the shadows. The footsteps pause and I hold my breath, not daring to move.

When they continue down the hall, I heave a sigh of relief, steadying myself. That was too close. I can see the front door but my heart sinks when through the glass, shadowy figures stand talking outside.

Scanning the space, my eyes land on something familiar—a small table tucked against the wall, cluttered with miscellaneous items. And there, half-spilling over the edge, is my bag. I thought it was lost. My pulse spikes when I remember my phone, daring to hope it may still be tucked inside.

Carefully, I ease forward, only to dart back into hiding as yet another set of footsteps interrupts me. On my second attempt, my trembling fingers manage to reach inside, landing on the familiar shape—the device cold against my skin. I gently pull it free, leaving the bag exactly as it was.

As I do, the photo I stashed there slides out, fluttering to the floor and landing face down. My breath catches as I pick it up, my eyes drawn to the inscription on the back. The deep, swirling handwriting is unmistakable now. It matches the writing in the Valentine's cards I'd recently seen. It *was* Josh who left it at the hospital, a quiet plea for me to never forget him.

The realisation makes me smile, a flicker of warmth cutting through the tension. Even more determined now, I snatch the photo up and, with nowhere else to put it, tuck it into my bra, keeping it close to my heart.

Retreating back into the shadows, I search for a hiding spot. There's a small alcove near the staircase and beyond it a door. I dash across the hall and into the recess. I'm still afraid I'll be heard if I try to make a call so gingerly open the door. There are a set of steps leading down to a basement. It's too dark to see much beyond that, but its eerie calmness makes me thinks its deserted. I hide behind the door, pulling it to. Remaining alert, I leave a small gap to peek through, pressing the phone to my ear. It bleeps and I check the screen to see the battery indicator flashing red. It's low. Too low. I'm not sure if there is even enough charge to make one call. In that second, it doesn't even occur to me to call the police. There's only one person on my mind. I have to end his suffering and let him know that I'm okay.

I scroll down my contacts until I see the entry he saved and smile at the title he amended the same night he proposed, my smile fading as I remember it was the same night I was taken. I hit the name— reminiscent of the words he wrote in my Valentine's cards all those years ago. *Your secret admirer- not Kurt,* followed by a heart emoji and a cheeky artichoke. A bittersweet reminder of the night we have yet to share.

It rings. Once. Twice. Three times. I pray the phones battery lasts long enough for him to answer. When I hear the connection, I don't wait, "Josh?" My voice is barely a whisper.

"Maeve?" His response is instant, filled with relief and panic all at once. "Jesus, baby, are you okay?"

"I'm okay..." I start but stop myself as the tears threaten to fall. "But Tony Castillo. He..."

"Tony?" He snaps interrupting. "Don't you mean Vince?"

"No Tony..." I try again, but he stops me once more.

"Are you sure?" His tone shifts—urgent, calculating.

"Of course I'm sure," I snap in frustration before the words that unwittingly seal Tony's fate slip out. "I looked him straight in the eye before he started groping me."

There's a moment of deadly silence before my phone beeps urgently, letting me know I'm almost out of time. "Josh, I don't have much time, my phones dying…"

"I'm close, baby." Josh's voice steadies, firm now. "Closer than you think. I'm coming to get you. Don't try to escape. They'll see you if you try to leave. Find somewhere safe to hide. Wait there. I'll find you."

Then—silence.

The phone finally dies in my grip.

My pulse thunders in my ears. I'm alone again. But he's coming. He's close. Hope blooms in my chest. He must know where I am—how? The plane I was bundled on, did it never actually leave? Was it all an elaborate illusion? But why? My mind goes into overdrive as I try to make sense of everything. One thought churns over and over, relentlessly. He's coming. All I need to do is find somewhere safe to keep hidden until he arrives. My knight. My protector. My all.

Through the crack in the door, I see more people passing by. To risk heading back into the open would be foolish. I turn and look at the steep steps dropping into the depths below. Maybe my best chance lies down there. With no time to hesitate, I count the steps before softly closing the door and throwing myself into utter blackness. I step carefully, counting each one as I descend into the unknown.

The darkness is suffocating. I shuffle forward, hands tracing the rough texture of the wall as I inch forward. Each step a risk.

Finally—I hit something with a sudden bump.

I jolt back, my heart hammering. It's another wall.

A dead end? No—the surface is smoother; there's a handle, it must be a door. With trembling fingers, I grip the cool metal and twist. It gives way. I push it open, expecting resistance—but there's none.

It's still pitch black and my stomach tightens. Is the room empty? I freeze listening intently but there's only silence. I step forward cautiously, sliding my hand along the wall until my fingers ghost over the familiar shape of a light switch. I hesitate, wary. If someone's here... if they're asleep... if they're lying in wait...

But I can't stay in the dark. I take a deep breath and flick the switch on. Light floods the room causing me to blink rapidly, the sudden glare stabbing at my eyes. My breath catches in my throat as I fight to focus on my surroundings.

As my vision sharpens, I see I'm facing the wall, I turn slowly, dread pooling in my stomach.

The room is cold, the air heavy with the faint metallic tang of something long dried. If I didn't know better, I'd say it was blood. The fluorescent light flickers overhead, its erratic hum breaking the silence. Shadows stretch and distort across the walls, twisting into shapes that almost seem alive and reaching for me.

My breath catches again as I take in my surroundings. The walls are lined with hooks and chains, their surfaces scratched and stained, as though they've been used to hold something—or someone. A table sits in the corner, its surface cluttered with tools. Some are rusted, their edges jagged and cruel, while others gleam under the flickering light, sharp and ready. I recognise some of them—tools I've used in surgery to help animals—but here, they feel sinister, their purpose twisted.

The evidence is undeniable. Some of these tools have been used recently—clumsily cleaned in a beaker of liquid before being left to dry on a blood-stained sheet of sandpaper. My stomach twists violently, bile burning in my throat as I fight the urge to throw up.

Three identical, white, steel boxes draw my attention. Larger than any chest freezer I've ever seen, their surfaces are smooth, unmarked, and unnervingly pristine. Like they're new and haven't been in place long. I step in closer, my pulse quickening. Two of the boxes are locked, their metal loops secured by thick pins. The third, however, is unfastened. I hesitate, my fingers trembling as I reach for the lid. The silence presses down on me, the rush of blood in my ears, deafening. Slowly, I lift it. Despite its weight, the greased mechanism allows it to glide open with ease. I brace myself, afraid of what I might find.

It's empty. My relief is fleeting. The emptiness feels wrong—like it's a void waiting to be filled. I turn to the second box, it's a crude lock, not designed to keep people out. What if...What if it's designed to keep people in? As much as the thought terrifies me, I pull the pin free. The lid resists slightly before flipping back.

A body lies limp inside. My stomach lurches, bile

burning my throat. The man's face is distorted—wounds old and new carve cruel patterns across his skin. Deep purple bruises mingle with raw, angry lesions. He is barely recognisable, but even after so much time apart how could I fail to know my own brother.

"Jimmy," I sob. Swaying as the room starts tilting around me. He looks lifeless, barely clinging to existence, I press my shaking fingers to his throat offering the universe a silent prayer until I find it—A pulse. Faint. Thready. But nevertheless there. If I hadn't found him soon, he would have suffocated in that box. I have no idea how long he's been trapped inside, but I can't waste time thinking about it now. My panic kicks into overdrive as I rush to the third box, yanking the pin to flip the lid back.

"Kurt?" I cry, my hand flying to my mouth in shock. His still body is sprawled unnaturally in the confined space, his features as battered as Jimmy's. I check for a pulse. When I can't find one a strangled noise escapes my lips. He's too big for me to pull out. Without thinking I jump right in.

I fumble around, trying to position him as best I can to force air into his lungs. "Come on, Kurt. Please," I beg.

A second attempt.

A third.

I can't lose him. I won't!

Then—a jolt followed by a gasp and a groan.

Kurt's chest rises sharply, before his eyes snap open, their usual mischief struggling through the haze of near-death. He blinks, dazed, before his swollen lips curl into something terrifyingly familiar and rarely bestowed—a grin.

"You took your time." His voice is hoarse, but undeniably smug.

I let out a breathless, choked laugh—half-relief, half-exasperation—then the tears come.

Kurt smirks, blinking sluggishly. "I bet you've been waiting years to catch me unawares so you could throw yourself on top of me and steal a kiss."

I let out something between a sob and a curse, pressing a shaky hand to his chest. Just to make sure I can feel his heart beating and I'm not having some weird hallucinatory dream. "Shut up, Kurt. Just be grateful I decided to save your sorry ass." We smile at each other. The seriousness of the situation buried beneath the weight of a thousand silent thankyous.

His smile lightens the heaviness in my chest, even if just for a second.

I haul myself out of the box, my legs trembling, and lungs burning under the pressure of everything I've just witnessed. I turn, pulling at Kurt, helping him upright and bearing the weight of a man twice my size. He grimaces, and I notice one of his arms is bent at an unforgiving angle. It's definitely broken and the pain must be unbearable, but he says nothing.

Despite Jimmy being smaller, he's so much weaker and it makes him seem heavier. He's coming around, but barely conscious. Together, Kurt and I manage to lift him, easing him out onto the cold concrete. He stirs, giving the welcome flicker of life—but his body is too wrecked for anything more.

Kurt exhales sharply, leaning against the nearest wall, catching his breath before turning his gaze on me. "Not that I'm complaining, but what the hell are you doing here?"

"I could say the same to you," I reply, giving him the abridged version, letting him piece the rest together himself.

Kurt's expression hardens instantly. He straightens, rolling his injured shoulder with a wince—a sharp, sickening crack breaking the silence. His jaw tightens, his breath coming slow and measured.

"Jesus," he mutters under his breath. Then, he looks up. The smirk is gone. His features are set —cold and grim. "I'm sorry, Maeve. We got it all wrong."

I frown, not understanding. Kurt sees my bewilderment and presses on.

"Jimmy called us, said people were after him, made us promise to protect you. We thought he was in hiding. Turns out, he never got away like we thought. When he failed to meet us as planned, he knew we'd come looking—and he did what he had to do to stay alive."

Kurt's gaze drops to the floor, frustration flickering across his face.

"I don't follow."

"The idiots upstairs knew Jimmy, Josh and I were

all close when we were younger. So Jimmy made it seem like, after cleaning up his act, we reconnected. He convinced Tony and Vince he'd spoken to Josh and me about what they were up to—but never let on how much information he'd actually shared. Vince and Tony have been trying to lure us here ever since—to find out what we know and silence us."

"What are they up to?" I ask, my brain scrambling to keep up.

"Smuggling drugs." Kurt sighs, shaking his head. "Everything pointed to Vince, but it was Tony all along."

"Tony? Wait—what do you mean? I'm losing the thread here."

"Your brother's a good man, Maeve. He's been helping kids—the kind who might've gone down the wrong path, just like he did all those years ago. Giving them something real to focus on, a chance to turn their lives around.

He was making a difference—until Vince showed up, trying to pull him back into his world. Vince wanted Jimmy to recruit those vulnerable kids into dealers, expanding the Castillo brothers' distribution network.

At first, we assumed Vince was trying to edge Tony out. Turns out, it was Tony's idea all along. The man's merciless—he'll do whatever it takes and use whoever he can to get what he wants. Probably even his own brother, given half the chance. Honestly, I wouldn't be surprised if he was the real reason for Vince's most recent incarceration.

Tony likes being king. And he doesn't share his empire. Since Vince got out, he's been constantly undermining Tony, trying to knock him down a peg and disrupting his cushy life. I wouldn't be shocked if Tony's about to put a stop to it."

"Vince has been in prison?" I'm not sure why that revelation lands harder than anything else Kurt is saying.

He nods. "When Jimmy refused to put the kids at risk, the Castillo brothers didn't take it too well. Tony got Vince to start pulling the kids in anyway. Things got heated between Vince and Jimmy. Then Vince got put away, and Jimmy thought that was the end of it.

But when Vince got out, everything flared up again. Jimmy became a liability—one they needed to eliminate."

"And that's when he got picked up and dragged your names into the frame?"

"Exactly." Kurt's voice is tight, jaw clenched. "Jimmy was on his way to the authorities when Tony's goons started closing in. He called Josh because he knew—whatever happened—we'd keep you safe. That call saved his life.

Tony's men snatched him up just feet away from the local cop shop. They brought him here, where Tony planned to finish him off."

I flinch, and Kurt's voice softens.

"Just before Tony was about to—"

I flinch again, and Kurt skips the words I can't bear to hear.

"…Jimmy started goading Tony, telling him he'd called Josh. He said that no matter what happened to him, Tony was on borrowed time anyway.

The Castillo brothers decided to keep Jimmy alive, hoping to dig out how much information he'd given us. But when he wouldn't talk, they decided Josh and I had to go too."

I swallow hard. The box—the one that was empty when I found it. It *was* waiting to be filled.

"I'm bait." The words barely make it past my lips, the truth sinking like lead in my gut.

Kurt nods, his eyes darkening. "They figured we'd come looking for Jimmy, ready to bargain. So they've been lying in wait—ready to take us down.

But Jimmy lied. He only called us out of concern for you. So we took longer to appear than the Castillos expected. We needed time to piece together what was really happening."

I blink, trying to process everything, but the pieces keep twisting, shifting in ways I can't quite catch.

"Then, when I finally turned up, I was alone— without Josh. Tony and Vince have a delivery due, and they want everything tied up before it arrives. With both Jimmy and me unaccounted for, they know Josh won't risk going to the authorities. Not yet.

But they're getting nervous. And now, they're trying to force his hand and make him show—by taking you."

Kurt's frown deepens. "There's something not

sitting right. I understand why they want to lure Josh here—to take him down quickly and quietly, on their own terms. But from what you've said, something doesn't quite add up. How did Vince know *exactly* when and where to strike to grab you? Douglas Dawson is involved in all this; he must have told him you and Josh had reconnected after he learned you'd split with his son.

Finding out where you lived wouldn't have been hard for them. But Josh got you out of dodge—yet somehow, they still managed to track you down fast. Too fast. Then, the *one* moment you were out of his sight... Vince snatched you. It's too convenient. Too precise. Their reach might be even greater than we thought."

A chill tightens around my ribs, sharp and unforgiving, as Kurt pushes off the wall. He glances down at Jimmy, then back at me, his voice dropping and edged with pity, but not for us. "They have no idea the wheels they've just set in motion. They'd better be ready—because they've just made the worst mistake of their miserable lives."

Of everything Kurt has told me, one realisation cuts the deepest. I stare at him numbly. "Is that why Josh showed up at my door after all this time? So he could watch over me, keep me safe—because Jimmy asked him to? Has he been manipulating me all along? Pretending he wanted to be with me just so he could move me around at his will? Are you saying our relationship is nothing but a ruse? Is that why he wouldn't have sex with me?"

Kurt smiles, his surprise genuine. "You guys haven't done it yet?"

"He said he wanted to wait," I mutter. I try not to, but I can feel myself blush.

"Wait?" Kurt murmurs, like the concept is foreign to him, before he breaks into a mischievous grin. "No wonder you threw yourself on top of me trying to get some action," he says, smirking like he's just solved a mystery.

My look tells him he's clearly missing the point of our conversation.

He chuckles. "Maeve, that man's been in love with you for as long as I can remember. Why do you think I kept you at arm's length when you had a crush on me? It would've been more than my life's worth to make a move. Everyone could see how he felt about you. Everyone—except you! Jimmy may have been the catalyst in bringing you back together, but the last time I saw you, you weren't wearing a rock like that on your finger."

He steps forward, lifting my hand to show off the engagement ring. "Does that look like a ruse to you?"

"No," I admit, smiling softly. Then I add in a slightly harsher tone, "I'm still mad at him though, for not telling me what was going on. And you for that matter."

He smiles back—a real, gleeful thing, sharp with anticipation. "By taking you, Tony and Vince invited the kind of wrath they can't even begin to imagine. Josh isn't coming for Jimmy and me anymore. He isn't even coming just to save you." He exhales, shaking his head. "No. He's coming for absolution. The moment you let slip the real reason you barricaded yourself in your room the night of the fire, I knew the Castillo brothers were on borrowed time. No one messes with anyone Josh cares about... especially you... without being made to atone for their sins."

He pauses, gaze darkening.

"But now... now he'll be blaming himself for every bad deed they've gotten away with since that night—every crime, every horror. He'll believe, with absolute certainty, that if he had brought them to justice back then, none of this would be happening now."

His voice drops, grim and final.

"He's coming to make them pay. And when he does... there won't be anything left to salvage. Not their empire. Not their reputation. Not even the wreckage of what they used to be."

He exhales, just once.

"Trust me... it's not going to be pretty."

A knot tightens in my chest. "But if they're expecting him, he's walking into danger."

"True," Kurt grins again, something dark flickering in his expression. "But you're forgetting two vital pieces of information."

I tilt my head, searching his face, trying to piece together what I'm missing. He lets me linger in uncertainty for a few moments, then finally puts me out of my misery.

"One. If you think he'll be coming alone, you're

wrong. Josh has friends just like Tony. But unlike his, Josh's are highly skilled, lethal, and don't need to get paid to stand by his side. And two—he now has help on the inside. Tony and Vince don't know the pair of us are free."

Chapter 22

Josh

It's 3 a.m. The night is thick with damp air, carrying the sharp scent of dew. A lone owl screeches somewhere in the distance—a haunting cry that fades into the hushed rustle of the leaves around us.

We sit crouched in the undergrowth, waiting. Foxy will give the signal through our earpieces any moment now. Nico and Ace flank me, each positioned a few feet away, tense but composed. Blake is farther out, unseen, holding the perimeter, ready to strike when the timing is right. He has two assignments—one the team knows about, the other they'll find out about later, a personal request to settle an old score.

The air is heavy with anticipation—the kind that coils in a man's gut before the first bullet flies. Every breath is measured, every heartbeat synced to the silent countdown ticking in my head. The team is locked in, prepped for the assault.

All except one.

He thinks the mission was postponed by twenty-four hours. And if Maeve hadn't escaped and sent out that warning call, I might never have uncovered the traitor selling us out for a quick payday. That mistake would have cost us more than I care to think about, especially given the numbers stacked against us—we're outmatched at least five to one.

It's a problem for later. Right now, the people I care about are priority one. The double-crosser is over an hour away, chasing phantom supplies after swallowing a bogus story designed to get him off the grid. I couldn't risk him catching wind of our revised plan, so Ace and I made sure he wouldn't. The missing SIM card in his phone also guarantees he won't be calling anyone with information that could dismantle our op before it even starts.

Still, it burned when Ace voiced what had been gnawing at my gut—the realisation I'd been betrayed by one of my own. Betrayal has a way of hollowing you out, leaving nothing but the slow, sick churn of resentment in its wake. And this wasn't some ambiguous suspicion.

It wasn't hard to work out who had done it. There was only one person watching Tony's place during the timeframe Maeve could have arrived there, and he's far too good at his job to make the mistake of missing such a crucial development. Which means he didn't miss it. He withheld the information—deliberately. He also had all the necessary access to be able to track my movements, to monitor Maeve, so he could report back to whoever was greasing his palm. And that meant every step I'd taken, every choice I'd made had been under my enemy's watchful eye long before I realised it.

Only Ace and I know. If the others found out, there'd be blood in the water, and I can't afford anyone losing focus—not now. So I gave them a clean lie: he was reassigned. They didn't question it, though I saw the flicker of surprise in their eyes. They know this mission is personal. But they also know better than to challenge me on the fact we are now a vital resource down.

Tonight, we get the job done. Everything else—including outing false friends—can wait.

I close my eyes and picture Foxy hunched over his console, tucked away in the safety of an unmarked transit van, nestled just off the road. His fingers fly across the controls, his gaze flicking between feeds. The mansion looms on the screen—pristine, sprawling, a fortress built on blood money.

"Showtime," Foxy murmurs in our ears.

Six drones deploy in silent synchronization above our heads, taking off across the sky in sleek formation before peeling off in different directions. A few moments later smoke grenades rain down like rolling thunder, spilling thick plumes with ruthless precision. Perfectly timed to blind security cameras and cloak the true threat. Alarm klaxons wail. Fire suppression systems kick in. The illusion is flawless —an attack with no attackers.

Inside the mansion, confusion spreads like wildfire. Shadows spill from the building—mercenaries, armed and wired, rushing out to face an enemy that doesn't exist.

While they chase Foxy's ghosts, Nico, Ace, and I slip in through the front door—left ajar in the chaos. We move swiftly. Silent predators slipping through the cracks, firearms ready to meet any challengers head on.

As soon as we move Foxy barks "Now."

Outside, Blake kills the electrics. The sirens cut off, allowing us to listen for approaching threats. The lights die, plunging everything into darkness. Our black outfits blend seamlessly into the abyss. We're prepared for the blackout. In one fluid motion, we flip our night vision goggles down, the green hue sharpening the shadows into clarity. Now, we move with the advantage—silent spectres cutting effortlessly through a dark void designed to render our enemies blind.

Every footstep is deliberate. Every breath controlled. There's no time for wasted movement. As good as the distraction is, it won't last forever. Soon, the hired help will storm back, primed for battle. We can all feel how fast the clock is ticking.

I give three signals.

Nico stealthily takes the stairs, weapon steady, scanning each landing for movement. Ace and I split, sweeping the lower floor, stalking like panthers on the hunt. Using furniture for cover, we clear each room in synchronized silence. The house is eerily quiet, though the chaos outside still echoes through the walls.

In my peripheral vision, I see movement—a silhouette in the doorway. I swing, gun raised, finger tightening on the trigger—until I recognise Ace. He signals—a faint nod toward the footsteps rushing in my direction. A guard appears, rifle slung low. He sees me at the last second—but his shock stalls his reflexes. I don't hesitate. My blade flashes, slicing under his ribs in one smooth motion. He doesn't even register the threat. I ease his body down, silently dragging it into the shadows before the blood can start to pool. Ace and I press forward, circling back, confirming one vital fact—our targets aren't on the ground floor.

Back in the entrance hall, a body crashes at my feet with a sickening thud—hurled from the balcony above. Nico sprints down the stairs shortly after, gesturing sharply. "Not upstairs," he signals. The targets we're searching for aren't there either.

Shouts from outside confirm what I already know —we're running out of time. I signal retreat.

Nico and Ace exchange glances—then lock eyes with me, unwavering. They know I'm not leaving. And they're telling me neither are they. Annoyance flickers through me at their insubordination, but I push it aside, reluctantly acknowledging the surge of respect that follows. I'll let their refusal to follow orders slide—for now.

Scanning the area, I spot a door tucked into an alcove and signal that I'm going in. Ace and Nico flank me, retreating into the shadows as I ease the door open.

Two men surge forward, poised and ready— strategically hidden, lying in wait. The first in a line of defence that tells me I'm close.

Neither gets the chance to fire off a shot. Ace lunges, catching the first attacker off guard, dragging him into the shadows with a forearm pressed hard against his windpipe.

The second takes a swing at me—his mistake. I grab his wrist, twist hard, and drive an elbow into his throat. He crumples, unconscious, tumbling backward to land in a twisted heap at the foot of a steep staircase.

Foxy's voice crackles in our earpieces. "They're heading back. You've got seconds."

Serious trouble is heading our way. I signal for Ace and Nico to fall back. This time I'm prepared and pretend to follow. Only once I'm sure they've slipped through the downstairs window, vanishing into the night, do I turn back. Returning to the staircase, I start down, closing the door behind me to erase my trail as I push deeper into the mansion's depths. I remove my earpiece to focus on the sounds around me. I'm on my own now. Urgency and adrenaline merge, pounding through my veins. Maeve and Kurt must be here. Somewhere. I'm not leaving without them. I just have to find them and get us all free—before the house becomes a trap.

As I descend the final step and round a corner, the power surges back on. Bright light flares in my eyes. I rip off my goggles, recovering just in time to see the glint of metal hurtling toward me. Reflexes kick in. I capture the hand lunging toward me, twisting hard to snap at least one bone as I deflect the knife straight into my attacker's chest. He recoils, but comes at me again. This time he's weak and in shock. One swift, well-placed strike immobilises him before he can sound the alarm.

Behind him, another door looms—tall, heavy, waiting to reveal its secrets. I press my ear against its surface. I hear nothing but stillness.

Cautiously, I turn the handle, pushing the door open—ready for whatever comes next.

Vince and Tony Castillo stand in the middle of the room, flanked by eight goons. Their expressions drip with amusement—smug, certain, like they've already won. Like I've walked straight into their snare.

Tony chuckles, slow and deliberate, the sound grating like nails on glass. Vince leans forward, a smirk curling at the edge of his lips, his eyes gleaming with cruel satisfaction. Then, with a sneer, he starts to clap—slow, measured, each beat echoing through the space like the toll of a bell.

"I'm not afraid to admit it," he says, voice thick with mock admiration. "I'm impressed you made it this far."

The sight of their faces turns my blood to lava. My pulse hammers, but I keep my stance controlled, unreadable, as I take in the room. It's a concrete torture chamber—straps and chains fastened to the walls, three large white containers lined up along one side. Two are locked with metal pins, and my pulse spikes as I think about what—or who—could be lying inside.

"We've got your girl upstairs," Tony announces calmly, his tone laced with a veiled threat meant to keep me in check. "Drop your gun."

He doesn't know I'm reassured. If they think she is still upstairs she isn't locked in one of the boxes. They also can't know she escaped, so they only think they have power over me.

I quickly assess the situation. Surprisingly, none of my enemies are visibly armed. Either their weapons are concealed, or they believe threats and sheer numbers will be enough to subdue me. But I still need to find Kurt, so I let them think they have the advantage.

Calmly, I release the ammunition from my gun, ensuring it can't be used against me, then cast both items aside in different directions.

"She's a good-looking woman. When you're out of the way, I'm sure she'll be up for a little fun."

Tony's sleazy insinuations ignite something deep, raw, and uncontrollable.

I launch myself at him, but half his lackeys hustle to form an impenetrable shield while the rest scramble to take me down.

I come out fighting like an avalanche, destroying everything in my path.

The first strike sends a man flying against the wall.

The second shatters a jaw.

The third crushes ribs before the man even hits the floor.

The fourth slams a head into one of the white

metal boxes, breaking a nose and stunning its owner.

There's an unstoppable force tearing through me, a primal fury that only halts when the next four men unify their attack.

Hands grab, fists swing, bodies pile in—pressing against me like an unrelenting tide.

I snarl, thrash—fighting like a grizzly until they finally manage to overpower me, forcing me down on my knees, pining my arms to contain me.

"Do you want to have your fun now, brother?" Tony asks Vince casually, nodding toward the chains hanging ominously from the walls behind him.

"Later," Vince replies, his tone as nonchalant as if he were discussing tea. "I have a date waiting for me upstairs—it'd be rude to keep her waiting."

Tony chuckles, the sound low and menacing, before jerking his head toward the one metal box that isn't locked.

"Put him in there for now, boys," he says, his voice dripping with cruel amusement. "Let him relax. Give him time to let his imagination run wild."

Even though I know she isn't where they expect her to be, the thought of them going anywhere near Maeve ignites a fury like no other deep inside me. A roar escapes my lips—primal and uncontainable. I flex my muscles, pouring every ounce of strength into breaking free. The men holding me falter for a split second, their grip loosening—but not quite enough.

I can sense their fear, like a lion catching the

trembling heartbeat of its prey.

They flip the lid, expecting the box to be empty. Inside, Kurt lies in wait—coiled like a spring, his face a mask of fury as he brandishes a straight razor he must've stolen from the table in the corner of the room.

He explodes out of the box, catching everyone off guard. The injuries he's sustained only make him appear more terrifying—wild, unhinged, unstoppable. One arm hangs at an unnatural angle, clearly broken, but he doesn't let it slow him down.

He moves fast—two sharp slices, perfectly placed across a throat of one guy, the brachial nerve of another. The thin material of his T-shirt offering no resistance to Kurt's attack. It's enough. It's the opening I need to break free.

Together, we tear through the last of the hired help. One-on-one, they're no match for Kurt and me.

Two fists fly. Two bodies hit the floor.

Vince does a better job than Tony at masking his fear when Kurt and I turn to face them. It's a skill he must have mastered while inside—where any sign of weakness was as good as painting a target on your back.

Kurt lets out a sharp laugh—low, amused. Dangerous.

Vince barely has time to brace before Kurt lunges, his movements fuelled by sheer resolve. The man who butchered him is now about to face the consequences.

Kurt's first punch connects hard, snapping Vince's

head back and stunning him. Another lands in his ribs making Vince stagger back, off balance.

Kurt dances around him, landing jabs with his one good arm, each strike calculated, relentless. He manoeuvres Vince into the perfect position—then delivers a final crushing blow.

The force sends Vince stumbling, feet skidding backward.

With a little help from Kurt, he topples into the very box meant for me.

Before Vince can scramble out, Kurt moves fast, slamming the lid shut and threading a metal pin through the loops, locking him inside.

Vince pounds against the walls, his rage muffled by thick steel.

Kurt exhales, shaking out his fist, before casually dropping onto the box, lounging like it's a throne built for him.

"What's it feel like, Vince?" Kurt calls, his voice edged with dark amusement. "All that time with your feet up in a cushy cell, taking a stroll in the yard, breathing in all that fresh air—bet that feels like a holiday camp compared to this." He raps his knuckles against the box, smirking as Vince thrashes against the steel walls. "This is a little smaller. Tighter. More bijoux. I'm afraid vitamin D and oxygen are a little lacking, but it's nothing less than you deserve. Being boxed up like the cargo you import."

Kurt shifts, making himself comfortable as he lounges atop the crate.

I smile at the brutal shift in power.

Kurt glances at Tony, who has his back—both figuratively and literally—against the wall. Then he looks at me, sweeping his arm in Tony's direction.

The gesture is clear.

Tony is marked as mine.

The final reckoning is about to begin.

Tony shifts uneasily, his eyes darting toward the basement entrance, silently willing reinforcements to storm in and save him. But upstairs, they're still scrambling—restoring power, rebooting security systems, and chasing the source of the drones.

No cavalry is coming.

I step forward, slow and deliberate, my gaze boring into Tony Castillo like a blade pressed to his throat.

"You always made sure your victims were restrained, didn't you?" I muse, lifting one of the chains conveniently hanging near him.

Tony swallows audibly, his Adam's apple bobbing as I lash out, collaring his throat against the wall. He thrashes, but the only person he harms is himself as I secure him in place with the very chains meant for his prey. The final fixing snaps around his wrist, and he's trapped.

I turn, scanning the array of torture tools displayed like trophies. My hand hovers over a scalpel. Picking it up, I hold it in front of Tony's face, pretending to survey it. The blade glints under the dim basement light, and Tony's eyes widen, fear flickering behind his forced bravado.

"What's this for?" I taunt, weighing the scalpel in my palm.

Tony swallows hard, forcing a smirk. "You don't have the guts."

I tilt my head, pretending to consider his words, before stepping closer and letting the cold steel hover just below his chin.

Only when a bead of sweat trickles down his temple do I lower the weapon.

"Nah," I murmur. "I've got something much better planned for you."

Tony exhales sharply, relief flashing across his face for half a second.

"Where's Maeve?" I ask, my tone almost cordial, the question laced with quiet menace.

Before Tony can respond, Kurt straightens, wiping an errant trickle of blood from his lip.

"I can help with that," he chuckles, his voice dark and amused.

Tony frowns—then freezes as Kurt strides toward the locked boxes. The only hiding place in the room.

Kurt flicks the latch, swings open the lid—and despite the circumstances, my heart sings when I see her.

She stands looking a little dishevelled. Whole. But furious.

"When you said I needed to hide in here, I didn't think you meant for sodding hours," she grumbles, shooting Kurt a glare. He just grins back.

"I could have survived this terrible ordeal only to be suffocated by the very man I rescued in the first place."

"You wouldn't have suffocated," Kurt retorts casually. "That box is at least seven foot long, four wide and four high, giving you approximately one hundred and twelve cubic feet of space. Take away your approximate body mass and your tiny little panting breaths, I'd estimate you had nearly two full days' worth of oxygen in there."

Maeve stares at him, incredulous at his impromptu lesson in the law of physics. "Who *are* you?" She sees Tony fastened to the wall and pouts, "You were supposed to let me out so I could help."

"Sorry," Kurt chuckles, glancing at me, not sorry at all, "Must've forgot in all the excitement."

I'm in front of her in an instant, gently lifting her out of the box as though she's fragile enough to break in my arms.

She frowns at me as I set her down.

"And *you*, mister, are in big trouble. B.I.G."

I don't care as long as she is okay. I look her over, holding her hands in mine. Red rings mar her wrists and ankles—marks of her captivity.

"What did they do to you?" I demand, my breaths deepening as relief gives way to rage.

Tony stiffens. Fear flickering in his eyes. "No," he whispers. "She was upstairs—she was locked—"

A faint tapping turns our heads to the last box.

Maeve rushes forward, unsealing it and throwing the lid back with Kurt's help.

"Jimmy?" I exclaim in surprise.

"I'll explain later," Kurt says simply.

I turn back to Maeve, my voice dropping.

"Did they... hurt you in any other way?" The words taste bitter. I can't bring myself to voice my real fear—but she understands.

"No," she whispers. "Vince drugged me and bound me so I couldn't escape. Tony... Vince interrupted him before he could take things too far."

Heat coils in my chest. My fists clench involuntarily.

The weight of vengeance presses against my lungs, blurring my vision until all I see is red.

"Don't." Maeve murmurs, reading my mind. "He's not worth it."

I exhale sharply, lowering the tensed arm I hadn't even realised I'd raised ready to smash Tony's face to smithereens.

"You should be grateful," I tell Tony, my voice edged with warning. "She just saved your sorry life."

Tony snarls, but his body remains shackled to the wall.

Maeve turns to help Kurt free her brother.

Only then do I step forward—leaning in, just close enough for Tony to hear the venom in my voice. "For now. But make yourself comfortable." I let the threat linger. "I've got something much more imaginative up my sleeve. I think you'll like it."

As soon as Jimmy is out, I take Kurt aside, far enough that Maeve and Jimmy won't overhear.

"Bring up the rear," I murmur.

Kurt narrows his eyes, listening.

"When we're gone, do what you want—but make

sure he's conscious when you leave."

Kurt nods once, confirming he'll obey without needing to know why.

I shift my focus, collecting my discarded firearm from the floor and reloading it, before looping Jimmy's arm over my shoulder and half-carrying him out of the basement. Maeve follows, her sharp eyes fixed ahead, scanning for movement, listening for danger.

At the top of the staircase, I pause, waiting for Kurt to catch up before I attempt to open the door.

Every second feels like an eternity before I hear the soft shuffle of footsteps and Kurt appears. Carefully, I crack open the door leading back into the hallway. It's too exposed. If we're spotted, we're done. Every distant noise, every shifting shadow feels like a threat waiting to strike. I tighten my grip on Jimmy. Maeve stays close, her breath controlled but shallow. We need a distraction. I look at Kurt and he knows what I'm thinking.

He shakes his head—a clear message: *stick together.*

Maeve watches the exchange, eyes searching. "Don't leave me," she whispers, gripping the back of my pants, holding me in place.

I look into her pleading eyes and surrender. We go together or not at all.

Suddenly chaos erupts outside. A myriad of flashing lights. Shouts. The sound of glass shattering upstairs. Bedlam takes hold—men scurrying every which way, unsure which direction to turn.

I smile. *Foxy.*

Seizing the moment, I signal for the others to stay in sync. We slip from cover, moving toward the front door in quick, measured strides.

A distant voice cuts through the air—orders being barked, men scrambling upstairs, still hunting ghosts.

Now.

We push forward, but just as we're about to slip into the night—Maeve stops.

I turn, heart hammering—only to watch her pluck her purse from a side table.

I stare at her. Gobsmacked.

She meets my gaze, wide-eyed.

"What?" She whispers. "It's one of my favourites."

I roll my eyes at the absurdity, dragging her behind me as we bolt through the door.

As we make our final break for freedom, adrenaline spikes, propelling us forward into the cover of the greenery a few feet away.

We're not safe yet. But we're close.

Keeping low, we creep further away. Kurt and I shield the others, forcing them to duck as car lights slash across the terrain, threatening to expose us.

Then—Ace and Nico emerge from the shadows, helping Maeve and Jimmy until we're fully clear.

Seconds later, Foxy appears beside us, driving the transit he used as his base.

Blake throws open the doors, grinning as he helps Maeve inside.

"What the hell are you doing here?" she exclaims, startled.

"Just passing through," Blake replies smoothly. "Thought I'd check on my cat."

Maeve's glare locks onto me. The trouble I'm in just got bigger. If she catches wind of what I'm about to do next, bigger might just explode into apoplectic rage.

Foxy drives to a remote location at the top of a hill, then pulls the handbrake, slouching back into his seat.

Blake opens the back door and climbs out.

Maeve, tending to her brother, turns on me the second I step down.

"Why have we stopped?"

"I need to take a leak," I tell her. It's not a lie. I do.

"What about you, Kurt?" I ask. Kurt meets my gaze, understanding the silent message I'm sending him.

He climbs out to stand with Blake and me.

As I shut the door, Ace moves smoothly into position, sliding between us and Maeve—blocking her from following.

Not that she looks like she's about to try.

Kurt watches me. "What's going on?"

I jerk my head toward the mansion, still visible in the distance. Kurt follows my gaze.

"Think Vince and Tony are still down there?" I ask.

"I'd bet on it. There was so much going on, I doubt anyone's thought to check the basement yet. When

I'd finished saying my goodbyes, I stuck some tape over Tony's mouth—to buy us more time."

"Good."

I turn to Blake.

"Did you get it done?"

Blake nods, reaching into his jacket.

"As per your specific instructions."

He hands me the item I've been waiting for.

Kurt recognizes the device instantly, a satisfied smirk gracing his lips.

"I thought you were letting them get away lightly," he mutters.

"A house for a house," I reply, pressing the detonator.

The explosions ripple through the air, shaking the ground beneath us.

We watch in silence as men scatter like ants, the fire tearing through the building until it's nothing more than a ball of flames. Smoke billows upward, blotting the horizon—a stark, violent contrast to the serene beauty of a bright new dawn breaking over the landscape.

Foxy starts the engine, and we all climb back into the van.

"Took you long enough," Maeve grumbles, her tone sharp but exhausted.

"You're right," I sigh, leaning in to kiss her temple. "It did."

Epilogue

Maeve

T he weather in Vermont is on our side— bright, clear, and crisp enough to keep us awake. I'm back at the Serenity Springs Tavern, but this time, I'm standing on a large floating raft on the pond, beneath a stunning arch of red and white carnations. Josh holds my hands in his, his grip warm despite the chill in the air.

Kurt stands just behind Josh, looking sharp in his suit, his jacket draped over one shoulder to accommodate the cast on his broken arm. The bruises on his face bloom in every colour of the rainbow as they heal, ensuring our wedding photos will be far from conventional—but I don't care. Having him by Josh's side means more to me than the opinions of anyone who might see the pictures and judge.

Tina, my maid of honour, stands behind me in a flowing navy gown that perfectly complements the queen's dress. The queen, regal as ever in her bridesmaid attire, is somewhat undermined by a neon-orange lifesaver—a non-negotiable addition from her father. In his infinite caution, he insisted she wear it, despite the fact that we're barely a few feet from shore and the water is embarrassingly shallow. It also seems to have escaped him that she's under the watchful eyes of two ex-Navy SEALs—who just happen to be excellent swimmers.

Josh, dashing and composed in his suit, looks far warmer than I feel. I can't help but envy his layers. My wedding dress, stunning as it is, offers little defence against the cool air slicing across my exposed skin. The daring neckline suddenly feels like a bold mistake. Not only because of the weather, but also the fact that it seems to be holding my future husband's attention more than my face.

Tiny lies sprawled beside Mr. Josh on the shore, while on the Tavern's veranda, our friends and family gather to watch the spectacle unfold. The only other person on the raft is our celebrant, guiding us through our vows. Mac convinced Jared to rent out the entire venue for the day, ensuring everyone could relax and enjoy themselves without interruptions.

Since we returned from Maine, Josh has been trailing after me like a lost puppy, much to everyone's amusement. He knows he's in trouble for not being honest with me from the start and has been desperate to make amends, tail firmly tucked between his legs. He even asked if I wanted to call off the wedding. I watched disappointment and apprehension flicker in his eyes, his voice barely steady as he struggled to get the words out.

I could have told him the truth—that there was

no way I'd let him go. But that would've completely undermined his punishment. If he knew my resolve was all for show, where's the fun in that? After everything I've been through, I'm entitled to a little mischief. It's not like I'll make him suffer forever. Tonight, I'll put him out of his misery—just before he puts me out of mine. Instead, I told him we had to go through with the ceremony. After all, Mac and the others had spent too much time and money setting this up for either of us to back out now.

"Do you, Maeve Mercer, promise to love, honour, and obey..."

"Whoa!" I hold up my hand, interrupting the celebrant mid-flow. A brief look of fear flashes across Josh's face, as if he thinks I've changed my mind and am about to back out. "Can you rephrase the question? I'm not happy with that last word."

The celebrant looks at me quizzically, and Josh relaxes slightly, his lips quirking at the corners.

"Um... Do you, Maeve Mercer, promise to love, honour, and..." She pauses, searching for the right word, so I help her out.

"...and respectfully listen to Josh Stone's opinions before deciding if he's being an idiot and setting him straight." I pause, then add with a grin, "I do."

A ripple of giggles spreads through the gallery as the celebrant turns to Josh.

"And do you, Joshua Stone..." I raise a finger, cutting her off again. "Promise to love, honour, and *obey* Maeve Mercer. To be completely open and honest with her at all times, even if you think the truth will hurt. Because you understand she's not a child, and lasting relationships are built on faith, loyalty, and trust. Plus, you acknowledge that she doesn't want to waste the next thirteen years building a life with the man she loves based on misunderstandings and false hope."

Josh hesitates, clearly trying to stifle a laugh, before answering solemnly, "From this moment on, I do."

The celebrant opens her mouth to speak, but Josh raises his finger this time, picking up where I left off.

"Do you, Maeve Mercer, promise to eventually put Joshua Stone out of his misery and stop busting his balls at every opportunity?"

I pretend to think about it for a few seconds before answering just as solemnly, "I do."

The celebrant looks between us, clearly confused, as I continue.

"Do you, Joshua Stone, promise to try and stop mistaking my contraceptive pills for painkillers then taking them every time my back is turned?"

The giggles grow louder as Josh rolls his lips and answers, "I do. Do you, Maeve Mercer, promise to *consider* relocating to California, where my business is based? Half my unit is empty and could be converted into a veterinary surgery for you to work in next door."

I wasn't expecting that. But since he's just promised total honesty, it must be something weighing on his mind. There has to be compromise, though—we can iron out the details later.

"I do. Do you, Joshua Stone, if I did agree to relocate, promise to support me should I decide to keep my cabin and return to Vermont regularly to assist Aiden in expanding my business there? Which may include one or both of us becoming licensed wildlife rehabilitators."

He doesn't blink before answering, "I do."

We both turn to the celebrant and smile.

"Are you done?" She looks between Josh and me until we both nod.

As the celebrant is about to continue, I think of one more thing. She snaps her mouth shut as I raise my finger again.

"Do you, Joshua Stone, promise to never complain if I have to bring my work home with me—or about the fact that my dog is likely to shed all over your home?"

"Our home," he corrects me.

"Our home," I repeat, trying not to smile.

"I do. Do you, Maeve Mercer, promise me the same—or about the fact that Kurt is nearly always hanging around with his smart mouth and questionable attitude?"

"I do," I giggle.

Kurt steps forward and kisses me on the cheek. "Aw, love you too, babe." I catch the faintest flicker of jealousy flash across Josh's face.

"Do you, Josh Stone, promise to never get jealous of other men paying me attention, knowing that since we agreed to be mutually exclusive, I have been —and will always be—100% faithful to you?"

"I do not!" Josh growls.

It was a long shot. "Fair enough," I chuckle, knowing it's a vow I'd probably struggle with too. I think back to the first flight we took together from Vermont to LAX, and how my gut twisted when it was obvious he was drawing a lot of female attention. "Me neither."

We both grin at each other goofily as I tell the officiant confidently, "We're finished." She looks at me doubtfully. "Promise," I add, to reassure her.

"They're the most... unusual vows I've ever heard," the celebrant mutters, scanning her book to figure out where to pick up.

Kurt smirks, leaning in to whisper loudly enough for everyone to hear, "They're sexually frustrated. It's messing with their minds."

Tina giggles while Josh and I both turn to glare at him.

The celebrant finishes up, and as she pronounces us husband and wife, our guests erupt into cheers. Glasses are raised, biodegradable confetti cannons fire, and laughter ripples across the water.

"You may now kiss the bride."

Josh leans in, but at the last second, I turn and offer my cheek instead. He wanted to wait for us to be together—so he can wait on all levels. He gives me a peck, and though I can tell he's disappointed, I'm unbothered. I know I'll make it up to him later.

Dropping one of my hands, Josh lifts the other in triumph—not toward our guests, but toward a boat stationed across the lake. I know exactly what he's doing.

Derek sits between Ace and Nico, watching the scene play out. I read in the papers that following an anonymous tip-off by a Mr Justin Time, Douglas Dawson had been arrested after the DEA intercepted a shipment of his so-called 'souvenirs' at Searsport docks in Maine. They found enough narcotics to destroy more lives than I care to count. He's currently being held on remand, and the evidence against him keeps piling up.

I can't say I'm surprised. Deep down I always thought there was something shady about him, though I could never quite pinpoint why. Apparently, after being caught cooking the books to cover his father's misdeeds, Derek tried to go on the run with Felicia. Luckily, Ace 'happened' to be in the neighbourhood to foil their plans.

Josh was so determined to have Derek at the wedding that he enlisted Ace and Nico to keep watch over him and deliver him straight to the local PD after the ceremony. As I watch the boat take off, I assume that's exactly where they're heading.

I also read in the news that the Castillo brothers' house burned to the ground. I told Josh they must have gone on the run, torching the place to destroy any evidence. The thought makes me uneasy—knowing they're still out there—but when I brought it up, Josh looked uncomfortable for just a moment before assuring me, with quiet conviction, that I'd never have to worry about them again. I trust his judgment, so I refuse to let them ruin my day—or any part of the future I'm in the process of building.

Josh spins us around, raising our joined hands toward the people we love most—the ones we're truly grateful to have here, sharing our day. More cheers erupt, and the pop of several bottles being uncorked fills the air.

Jimmy stands between our parents, steady yet changed by everything we've been through. Our mother's arm is linked firmly in his, her gaze flickering between pride and worry as she studies the external bruises that are already starting to heal. The internal scars forged from guilt and regret will take longer. Our father, never one for grand gestures, rests a reassuring hand on Jimmy's shoulder—a silent acknowledgment of battles fought and bonds reforged.

Jimmy talks about moving back to Vermont permanently, and though I haven't told Josh yet, I've already made my decision—of course I'll relocate with him. Once he knows, I'll offer Jimmy my cabin. It'll be good to know he'll be close to our parents when I leave. And maybe, it's my way of trying to ensure I'll always know exactly where I can find him. Still, I'd hoped, maybe selfishly, that he'd consider California instead. There's so much lost time to reclaim, but looking at our mother now—the way she holds onto him like she's afraid to lose him again —I'm not sure she'll ever let him go.

Josh offered him a job at his firm but Jimmy says he just wants a quiet life now, and I understand that more than most. My cabin gave me solace when I needed it—now it's his turn. I hope it can give him the peace I found there. Liam has also offered him his old job back at the garage. He's considering it, but I think he needs some time to heal and decide whether going back is truly what he wants, or if starting anew entirely would serve him better.

He raises his glass to Josh and me, and I meet his eyes, a rush of sibling love tightening my throat. Having him here—not just as a guest, but as my brother again—is the gift I never thought I'd have.

Out of the corner of my eye, I see Kurt grab the back of Tia's life jacket to steady her before planting his feet wide and waggling the raft, sending ripples across the water. The celebrant grabs hold of the arbour as I fall safely into Josh's strong arms.

"Hey, baby," he whispers as I land, confirming what I already knew. "I've got you."

I smile at him goofily. Then, everyone's attention shifts to Tina, who is cursing at Kurt as she stumbles, teetering on the edge of the raft, trying not to topple into the water.

The queen erupts in laughter, clapping her hands and squealing in excitement. "Do it again! Do it again!"

Tina just manages to stabilize herself—until we get an unexpected visitor. A frog leaps out of the pond, landing squarely on the exposed part of her foot.

"Urgh!" She screams. "Get it off!"

She hops about in disgust, missteps, and this time, there's no saving her. Arms flailing, she plunges backward, landing on her ass in the water.

She fully submerges before standing in the thigh-high water, coughing, spluttering, and loudly threatening to end poor Kurt's life. It's impossible not to laugh at the situation—or at her thoroughly aggrieved expression.

"Well, that's just great!" Tina pouts, pushing the remnants of her previously perfect hair back from her face. "This is all your fault!" She yells at Kurt, flapping her arms in exasperation.

Without a second thought, Kurt hands Tia off to Josh before jumping into the water to join her. Encumbered by his broken arm, he can't scoop her up like a bride, so he simply tosses her over his shoulder and heads for shore—much to the delight of everyone watching, and the exasperation of the woman he's pretending to rescue.

"Don't worry, sweetness," Kurt smirks, giving Tina a playful tap on the backside as he carries her off to who-knows-where. "I'll dry you off and help you get changed."

"Tina Marie Collins!" I yell with a smile. "You'd better be back at the table, ready for dinner, in ten minutes."

"Five!" Liam growls, craning over the balustrade of the veranda, scowling at Kurt as he manhandles his sister.

Kurt answers us both on her behalf, completely unfazed. "I'll see what I can do, but timing isn't really my strong suit." Then, turning to Tina, he adds, "I perform best under pressure."

"Who told you that?" Josh calls back—only for Kurt to flip him off in response.

By the time Kurt and Tina make it back, everyone has finished their starters and moved on to the main course. Tina looks distinctly flushed, while Kurt wears the self-satisfied smirk of a man who's been up to no good. Josh leans over and starts whispering to Kurt. He doesn't look amused, but Kurt just chuckles like a naughty schoolboy. I catch Tina's apologetic glance and meet it with my amused one. She flaps her hand under her chin and blows out a deep breath, making it clear that whatever she's been up to was somewhat... hot.

Later, Mac pulls me aside. "What's the story there, then?" She nods toward Tina and Kurt, who are standing with their backs to one another across the room. Tina is talking to Blake, who appears to be shamelessly flirting with her, while Kurt pretends to talk to Josh, repeatedly side-eyeing them and throwing silent daggers at the smirking Blake.

"There isn't one," I laugh. "Tina lives and works in New York. She loves her job, and living there would be Kurt's worst nightmare. Not much can happen long-term."

"No," Mac muses thoughtfully.

"What are you thinking?" I giggle.

"I knew a girl once. She lived in and loved her job in Vermont. Never thought she'd leave, but the right guy came along. They got married, and now she's considering moving across the country to be with him in L.A." I cast Mac a startled look. "I really hope she does come. She's become a good friend, and it would be lovely to hang out and see her more often."

I smile softly as Mac nods back in Kurt's direction. "He's different when she's around."

"Different? How?"

"Hmm... Softer."

As Mac says the words, I look over just in time to see Kurt poised to drop an ice cube down the back of Tina's dress, while she giggles and blushes at whatever Blake is saying to her. He's stopped just in time by an unamused Liam grabbing his wrist.

"Softer?" I widen my eyes at Mac as a piercing scream draws everyone's attention to Tina. She hops about until a piece of ice falls from her dress onto the floor. Without hesitation, she instinctively rounds on Kurt, slapping him across his already bruised cheek.

"Ow," he clutches his face, appearing to be in genuine pain. "Jeez, didn't think I'd suffered enough recently," he moans.

Tina rushes to Kurt's side, fussing over him, guilt written all over her face. Behind her back, Blake flips Kurt off, irritated at losing the girl. As soon as Tina is distracted, Kurt winks at him, smirking smugly —letting him know his little stunt was entirely premeditated and meant to remind Blake who's boss.

"Forget it," I tell Mac. "Together in small doses, they're fine. Put them together long term, and I'm pretty sure they'd end up killing each other."

"We'll see."

"What's that supposed to mean?" I ask, but before Mac can answer, Josh meanders over, interrupting whatever thoughts are percolating in her mind.

"Thanks for putting this all together." Josh kisses Mac's cheek before pulling her into a hug.

"I didn't do it alone. I had help," she replies, gesturing around the room at the new friends I've recently made.

"I know. I've thanked them already."

"Good." Mac sighs, her happiness tinged with a hint of sadness. "Because you guys need to make a move. It might be better if you slip away while no one's looking, or else it'll take you an age to get out the door—and that plane won't wait forever."

"Plane?" Josh tips his head quizzically. He has no idea where we're heading.

Mac looks at me and smiles. "There's a car waiting for you outside. Your bags are already inside."

"Thanks." I hug her tightly, kissing her cheek. "Are you sure about taking care of Tiny and Derek until we get back?"

"Of course. They're no trouble. In fact, Tiny keeps Mr. Josh occupied and out of mischief, while Derek does the same for Tia." She beams at me before pointing toward the door and switching into her mom tone. "Now, go!"

I don't need to be told twice. I grab Josh's hand and attempt to pull him after me as I make to leave.

He digs his heels in for a moment before conceding, turning to Mac with a final few words. His tone shifts into the one that brooks no argument, the one he uses when he means business.

"Remember what I said about Bear. I don't expect he'll be in touch, but if you hear from him, let Kurt know immediately. All his access within the firm has been revoked."

Mac nods in understanding.

"Who's Bear?" I ask as we step outside.

Josh growls. "Someone who used to work for me. He took off in the middle of a job, Kurt—and a few guys we work with—want to have a word with him about it."

"Don't worry," I say, raising Josh's hand to my lips, kissing it gently. "He's bound to turn up eventually."

"You can count on it," he mutters before his face softens, letting me lead him away from our partying guests.

By the time we step through the doors of a private villa on the island of Nevis, it's late evening. While I'm eagerly taking in our surroundings, Josh doesn't waste a single second after the door closes before shrugging off his shirt, discarding his shoes and socks, and by the time I turn, he's already unfastening his trousers. Trying to remain stoic becomes an almost impossible task.

As I wheel the suitcase into the bedroom, he growls behind me, "You won't be needing that."

I grin, then quickly compose myself, adopting a neutral expression as I turn to face him.

"You think you're forgiven, just like that?" I shut the bedroom door in his face before he can enter—I need time to prepare. A thud follows, suspiciously sounding like his forehead hitting the back of the door, before he whines, almost pitifully, "But babe. It's our wedding night. We had plans. Can't you put being mad at me on hold—at least for the next twenty-four hours?"

"No," I call through the door. "When I forgive you, it's going to be permanent. No rehashing the past if we get into an argument."

"What can I do?" He murmurs dolefully.

"I was told the fridge would be stocked. Can you make me a sandwich and bring it in with some fruit and a couple of bottles of water?"

"Sure."

I listen at the door until I hear him retreat—then I spring into action. The bedroom is sumptuous, with patio doors opening onto gardens lit with soft solar lights. *I could spend a few days holed up in here,* I muse. *With a little food and water.*

The moon hangs high in the clear sky, casting a silver beam of light down to the tranquil sea, its gentle waves rolling onto the beach just beyond the garden. I crack the doors open slightly, releasing some of the heat built up during the day.

Once that's done, I open my suitcase to find the sexy lingerie I packed specifically for this moment, changing and draping myself seductively across the bed just in time for Josh's return and his tentative knock on the door.

"Come in," I purr.

Josh pushes open the door holding a tray crammed full of goodies, stopping in his tracks as soon as he sees me. His eye's flame with heat and desire as his eyes rake over my body.

"I've decided to forgive you, on one condition," I say, my voice impassive and even.

Josh swallows audibly before murmuring, "Name it."

"You make good on your previous promises about what I could expect on our wedding night, and you agree to stay in this room with me for as long as it takes you to give me one orgasm for every day you've made me wait to have my wicked way with you."

"Thirteen years is a lot of orgasms," Josh smirks, discarding the tray onto a dressing table before undoing his trousers with such speed and dexterity, they fall to the ground for him to step out of in seconds. He's gone commando and my eyes widen as I see just how ready he is to take my challenge.

"I didn't mean thirteen years," I bluster, sitting up in bed nervously, "I meant…"

Josh is on me in a flash, silencing me with a kiss.

He pulls back briefly to whisper, "Relax baby, I'm about to take you to places you've never been before."

"That shouldn't be too difficult," I chuckle.

When he kisses me a second time, I relax instantly. He deepens the kiss and as he explores my mouth with his tongue, my arousal takes hold. I become as eager to please him as he is to please me. As our passion starts to escalate, I'm suddenly struck be a worrying thought. "Wait. Stop," I force the words out unwillingly.

"What?" Josh pulls back, but I can tell it's a struggle. He looks at me, panting and breathless.

"I just remembered—with you repeatedly taking my pills, and the whole being kidnapped thing meaning I've missed a few—we might not be as protected as we think."

Josh smirks. "I'm used to dodging bullets."

"Like this one." I raise an eyebrow, running my finger over the scar on his shoulder.

"If we took a hit, it wouldn't be the worst thing in the world for me. I'm in this for keeps. But if you're not ready…"

I don't need long to think. Seeing him staring down at me with nothing but pure love, his expression brimming with warmth and affection, gives me the answer I need. "Let's play a little Russian roulette, shall we?" I snigger.

Josh grins back at me before picking right up where we left off and making good on those promises.

Again.

And again.

And again… until I lose count.

Books By This Author

Stone's Security Series:

When danger and desire collide, love can prove to be the most unpredictable threat of all.

Marked by Stone

Healing Hearts Series:

When love and laughter collide, sparks fly, hearts heal, and Hollywood's brightest stars learn that fame is no match for fate.

Healing Hollywood Hearts
Meeting Mitchel's Match
Lovin' 2 Leading Ladies

Printed in Dunstable, United Kingdom